# THE
# GOOD
# PEOPLE

BY STEVE COCKAYNE

*Legends of the Land*
Wanderers and Islanders
The Iron Chain
The Seagull Drovers

The Good People

# THE
# GOOD
# PEOPLE

## Steve Cockayne

atom

www.atombooks.co.uk

ATOM

First published in Great Britain in 2006 by Atom

Copyright © MetaVentures 2006

The moral right of the author has been asserted.

A CIP catalogue record for this book
is available from the British Library.

Hardback ISBN-13: 978-190423-362-6
Hardback ISBN-10: 1-904233-62-7
C format ISBN-13: 978-1-90423-392-3
C format ISBN-10: 1-904233-92-9

Typeset in Fournier by M Rules
Printed and bound in Great Britain by
Mackays of Chatham plc

Atom
An imprint of
Little, Brown Book Group
Brettenham House
Lancaster Place
London WC2E 7EN

A member of the Hachette Livre Group of Companies

www.littlebrown.co.uk

I would like to express my thanks to the many good people who have, consciously, unconsciously or post-humously, provided help in the writing of this book. In particular, I want to mention Katharine Briggs, Roger Bunce, Frank Cook, Anne Dewe, Tim Holman, Kathy Hutchinson, John Kemp, Fiona Lock, Laura Murphy, Gabriella Nemeth, Oliver Sparks, David Still, and, as always, Pauline Cockayne.

Perhaps writing is not such a lonely job after all.

S.V.C.

# CONTENTS

# PROLOGUE

*Y*ou are young, Jamie. You are young and I am old, and there are so many things that I need to tell you. Things that will be lost for ever if I don't tell them to you now.

By the time that you read these words, you will be twelve years old and, by that time, Hedley House will have been pulled down, the forest behind the house will have been uprooted, and the lake will have been drained. Instead of the house, there will be a new estate of executive homes, and instead of the forest and the lake there will be a row of neatly kept suburban gardens. So you'll need to know all about Hedley House, Jamie; you'll need to know its story, and you'll need to know about my family and about all the other people who lived there too. You'll need to know about the garden gate, and you'll need to know about the forest on the other side of the garden gate, and you'll need to know about the lake that once lay at the heart of the forest.

And, of course, in order to understand about the forest, you'll need to know about the Land of Arboria, and then you'll need to know about the war between the Arborians and the Barbarians, and then, of course, you'll need to know about the Good People. More than any of that, though, you'll need to know about Janny Grogan, and about what happened when Janny came to Hedley House.

So here I am, sitting here day after day at this grubby table, writing it all down for you, writing and writing and writing until my head throbs and my fingers ache and my eyes glaze over with exhaustion. At times, I have felt that I would never reach the end of my task, but I know now that it will soon be done. Then, at last, I shall be able to parcel up my work and consign it to a place of safety until it is time for it to pass into your hands.

After that, I shall return for the last time to Hedley House, and there I shall wait patiently upon the will of the Good People. Perhaps I must face the full fury of the Hand of Fire, or perhaps I must face some other fate altogether. Soon enough, though, I shall know. Bad things have happened at Hedley House, Jamie, wicked things have been done, and soon it will be time for me to face up to my retribution. By then, though, my task will be complete, and the burden will slip at last from my weary shoulders. One day, perhaps, it will be your turn to take up that burden. One day, perhaps, you will be ready to learn what happened here and why it was that it had to happen.

One day, perhaps, you will understand.

*One*

# THE LAND OF ARBORIA

**SOUTH MIDLANDS TODAY**
**Camera Script Wed 19th May**
**Reporter JOAN HILDEGAARD**

**JOAN:**

Well, good morning to you from Helsing Wood, where today I have witnessed the end of a long and bitter struggle, a struggle that has divided the neighbourhood and brought chaos to what was once a peaceful, rural backwater.

Of course, if you're a regular viewer of this programme, I need hardly remind you that the sleepy hamlet of Upper Helsing has for months been at the forefront of a campaign to save Tollcester District's most ancient woodland from destruction. But today, finally – and some will say tragically – the battle has been lost; the men with the tractors, the chainsaws and the excavators have begun to move in and, as you can see, the first of the ancient oak trees have begun to fall. But not, of course,

3

without protest. As usual, the demonstrators are out in force. I can see some people carrying placards over there, there are people banging drums, there's a group of people wearing black and carrying a coffin, and I've even spotted someone sitting up there in that great big tree right at the top of the wood.

I think you can see a close-up of him now. He looks like quite an elderly man, he's got a long, bushy white beard. His clothes are all in tatters, but there seems to be some kind of faded flower pattern on them and he's wearing an old tin helmet on his head. Yes, and there's some writing on the helmet, and I think if our camera could zoom in a bit more . . . I can see it now, it's three letters – 'ARP' – does anybody know what that means?

I think the man's seen us, he's getting very excited now, he's shouting and he's waving his arms. I suppose he must be one of the demonstrators, but he looks more like some kind of wild man. Perhaps we can get a mic over there and hear what he's saying. Hello, what's that?

Well, I'm truly sorry, viewers, it seems that we've run out of time for now, we're just coming up to our commercial, so we're going to have to leave these dramatic scenes and bid you farewell for the time being. But if there are any new developments from Helsing Wood, or if we learn any more about the wild man in the tree, then I promise that you'll be the first to hear about it.

You've been watching Joan Hildegaard, here in

Upper Helsing. Don't forget to stay with us on *South Midlands Today*. We'll be back with you again - right after the break!

It was quite a shock to see myself on television. I no longer have a television set at home, you see. My old black and white set broke down some years ago, and somehow I never got around to replacing it. And then the electricity got cut off, so there didn't really seem any point. So now I only get to watch television when I'm out of the house, and that usually means when I'm here, in the café at the bus station. I don't like the place very much, but at least they will let me sit here for as long as I want without having to spend more than a couple of pounds. I can sit here all day if I like, drinking lukewarm instant coffee, or perhaps eating a stale doughnut with magenta-coloured jam in it.

On the café wall, the menu is spelled out in white letters on a perforated black plastic board. There is a tiled floor and a big, dirty, plate glass window and a pair of dirty plate glass entrance doors. The window looks out across the dingy underpass that leads from the Broadgate to the bus station. I can watch the people as they come and go and, when there aren't any people, I can look out at a vandalised payphone, a kiosk that sells hair extensions and a row of left-luggage lockers, their doors defaced with incomprehensible graffiti.

Above the counter, there are photographs of the various meals on offer. Over the years the colours in the photographs have faded, so that now everything looks pale brown. Sometimes, if I look hard enough, I can detect the same arrangement of chips in two adjacent pictures, the same sliced tomato appearing time after time on a sequence of plates. If I could be bothered, I could probably work out the exact order in which the pictures were taken.

The best thing about the café, though, is that the tables are quite big, and I always get a whole table to myself because, for some reason, nobody ever wants to sit next to me. That means that I can spread my work out around me, and I can carry on in peace doing what I have come here to do.

I have to come here, you see, because I find it so hard to concentrate when I'm at Hedley House. Hedley House, my house, the house where I have lived all my life, lies at the edge of the sacred land of Arboria and, for as long as I can remember, Arboria has been my real home. Arboria with its woodlands and its glades, its lakes and its crags, its tree houses and its secret paths, its voices and its scents and its memories. But now the wreckers and their machines are moving into the Arborian forest, and I know that the forest isn't going to be there for much longer, and of course once they've felled the forest they're going to demolish Hedley House, and after that there won't be an Arboria any more and there won't be anywhere left for me to go.

But in the town, with all its noise and its frenzy, I can forget about all that for a while. For a time, the dim voices and the faded scents and the hazy memories will cease to trouble me. So I catch the bus into the town, and I sit here in the little café at the bus station.

At a table on the far side of the room there sprawls a group of teenagers: four boys and two girls. They are perhaps fourteen or fifteen years old, and they are wearing something approximating to school uniform. They seem to be trying to make their Coca-Cola last as long as my coffee. Two of the boys and one of the girls form a close, noisy huddle, the boys competing aggressively for the girl's attention. A little way away from them sit another boy and girl, their arms wrapped around one another, their faces and bodies touching, the girl whispering something into the boy's ear. I feel uncomfortable looking at these two. They remind me of some of the things that have passed me by in my life, things that it is now too late for me to enjoy.

Slightly detached from the group sits the fourth boy. He seems smaller, and perhaps a little younger than the others. He doesn't take part in whatever the group is doing, but he watches them, he listens to them, and he misses nothing. This, it occurs to me, is how I might have appeared when I was fourteen: watching, listening, taking everything in, but somehow never really wanting to join in. Perhaps, Jamie, this is how you will be when you are fourteen, half a lifetime from now.

Now something else catches my attention. Attached to the café wall, next to the entrance doors, is a large colour television set. The screen, which a moment ago carried a picture of a young female reporter with a microphone, now carries, astonishingly, a picture of myself. I listen for a moment to the reporter's commentary and I am rather shocked to realise that this is how the world must now see me. A wild man in a tree, a crazy old fool in a tin hat, a lunatic screaming abuse at workmen and hurling branches at bulldozers.

But of course I am the last survivor of Arboria. I, Kenneth Storey, am the Keeper of the Great Book. I am the one charged with the duty of preserving the history and traditions of the sacred land. I am the one who must defend Arboria against the machinery of the wreckers. I must defend my beloved Arboria, I must defend her to the death!

For now, though, I stay here in the cafe. I stay here partly to finish the task that I have set myself, and partly because I am afraid to go home. It is not just because of the machines that I am afraid. I am afraid because Hedley House, and the forest, and the lake, have too many ghosts. There is not a room into which I can walk, not a staircase up which I can climb, not a path along which I can stroll, without coming face to face with an invisible someone, an intangible something. From the depths of the past the ghosts reach out for me, from every obscure corner of the house they whisper to me, from every secret glade of the forest they murmur my name, mocking me, daring me to confront them. So I am afraid, yet confront them I must, and quickly too, for time is running away from me, fleet-footed, and soon, very soon now, it will be too late.

So I must tell you about the land of Arboria and, first of all, I must explain what we had to do to get there. Outside my grandmother's kitchen door, just across the vegetable patch, set in a high brick wall, was the garden gate, although the garden gate wasn't actually a gate, it was really a tall wooden door. Sometimes the garden gate was latched, but sometimes it seemed to hang slightly open on its hinges, as if it were tempting you to step through. And somehow the ground around that garden gate always seemed to stay dry, even when it had been raining a lot, and that made it all the more inviting. I don't know why we called it the garden gate because it didn't lead into a garden, it led down to the wood and the pond. The wood was quite a small wood really, and the pond was quite a small pond but, when I went through the garden gate, the wood became the great forest of Arboria, and the pond became a long, deep, dangerous lake at the bottom of a deep, beautiful valley.

It was my brother Robert who first showed me how to get to

Arboria. All you had to do was to step through the garden gate.

'Good morning, Master Kenneth! Lovely morning, don't you think?' It was the thin, husky voice of Tommy Pelling. My first job when I arrived in Arboria was always to say hello to Tommy. Tommy was in charge of the log store, and the log store stood just on the other side of the garden gate, on the left-hand side against the wall. The store was a brick hut, rather tumbledown, with a rickety red tiled roof, a window with no glass, and a doorway with no door. Inside the hut, up against every wall, were tall, orderly, musty-smelling stacks of logs. It was Tommy's job to look after the logs, and this he did with great devotion, dusting them and airing them and rearranging them every single day. The inside of the log store was Tommy's private domain, and neither Robert nor I would have dreamed of venturing inside without an invitation.

Tommy himself was a small, slight creature with thin, wispy hair and very large ears. His clothes were ragged and worn, and his toes peeped out through gaping cracks in his large, flat shoes. It would have been very hard to say how old he was. He was one of those people who always seem to have been the same age. It was always worth talking to Tommy, though, because Tommy always seemed to know what was going on in Arboria.

The little man propped his broom up in a corner of the store and leaned back against the stack of logs, the doorway framing his narrow form. He beckoned to me and I stepped inside the store, while Robert waited impatiently at the doorway. 'So what might you be thinking of doing today, young master?' Tommy asked confidentially. He was very well-spoken, certainly as keepers of log stores go.

'I don't know, Tommy,' I replied. 'What do you think? Is there anything special going on?'

Tommy leaned his head to one side and rubbed the tip of his ear before replying. 'I should certainly think about steering clear of the water today,' he said finally, 'that is, Master Kenneth, if I were in your position.' I gazed at him, willing him to continue. After a long pause, he gave me a faint smile. 'I've heard some peculiar noises from the other side of the water,' he said finally. 'Most peculiar. I have the distinct feeling that there may be *plans* afoot. Plans of a sinister nature, perhaps. I would advise caution, young sir, great caution, before proceeding in that direction.'

'Come on, Ken,' Robert called from outside. 'Haven't you finished yet? Let's head for the House in the Air. I can have a good look through the binoculars. See if I can spot any signs of trouble.'

'A most sound move, Master Kenneth,' Tommy commented. 'A most sound move indeed. And now, if you'll excuse me . . .' He eased himself to his feet and picked up his broom from its place. This, I knew, was my signal to rejoin my brother. A moment later, I could once more hear the brisk sound of sweeping from inside the hut.

'The House in the Air, then?' I checked.

'The House in the Air it is,' Robert replied crisply.

'Tommy says there might be danger.'

'Perhaps we'd better be armed, then,' my brother replied.

Nodding, I looked back inside the hut. 'Oh, Tommy? Have you got a couple of bows that we could borrow?'

The sweeping stopped again. 'Yes indeed, Master Kenneth. I'm sure I can oblige.'

A few moments later, we were shouldering our bows and our quivers of arrows, and setting off on our way. Robert strode ahead of me, his bow and arrows slung over one shoulder, his knapsack bumping up and down on his back.

It was a fine spring day. The tall trees were in full leaf, their branches forming a long, curving colonnade ahead of us. Huge drifts of wild flowers had started to appear on the banks and beside the paths, and the clamour of birdsong erupted from every direction. We strode down the broad, undulating track.

'No signs of trouble in Arboria,' Robert remarked. 'I think Tommy Pelling might have been barking up the wrong tree. Still, best take a good look round.'

The track started to fall away, leading us gently downhill, then it curved gradually off to the right, taking us along the flank of a steep valley. Below us, a swift-flowing mountain stream splashed and bubbled over rocks and boulders. As we rounded the next bend, the valley floor fell away sharply and the stream suddenly cascaded down before widening out into a broad lake. In the distance, we could just make out a waterfall and a narrow wooden bridge. I paused for a moment at the bend, partly to recover my breath, but partly to take in the view across the lake to the land of the Barbarians.

The forest continued on the Barbarian side, but the trees there were not as tall as the Arborian trees. Their trunks were crooked, their branches gnarled and twisted. They looked as if they were fighting one another for a glimpse of light. In the far distance, beyond the forest, I thought I could just make out the purple outline of the mountains. They didn't quite look like solid, believable mountains, though. They looked more like a silhouette that had been cut out from a strip of purple card.

'Come on, Ken!' Robert's impatient voice broke my

thoughts. 'No time for dawdling! Look sharp, or you'll miss the way!' Obediently, I followed my brother up a side turning. Now we were heading away from the lake, heading back up the slope of the valley towards the Great Tree.

The Great Tree was a huge, ancient oak which stood at the centre of a clearing close to the top of the Arborian forest. A few of its branches hung over the wall into the garden of Hedley House, but the House in the Air was on the opposite side of the tree, facing away from the wall. It commanded a panoramic view across the whole forest of Arboria. In the distance, I could see the lake and the mountains. Closer to me, I could imagine other tree houses, the houses where the Arborians lived. In my mind, most of these tree houses had canvas sides so that at night, when the lamps were lit inside, I could see the shadows of the Arborians as they went about their business: eating and drinking and sleeping and making love.

The House in the Air, though, did not have canvas sides. The House in the Air was built entirely from wood, mainly chestnut wood. Every piece of wood that had gone to build that House was of a different shape, because every piece had been hewn from the trees in the forest. Arborian wood does not come in neat strips and blocks and rectangles like the ordinary wood that you get in a timber yard. Arborian wood is living wood, and every piece is curved or rounded or twisted or knotted and, for every piece of wood, there is always another piece that will fit snugly beside it. Every piece can be whittled and carved and curved and shaped until it is just the right shape. And all those pieces of wood fit exactly together to make a house that has doors and windows and boards and beams and purlins and shingles and gutters.

But the House in the Air was not built like an ordinary tree

12

house. An ordinary tree house would have been built on a wooden platform nailed to the lower branches of the tree. The House in the Air didn't stand on a platform. The House in the Air hung on four stout ropes from the high branches of the Great Tree and, as the branches of the Great Tree moved gently with the wind, the House in the Air rocked all the time gently to and fro.

Heaving ourselves off the top rung of the ladder, we scrambled in through the doorway, tossing our bows and arrows into a corner. Robert reached into the depths of his knapsack and pulled out an old pair of binoculars. 'Right then,' he said. 'Let's take a look.'

Side by side, we knelt up against the windowsill, Robert squinting through the binoculars while I shaded my eyes with my hand. I peered at the trees on the Barbarian side of the lake, searching for signs of activity. 'Is that smoke?' I said after a time. 'It's coming from down there, quite near the water.'

Robert tried to re-focus the binoculars, while I tried to guide him in the right direction with a touch on the elbow. 'It's all right, Ken,' he said rather sharply. 'I've got it now.' He stared through the lenses for quite a long while. 'You're right, though,' he said finally. 'It is quite near the water. I wonder what's going on?' He continued to stare in the same direction for some time longer, his forehead wrinkling in concentration.

'Perhaps the Barbarians are marshalling their army,' I suggested. 'Perhaps Tommy was right and they're planning to attack us.' Leaning towards him, I reached for the binoculars. 'Let's have a look, Rob,' I begged. But Robert tightened his grip.

'You're not allowed to,' he told me firmly. 'Father gave them to me, not to you.'

13

'It's not fair!' I complained, reaching across to wrestle them away from him. But my brother was too quick for me. He thrust them into his knapsack and sprang to his feet, holding the bag behind his back. 'You can't have them!' he jeered. 'You can't—'

At that moment, though, we were interrupted by the distant sound of my mother's voice, anxiously calling to us from the far side of the wall. 'Robert! Kenneth! Where are you? What are you doing? Hurry up, your lunch is nearly ready!'

So our fight was abandoned before it had really begun. 'Come on, then,' ordered Robert curtly. We'd better go. Never mind the Barbarians for now. We'll be in real trouble if we're late for lunch again.'

It's funny, Jamie, if I ever mention the war to someone of your age, they don't seem to know which war I'm talking about. 'The Vietnam War?' they ask me. 'The Gulf War? The Iran-Iraq War?' I suppose your school history books mention all of those wars but, for someone of my age, the war can only mean one war, and that is the Second World War, the war against Adolf Hitler.

I was eleven years old at the start of that war, and I was seventeen by the time Germany finally surrendered. The war years were my years of growing up, of growing from boy-hood to manhood. Although I was too young to join the army and fight, the war still left an impression on me, an impression that has stayed with me for the rest of my life. Because, even in the garden of Hedley House, even in the forests of Arboria, the guns and the bombs and the armies never seemed so very far away.

By the time that war was actually declared, the preparations

14

had been going on for more than a year. My father, Hugh Storey, was too old for active service. He was a businessman, and we were quite well off in those days, but he still wanted to do his bit, so he volunteered to train as an air raid warden. He seemed quite happy strutting to and fro in his tin helmet and messing about with the gas masks and stirrup pumps and sandbags. He gave my mother the task of sticking brown paper crosses on every window pane in Hedley House. This was supposed to protect the glass from shattering if a bomb fell nearby.

My mother's name was Antonia Storey, or Toni for short. Before she married my father, she had been quite a famous actress. Her professional name was Antonia Vale, but I don't suppose many people would remember her now. You're certainly too young to remember her, Jamie. Anyway, she had always suffered from rather delicate nerves, and, at the thought of the troubles to come, her behaviour had really started to become quite erratic. If she was having a good day, though, she would try to help my father in whatever way she could, so perhaps the brown paper crosses kept her occupied during those long sultry afternoons.

The fifth person in the house was my grandmother, my mother's mother. Her name was Mrs Hedley, and she had her own little set of rooms at the back of the house next to the kitchen. She was quite an old lady, and she used to keep mostly to herself, but even my grandmother ended up being drawn into the preparations for war. Her particular job was to make up the thick blackout curtains which would prevent any chink of light being seen by the enemy bombers. Robert and I helped her to fold up all the old flower-patterned curtains and pack them away in trunks 'for the duration'.

My father decided to build an air raid shelter in the garden.

Many of our friends were using the prefabricated Anderson shelters that the government had issued, but my father for some reason wanted to open up the old abandoned ice house and use that instead. The ice house was an odd structure that had been built in the grounds of Hedley House in the long-ago days before people had refrigerators in their kitchens. It was built into the side of a little hill, and it consisted of two underground chambers with brick walls and vaulted ceilings, linked together by a low archway. Its entrance, set between two sloping banks of earth, was partly overgrown. I had always thought that it looked rather like a cave. Anyway, the ice house certainly made a good air raid shelter. Apart from patching up some of the brickwork, the only real work that was needed was to fit it with a pair of heavy iron doors.

I still remember the afternoon when the doors arrived. They were delivered by horse and cart, and I suppose they must have come from the family print works, or one of the other factories that the Storey family ran in Tollcester. My father took charge of the operation, assisted by my Uncle Magnus, my brother Robert, and Davy Hearn the gardener's boy.

Robert and I nodded warily in Davy's direction, and Davy nodded back at us. Davy Hearn was a year older than me, but a year younger than Robert. He was a tough-looking boy with dark tangled hair, darting eyes and crooked teeth, and he wore a pair of torn corduroy breeches and a dirty shirt with rolled-up sleeves. I knew that if I got too close to Davy Hearn I would notice an odd, slightly musky scent. But I usually tried to avoid getting too close to Davy, because there was something about him, some indefinable quality, that always made me feel rather uncomfortable.

Of course, I was really supposed to be helping the others

with their work, but I had never had much aptitude for practical tasks. In the end, I spent most of that afternoon sitting on the sidelines, trying to adjust the straps of my new gas mask. The strange rubbery smell inside it made me feel rather sick.

After everyone had been at work for an hour or so, my mother came down from the house to bring refreshments. She tottered uncertainly along the path in her high heels, carrying the tea things on a tray. My father, though, was not in a good temper. 'For heaven's sake, Toni,' he complained. 'Where's the milk? Can't you ever get anything right?'

'I'm sorry, Hugh, I'll go back for it,' my mother replied unhappily.

'Oh, what's the point?' my father replied wearily. 'By the time you've got yourself organised, the tea will probably be cold.'

A few months after this, the first evacuees started to arrive in the village. I hadn't imagined my mother wanting to take anybody in at Hedley House. Perhaps because of her nervous condition, she sometimes seemed rather a selfish woman, but I suppose that she must have had some sort of sense of duty. She had decided that, in principal at least, it would be a good idea to offer a temporary home to a child. To a nice child, at any rate.

'They're going to be arriving on the train at Helsing Halt and waiting in the village hall,' she explained to Robert and me. 'I thought we might go down there and see if we can find one that we like.'

We had to travel the two miles to Lower Helsing on foot, because my father, anticipating the start of rationing, had already started being 'careful' with petrol. We set off in the mild September sunshine, my mother, as usual, in unsuitable shoes, having to stop for frequent rests. Robert and I dawdled along picking blackberries from the hedgerows. But when we arrived at Lower Helsing, we were quite unprepared for the sight that greeted us.

The hall was packed with dirty, ragged, tired-looking children. Some were sitting cross-legged on the floor, but many, exhausted from their journey, were lying huddled in blankets or raincoats, sleeping, or trying to sleep. Each child had with them a small suitcase and a gas mask, and wore a label inscribed with their name. Here and there I noticed a couple of boys fighting, a group of girls playing with their dolls, someone scribbling with a pencil stub on a postcard, someone else leafing through a dog-eared *Tiger Tim* comic. A policewoman and a couple of ladies in Women's Voluntary Service uniforms were making their way to and fro along the lines, handing out mugs of hot milk. Several of our neighbours from the village were casting a doubtful eye over the potential guests on offer. From all directions I could make out the sound of muffled sniffing and crying. The atmosphere in the hall was stuffy and carried an unpleasant whiff of urine.

My mother drew her breath in sharply. 'But it's horrid!' she gasped. 'They all look so . . . so . . . I didn't think they'd be . . .' In dismay, she turned around and started to walk back the way she had come.

Over the next few days, that first group of evacuees did all manage to find places to stay, but the activities of the billeting officers did not, apparently, extend as far as Hedley House.

'I'm so glad we didn't have to take anyone in,' my mother said later. 'I've heard such stories. They wet the beds, they've got lice in their hair, horrible rashes on their skin. You can't understand what some of them are saying, and they don't know how to behave, some of them don't even know how to use a knife and fork. I'd be happy to have someone nice, of course, for someone nice I'd be the first to help.' In the end, of course, we *did* help, but it wasn't until the following spring that Janny Grogan arrived.

Janny came in the second year of the war, and I know that she came in the springtime, because I remember noticing, on the day that she came, that the trees and bushes in the garden did not yet have all their leaves. It was raining too, not hard, but a gently persistent spring rain, persistent enough to wet Janny's face. Because of the rain on her face, I could not, at first, detect her tears.

It was because of the rain too, that Robert and I had decided not to venture into Arboria that afternoon. Instead, we were exploring a corridor of unoccupied bedrooms in the north wing of the house that had not been used since my grandfather's day. The room in which we were playing had a row of old history books on its dressing table. I was sitting on the narrow bed, leafing though the pages of a book about the Stone Age, probably looking for pictures of scantily clad cave girls. Then, through the rear-facing window, I caught my first glimpse of our visitor. She was standing at the back door of Hedley House, flanked by two middle-aged ladies, one in a tweed suit and the other in the uniform of the Women's Voluntary Service. The kitchen and the back part of the house were my grandmother's domain, and so it was my grandmother who went to answer the door. 'You'd better come inside,' her voice echoed faintly from below. 'I'll have to fetch my daughter. *Antonia?*'

A moment later they were all out of sight, but I could hear the ring of their footsteps as they made their way through the back porch and across the stone flags of the kitchen floor. Robert and I swiftly made our way along the landing, to a position from which we could observe things at first hand. We knelt side by side clutching the banister railings, our bare knees wedged between the carved uprights. Below us, the empty hallway echoed with the solemn tick of the old grandfather clock that stood facing the front door. All the way down the staircase, the dark and forbidding portraits of our ancestors hung in their frames, looking on impassively at the scene that was unfolding below.

'I bet you she's an evacuee,' whispered Robert. 'Those ladies will be billeting officers. They'll say that we've got to take her. Mother won't like it one bit. Just you wait and see.'

'An evacuee?' I replied. I could feel my voice rising. 'How long will she be staying with us, Rob? Will we have to tell her about Arboria?'

'Just keep quiet, can't you?' Robert hissed. 'Never mind about Arboria just now. I'm trying to hear what they're saying.'

But from our elevated position we could make no sense of the hushed voices. After a few moments, though, the small party made its way out of the kitchen and up the step to appear below us in the hallway: three women, and a thin, silent little girl. The adults gathered around the hall table, leaving the girl for a moment on her own. I could see papers being produced, the lady in tweeds reaching into her handbag for her fountain pen, my mother signing three copies of a document. On the other side of the hallway, the girl stood quietly apart, head hung, hands by her sides.

'Can we offer you a cup of tea?' my mother said.

'How kind,' replied the tweedy lady, 'but I'm afraid we really must hurry along. There are just so many things to do nowadays. But thank you for being so helpful.' And then they were gone.

'Robert? Kenneth?' my mother called. 'I know you're up there. You'd better come down and meet your new little friend.'

Cautiously, we made our way to the bottom of the stairs, Robert stepping ahead, while I sheltered behind his broader frame, peering nervously over his shoulder. Across the width of the hallway we stared at our uninvited guest.

'This is Robert – and this is Kenneth,' said my mother to the girl. 'Boys, this is Janet Grogan. Say hello nicely.'

'Hello, Janet,' Robert said politely.

'Hello, Janet,' I repeated.

'Janny,' said the girl. 'People call me Janny.' I noticed at once that her speech had an unfamiliar, metallic twang.

Janny Grogan stood about the same height as me, and I guessed that she was about my age. She was wearing a dark green gabardine raincoat with the belt drawn tightly about her narrow waist, and on her head she wore a matching dark green school beret. She was carrying a small suitcase and a gas mask. The legs that I could see beneath the raincoat were thin and white with angular bony knees, and the face beneath the beret was thin and white with pale scattered freckles and a rather long, rather red nose. Her lank hair and her eyebrows were of a light, sandy colour, and her lips were thin and chapped and tightly drawn together. Her eyes were of a very pale grey, so pale that they appeared almost colourless. As Robert and I drew closer to her, I could see that the rims of her eyes were sore and red, presumably from recent weeping. Although her clothes were worn and shabby-looking, she wore them with dignity, managing somehow to convey an air of impoverished respectability.

'Would you like a biscuit, Janny?' my mother suggested

timidly. Despite her unstable nature, my mother was at heart a well-meaning person, but even I could tell that biscuits were not what the girl needed at that moment.

'I don't know,' Janny replied. Her head tilted fractionally down and she started to sniff back a sob. 'I don't think so.' At this moment, my grandmother appeared from the kitchen.

'The girl's worn out,' she said sharply. 'Can't you imagine what it's like on those trains, Toni? Come on, duckie, bed's what you need. Let's get you a hot water bottle.' And, brushing past Robert and myself, she briskly conducted Janny up the stairs and along the landing towards the empty bedrooms.

Janny ended up in the very end room in the front part of the house, the room that adjoined Robert's. Her door remained closed for several days and, during this time, Robert and I worked ourselves into a frenzy of speculation. Tiptoeing along the corridor, we would pause at her doorway, taking turns to place an ear to the keyhole. All that we ever heard, though, was faint, muffled weeping.

So who was this odd little girl with her strange-sounding speech? Where did she come from? What were her family like? And, above all, how long would she be stopping with us? My mother, although content to do everything that the wartime state of emergency obliged her to do, seemed uninquisitive about our guest, and we soon exhausted her meagre store of knowledge. My grandmother, though, proved a more fertile source of information.

'She's sitting up in bed now,' said the old lady on the second day of Janny's confinement. 'Looking out of the window. I don't suppose she's ever seen fields before. I've said she should write a postcard home, but she says that she doesn't have anyone to write to. Poor little thing.'

'Maybe she's an orphan,' suggested Robert.

'Perhaps her parents are foreign spies and they've been sent to prison for the Duration of Hostilities,' I speculated. 'Don't you think "Grogan" is a funny-sounding sort of name? I don't think it sounds very English. Actually, I thought her voice sounded a bit German.'

'How would you know that?' Robert jeered. 'You only heard her say a couple of words. She might have been from Scotland. Or Ireland. Or anywhere.'

'I don't think she's from any of those places,' my grandmother contributed. 'I think she comes from a different kind of place altogether.'

'We don't really have any idea where she came from,' retorted Robert. 'Do we? In any case, I thought all the evacuees came from London. Wouldn't that make her a cockney?'

'I expect the Germans are going to bomb lots of other cities as well,' I said. 'Cardiff. Edinburgh. Even Birmingham.'

'You're right, Ken,' Robert conceded. 'I suppose there'll be evacuees from all over the shop. Look, the rain's stopped now. Do you fancy going up to the House in the Air?'

'Race you there!' I shouted. Suddenly, we were bounding down the stairs, three at a time, tearing across the hallway, elbowing each other aside in the tussle to be first into the kitchen, first out of the kitchen door, first through the garden gate.

'Rob, have you ever noticed anything odd about the black fish?'

It was the next day. The weather had turned warmer, and my brother and I were basking on the flat rocks at the foot of the lake, our thighs and elbows baking on the smooth surface. We had wearied of stalking the Barbarians and, for the time being, our knapsacks and our bows and arrows lay abandoned on the rocks beside us. Janny, meanwhile, remained in her room, her mystery for the moment still unresolved.

'How do you mean, odd?' Robert was staring across the surface of the lake at something on the far bank, and he didn't seem particularly interested in anything that I had to say. 'They're just fish, aren't they? They're just like any other fish.'

But I wasn't going to be fobbed off so easily. 'Well, why do we never see them in the stream?' I persisted. 'The stream flows into the lake at the top, doesn't it, and then it flows out into the waterfall at the bottom. So why do we only see the black fish in the lake and never in the stream?'

Robert turned to face me, his face screwed up into a scowl. 'I don't know,' he replied. 'Have you ever really looked for them in the stream? And anyway, what does it matter? They're only fish!' He returned to his scrutiny of the far shore, shifting his position fractionally as he did so. 'I'm sure I saw somebody moving about near the water again. Perhaps you were right about what Tommy said. It does look as if those Barbarians are up to something.'

'I've only ever seen them in the lake,' I persisted. 'The fish, that is, not the Barbarians. And that's not all. Sometimes they make patterns. I've watched them. It's like a great dance, or a sort of geometric design. Something, anyway. I don't know.'

'For heaven's sake, Ken.' Robert didn't look at me this time. 'How could the stupid fish manage a thing like that? And anyway, what if they did?'

'I don't know,' I replied sulkily. 'I just thought you might . . .'

'Ssshhh!' Robert hissed me into silence. 'I can see someone now! Where did I put those damned binoculars!' He pointed his finger towards a spot on the opposite bank. I peered in the same direction, screwing up my eyes against the broken light that flashed from the surface of the water. Then, at last, I too caught a glimpse of movement among the distant branches.

'It's only Davy Hearn,' I said finally. 'But what's he doing, Rob? What can he be up to?'

Robert heaved himself into a sitting position, reached down into the depths of his knapsack and, after a few moments, produced the binoculars. He raised them to his eyes, adjusting the screws as he did so. 'You're right,' he said after a moment. 'Here, see for yourself.' With an air of lordly condescension, he handed them to me.

'Thanks, Rob.' I fiddled with the focusing screw, until the image finally shuddered into view. Sure enough, there in the distance was Davy Hearn. I stared at him. He hadn't seen me and, watching him through the binoculars, I felt safely detached from the threatening force of his presence.

'Is he on his own?' Robert's brisk voice cut in. 'I thought I saw him turning round. Is he talking to someone?'

Startled out of my reverie, I edged the binoculars slowly to the left, then slowly back to the right. 'Yes, I think . . . No, hang on . . . Good Lord! It's . . .' Speechless, unable to believe what I saw, I pressed the lenses even closer to my eyes.

'Here, let me look!' Unable to contain his frustration, Robert snatched the binoculars away from me. I struggled furiously to get them back and, during the tussle that followed, a flailing foot landed an unlucky kick on one of the quivers. With an untidy rattle, the arrows cascaded down the side of the rock. Alerted by the noise, Davy spun around in alarm and at once caught sight of us. For a moment, he remained frozen, then, abruptly, he turned and vanished into the undergrowth.

'You idiot!' Robert exclaimed. 'You've scared them away now!'

For a moment I stared at him. Then, slowly, comprehension began to dawn. '"Them" . . .' I repeated. 'Rob, you said *them*. Not him. *Them*. You saw them too, didn't you?'

Because I knew what I had seen and, indeed, there had been two of them. Two stocky figures half-hidden in the bushes behind the place where Davy had been standing. Two dark-faced men in softly gleaming helmets and breast-plates. Two Barbarian warriors with lank moustaches and copper-pointed spears.

'Yes,' my brother replied, half-reluctantly. 'I did say "them". I saw them too, Ken. I saw them too.' For another long moment, we stared at each other. Then the silence was broken by the sudden patter of raindrops on the rocks. Robert jumped to his feet. 'Come on!' He aimed not too gentle a kick at my side. 'Race you back to the house!'

Up until that day, Robert had always been the leader in our Arborian adventures. Robert had been the one who worked out the plans, Robert had been the one who made the decisions. I, on the other hand, had been the one blessed with the power of imagination. I had been the one who heard voices, I had been the one who saw things, I had been the one who knew what sort of clothes the Arborians and the Barbarians wore, what sort of weapons they carried. But all that started to change when Janny arrived. When Janny arrived, Robert began to see things too.

The teenagers have left the café now. The two boys and the girl were the first to go, a boy hanging on each of the girl's arms, while the solitary boy, the one who listened and watched, tagged along behind them. The final two, the boy and the girl who could not keep their hands off each other, stayed for a while longer, eventually making their departure when the woman behind the counter started to mop the floor. Now I am the only one left, and I can see from the woman's hostile glances that it is time for me to leave too.

Slowly I gather together my papers, stacking the loose sheets, rolling up the big scroll, finally stuffing the whole pile into my ancient briefcase. My work is progressing well, but there remains much to be done. I wish that I had begun my work sooner but that, of course, is a mistake that I cannot undo. It is too late now to do anything except finish writing my account, my account of the last days of the land of Arboria.

Then, Jamie, my work will be done. And then, it will be your turn.

## *Two*

# THROUGH THE GARDEN GATE

$\mathcal{A}$ couple of days after Janny's arrival, my grandmother gave me and Robert an errand to run. 'The girl needs some ointment for her eyes,' she explained. 'They're still very sore.'

'Isn't that just because she's been crying?' I suggested.

'I think there's something else as well,' said my grandmother. 'She says she's got pink-eye, and she's supposed to have some special stuff for it.'

'Didn't she bring any with her?' Robert enquired.

'She didn't have anything in her suitcase,' said my grandmother. 'Just a few clothes. Perhaps she had to catch the train in a hurry. Anyway, I need you to get the bus into Tollcester, and go to the chemist, and ask for some boracic solution, and a tin of boracic and Vaseline ointment.' She caught my startled look. 'It's all right, you won't have to remember anything. I've written it all down for you. Here's the money. Oh, and you can take some of these old tins back for salvage while you're about it. And you're to catch the bus straight home after.'

This excursion offered me a rare chance to take a break from routine. Although Robert was by this time travelling each day to Tollcester to go to the grammar school, I was still attending the village school at Lower Helsing, and would continue to do so until the coming September. A visit to the nearby cathedral city would give me an opportunity to see some different sights, to breathe some different air. Arboria, just this once, could wait until another time.

'She'll be up and about before long,' my grandmother reported the following day. 'She's a tough wee thing, more than you'd think to look at her, and she's starting to feel stronger. She's had some sorrows in her life, though, so I want you boys to be kind to her, make her feel at home here.' She looked at me sharply. 'And Kenneth – try not to bother her by asking too many questions.'

'Did the ointment do any good?' I asked.

'A bit,' my grandmother replied. I noticed that her lined features had taken on a slightly absent air. 'But her eyes are still quite red. I'm beginning to think that it's not the boracic that she really needs.'

After a few days, Janny started to make tentative appearances at mealtimes, sitting at the big kitchen table, at the far end from Robert and myself. She continued to occupy a private, silent space of her own, protected by an almost tangible barrier that we boys were reluctant to violate. Robert, more adventurous than I, was the first to speak to her.

'How are you today, Janny?' he ventured.

'A bit better, thank you,' Janny replied. She did not look up, but continued to tap away at the shell of her boiled egg, this task seemingly requiring all her concentration. Her pale, sandy head and narrow shoulders were silhouetted against the window, the expression on her narrow face indecipherable.

'What are you going to do this morning?' Robert persisted.

'I'll go back to my room in a little while,' said Janny. Neither of us could think of any reply to this, so conversation lapsed again, the silence punctuated only by the chink of cups and the tapping of spoons on eggshells. After a while, the girl rose silently and took her leave. Robert and I deposited the plates and egg cups in the sink and made our way out by the back door, across the vegetable patch, and through the garden gate.

'Good morning Master Robert, good morning Master Kenneth.' It was Tommy Pelling, calling out to us from somewhere within the dank recesses of the log store. I paused for a moment, peering through the doorway. Inside, I caught a glimpse of Tommy's slight form, as he bustled about amongst the neatly stacked wood. I waited for a moment to see whether he was going to come out and speak to us, but he did not appear. 'I'll leave you to it, young masters,' he called out after a moment. His tone sounded more muffled. 'I've got a busy day today.'

We continued on our way. After a time, as we approached the shores of the lake, the track started to slope downwards. As the ground became steeper, we found ourselves breaking into a run. I was struggling now to keep pace with my longer-legged brother; a painful stitch beginning to rake at my side.

'Slow down, Rob,' I called. 'What if there's an ambush?'

'Don't be such a baby,' Robert called back over his shoulder. 'There won't be any ambush today. Can't you see how peaceful everything is in the forest? Come on, I'll see you down at the hiding place.'

A few minutes later, I caught up with him. He had arrived at the shore of the lake and was scrambling across the boulders to the place where we sometimes used to sit and watch the black fish. At the end of the row of boulders there lay a patch of flattish ground on which there grew an irregular row of willow trees, their branches drooping down over the gently rippling surface of the lake. Ducking his shoulders, Robert wriggled his way between the branches of the first tree. Moments later, I followed him, finally emerging into a dry, secret hollow that was protected from the weather and shielded from the sunlight by a densely woven canopy of branches. We were alone now, this was our private hiding place, and from here we could peer across the waters of the lake and observe the comings and goings of Davy Hearn and the Barbarians on the opposite bank. I looked out anxiously, alert for any sign that the enemy might be making ready to attack. Robert drew the binoculars from his knapsack and squinted through them, scanning the lakeside from end to end. After a little while, he nudged me.

'Look, off to your left,' he hissed. 'I can see them up there on those crags, staring down into the water. And there are more of them this time? What do you think they're doing?'

I followed the direction of my brother's pointing finger. Sure enough, I could see six or seven of the Barbarian warriors. They were crouched at the lip of the crags, staring intently down into the water. 'They might be watching the black fish,' I replied at length. 'But I don't think they're trying to catch them. They're too high up. I wonder what they *are* up to? Here, give me those . . .'

Reluctantly, my brother handed me the binoculars but, in my excitement, my clumsy fingers failed to connect, and the instrument fell with a clatter onto the ground. From the far side of the lake, a row of dark, startled faces swivelled around to stare at us. The next moment, the Barbarians sprang to their feet, turned tail and vanished once more into the undergrowth.

'Damnation!' said Robert. 'You're such a butterfingers! And now they've gone again. It's all your fault.' He picked up the glasses and examined them anxiously.

While my brother was doing this, I started to think about the Barbarians. Of course, I reasoned, they won't spend all of their time staring at the black fish. Nor will they spend all their time thinking about attacking us. They must have homes somewhere, perhaps in a camp in one of the clearings. They must have wives and sons and daughters. Perhaps their daughters might sometimes come down to the lake to bathe. If I was lucky, I might catch a glimpse of a naked Barbarian girl . . . but, of course, if that happened, I should really hide my eyes, or look the other way. My grandmother would have warned me that, if I gazed for too long, I would be struck blind. I didn't really believe this, though. It had certainly never happened to anybody that I knew.

'No sign of anyone now,' said Robert suddenly. Satisfied that the binoculars were undamaged, he was once again scanning the opposite shore. 'But I didn't like the look of them one bit. Where have they all come from? We ought to make some preparations, in case they do decide to attack us.'

'Do you think they'll come soon?' I said doubtfully.

'It's anybody's guess,' Robert answered. 'But we should be sure and maintain a state of alert for the foreseeable future. Keep watching the far shore.'

'Perhaps we could start an Arborian army,' I suggested. 'We could have our headquarters at the House in the Air. Then we could be ready to defend Arboria. If they ever did come across.'

Robert considered this for several moments. 'Good idea,' he said finally. 'And of course we've already got our bows and arrows. We'll have to remember to carry them at all times. Then we'll be safe.' Secure in this knowledge, we felt able to relax a little. Robert reached down among the roots of the tree and produced a bottle of ginger beer.

'Refreshments?' he suggested.

'Refreshments,' I agreed. My brother popped the cork and took a long, gurgling draught from the bottle. When he had drunk his fill, he wiped his mouth on the grey sleeve of his pullover and passed the bottle to me. 'Here, you can have what's left.' He waited while I swallowed the dregs, then started on a new topic. 'Hey, what do you think of Janny Grogan? She's a bit strange, isn't she? Do you really think she might be a spy?'

I conjured up a mental image of Janny's pale, tear-streaked face, her silent, remote demeanour. She did not at all resemble the dark, sinister undercover agents who appeared in the comics that we read.

'No, I can't really imagine it,' I conceded finally. 'But of course we can't be too careful. I suppose the best spies wouldn't look the way you'd expect them to look. Perhaps she's a master of disguise.' I sniggered. 'Or should I say, a mistress.'

Robert ignored this. 'She's certainly different from us,' he mused. I stifled another snigger. 'No, not just because she's a girl, stupid. I mean, I don't think she sees things the same way we do. She somehow never really seems to be *with* the rest of us, if you know what I mean. It's as if she was really some-where else. Gran would probably say that she's away with the fairies.' We both considered this for a while. 'Anyway,' Robert concluded, 'probably best not to tell her too much about

Arboria. For the time being, at least. Until we manage to find out a bit more about her.'

'Yes, probably best,' I agreed. 'What about the Barbarians, though? Can I have another look through the binoculars?'

'Here,' said Robert grudgingly. 'Just try not to drop them this time.'

That summer, the first summer of the war, was the time of the Blitzkrieg, the first big attack by Hitler's bombers on the cities of Europe. Although an assault on England was expected nightly, to begin with none came, and for many weeks the air raid sirens remained silent. It was because of the sirens, though, that Robert and I were finally thrown together with Janny.

On the night when the air raid warning finally sounded, my father was not in the house. I am not sure whether he was patrolling the village streets in his air raid warden's helmet and greatcoat, or whether he had simply been detained by some crisis at the print works. My father spent long hours looking after the works, while my Uncle Magnus devoted most of his time to a factory that made women's underwear and was therefore generally known as the 'knicker factory'. The family owned a shoe factory too, and quite a few other businesses in Tollcester. When my father came home he would usually be tired and bad-tempered, and his clothes would smell of printer's ink. At these times, he wouldn't want to talk to Robert and me, he would just want to get into a hot bath with a glass of gin.

In any case, on the night of the air raid warning, it fell to my mother to organise, as best she could, the safe transfer of the occupants of Hedley House to the shelter. The shelter, of course, was situated a little way beyond the garden gate at the edge of the Arborian forest, and this meant that, in order to enjoy the protection of its reassuring walls, my mother, my grandmother and Janny would have to be granted safe passage through Arboria. So, while my grandmother was busy in the kitchen filling the Thermos flask with hot tea, and while my mother was scurrying from room to room frantically collecting armfuls of blankets, Robert and I, waiting in the back porch, were able to hold a hastily whispered conference.

'Mother and Gran will be OK,' said Robert firmly. 'But I'm not sure about Janny.'

'Perhaps we should blindfold her,' I suggested.

'Don't be daft,' said Robert. 'What would we say to the grown-ups? Anyway, look, it's getting dark. She won't see much. And she'll be confused. I bet she won't even remember which way we came.'

'What are you boys muttering about now?' my mother interrupted. 'Come along, it's high time we were getting down to the shelter. Robert, you'll have to carry these things. And you'd better take the torch and go in front. Has anyone got the alarm clock? Oh dear, it would be so much easier if Hugh was here. But you know the way, darling, so we can all follow you. Mummy and I will bring up the rear. And Kenneth, you and Janny can be in the middle. You'd better hold hands with her, Kenny, just to make sure that she keeps to the path.' Janny and I exchanged apprehensive glances but, after a moment, she meekly offered me her hand.

With the wail of the air raid siren scything mournfully through the twilight, our small party made its way across the vegetable patch, through the garden gate and past the log store. If Tommy Pelling noticed our passing, he did not make any response, for the small building remained inscrutably silent and dark. As the gloom of the forest settled around us, I sensed the nervousness of the others and gave a firm grip to Janny's cool, slender hand. Did I feel a faint answering pressure? Perhaps I did but, there again, perhaps all that came later. Drawing Janny along with me, I followed my brother up the narrow path to the left. When we arrived at the entrance to the shelter there was a sudden moment of confusion.

'Drat!' said Robert. 'There's a beastly great padlock on the doors.'

'Oh yes,' my mother remembered belatedly. 'Hugh put it there. I think he was worried about people getting in, he said that tramps might go in there for something or other. He's always worrying about tramps. Robert, you'd better run back with the torch, you can put those other things down for a minute. I remember now, the key's on one of those hooks by the back door. We'll wait here. Off you go.'

While my brother was away on his errand, it fell to my mother to keep the rest of us entertained. Fortunately, she was having one of her better days. 'Let's have a sing-song,' she suggested. '"Make the gallery ring"', that's what we used to say in the old days. What about one of those songs from the wireless?' By the time we'd got through a couple of verses of *Run, Rabbit, Run*, Robert had reappeared with the vital key and we were soon ensconced in the safety of the shelter.

The wail of the air raid siren was soon to become a familiar sound, and we were to spend many nights huddled in the ice house as the enemy aircraft rumbled overhead, on their way to attack Birmingham or Wolverhampton or Liverpool. Luckily for us, our air raid shelter was better appointed than the one-room Anderson shelters that most other families had. At the bottom of the stone steps there were two separate chambers, one leading off the other. The first area was our sitting room, and that had been kitted out with some battered old armchairs and an ancient sofa. At the end of this was an archway, across which my mother had hung an old set of curtains. Through the archway was the sleeping area, a narrow, bare room equipped with three sets of iron bunk beds. At the far corner of the bunk room there had once been a low doorway that led to some of the abandoned vaults of the ice house, but this portal had been bricked up when the alterations were being done. The mysterious underground realms were, at least for the time being, beyond our reach.

'I've got some matches and candles,' said my mother. 'You three children may as well go straight to bed now. Gran and I will sit up in here for a while. We'll probably have a little drink before we turn in.' Clutching our candles obediently, the three of us made our way through the arch and pulled the curtains across the opening.

In the bunk room, Robert and Janny and I struggled through the clumsy and embarrassing process of changing into our night things in the half-light. We boys had agreed without discussion to occupy the set of bunks nearest to the curtained archway, Robert on top, myself below. Meanwhile, Janny had chosen the top bunk on the opposite side of the room, shinning up the end of the iron bed-frame with a display of agility that momentarily startled me.

'Can you tuck yourselves in?' It was the muffled sound of my mother's voice behind the curtain in the adjoining room.

'Leave it to us,' Robert shouted. 'All right, everyone, candles out in thirty seconds.' For a few brief moments I lay there staring at the flickering shadows on the ceiling, then all was darkness.

I didn't go to sleep of course. Everything was far too strange and exciting for that. My mattress was thin and hard and lumpy, and the grey blanket that covered me was tickling my cheeks and my nose. From the other room I could hear the faint murmur of the grown-ups' conversation, the muffled clink of glasses. Further away, the siren continued to howl its lament.

'Rob,' I whispered, 'are you awake?'

'Shut up,' hissed Robert. 'Go to sleep. You'll wake Janny.'

'Rob,' I persisted, 'if the Germans bombed the forest, what would happen? What would happen to Arboria?'

Robert did not reply.

'And what about the Barbarians?' I persisted. 'Could they ever make bombs like Hitler's? What if they tried to bomb us too?'

'What are you talking about, you boys?' This was a different voice; it was Janny's small sleepy voice, just audible on the far side of the room. 'What do you mean? Who are the Barbarians? Do they live in the forest?'

'They live in a clearing on the far side of the lake . . .' I began.

'Shut up, Ken,' Robert interrupted me. 'Look Janny, we can't tell you. It's a secret. And it's nothing to do with you anyway. Now will the two of you both be quiet?'

Soon, from the gradual change in Robert's breathing, I knew that he had fallen asleep. Somehow, though, on the far side of the bunk room, I could still sense Janny's silent, wakeful presence. I suppose I should have felt sorry for her and, to some extent, I did. My main feeling, though, was something that was new to me, something that I hadn't felt before. It was a bit like excitement, and it was also a bit like fear, but it wasn't quite either of those things. In the end, though, I must have fallen asleep, because I don't remember hearing the grown-ups come to bed. That first air raid turned out to have been a false alarm, and it was to be some months before we heard the sound of the sirens again.

'I think Janny might be feeling a little bit lonely,' said my mother tentatively. 'Being taken away from her family and her home, and then coming to a strange place. Don't you think it would be nice if she could join in with some of your games? We really ought to try harder to make her feel welcome.'

It was a few days after the sirens had gone off. Robert and I were sitting side by side on the old stone bench by the rear porch of Hedley House. Robert was whittling away at an ash twig to make a new arrow for his bow. I had a large pad of cartridge paper on my knees, and on this I was trying to draw a map of the forest. Here were the Arborian tree houses, here was the lake, and here was the Barbarian camp . . . A little way away from us, my mother was pottering about in the vegetable patch, in the corner where the chives grew. At the far side of the garden, where the branches of the Great Tree overhung the wall, I could just make out Janny's insubstantial figure. In the dappled shade cast by the branches, she was drifting aimlessly about among the long grass, her cardigan and her grey pleated skirt wilting tiredly in the spring warmth. I was annoyed with my mother for referring to the affairs of Arboria as games, but I felt it wiser not to make a fuss.

'I suppose so,' replied Robert ungraciously. He turned to me then and continued in a lower voice, 'I suppose we could let her come into the forest. What do you think?'

For a moment I considered this. 'Perhaps we should give her an initiation test,' I ventured. 'Some kind of task to accomplish, some kind of ordeal to see whether she's fit to become an Arborian. What kind of ordeal, though? I'm not sure. Perhaps if . . .'

'What have you got to discuss, boys?' my mother interrupted us. 'Can't you see the poor girl's homesick?'

'All right, Mother,' Robert called back. He turned back towards me. 'Ken, I think I've got just the thing. Janny?' The distant Janny turned slowly to face us. 'We're going for a walk in the forest. You can come with us if you like. Have you ever used a bow and arrow?'

So, after some brief but essential discussions about what shoes and hats to wear and what time we needed to be back for tea, the three of us headed out of the back door, across the vegetable patch and through the garden gate.

Janny's presence must have come as a surprise to Tommy Pelling because, when we paused at the log store to collect the bows and arrows, Tommy handed them to me with no word of greeting, with nothing more than a pair of abruptly raised eyebrows. At the doorway, Janny hesitated for a moment, a puzzled look on her narrow face. Robert and I exchanged glances at this. 'Let's keep going,' I said quickly. So we boys continued on our way with Janny following close behind.

As we approached the turning for the ice house, the path began to broaden out and slope gently downwards. We wound our way between the tall stems of the trees, the sun's rays slanting between the branches in long wedges of light. The clumps of knotted tree roots were softened by long drifts of bluebells, and the scent of the flowers hung heavily in the air. Down the track the three of us strode, past the path that led up to the two tightly padlocked iron doors of the ice house, down the steeply sloping track towards the near shore of the lake. Once or twice, I heard a rustle in the undergrowth, as if some unseen being were silently keeping pace with us. Perhaps it was a detachment from the Arborian army, it occurred to me. Yes, that was it. The Arborians were watching over us. The Arborians were keeping us safe.

As we strode on towards the lake, I found myself starting to wonder what form of ordeal Robert had in mind for Janny. Was he going to ask her to shoot a pigeon or a rabbit at twenty paces? Was he going to ask her to reach into the water and bring out one of the black fish? But we didn't take the path that led down to the lake. Robert led us instead along the high ground that skirted the shoreline. Down below us to our left, the tops of the six willow trees nodded gently, like a row of gigantic shaggy heads.

The three of us were well spaced out by now. Robert, as always, was walking in front, with his bow and arrows slung over his shoulder. Janny was following a little distance behind him, while it was left to me to bring up the rear. Watching Janny from the back, I could see at once that this wasn't the first time that she had walked along a woodland path. The stones and roots and puddles formed a miniature obstacle course for the unwary, but she picked her way among them with light, sure feet, scarcely wavering in her path as she followed in my brother's wake.

As we drew level with the wooden bridge that spanned the stream, I began to wonder whether Robert had in mind for Janny some daring confrontation with the Barbarians. The Barbarians, though, were skulking out of sight, waiting perhaps to see what surprises this strange new visitor might be bringing with her to the forest. At any rate, Robert did not approach the bridge but veered off, at the last moment, along a narrow track that led back uphill and away from the water. Janny, unfaltering, took the sudden change of direction in her stride, but I was getting out of breath and flustered, and I nearly lost my footing. We continued on our new course. For a few moments I was perplexed until, suddenly, I realised that my brother was leading us back through the forest in the direction of the Great Tree. This must have been his goal all along. He had taken the long route on purpose. Robert wanted to impress our guest with the extent of our kingdom.

A short time later, we arrived in the clearing. Beneath the branches of the Great Tree, the three of us formed a loose circle, not sitting but standing. Robert and I both knew instinctively that this would lend a sense of occasion to the gathering. Janny must have sensed it too, for she stood straight, silent and grave, waiting to see what was about to happen.

'Janny Grogan,' said Robert finally. 'We welcome you to the Kingdom of Arboria.' Janny said nothing. She did not laugh or giggle, as many children would have done. She maintained her air of solemnity. 'However,' Robert continued, 'before you can aspire to the full status of an Arborian citizen, you will be required to undergo an ordeal.'

Janny bowed her head fractionally. Robert then turned away from us and began to walk slowly around the tree. Janny followed him, and I once again brought up the rear. On the far side of the massive trunk, there dangled the long rope ladder, extending far above us into the branches. For its rungs, the ladder had curving, irregularly shaped pieces of tree branch, and for its ropes it had knobbly, hairy lengths of twisted twine. Of course, if ever the Barbarians decided to attack us, the ladder would have to be hauled up out of the way but, just at the moment, it dangled down invitingly. The rope ladder led up to a wooden platform that rested upon the lower branches of the Great Tree, and from that platform there rose a stronger, wooden ladder that led up to the next platform. From here there extended another, narrower ladder, and so it continued, until eventually you got to the highest platform of all.

'This is the Great Tree of Arboria,' Robert was explaining. 'And at the top of the Great Tree is the House in the Air. That's where the Arborian headquarters is. You can't see it from down here and it's quite a long climb to get there. I'll go first, then Ken will follow me. Then you're to climb up after us. Do you think you can do that?'

'I'll try,' said Janny. I had expected to detect at least a glimpse of apprehension in her grey eyes, but there was nothing.

'Very well,' Robert declared. He turned smartly around and grasped the rungs of the ladder. My brother was a good, practised climber. He made his way briskly and efficiently up the tree, hand over hand, foot over foot. Such was Robert's economy of movement that the ladder hardly swayed beneath his weight. In only a few seconds he had disappeared among the branches of the tree, and only the faint rustle of the leaves above us told us that he was still climbing.

'It sounds like a long way up,' Janny observed.

'It is a long way, yes,' I replied. 'And there are other ladders further up in the branches. But the rope ladder can only take the weight of one at a time. We have to wait for Robert to call down.'

Janny nodded. For a few long moments we waited.

'Next!' came Robert's voice from far above us. I turned to the ladder and started to climb. I was not as good a climber as my brother. I had never been naturally well co-ordinated, and I suffer sometimes from shortness of breath, but I had at least no fear of heights, and I had learned through long practice to heave myself up from rung to rung without mishap. I lacked the discipline of Robert's technique, though, and the tail end of the rope ladder lashed around wildly below me. Eventually, though, I reached the top of my climb. At the threshold of the House in the Air, I found Robert lying on his front, peering down at the scene below. I threw myself down next to him. A light breeze was blowing, and the house was swaying gently to and fro on its ropes. We lay there side by side for a few moments, enjoying the soothing sensation of weightlessness.

'Let's make her wait a bit longer,' my brother whispered. 'Just to keep her on her toes.' Far below, through a gap in the branches, I could just make out Janny's foreshortened form. She was standing exactly where we had left her, her head tilted up now, straining for a glimpse of her destination.

'Isn't that long enough?' I suggested after an interval.

'I suppose we don't need to scare her out of her wits,' said Robert. 'OK. Are you ready?' I nodded.

'Next!' we shouted in unrehearsed unison.

For a moment, Janny didn't move. Then, slowly, she took a couple of steps, not towards the rope ladder, but towards the mighty stem of the tree itself. Robert and I exchanged bewildered glances. Janny appeared to be studying the tree, casting her gaze over the knobbly surface of its bark. As she did this, her feet were busy too, wriggling their way out of their sandals and ankle socks, flexing themselves on the short grass of the clearing. Finally, Janny shed her drab cardigan and rolled up the sleeves of her blouse. For a long moment, every creature in the forest seemed to hold its breath. Then, bare-legged and bare-armed, Janny Grogan stepped towards the Great Tree and started to climb.

It was like watching a cat shinning up a wooden fence. The girl seemed to be ascending almost vertically through the air. Gravity had become simply an inconvenience to be ignored. Her eyes were focused on the way ahead of her; her long fingers and feet unconsciously sought handholds and toeholds; her supple limbs propelled her spare body upwards with fluid, unconscious co-ordination. As she reached the lower branches of the tree, I could see that her face was slightly flushed, but her breathing did not appear to be any faster than normal. I noticed that Robert's jaw was hanging open, and I realised that mine was too.

'She's past the top of the rope ladder now,' breathed Robert. 'But she's not using the steps. How's she doing it?' We exchanged baffled looks. 'Look lively, though, she'll be here in a sec.'

Spontaneously, we both rose to our feet. A second later, Janny's tousled head appeared over the edge of the platform, followed by her two hands, followed by an ivory knee, followed by another knee, and then she was standing erect before us with the whole of the forest of Arboria spread out below. She smoothed down the pleats of her skirt. Her eyes were glistening, her lips slightly parted. She was not smiling, she was not laughing, but the look on her narrow face was, unmistakably, a look of triumph. We stared at her dumbly. There was a long, long moment of silence. Her slender form seemed aglow with energy.

'Well, boys,' said Janny finally, 'are you going to let me join in your games now?'

*

45

So Janny was allowed to join in. Within the gloomy confines of Hedley House, she remained the same sad, pale withdrawn creature who had been delivered to us by those two kind ladies on that damp spring day. But, set free to roam in the forest of Arboria, she was transformed into a different being: a quick, vibrant, mercurial creature who was somehow almost an integral part of the forces of nature that encircled us. She could run as fast as Robert, and she could climb trees like a squirrel. At archery, she would have been fit to lead the Arborian army while, crouched by the side of the lake, she could pluck the black fish from the water with all the startling dexterity of the Barbarian girls whom I sometimes imagined fishing there. She had sharp eyes too, sharp enough to spot a rabbit or a weasel hiding from us in the undergrowth, sharp enough to count the eggs in a nest in the high crook of a bough.

At the House in the Air, at the Arborian headquarters, Janny found herself a natural place. I had come up with the idea that we should all give ourselves Arborian titles, and the others had enthusiastically agreed with this. Robert, as the eldest, was elected High Lord, while I, with my extensive knowledge of Arborian history and customs, was to be known as Keeper of the Lore. For Janny, we devised the position of Chief Scout. It was Janny who could steal out into the night from the House in the Air, it was Janny who could crawl on her stomach along the branches of the Great Tree, it was Janny who could skip her way from treetop to treetop. It was Janny who would catch the first glimpse of the Barbarian hordes as they assembled with their spears to invade our sacred land, and it was Janny who could hurry back to bring word to the Arborian army of the danger that threatened.

'Send word to the Arborian bowmen,' Robert instructed her

one afternoon. 'Let them know that they can stand down for the night.'

'The bowmen have been informed,' replied Janny. For a moment, something like a smile seemed to cross her features. She must have noticed me looking at her, though, for she quickly composed herself.

'Good work, Chief Scout,' said Robert. 'Now, how about some refreshments?'

I fetched the picnic basket from its corner, and Janny and I knelt beside it to open a bottle of lemonade and to butter some slices of bread. The first ration books had been issued by this stage of the war but, in the country district around Lower Helsing, it was still quite easy to obtain butter and other such necessities. Robert watched while Janny and I prepared the feast.

I enjoyed buttering bread with Janny. As a matter of fact, I enjoyed doing just about anything with Janny. Where once I had followed my brother about like a small eager dog, I now found myself forsaking his company and looking for excuses to spend time with the girl. So it was that I contrived to be with Janny to carry out the various tasks that were necessary for day-to-day Arborian life. We prepared the refreshments, we collected the sticks for kindling, we cut down the brambles where they were blocking the paths, we fitted the new rungs to the ladders when the old ones began to split.

While carrying out such work, we exchanged few words. Our companionship seemed to go beyond mere language. I found deep satisfaction in a duty wordlessly shared, in a task carried out without the need for discussion, in a small project brought to completion in companionable silence. Sometimes, at the point of fulfilment, there would be an exchange of glances, a conspiratorial moment that conferred brief union between us. But Janny seemed always to check herself, always to draw back at the last moment from anything that felt too much like intimacy. Even here in the forest she remained a private person. There was some inner part of herself around which she seemed to have built a fence and, whatever it was that was inside that fence, it remained inviolable. More and more, though, I found myself becoming curious about what exactly it was that she was protecting.

Meanwhile, I was beginning to realise, not only my brother, but Janny too could easily outstrip me both in strength of arm, in fleetness of foot and in sharpness of eye. With their superior physical prowess, the two of them seemed in many ways to be natural allies, and I realised that I was in danger of becoming merely the child in this little family of three. What saved me, though, what kept me as an equal partner, was that in matters of Arborian knowledge and lore I was accepted as the ultimate authority. If the girl detected anything in me that was of interest to her, I concluded, it can only have been my secret wisdom and the jealously guarded power that it had started to confer. But, truthfully, I doubted whether she really saw much in me at all.

'I've got to go now,' said Janny suddenly. We had finished our picnic and, without saying goodbye, she disappeared over the edge of the platform and vanished into the foliage below.

'It's odd, isn't it?' Robert observed sharply. 'Have you noticed that she's always the first to leave? I wonder what it is that she has to rush off for? Do you think she really is one of us? Really one of the Arborians?'

I thought about this for a few moments. 'She is and she isn't,' I said eventually. 'When she's here, she's like an Arborian, but it's as if she . . . she sort of needs to remind us that she has other things to do too. I wonder what sort of things they could be?'

'I wonder,' Robert echoed, but something in the tone of his voice told me that he already had half an idea of the answer. 'Is there anything left in that bottle?

You've probably realised by now that my brother and I were very different from one another. Although he was only two years older than me, Robert remained the leader in everything that we did, while I was content to leave the last word to him. As far back as I can remember, Robert had always seemed to know what he wanted from life and what he needed to do in order to get it. At school, his reports used to say that, although not 'naturally gifted', he was nevertheless capable of 'exemplary application'. He worked hard at his lessons and he played hard at his sports. Later, when he was called up into the army, I'm sure that he must have fought hard, but by then we had begun to lose touch with one another. Later still, when he went into the family business, he worked hard at that too; in fact he ended up running the print works for almost forty years.

But I never really had any idea what I wanted. I hated school and I couldn't see the point of most of the things that I was expected to learn there. My reports used to say that I had 'some ability but lacked concentration', and I was forever being told off by my teachers for reading books that I shouldn't have been reading, or for playing cat's cradle, or for staring out of the window instead of concentrating on the lesson. One of the teachers, Mrs Deakins, was constantly making an example of me, screaming at me with her furious face inches away from mine, forcing me to stand in the corner for being lazy and then smacking the backs of my legs when I wasn't expecting it. Eventually, I became so frightened of her that I started to have temper tantrums when it was time to go to school in the morning. Sometimes I would throw myself on the floor and punch the skirting board until my knuckles bled. Once I clung onto the leg of the kitchen table and defied anyone to drag me out of the house. When these things happened, my mother would write a note to Mrs Deakins, and I would be allowed to stay at home. I never saw the contents of these notes, but Robert had the job of delivering them to the school, so he was usually able to discover what my mother had written.

'She says that your nerves are in a delicate state and you must be allowed to rest,' he quoted derisively one afternoon. 'What it really means is that you're hysterical and you're spoiled. I'm the oldest, so I'm expected to work hard and set an example, but you're the baby, so you're allowed to do just as you please.'

Although I resented being called a baby, I suppose it is true that I was spoiled. As time went by, I spent less and less time in the schoolroom. Now and then I was taken to see the doctor, and he would prescribe me this tonic or that, but none of the medicines seemed to make any difference. The little notes to Mrs Deakins continued, and the periods away from school grew longer and longer.

'Even though you're at home, Kenneth, you still mustn't neglect your lessons,' my mother would say occasionally. 'But perhaps you might spend a little time with your grandmother this afternoon. I think I need to have a lie down.'

When it was one of her bad days, my mother would often have to go upstairs to lie down. When she married my father, he had made her give up the theatre but, without her acting, she was never really happy. True, she sometimes seemed lively and full of bright ideas, but on some days she didn't even have the energy to get out of bed. Her nerves, like mine, were in a delicate state of balance and, as she often pointed out to me, 'this wretched war hasn't helped one little bit.' I suppose that while Robert took after my father, it would be fair to say that, in many ways, I took after my mother.

But, with my mother so often indisposed, it was with my grandmother that I came to spend many of my daytime hours, and it is my grandmother whom I must thank for what little education I had. I think I mentioned that my grandmother was called Mrs Hedley, Mabel Hedley, actually. It was the Hedley family who had built Hedley House many generations ago, but at various periods my father's people, the Storeys, had occupied the house too. When my parents got married, Hedley House had passed once again to the Storeys, although my grandmother continued to live there. I remember her brewing her strangely scented green tea in the downstairs back kitchen. Next door to the kitchen was her little parlour, whose air was heavy with the fragrance of the tobacco that she smoked in her porcelain pipe.

I spent many hours with the old lady. We would sit facing each other in the two old Windsor chairs on either side of her fireplace, and, soothed by the tang of her tea and lulled by the aroma of her tobacco, I would listen entranced to everything that she had to tell me. I didn't learn anything about exothermic reactions or about irregular verbs or about South America, but I heard a lot of stories about Lower Helsing and Upper Helsing, about the Saxons who used to farm there, and about the Romans who built the Tollcester Road and Langham Street. I learned about Hedley House too, and about the lake behind the house, and about the forest and about the ice house that my great-great-grandfather had built. And I learned other things too: strange, unsettling things.

'Once upon a time,' said my grandmother, 'Arboria was my country. It's your country now, but years ago, when I was just a little girl and your mother and father hadn't even been born, Arboria was mine. It was given to me by the children who came before me, and in time I passed it on to the children who came after me, so I can tell you all about the Arborians and the Barbarians. It was all recorded in the great Book of Arboria,' she added, 'and one day, Kenny, that book will be yours. And the book will tell you about the Good People, too.'

'The Good People?' I interrupted her . 'Who are they? Where do they live?'

'They live where they've always lived,' the old lady replied. 'Beneath the hill at the top of the forest. Deep under the earth below Hedley House. They've been here since long, long ago. They were here even before the Romans came to Tollcester.'

'Wasn't it the ancient Britons who were here before the Romans?' I asked her. I had been reading a history book a couple of days earlier.

'Even before the ancient Britons,' she said quietly. 'The Good People were here long, long before that.' For several moments she sank into reflective silence, as if unsure whether to continue. She took a short sip of her tea, followed by a long pull at her pipe. 'The Good People,' she repeated at last. 'They were here long before all of the others came, and some folk say that they'll still be here long after all the others have gone.'

'Have you ever seen them?' I said.

'Only once,' she replied, 'and that was a long time ago. I was just a young girl.' Once again, she fell silent. 'I'm old now,

Kenny,' she continued finally. 'I don't suppose I'll see the Good People again in this lifetime. But perhaps one day you might see them.' For a moment, she looked almost angry, as if she regretted having spoken. 'But that's enough for today,' she said suddenly. 'Why don't you go and see if your mother wants a cup of tea?' I turned away from her, uncertain how much of her story to believe.

Of course, history books weren't the only books that I read. The house was full of story books too, shelf upon shelf of them. I used to love the power of those books to draw me into their fantastic imaginary places, to transport me to wonderful realms that stood quite apart from the everyday world. When I was very young, I read books of fairy tales, of folk tales, of sleeping princesses and enchanted castles and goblins and witches and demons. As I grew older, I started to read books of adventure, books about pirates, desert islands, hidden treasure and ships flying the skull and crossbones. And, after that, I started once more to read books about magical kingdoms, about people who could fly, people who could change their shape and about other strange creatures with terrifying powers.

For each one of these magical worlds, of course, there was a special way of getting there from the ordinary world. Perhaps you had to jump off a windowsill and fly. Perhaps you had to slip down a rabbit hole or walk through a magic mirror. Perhaps you had to step through a magic amulet or through the back of a wardrobe.

From reading these books, I started to understand that Robert, Janny and I were not alone. It seemed that other children, too, had their own secret, magical places, places in which they could find refuge from the everyday routine of mealtimes and teachers and rules. But perhaps books of that kind seem a little old-fashioned to you, Jamie. Perhaps you read a different kind of book altogether. Perhaps you'd rather look at a computer screen than the pages of a book. For me, though, whenever I could manage to slip away from Hedley House, Arboria lay, in all its seductive glory, just on the other side of the garden gate.

What was so special about Arboria and all these other worlds, you see, was that they were places to which adults were forbidden to go. Arboria belonged to the children of Hedley House, and at Hedley House, my grandmother told me, there had always been children. There had been generations of Hedley children and of Storey children, brothers and sisters and first cousins and second cousins, all in the house together, and all of different ages. In the old days, when the families had been able to afford servants, there had been yet more children, the bright young housemaid and the dim-witted scullery maid, the boy who sharpened the knives and the boy who polished the boots, the fair-haired stable boy and the dark-haired gardener's boy. From generation to generation, the history and the geography and the secret lore of Arboria had passed from child to child. The story of Arboria stretched away behind us into the depths of the past. Once, it had belonged to my grandmother. Now, though, it belonged to Robert, to Janny, and to me.

Janny's attitude to her education, it turned out, had a lot in common with mine. She had no wish to attend school if she could avoid it but, unlike me, she didn't have to rely on notes from my mother. Since the start of the war, two schools had shared the one schoolroom at Lower Helsing. The morning school was for the village children, while the afternoon school was for the evacuees. Thanks to a couple of carefully forged letters, each school, it seemed, now believed that Janny's proper place was at the other. So, while Robert was travelling to and fro to the grammar school in Tollcester, I was managing to spend quite a lot of my daytimes with Janny. And, although Janny had made it clear that our adventures in Arboria were only one part of her life, during the hours that she did spend in Arboria she always gave herself to it wholeheartedly.

One day, though, I discovered that Janny had been learning much more about Arboria than Robert or I had meant to tell her.

'Where does Tommy Pelling live?' she asked me. 'Does he really sleep in that little hut by the gate?' We were down at the lakeside, making our stealthy way along the line of willow trees, creeping from the shelter of one tree to the shelter of the next, ever alert for sight or sound of Barbarian spies. It had rained hard for the previous few days, the stream was flowing swiftly and dangerously along its deep valley, and the paths were treacherous with mud.

'Tommy's not like us,' I replied cautiously. 'He doesn't live the same way that we live. He belongs in the forest. He doesn't need to come indoors. He's quite comfortable in his hut. And the grown-ups don't know about Tommy. Well, I think my grandmother might know. But not the others.' I paused for a moment, clinging on to a low branch for support. 'He's like a friend . . . or a guide . . . He knows all about the forest. And he's lived here for a long time, probably longer than any of us.' As this phrase escaped my lips, something about it seemed to snag at my mind, something that struck a distant bell somewhere in the recesses of my memory. For the moment, though, I was forced to dismiss it, and instead to concentrate on the tricky business of remaining upright on the soggy ground.

The two of us emerged from beneath the willow where we had been hiding and half-ran, half-skidded down a length of muddy track to the safety of the next tree. Under its canopy, we crouched down side by side, peering out across the water. Our bodies, hot from our recent scramble, were just touching at the flanks. Janny was wearing a thin summer dress and I found myself suddenly aware of her warmth and her scent.

'Is he real?' said Janny after a while. I looked blankly at her. 'Tommy Pelling. Is he real? I don't think I've ever seen him.'

I hesitated. 'He's as real as any of us,' I said finally. 'He's real, but he's just . . . different. And he's quite shy, he doesn't like to be seen, so he usually manages to hide himself from people's eyes. I don't think he's quite sure about you yet. But I'm sure he'll like you. When he gets to know you, that is.'

Janny considered this, then changed the subject. 'Can we get to the other side of the lake?'

'It's dangerous,' I replied quickly. 'The Barbarians have their camp there. They watch the water all the time.' I glanced out across the lake. Sure enough, among the bushes on the far shore, I caught a glimpse of the dull glint of copper, a breastplate, perhaps, or the tip of a spear. I pointed a finger. 'Look, there's a couple of them over there, just under that tree. Can you see them?'

'I'm not sure . . . I think I saw something . . .' Janny shielded her eyes against the glare from the surface of the water. 'Are you frightened of the Barbarians?' she said suddenly. There was a faint hint of mockery in her voice.

'Of course not,' I replied hurriedly. 'But we still have to beware of them, because they're powerful and they're dangerous. They have to be respected. Anyway, we're not supposed to go over there. Not without telling Robert.'

'I'm not scared,' said Janny carelessly.

'I suppose we could go and have a quick look,' I conceded. 'Just as far as the bridge, though. We mustn't go across.'

Janny seemed content with this compromise so, cautiously, we continued on our way to the foot of the lake, scrambling down over the angular rocks that skirted the waterfall, our ankles and knees protesting at the violence done to them. A minute later, we were standing at the end of the wooden bridge, staring down at the waters of the stream. It was a cold, swiftly moving stream that sometimes flowed and bubbled over rocks and boulders, and sometimes rushed and tumbled down waterfalls and crags.

'Let's go across,' cried Janny daringly.

'We really shouldn't,' I countered anxiously. 'We ought to call up the Arborian army. So that they can look out for us.' But Janny had already taken her first step onto the decking of the bridge. Nervously, I followed her but, as I did so, a sudden plume of spray blew across from the waterfall, and our hands unconsciously sought the reassurance of the rail.

Just then, a familiar figure appeared at the far end of the bridge, a boy who was slightly taller than me, perhaps nearly as tall as Robert, but darker haired and more muscular in build. He was wearing a tattered shirt that had probably once been white and a pair of ragged corduroy breeches that had probably once been brown. The breeches ended just below his knees, exposing his brown shins and his bare feet. Beneath his leather belt there winked the coppery blade of a knife. 'Who's that?' Janny whispered to me. 'Is it Tommy?' She stared at the boy and the boy stared back at her, tangled locks of hair half-obscuring his eyes.

The forest had fallen silent. It seemed almost as if the birds had stopped singing, as if the wind had ceased to blow, as if the waterfall itself had become petrified in mid-movement, as if the whole of Arboria were holding its breath, awaiting the next moment of time with trepidation. At the centre of the silence though, Janny's narrow frame seemed to grow fractionally and to tauten, as if charged with electricity.

'No, it's not Tommy,' I whispered back to her. 'It's Davy Hearn. The gardener's boy. I've seen him talking to the Barbarians. Be careful of him.' Janny took half a step forward and, simultaneously, the boy mirrored her action with a half-step of his own. He was close enough now for me to see the fine, dark hairs on his forearms and shins. 'Janny?' I placed a restraining hand on her shoulder, willing her not to take another step.

But just then a large cloud of spray exploded across our path, wetting our clothes and drenching our hair. The silence was abruptly broken. The water flowed again, the wind started to blow, the birds sang once more. Startled, Janny stepped back and, at the same moment, the boy turned and darted away among the trees on his own side of the stream.

Suddenly, I realised that I'd had enough of Arboria for the day. 'I think it must be nearly teatime,' I said, my voice a little unsteady. 'Shall we go back to the house? We've probably had enough excitement for now.'

'Yes . . .' Abstractedly, Janny started to rearrange her dripping hair.

Back indoors, we settled ourselves at opposite sides of the kitchen table, mugs of hot milk in front of us. Tentatively nibbling at a slice of my grandmother's seed cake, Janny returned to the subject of Davy Hearn. 'Does Davy – I mean, do the

Barbarians – ever come across to our side of the stream?'

'Not usually,' I replied. 'He's – they are – frightened of running water. Grandmother says that the Barbarians are ignorant people. They're superstitious. So they try not to come across.' Suddenly, I found myself very anxious for Davy and the Barbarians to stay on their own side of the water.

'Don't they *ever* come?'

'Well, perhaps they would if they really wanted something. Perhaps if they decided to invade Arboria. Then they might find the courage to cross over.'

Janny bit off a small piece of cake.

'Or perhaps,' she suggested, 'if somebody on this side invited them across.'

'I suppose so,' I agreed reluctantly. 'But who would invite the Barbarians? They are our enemy. I don't think anyone would want them.' In reply, Janny offered me only a brief, enigmatic glance. Later, when she had left the kitchen and gone upstairs, I started to wonder what it was that had passed between Janny and Davy Hearn, what unknown force it was that had seemed to draw them towards one another across the narrow expanse of the bridge. But then the back door banged open, and Robert had arrived home from school, and there were stories to be told, and games kit to be unpacked, and tea to be made. So, for the time being, these puzzling things passed, once more, from my mind. But, as I later came to understand, it was in the company of Janny Grogan that the first faint, threatening stirrings of adolescence had begun to trouble me.

*Three*

# THE MIDNIGHT DANCE

*A*ll of these things happened a long time ago, Jamie, but sometimes things seem clearer when you are able to look at them from a distance. Sitting here in the café, looking at that group of teenagers at the table opposite mine, I am reminded once more of my own, long-vanished teenage self. For I entered the war as a boy, but I emerged six years later as . . . what? I was going to say that I emerged as a man but, in truth, I am still not too sure about that. When a boy grows up, my father was constantly telling me, he must learn to do what the Bible tells him to do. He must learn to put aside childish things. And he was right, of course. The other children that I knew were growing up quickly but, for me, the closer I approached the end of childhood, the more reluctant I became. Even now, I am not even sure whether I really have put aside my childish things. I have certainly never left Hedley House, and nor have I left Arboria. These days, though, I do not find it so easy to make my way about the Sacred Land. The trees in the forest have grown unchecked, their branches weaving one into another to form an impenetrable ceiling through which scarcely a chink of sunlight can penetrate. The undergrowth has spread out too, it has spread out little by little to choke the lanes, to obscure the tracks so that, where once there were broad highways, there now remain only low, narrow, twisting paths. Even where the paths are clear, though, my progress remains slow, and for this I can only blame the passing of the years. Because, as the years have flown by, so has my frame grown more stooped, my stride less swift. My progress through the forest is more halting now, more painful.

But, even at my advanced age, I can still climb up the Great Tree to the House in the Air. I have made certain that, above all things, the path that leads to the Great Tree has remained unobstructed, that the rope ladders, staircases and branches that lead me to my vantage point have remained securely in place. Because, from the House in the Air, I can keep watch. Sometimes Tommy Pelling comes with me, and he keeps watch too, for faithful Tommy loves the forest of Arboria just as I do. From the House in the Air, Tommy and I can watch the men with their chainsaws and their bulldozers and their excavators, we can watch them as they blunder their way ever closer to the secret heart of Arboria. From the House in the Air we can watch, and from the House in the Air we can prepare ourselves for the confrontation that is soon to come.

I am almost alone in the forest now. All the others have gone, every one of them except for Tommy Pelling. Now there's just Tommy and me.

Of course, I did not realise it at the time, but that moment, the moment at which Janny Grogan and Davy Hearn stood face to face with each other at opposite ends of the wooden bridge, was the moment at which the forest of Arboria began to stir. It was as if the presence of Robert and myself, even the presence of Tommy Pelling and Davy Hearn alone, had not been enough. The forest had been asleep. Even with the rising sap of spring, it had not truly discovered its own nature. It had needed something more than that, something that would act as catalyst in the wild intermingling of elements, and that something had been the presence of Janny.

In that moment, on the bridge, it was as if the sap had started to pulse more determinedly through the stems of the trees, it was as if the roots had started to burrow more deeply into the black earth. It was as if the birds on the branches and the fish in the lake and even the insects in the air had started to be aware of their world with sharpened sensations, with heightened consciousness. Arboria had started to awaken from its long slumber. Arboria had started to prepare itself for what was to come.

But as Janny began to work her magic on the forest so, at the same time, did the forest begin to work its magic on Janny. Within the cold walls of Hedley House, Janny remained a sickly creature, barely possessed of the energy to drag herself from one task to the next. She was pale and red-eyed and she still wept often. Her lank sandy hair, and the drab clothes that draped her bony frame, gave her the appearance of a scarecrow, and her monosyllabic utterances conveyed an air of isolation that did nothing to invite further communication.

Passing through the garden gate, though, into the brighter, sharper air of Arboria, Janny seemed at once to be transformed into a different being. She carried herself more upright, she walked with her shoulders held back and a spring in her step, and a touch of colour seemed to infuse her freckled cheeks. Her hair appeared thicker and healthier, and even the red blotches around her eyes became less noticeable. She spoke more forcefully, more cheerfully, even. In the forest of Arboria, Janny blossomed.

Of course, we couldn't spend all of our time in the invigorating surroundings of the forest. Back inside Hedley House, Janny lapsed quickly back into her old ways. The month of May arrived and, with the dust carried on the wind from the haymaking, her eyes started to itch and stream. Robert and I were constantly being sent on errands to the chemist's in Tollcester to fetch more jars of the boracic ointment. Each night, Janny had to sit at the sink facing the kitchen window, her white legs protruding from her nightgown, their fine, pale hairs standing fearfully erect in the chilly evening air. My grandmother dipped her finger into the jar of boracic ointment. 'Put your head right back, duckie, and look into that corner,' she ordered and, as the girl arched her thin white neck over the back of the wooden chair, the old lady delicately wiped around the outline of each sore eye with a cracked fingertip. 'Does that feel any better?' she enquired.

'It does feel a little better, Mrs Hedley,' Janny replied, cautiously opening and closing her eyelids to make sure that the soothing solution was evenly spread about.

'Off to bed with you, then,' my grandmother replied. 'I've made you a mug of hot milk. Take a biscuit too. You need a good night's sleep.' She ushered the girl out of the kitchen with a gentle pat on her bony backside.

Despite my grandmother's best efforts, though, the sound of weeping could still be heard as I tiptoed past Janny's bedroom door.

I have noticed that different people have different names for the main downstairs room in their house. Some people call it the sitting room, some people call it the living room. In some houses it is called the parlour, in other houses it is called the lounge. At Hedley House, though, the room was always called the garden room. The reason for this is that the room had a set of French windows that opened onto a wide stone terrace that was fringed with big bushes and stone urns. There were even a couple of statues. From the terrace, there was a flight of broad stone steps that led down onto the lawn. You couldn't quite see the forest of Arboria from the French windows but, if you stepped out onto the terrace and turned to your left, you would have been able to get an excellent view of it. If you had continued to walk in this direction, you would have ended up on the piece of terrace outside the kitchen door, the terrace that led you towards the vegetable patch and the garden gate.

The garden room was a large, rather old fashioned sort of room. At the centre of one wall was a wide fireplace with an ornate mantelpiece. Above the fireplace, and around the other walls of the room, there hung a number of large, gilt-framed oil paintings. Unlike the family portraits that hung in the rest of the house, these paintings mainly depicted country landscapes. Around the room were placed several chintz-covered armchairs and sofas, as well as a pair of oak bookcases and, striking a somewhat discordant note, a racy-looking cocktail cabinet. All of these pieces were large and solid and somewhat battered-looking. The ceiling of the room was high, and at the centre of it there hung a large chandelier. This chandelier was rarely lit, as my father said that it had too many bulbs and that the electricity would be too expensive. Instead, there were half a dozen standard lamps scattered around the room. These provided rather inadequate pools of dim yellow light, pools of light that did not quite meet at the edges. In between the pools of light, there were always sombre patches of shadow. The French windows faced south, but the curtains on the other windows were never properly opened, so it always seemed dark in there, and the lamps had to be lit for most of the day. In these gloomy surroundings, the Storey family spent its hours of domestic leisure.

Next to the French windows there stood a grand piano. This had been an impressive instrument in its day although, like everything in Hedley House, it had suffered from years of neglect. The piano was made from a light-coloured wood with a swirly pattern in the grain and had elaborately turned legs and yellowing keys. Over the keyboard, the maker's name was inscribed in illegible gothic script.

In her days as an actress, my mother had learned to sing and play and, if she was having one of her better days, she would sometimes wander across to the piano in the afternoon. Then, placing her drink on top of the instrument, she would settle herself on the worn leather stool, strum a few introductory bars of music, and launch into a song. My mother's repertoire consisted in the main of the cabaret tunes of her youth, half-jaunty, half-bluesy ditties by the likes of Cole Porter and George Gershwin. She liked to have the French windows open while she played, allowing the plaintive tunes and their rueful, melancholy lyrics to drift out across the terrace, 'so that the gardener can enjoy them too', as she used to say. In my memory, it always seemed to be raining outside the windows on these afternoons, the delicate percussion of the raindrops providing a gentle rhythmic accompaniment to Gershwin's languid syncopations. So the gardener would usually miss the show, having in all likelihood retreated to the safety of his greenhouse.

I hardly ever venture into the garden room now, but today I was reminded of my mother's music, perhaps by a song that I had heard playing on the wireless. Gently I pushed open the double doors, silently I threaded my way between the cobweb-draped pieces of furniture to the piano stool, my nostrils twitching at the heavy smell of damp. As I eased myself into position, I noticed that several pieces of cut glass from the chandelier had fallen to the floor and now twinkled forlornly among the dust and the dead spiders.

As boys, both Robert and I had been subjected to piano lessons but, as neither of us had shown much aptitude, the lessons had soon been discontinued. 'I think you get your musical talent from your father,' my mother had commented wryly.

Carefully, I lifted the lid of the keyboard. It did not open easily, having perhaps become warped or twisted by years of mildew and neglect. Experimentally, I pressed down a single white key: the G below middle C. Around the garden room there echoed a reverberant, out of tune note. The old piano tuner, I remembered, had died just before the war, and a replacement for him had never been found.

Hesitantly, I started to pick out a melody. I had not played for years, and I could feel my fingers protesting at the unaccustomed contortions. My music lessons had not been completely wasted, though. I had managed to retain a repertoire of one single tune. This tune had the great advantage that it could be played entirely on the white keys of the piano, without once having to brave the complexities of the black. It was an old folk song, and it was called *Over the Hills and Far Away*. I played it once, slowly, one-fingered. Then I played it again, slightly quicker, this time, my left hand offering a few tentative accompanying notes.

All at once, I was reminded of the day when Janny had played the piano.

'Why do I have to go to church?' Robert was complaining. 'Ken doesn't have to go. Even Janny doesn't have to go. So why me? It's not fair.'

It was a Sunday morning and a light drizzle was falling outside, as it so often seemed to do at Hedley House. My mother was standing by the kitchen door fidgeting indecisively with her umbrella, while my father was in the small back entrance lobby, rummaging through the jumble of mackintoshes and duffel coats that hung there. He was searching, as he searched every Sunday, for some article of outdoor clothing that would be appropriate both for the two mile hike to Lower Helsing, and for the weekly act of worship that would follow.

Robert and I were sitting at the kitchen table. I was nursing a mug of hot milk and trying my best to be invisible. The door to my grandmother's parlour was firmly shut. I imagined her cocooned in front of the fire, smoking her pipe contentedly. There was no sign of Janny.

'We've got a position to keep up in this village,' my father's voice boomed from the lobby. It's important to show the flag. You're fourteen, Rob. It's time you started acting like a man. Toni, do we really still need all this stuff?' He was now wrestling with a tangle of ancient shooting sticks and dog leads. 'It must be ten years since the last dog died.'

'Poor old Patch,' my mother replied absently. 'Your father's right, Robert,' she continued in a slightly more definite tone. 'The Storeys have to set an example. People seem to look up to us in this village, though heaven knows why. But surely we can't expect poor Kenneth to come out in this rain? He's feeling

67

a little peaky today, aren't you darling?' I winced as she ruffled my hair, but decided that it would be wisest to remain silent.

'Well, why do we have to walk?' Robert demanded sulkily. 'We could get there in five minutes in the car.'

'It's hard to get the petrol nowadays,' said my mother. 'Isn't that right, Hugh?'

'Oh, come along!' my father interrupted her impatiently. 'Robert! Toni! Coats! Boots! We're going to be late.'

'See you later then, darling,' said my mother, kissing the top of my head. 'Keep warm.' Robert, in a final, somewhat immature, parting gesture, poked his tongue out at me, and with that all three of them were gone.

In the quiet that followed, I allowed myself to relax a little, slowly sipping the last of my milk. I contemplated the two hours ahead of me and wondered how best I might occupy myself while the house and the garden were exclusively mine. It seemed a bit wet for a visit to Arboria. Perhaps some further exploration of the unoccupied wing? Maybe a visit to the bedroom with the book about the cave men? I had just started to consider the attractions of this plan when it occurred to me that Janny must still be somewhere in the house. Why didn't Janny have to come to church with us, I wondered. Perhaps she was Jewish? Or Roman Catholic? For a while I continued with this speculation until it dawned upon me that somewhere, in the distance, I could detect faint strains of music. I sat up and listened more attentively. It sounded as if someone was playing the piano.

Putting my mug down on the draining board, I left the kitchen and stepped into the hallway. The sound became more distinct. Drawn by the music, I made my way down the passage towards the front door, then turned left across the hallway towards the doors of the garden room. The music was much louder and clearer now. I could almost recognise the tune.

The double doors that led to the garden room were standing ajar. I stepped across the threshold, and there was Janny. She was sitting at the piano, her frail form silhouetted against the light that spilled through the French windows, her long spine curved slightly forwards, her slim white fingers meandering over the keyboard. I had never heard her play before, had not even realised that she was blessed with the gift of music. But I could tell at once that she was a good pianist and, although the piano sounded slightly out of tune, I could tell that she was doing far more than just playing the notes in the right order. Janny was making real music.

My heart pounding in my throat, I moved towards her, my feet seemingly drawing me forward of their own volition. At first she didn't see me, absorbed as she was in what she was playing. I recognised the tune now: it was the same tune that I had once learned, the only tune that I could play. It was *Over the Hills and Far Away,* but it sounded much fuller, much richer than the halting version that was my wretched party piece. I could hardly believe that the music was coming from our old, out of tune piano. While I could manage to play, at most, two notes at a time, Janny's fingers seemed able to coax multi-voiced chords and rippling arpeggios from the keys. The wistful trills and turns spoke to me of dreams long-forgotten, of loves long-lost, of other worlds far beyond the distant purple hills. Perhaps, I wondered, this is what the music of Arboria might sound like? I glanced through the French windows into the garden, half-expecting the shrubbery to be packed with Arborian musicians, joining in with dulcimer and fiddle and recorder. But there was nobody out there, only the terrace with its stone ornaments, only the shrubbery beyond. I shifted my gaze back towards the girl at the piano. Janny's thin face was rapt. She was almost smiling. She still hadn't seen me, although by this time I had approached close enough to reach out and touch her. I didn't touch her, of course, because if I had done that, the music would have stopped, and I didn't want the music to stop.

Mesmerised, I lingered there, suspended momentarily in space and time, wishing that the harmonies could continue unresolved for ever. But as I listened, it slowly dawned upon me that, along with the music of the piano, I could hear another sound too. While Janny was coaxing her chords and trills and arpeggios from the keyboard, something else was filling the gaps between the notes, some other, unseen instrument whose notes were long and cool and sharp and moist. A clarinet? A flute?

I felt my eyes drawn once more towards the French windows. They were standing slightly ajar, so that I could see the bushes in the shrubbery, could make out the stone urns that stood at the top of the steps. And there, among the group of statues, stood another figure, a figure that I had not noticed until that moment. It was the figure of a wild-haired, half-naked boy, a boy who was playing upon a battered old tin whistle, a tin whistle whose narrow stem was almost black with age and grime. For a moment, it seemed as though some young woodland god had stepped from the forest of Arboria to play his untamed music upon the very flags of our terrace, as though some wild faun had been enticed from his hiding place by the perilous enchantment of Janny's music. For a long moment I stood bewitched, trapped between the caressing, seductive tones of Janny's melody and the piercing invasion of this young intruder.

Slowly, the boy stepped towards the windows and, as he approached, I found myself hearing other sounds too, distant voices that rang out from field and wood, faraway instruments that echoed from forest and hill, sinister percussion that reverberated from cavern and lake. It was like being at the centre of a deep, alluring orchestra. The sound was enchanting me, wrapping me in dark folds of harmony, drawing me half-willingly, half-reluctantly, into strange, remote realms that extended far beyond my understanding. Agonisingly, inexorably, the music swelled to such a peak that I found myself wondering for how much longer I would be able to withstand the temptation. What would happen, I wondered, if Janny or I invited this boy to cross the threshold?

Then the boy saw me and, at the same moment, I recognised him. 'Davy Hearn!' I breathed. We were each as startled as the other. For an instant, he stood frozen. Then the whistle dropped from his lips and, abruptly, the music ceased. The boy turned around and fled. In an instant, he was gone from my sight.

Janny lifted her hands from the keys and turned slowly to face me.

'Kenneth,' she said in a matter-of-fact sort of way. 'I didn't hear you come in.'

'Oh,' I countered lamely. 'Sorry. I didn't mean to interrupt. Where did you learn to play like that?'

I didn't really expect an answer to that and, sure enough, I didn't get one.

For much of the time, of course, our lives were overshadowed by the events of the war. Hitler's aircraft had still not started to drop their bombs on England, and I heard my mother and father talking from time to time about what they called the 'phoney war'. Hedley House nevertheless remained in a state of alert for the bombardment that was still expected daily. My father was putting in long hours at the print works but, during his occasional spare moments at home, he continued to study hard for his duties as an air raid warden. His black tin helmet, bearing the letters ARP for Air Raid Patrol, squatted in permanent readiness on the small table next to the front door. My mother, as patriotic as her unstable nerves allowed, was constantly called upon for help. For hour after hour, she would listen patiently as my father recited the lists of poisonous gases that the enemy was expected to use, and the various ghastly symptoms associated with them.

Robert came home one day in a state of high excitement. 'The Head wants us all to become builders!' he exclaimed. Apparently, Tollcester Grammar School needed its own air raid shelter, and the boys at the school were to be enlisted to help build it. For a couple of weeks after that, Robert arrived home each day on a later bus than usual, his blazer pink with brick dust, eager to tell the household everything there was to know about sand and cement and corrugated asbestos.

Not even my grandmother was allowed to escape from the war effort. One of her jobs was to make sure that the scraps from the kitchen were thrown into a special bin which was known as the pig bin. The contents of this bin would later be collected by Mr Lazenby from Helsing Fold Farm to feed to his pigs and chickens.

Some of the women in the village donned overalls and took jobs on the farms and in the factories, but my mother decided that, for her, these would not be suitable occupations. 'My nerves wouldn't stand it,' she explained. 'All that dirt and noise.'

In the network of lanes that surrounded Hedley House, the signposts were turned around to point in every direction but the proper one. This, apparently, was intended to confuse the German invaders, should they ever get as far as Upper Helsing. Meanwhile, at the main gates of Hedley House, a signboard bearing the name of the property was, for the first time in living memory, attached to one of the brick gateposts. This was to avoid confusing the postman, who would certainly have suffered a degree of disorientation at the sight of the misleading signposts. There was even talk of the iron gates and spiked railings being taken away by the government and melted down to make guns, but neither of my parents was prepared to take this rumour seriously. My mother, in particular, cherished a great fondness for the tall gates, as the Hedley family crest formed the focal point of their intricate ironwork.

The air raid shelter in the old ice house remained unused. Since that false alarm in the early spring, the sirens had not sounded again but, following the delay in gaining access to the shelter on that unfortunate occasion, my father had decided that the key for the padlock should be kept close at hand, and had contrived a hiding place under a large stone next to the twin doors.

While all this was going on, Janny Grogan and I were pretty much left to our own devices. Of course we carried on with our Arborian adventures, and in these we were occasionally joined by Robert, Davy Hearn, and sometimes Tommy Pelling. Still intrigued by Janny's air of enigmatic self-containment, I continued to regard her with wary fascination.

One day, news came on the wireless that the campaign on the Western Front had run into difficulties. A huge contingent of

Allied troops had become marooned in the French port of Dunkirk, and it seemed that the only way in which they could be rescued from the surrounding German forces was by sea. A fleet of small craft was to be assembled at Dover and, with the assistance of this motley force, the men were to be saved.

'There's a call been put out for volunteers,' my father explained that evening. We were all sitting around the kitchen table digesting our frugal wartime supper of macaroni cheese and steamed pudding. Only my grandmother was absent from the table, having maintained her lifelong custom of eating alone in her parlour. 'Anyone who owns a boat is being asked to lend a hand,' my father continued. 'It's going to be called Operation Dynamo.' Having made this important announcement, he returned to his scrutiny of the poison gas manual, seemingly unmoved by the patriotic spirit.

'What about Magnus's boat?' my mother suggested. She had been having one of her more energetic days, and seemed suddenly alight with enthusiasm. Upper Helsing was about as far from the sea as it is possible to be in England, but my uncle Magnus was nevertheless the proud owner of a motor launch which he kept moored at Brancaster on the windswept Norfolk coast.

'Magnus won't go,' my father muttered, half to himself. 'Far too busy fannying around in his knicker factory. Toni, can you test me on these gases just once more?'

'May I leave the table, please?' Janny interrupted. She was not thriving on the austere diet, and her eyes and nose were red and streaming.

'Yes Janny,' said my mother. 'Scrape your leftovers into the bin before you go.' There followed a short silence during which my father continued to study his book.

'We could be in Operation Dynamo, Hugh,' my mother tried again. 'I hate to think of all those poor men besieged in the town. I'm sure Magnus would let us borrow the boat.' Exasperated, my father finally put his book down. Robert and I looked on in silent fascination.

'What about petrol?' my father demanded. 'It's much harder to get now that it's on the ration. We've hardly enough to get to Tollcester and back these days.'

'We could borrow some from one of the factories,' said my mother, continuing to warm to the idea. 'From the print works. Or maybe Magnus would let us scrounge some from the knicker factory. Oh, let's do it, Hugh! We haven't been away since this wretched war started. It'll be so exciting, and we'd really be doing our bit as well.'

'Can I come ?' Robert asked.

'No, of course you can't,' my father countered. 'We're talking about grown-ups' business, not a family picnic. Speaking of which, who's going to look after the boys?' It was obvious now that he was heading for defeat. 'We can hardly leave them alone with – what's her name?'

'Janny,' said Janny. She had been standing quietly by the pig bin, listening to the discussion.

'Yes, thank you, with Janny,' my father continued. 'As I said, we can hardly leave them alone with the girl. Not at the age they're getting to now. Do you understand what I'm saying? You'll have to stay behind with them, Toni.'

'Oh, Hugh.' My mother sounded crestfallen. 'I was so looking forward to going. But listen, Mummy will still be here. I'm sure she won't mind taking charge for a few days.'

'With her usual rod of iron,' my father observed sarcastically. He had finally given in to my mother, as he almost always

75

did. 'Oh well, I suppose the old Lanchester could do with a bit of a run. All right, Toni, I'll put our names forward. But don't blame me if the boat ends up hitting a mine.'

One by one, the members of the family left the kitchen. My father was the first to go, gathering up his book and his pipe and making his weary way down the passage to his study. 'Remember to pull the curtains before you put any lights on,' was his parting shot. Janny was the next to leave, slipping away quietly as always. My mother stayed behind to wash the dishes, while Robert dried and I put away. At last, satisfied with her work, she fetched the kettle from its place on the stove and made a pot of tea.

'Do you want a cup, Mummy?' she called out in the direction of my grandmother's parlour.

'No thank you, Antonia,' came the muffled reply. 'I've made myself some of my own.' The old lady did not care to share her private supply of green tea with the rest of the household.

'I'm taking mine through to the garden room, then,' my mother went on. 'I'll see you in the morning, Mummy. Sleep well.' Then she too made her way along the passage, leaving only Robert and myself. The curtains had not been drawn, so the lights remained unlit. For a time, the two of us stared out of the window at the darkening sky, watching it fade slowly in colour from navy to indigo to black. The branches of the Great Tree, at first forming an irregular dark latticework against the scudding clouds, finally merged imperceptibly into the encroaching gloom. Each of us was absorbed in his own thoughts, but there remained nevertheless a sense of easy companionship.

'Arboria?' I hazarded eventually.

'Maybe tomorrow,' Robert replied at length. 'It's too dark now.' There was another silence.

'Do you know what Janny's doing?'

'Search me. I don't know what she gets up to. Can't make head nor tail of her.' The silence reasserted itself for a period.

'I don't mind her,' I said at length. 'But you're right. She is strange.'

'She is that,' Robert concluded. He stood up, yawned and stretched himself. 'Think I'll turn in now. Seem to need my sleep since we started building that shelter for the Head.'

I ignored this invitation to discuss his favourite subject yet again. 'See you tomorrow, then, Rob,' I said.

'Yes, see you tomorrow, Ken,' said my brother, and then he too was gone.

I sat alone in the darkness for a while, allowing my senses to attune themselves to the summer evening sounds and scents that were drifting in through the open window. The honeysuckle outside the kitchen door, the birds in the branches of the Great Tree, the distant ripple and murmur of the stream, the black fish blowing the occasional bubble. Perhaps, somewhere in the distance, I could even hear, faintly, the eerie music of Arboria. I relaxed back into my chair. Slowly, my eyes began to close . . .

Then, abruptly, I was alert again. Because I had heard another sound, a sound that came from much closer at hand. I pricked up my ears. Sure enough, from behind my grandmother's parlour door, there came the sound of hushed voices, voices that seemed to be in earnest conversation. I listened hard, trying to understand what was being said, but I could make no sense of the muffled words.

Silently I rose to my feet. Obeying some unexplained instinct, I retreated stealthily to the darkest corner of the kitchen. The sounds continued for several minutes more then, just as my legs were threatening to buckle with cramp, the parlour door creaked open, releasing a shaft of yellow light into the gloom of the kitchen. There, silhouetted in the door frame, stood the narrow, unmistakable figure of Janny Grogan. She did not see me, and I remained motionless, not allowing my presence to reveal itself to her. I waited until she had made her way out into the hall, until my grandmother's door was firmly closed again.

Soon, apart from the muted tick of the grandfather clock, all was silent in Hedley House. Then, at last, watched only by the silent paintings of my forebears, I made my solitary way up to bed.

The next few days were dominated by the preparations for my parents' part in Operation Dynamo. Permission had to be sought from my uncle Magnus for the loan of his boat, and keys and passes had to be collected to ensure its release from its moorings. My father had to arrange for a temporary leave of absence from his duties as Air Raid Warden. My mother fretted endlessly about what food, clothing and bedding would have to be packed into the car. My father assembled a hefty stack of Ordnance Survey maps for the drive to Brancaster, and an equally hefty stack of maritime charts for the voyage around the coast to Dover. Petrol for the car had to be obtained by whatever means were available. Arrangements were made for the running of the print works to be overseen, in my father's absence, by the foreman Frank Carberry.

At the last moment, a leak was discovered in the radiator of the ageing Lanchester, and this delayed my parents' departure for several hours until a repair could be accomplished. While this was being done, my mother made a series of hasty telephone calls to various East Anglian cousins to try and arrange for a night's accommodation. By the time everything was ready, it was late in the day and twilight had begun to encroach.

'Remember to write a note to the school if Kenneth has to stay at home again,' my mother was explaining to my grand-mother as the family gathered in the front porch. 'Robert will get himself up in time for the bus, you won't have to worry about that. Oh, and make sure that Janny puts her ointment on at the right times, it's all written down somewhere. You'll have to get Robert to help you put the bins out for the dustmen. And if the vicar calls round . . .'

'Come on, Toni,' my father interrupted her. 'Get in the car. We want to get to Hunstanton before bedtime, don't we? And don't forget about the blackout, you lads. Rob, you'd better take charge of all that. You can wear my helmet if you like.' He tugged the car door shut, started the engine, switched on the hooded headlamps, and began to pull away from the house. Robert and I ran to the gates and held them open like twin sen-tries. Janny and my grandmother remained on the porch, waving in unison. Janny, I noticed, had a tear trickling down one freckled cheek. As the car moved away, my mother wound down her window.

'Remember to wash yourselves at least once a day,' she called. 'Hands, faces and knees at least. And don't forget your hot milk, Kenneth. And both of you look after Janny. Goodbye darlings. We'll be back before you know it.'

'Have you got those maps organised, Toni?' my father interrupted her. And with that, they were away, my father intent on the way ahead, my mother blowing frantic kisses out of the window. Robert and I stepped out into the road and watched the tail lights of the car as they disappeared in the direction of Tollcester. Then we pulled the gates shut and walked back towards the house. Janny and my grandmother were still standing on the front porch. My grandmother produced a handkerchief from her sleeve and silently handed it to the girl.

For the first time, I began to consider the possibilities for three lively children of a life free from parental supervision. Wondering how much I would really miss my mother and father, I found myself seized by a sudden fit of shivering. I drew my arms around my chest.

'It has turned a bit chilly, hasn't it?' Robert observed. 'Let's get ourselves indoors.' He picked up the ARP helmet from the hall table. It was a loose fit on his head, almost covering his eyes, but he tightened the strap under his chin so that it remained firmly in place. 'Come on, let's check the blackout like Dad said. Rob, Janny, you two do the upstairs. I'll do down here. And how about some supper, Gran?' As he shepherded the three of us into the hallway and allotted us our various tasks in his booming voice, I realised that my brother had already fallen into my father's role.

After supper I went up to my room. I was lying on my front on my bed, leafing through my dog-eared copy of *Swallows and Amazons*, when there came a tap at the door. It was Janny. 'Can you come downstairs?' she said. 'Your gran wants to see you.'

'All right.' I made my way down to the kitchen and knocked hesitantly on the door of my grandmother's parlour. There was a moment's silence, then she called me inside. As I seated myself in one of the battered old Windsor chairs, I suddenly noticed that there were not one but two empty cups and saucers in the grate. I knew at once that Janny had been there again. I wondered what the two of them had been discussing.

My grandmother saw me looking at the cups. 'Ah yes, Kenny,' she started. 'You must have guessed. I've been having a little talk with Janny. Now I want to have a little talk with you.' She reached into her big earthenware tobacco jar and started to fill the bowl of her pipe, her fingers working away while she talked. 'How have the two of you been getting along?'

'I'm not sure,' I replied, uncertain how to respond to this. 'I've never really met anyone quite like her before. Sometimes I can't make out what she's thinking. But she can certainly climb trees.'

'Climb trees,' my grandmother echoed. 'Yes. You like your walks in the forest, don't you?' I noticed that she used the word *forest*, rather than *wood*, which is the word that my father would have used.

'Robert comes with us sometimes,' I reminded her. 'And Davy Hearn. And Tommy.'

'Davy Hearn and Tommy Pelling are what they are,' my grandmother observed cryptically, 'and Robert can only be his father's son. But you, Kenny, I think perhaps that you might be a little bit different from your brother.'

'Different?' I was baffled by this. 'How do you mean, different?'

Before making any reply, the old lady picked up a spill from the fireplace, held it to her pipe and inhaled deeply. 'Well, let's just say that you and the girl have got something in common, maybe something that most ordinary people wouldn't understand. But when I was a girl, Kenny, a long time ago, perhaps I understood a little bit about it too. So why don't we just say that

81

all three of us are quite a lot alike.' She paused for a moment, fiddling once more with her pipe. Eventually, satisfied with her adjustments, she continued, more slowly now. 'The Hedleys have lived at Lower Helsing for a long, long time, Kenny, probably much longer than you imagine. I've got Hedley blood in my veins, and so has your mother, and so has Robert, and so have you. And at times the Storeys have lived here too, of course, and you and Robert have both got Storey blood from your father's side. But I think that your brother is probably a little bit more like the Storeys, and you are probably a little bit more like the Hedleys. Quite a lot like the Hedleys, really.'

I looked blankly at her. After a moment, her lined face relaxed into a faint smile.

'Never mind,' she said finally. 'You'll understand soon enough. But Kenny, I want you to promise me one thing. I want you to look after Janny, because she's a little bit different too, and I've got the feeling that you two might understand each other better than you know. You may not realise it yet, but you've got a lot in common. And, one day soon, she's going to ask you to do something for her, something perhaps a bit unusual. So if ever Janny Grogan does ask you to do something for her, Kenny, then I want you to be sure and do it. Can you promise me that?'

'Yes, I think so.' Through the cloud of fragrant pipe smoke, I noticed the gleam of flint in the old lady's eye. 'Yes, of course I promise,' I finished hastily. 'But Gran . . .'

'That's enough questions for tonight,' my grandmother interrupted me. 'I've asked and you've promised, and that should be enough.' She glanced up at the old wooden clock that stood on the mantel. 'It's late now. Off to bed with you.'

*

The next day, my mother telephoned to let us know that she and my father had got as far as Hunstanton, but she warned us that it might not be easy for them to get in touch from that point onwards.

'We'll phone from Brancaster if we can, darling,' her distorted voice echoed down the line. 'But you mustn't worry if you don't hear anything for the next few days. Oh dear, I've got to go now, you know how your father is when he wants to get started.' In the background I could hear my father's impatient voice, urging my mother to hurry up and get in the car. 'I love you, Kenneth,' breathed my mother hurriedly. 'I love you both. Take care.' Then, with a click and a buzz, the connection was broken.

For a day or two, I continued to puzzle over the promise that I had made to my grandmother but, with countless other things to occupy my time, the question soon drifted away to some neglected corner at the back of my mind.

Despite the absence of my parents, life at Hedley House continued more or less as usual. Robert caught the morning bus to school, but, by now, all attempts to get me to school had been abandoned, and my grandmother had taken over the task of writing my sick notes. During the day, Janny and I would while away our time exploring the forests and glades of Arboria, picnicking in the tree house, fishing in the stream. Some afternoons, we crouched beneath the old willow tree, spying on the comings and goings of Davy Hearn and the other Barbarians. On other days we would lie in the bracken staring up at the sky, hoping once more to catch a fleeting strain of the strange, unearthly music. Supper, such as it was, was prepared by my grandmother, and the washing up was done by Janny and me, while Robert lounged at the table reading the evening paper. We all went to bed at more or less the usual time, and we all slept as well as ever.

But on about the fifth or sixth night, my sleep was disturbed. Every time I started to drift off, I would find myself abruptly stabbed awake by jagged shards of threatening dreamstuff. I felt cold, so I fetched an extra quilt from the blanket chest. Then I felt hot, so I discarded all of my bedclothes apart from a single sheet. Then I still felt hot, so I discarded my pyjamas as well. Fitfully I tossed from one side to another, the bedclothes winding themselves around my naked limbs, my pillow refusing to mould itself to the shape of my sweating head. Just when I had finally started to fall into a deep sleep, I was jolted awake once again by a loud knock on my bedroom door.

I sat up in bed. The door was open and there, outlined against the dim light from the landing, stood Janny. She was wearing, not her nightclothes, but a light-coloured summer dress. Her pale, sandy hair hung loose about her shoulders. Her feet, I noticed, were bare.

'Kenny?' she said quietly. 'Are you awake?'

'I am now,' I mumbled. 'What do you want?'

'Will you come down to the forest with me?' said Janny. 'Down to Arboria?'

'What?' I replied irritably. 'Don't be stupid. It's dark. I want to go back to sleep.'

'Please, Kenny,' she insisted. 'You'll never regret it, I promise.'

When I heard that word, of course, I immediately remembered the promise that I had made to my grandmother.

'All right then,' I replied grudgingly. 'Just for a bit.'

'You'd better put some clothes on, though,' Janny giggled. She had caught sight of my bare, bony chest. I started to reach for my underwear.

'Oh, don't bother about those,' she said. 'It takes too long. Just your shorts and a jumper will do. I'll go and wake Robert.'

As I struggled into my clothes in the darkness, I could hear Robert complaining from along the corridor. 'Oh, I suppose I'd better come,' I heard him say finally. 'I can hardly let you two go out there on your own.' When he appeared a moment later, I saw that he was wearing the ARP helmet.

Janny led the way along the landing and down the stairs. Each time she came to a window, she threw open the curtains, and pale moonlight spilled through into the house, lighting our way to the kitchen. When we reached the back door, Robert and I started fumbling around for shoes.

'Barefeet's better,' said Janny. 'Shoes make too much noise. And anyway, we won't need them for what we're doing.'

Robert and I exchanged glances, but Janny had already unbolted the back door and stepped outside onto the terrace. Apprehensively, we followed her across the vegetable patch and through the garden gate. Outside the doorway of the log store, Tommy Pelling was waiting for us, hopping eagerly from foot to foot, his tattered breeches flapping loosely about his thin little legs.

'Oh Master Kenneth, Master Robert, Miss Janny,' he exclaimed, 'you've come, you've come! What a night it's going to be! What a night!' Instead of retreating to his bed among the logs, as he usually did, he started to run along with us, circling our small party in a state of high excitement.

Janny's jaw dropped open. 'Are you . . . ?'

'Yes, Miss Janny, I'm Tommy, I'm Tommy' he replied, jumping up and down as he spoke.

'Lead the way then, Tommy,' Janny called out to him. At

once, Tommy ran ahead of us, almost passing from our sight in his haste.

I had expected it to be dark, but the moon shone brokenly through the tangle of branches, offering an elusive, dappled light to the forest floor. The track shone before us like a ghostly ribbon, and Tommy's pale form bobbed in the gloom, seeming to glow with a dim light of its own.

As we made our way forward, I started to become aware of a slow, regular, rhythmic pulsation, like the pounding of a mighty engine. Where it came from I could not tell, I could not tell even whether I was hearing it with my ears or feeling it in my bowels. Perhaps, I thought, it was nothing more than the throbbing of my own blood in my veins. But, as we made our way deeper into the forest of Arboria, I realised that the rhythm was coming, not from inside me, but from beneath me, from the earth below, from the roots of the trees, from the sightless depths of the lake, from the fathomless pits of the caves. It was as if I could feel the pounding of the secret heart of the forest itself, as if, on this moonlit May night, the very land of Arboria were about to leap to its feet and dance.

Following Tommy's spectral form, we made our way deeper and deeper into the forest, following tracks now that we had never followed before, penetrating into realms that had, until this night, been forbidden to us. And the deeper we went, the harder we felt the throb of that mighty heart, the stronger we sensed that living pulse of the land. At last we arrived at a clearing, a clearing that I did not remember visiting before. Now, at last, we could comprehend the rhythm that possessed us because, in the clearing, we could finally hear the music. Here, at last, the melody and the harmony stood revealed.

From all around us came the noise of instruments and the

din of voices. From in front there came the twang of harp and lute. From one side there came the wail of fiddles, while from the other side there came the wheeze of concertinas. From somewhere below us there came the rattle of tambourines, the clatter of drums. All together, they wove a jagged tapestry of sound and, in among it all, to and fro between the warp and the weft of the fabric, there looped the agile, penetrating voice of Davy Hearn's tin whistle.

As I peered into the gloom of the surrounding undergrowth, it seemed that I could make out the pale blue, spectral forms of the musicians and singers themselves, men, women and children plucking and blowing and beating their instruments in accordance with some other-worldly design that lay just beyond the borders of my comprehension. But, whenever I tried to look directly at any of the ghostly musicians, they would swiftly dissolve into a blur.

'It's the night of the dance,' breathed Janny. 'It's the music of the Good People.'

'The Good People?' I replied in alarm.

Janny looked at me for a moment but did not reply. 'Come on,' she said finally. In silent terror I stood at the edge of the clearing. Its pale wide circle, spread out before me at my feet, seemed to offer an empty canvas that begged for the first stroke of a brush.

Then, from the gloom of the undergrowth, vague, tentative forms began slowly to emerge, each of them glowing with a faint, icy blue light. First one, then others, started to detach themselves from the darkness and to bob forward into the clearing, hesitantly at first, then with a gathering sense of purpose. As each of them passed across the corner of my eye, it seemed once more that it bore the faint outline of a man or a woman, the vague form of a boy or a girl. But if I tried to look directly at any of the dancers, their features and their form were lost to me, and I could see nothing but an unfocused patch of phosphorescence. Slowly at first, then faster and faster, the ghostly dancers began to circle, weaving and whirling in a complex pattern of interlinking trails, responding to a weird geometry that seemed to spring from the jagged melody of the fiddles, from the sour rasp of the concertinas, from the dark pounding of the drums, from the hypnotic moan of the voices, from the uncanny rhythm that pounded somewhere in the dark heart of the very earth itself.

After a time, my gaze alighted upon two dancers who stood taller and more lordly than the rest, a stern, bearded man and a slim, graceful lady. Somehow it seemed to me that I knew them. I tried to call their names; I could almost taste the words upon my lips. But my throat was paralysed, my lips were dry, and then the two dancers were gone. Bitter with regret, I gazed into the heart of the pattern that the dancers wove until, at last, I felt the light touch of a hand upon my forearm. It was Janny. 'Did you see them?' she breathed. 'Lord Owen and Lady Margaret? The Lord and Lady of the Good People? The Lord and Lady of the Night?' Her eyes were ablaze with hard fires. 'Come and dance with me, Kenny,' she begged. 'Come and dance with me. Then you can see the Lord and Lady too . . .'

I shook my head. My feet seemed frozen to the ground. 'I can't,' I murmured. I could not force myself to meet Janny's gaze. There was something in those eyes now, something that I hadn't seen until now, something before which I melted in terror, something in the face of which I found myself utterly depleted. 'I mustn't . . .'

Without another word, Janny turned away from me. 'Robert?' she pleaded. Robert hesitated. Janny took a step closer to him, devouring him with her eyes. 'Very well,' he said weakly. Then, at once, the girl seized his hands and whirled him away into the midst of the circling mass. In an instant, the two of them were lost from my sight. Rooted to the spot, I remained on the sidelines, half-fascinated, half-terrified, as the music grew wilder and wilder and the steps of the dancers grew faster and faster. As I watched, I knew in my heart that I had wanted to dance, I had wanted to dance more than anything in the world. But my feet had refused to co-operate, and now I had missed my chance.

After a time, the music began to slow, the dancers began to tire, and the lights began to dim. One by one, the members of the party slipped away, back to the dark places from which they had come, until at last there were just Robert and Janny and Tommy and me. Exhausted, we staggered back along the track in the fading moonlight. Tommy was the first to leave us, vanishing back inside his brick hut. Robert and Janny and I manhandled each other through the garden gate, lurched arm in arm across the vegetable patch, stumbled back up the stairs to our three narrow beds.

'I saw them,' Janny murmured as she collapsed into bed. 'I saw the Lord and Lady of the Night. Didn't you see them, Kenny? Didn't you see them?'

'Just for a second, ' I replied sadly. 'Only for a second.' But, as I drifted off to sleep, one thought continued to whirl around and around in my head. Janny might have been dancing with Robert, I told myself, but really she wanted to dance with me. It was me that she asked first. It was me that she asked first. But I was afraid. It was me that she asked first, but I was afraid.

Next time, I'll dance with Janny. Next time I'll dance with her. Next time, I won't be afraid. Next time, I'll be ready . . .

By the time I awoke the next day, the morning was well advanced. Lying in bed, the light slanting through the gap in the curtains, I began to recall the events of the night before. Everything that had happened to me seemed faint and distant now, the din of the instruments muted, the scheme of the dance obscured. Even the overwhelming pounding beneath my feet seemed no more than an elusive memory. I had even started to wonder if it had not, after all, been a dream but, as I finally sat up on the edge of my bed, I noticed with a start that my bare feet were caked with earth. So, I had, after all, been in the forest . . .

I pulled on my dressing gown and clumsily knotted the cord. My bedroom was the end one in the back part of the house. I stepped across the passage to the head of the stairs and shuffled along the main corridor to where the others had their rooms. Their doors were still closed. From Robert's room, I could hear a faint sound that might have been snoring, but from Janny's room I could plainly make out the sound of her weeping. What, I asked myself, had really happened the previous night?

Arriving in the kitchen, I cut myself two rather uneven slices of bread and started to make a round of toast. Having completed this task, I seated myself at my usual place at the table, my plate in front of me, a glass of milk to my right. But I didn't have time to eat or drink because, suddenly, my head began to whirl once more with the vertiginous motion of the dance. Back again came that unnameable sensation, half-longing, half-fear, that had seized me as I hesitated at the edge of the clearing. Surely, after all, the dance was a thing of danger, a thing to be avoided, a thing to be shunned. Surely my leaden feet had done me a kindness in rooting me to the spot at that terrible moment. Surely my clumsiness and my hesitancy had offered me protection, protection from things that were better left untouched . . .

'Your toast's getting cold.' I realised that Robert must have been standing in the doorway for some little time. I looked up at his face, just in time to see him glancing down at my feet. I could tell at once that he had seen the earth there and that he understood its significance. We exchanged glances, but neither of us spoke our thoughts aloud. 'It's nearly eleven o'clock,' he said finally. 'Why didn't you wake me?'

At that moment, though, there was another interruption, this time the noisy jangle of the front doorbell. Robert went to answer it, and he came back a moment later accompanied by the bulky, tweed-suited figure of our uncle Magnus. Magnus's expression was grim. A yellow telegraph envelope was clutched between his uneasy fingers, the thin paper crumpling in his unsteady grip.

Without anyone saying a word, Robert tapped on the door of my grandmother's parlour and, a second later, our uncle stepped inside and closed the door. I became aware of the pounding of my heart. Scarcely knowing what I was doing, I rose to my feet and moved across the room to stand side by side with my brother. Together we stood trembling, waiting for that door to open again, although somehow I think that we both understood what it was that we were about to hear. After what seemed like an eternity, although it could only have been a few moments, my grandmother emerged from the room. I could see Magnus fidgeting behind her in the gloom of her parlour, his gaze directed downwards at the carpet.

'You poor boys,' my grandmother began. She didn't have to go on. Robert and I knew that our mother and our father were both dead. We stood there in silence, uncertain what to do or what to say. Then, slowly, we once again became aware of the distant, sour noise of Janny's weeping.

I learned later that my parents had not died heroic deaths on the sands of Dunkirk, nor had their boat been holed in the Channel by a German mine. Indeed, they had played their part in the rescue of the British troops without mishap. The following day, they had returned my uncle's boat to its mooring. They had then chosen to drive back from Brancaster that same night, and on this journey their car had collided with a lorry on a bend in the road. They both died instantly.

Road accidents didn't stop happening during the war, of course. Because of the blackout, there were probably more accidents than there might have been in peacetime. Later on, cat's eye reflectors were fitted down the middle of the roads. They saved many lives, but they came too late to be of any help to my parents.

Uncle Magnus, as my father's next of kin, had the job of organising the burials, and the mourners were invited back to his house in Tollcester afterwards. Robert and I were not allowed to attend. My grandmother explained to us that funerals were not fit occasions for children. Neither of us really liked being referred to as children but, in the circumstances, neither of us felt much like arguing.

On that gloomy afternoon, it was Janny alone who wept for my mother and father, her sobs echoing from her room and blackening the air around Hedley House. Robert had shut himself in his room, presumably seeking whatever consolation his school books might offer. For my part, I did not feel inclined just yet to venture back into Arboria so, instead, I wandered into the old north wing of the house, kicking up a trail of dust as I drifted aimlessly from room to room. Eventually, in an abandoned scullery, I found some pots of paint and some old brushes, their bristles matted together with dried turpentine. I selected a tin of black paint and a tin of white paint, and then I made my way back down the passage and out of the front door to the tall iron railings that stood guard at the front of Hedley House. The two spiked iron gates hung from two stout brick columns and, attached to one of these columns, was the sign board that bore the name of the house. Kneeling on the ground in front of the board, I prised open the two tins with the blade of my penknife, then hacked my way through the thick, lumpy skin that covered the surface of the paint. Beneath the skin, the paint was thick and treacly and pungent. I chose a brush at random, dipped it into the white paint and gave it a perfunctory stir. Rapidly, I applied a thick coat of paint over the whole surface of the sign board. Then, dipping the same brush into the black paint, I inscribed, in clumsy freehand, the single word ARBORIA.

I took a step back to inspect my handiwork. The white background was horribly uneven, with brush strokes going randomly in every direction. The letters of the name were irregularly spaced, with the final three characters crammed into a gap that was really only large enough for two. As well as that, because I had not bothered to clean the brush, the letters, instead of being a solid black, appeared an irregular streaky grey. I had to admit that it was a ghastly mess, but at least the name stood out bold and clear. Then I suddenly remembered how meticulously my father had painted the original sign. And then, at last, I felt the tears beginning to well up inside me.

Later that day, my grandmother returned home. Instead of retiring to her parlour and her usual green tea and tobacco, though, she boiled a kettle on the kitchen stove and beckoned us to sit down at the big table with her.

'Your uncle and I have been having a talk,' she explained. 'He has asked if you two boys want to go and stay with him. So that your uncle and Aunt Dottie can look after you.' Robert and I exchanged uneasy glances over the rims of our mugs. 'I don't know what you think,' my grandmother continued, 'but I think we should all stay together, here at Hedley House. We all grew up here, and we've all spent our whole lives here. And perhaps there have been enough upsets in our lives for the time being. So, for now, I want to stop here, and I'm going to look after you.' I could see the look of relief on Robert's face at this news. 'But there's one thing that you must both do,' the old lady said finally. 'You must write to your uncle and thank him for being so kind.'

'Mrs Hedley?' It was Janny's voice. We all looked towards her. Her eyes were dry now, although their rims were still red. I noticed a thin streak of dried snot encrusted on the fine hairs of her upper lip. 'What will happen to me?'

'Oh, you silly girl,' my grandmother replied. 'Why, this is your home too. We're not going to turn you out. Of course you must stay here with us. Where else is there for you to go?'

'Oh, thank you so much, Mrs Hedley, thank you. I hope I won't be too much trouble.' For a moment, I thought Janny was going to cry again, but for once she didn't.

We remained in the kitchen for supper. At the end of the meal, Robert retired to his room to do his homework for the next day. Janny and I helped my grandmother with the dishes, after which I put the plates back in their places on the shelves of

94

the old Welsh dresser, while Janny excused herself and disappeared on some business of her own.

At last, the old lady beckoned me into her parlour with her. I stood just inside the door, while she picked her way through the clutter of ancient furniture to the narrow chest that stood in an alcove on the far wall. She retrieved something from its depths and made her way back to where I was waiting.

'It is time for you to have this, Kenny,' she said. 'Now that your father's gone. There are important things for you to do.'

'What about Robert?' I said.

'Yes, of course. Robert must be the man of the house now,' she replied. 'But for you, Kenny, there are other things. What I have here is for you, not for Robert.' She placed in my hands a fat, yellowing scroll of paper, tied up with faded ribbon. The paper crackled faintly where my palms touched it, and a musty smell pricked at my nostrils. My trembling fingers began to investigate the tangle of knots. 'Be careful,' the old lady warned me. 'It's very old. Best put it on the table.'

I did as she suggested. Carefully, I brushed away the layer of dust that covered the scroll. Carefully, I unpicked the knots, breaking a couple of fingernails as I did so. Then, at last, I began to unroll the paper. The first thing I saw, in capital letters, was the title of the scroll. This ancient roll of crumbling paper, I realised, was the Great Book of Arboria, the book that would tell me everything I wanted to know about the Arborians and the Barbarians and the Good People. 'It is for your eyes alone, Kenny,' said the old lady. 'Read it carefully. Do your best to discover its meaning. And then, perhaps, you will begin to understand.'

I could have asked her a thousand questions but, at that moment, our conversation was interrupted by the mournful wail of the air raid siren. Seconds later, Robert came pounding down the stairs in his tin hat. 'Air raid!' he called, his recently broken voice booming down the corridor. 'Everyone to the shelter.'

Although I did not realise it at the time, Hitler's aircraft had at last started to attack us in earnest. It was an attack that was to continue for many months to come. The Battle of Britain had begun.

*Four*

# THE GARDENER'S BOY

$\mathscr{I}$ had visitors at Hedley House this morning, although I am sorry to say that they were not very welcome visitors. Just after nine o'clock, there came a loud, rusty jangle at the doorbell and, the moment that I opened the front door, two women barged their way straight into the house. They were not exactly young, but they were not exactly middle-aged either. One of them was tall and dark-skinned, with straight black hair and a narrow, rather intimidating pair of spectacles. The other was smaller and fatter, with short, untidy hair. She wore a hideous flower-patterned skirt and clumsy-looking sandals with ankle socks. The tall one carried a slim, black document case, while the short one carried a clipboard with an untidy sheaf of papers attached to it. They were both wearing official-looking badges. Neither of them was smiling.

'We are from Tollcester District Council Environmental Standards Division,' said the tall one. The short one offered me a brief glimpse of some documents.

'Oh yes?' I replied politely, not yet suspecting the purpose of their visit. 'Can I offer you a cup of tea? A biscuit, perhaps?'

'We'd best not, thank you,' the tall one continued. I caught a brief expression of disappointment on the round face of her colleague. 'We've several more calls to make after this one. Now, Mister, er . . .'

'Storey,' the short one prompted her. She flicked through her papers. 'Hedley House, Upper Helsing. Kenneth Storey, sole occupant, is that right?'

'Yes, sole occupant for some decades now.' I offered another half-smile, hoping to establish a more cheerful atmosphere, but my effort was in vain.

'We'd better get started,' said the tall one. 'Mister Storey, this is a statutory inspection under the terms of the Housing Act of 1985. The department has received a number of complaints concerning the condition of this property . . .'

'Who has complained?'

'We're really not at liberty to say. Now, as I was explaining . . .' I found myself unable to concentrate on the woman's words. Who could possibly have made a complaint, I wondered. I don't have any neighbours, the nearest house is at least a quarter of a mile away. Who could it have been? And then, slowly, it dawned upon me that it could only have been the wreckers, the property developers who had come to destroy the forest of Arboria. That was it. They wanted the land for their new houses. They wanted to demolish Hedley House.

'. . . so perhaps we can make a start in the kitchen?' the tall woman was saying. In a daze, I led the way. Our glum little procession of three moved from room to room, leaving a triple trail of footprints behind us in the dust. The short woman made notes on her clipboard, while the tall one barked brusque remarks into some kind of miniature recording machine. 'Extensive staining of plaster,' she said. 'Wallpaper becoming detached. Suspected defective damp-proof course. Ground floor windows obscured by vegetation. Inadequate light for normal activities. Is there a toilet on the ground floor?'

After a time, we made our way upstairs. My two guests examined one abandoned bedroom after another, reacting in horror to the warped window frames and sticking doors, to the dust-shrouded furniture and the threadbare carpets, to the lop-sided portraits in their chipped gilt frames, to the collapsing ceilings and the invading branches. Eventually we arrived at the head of the long corridor that ran the full length of the old north wing. Our footsteps kicked up a fair cloud of dust, which started the tall woman coughing. A moment later, the short woman's bulk proved too much for the rotting floorboards, and one clumsy foot suddenly disappeared up to the ankle.

'Well, I think we've, oh, excuse me . . .' – the tall one broke into another fit of coughing – 'Is your foot all right, Sue? Well, don't forget to do an accident form when we get back to the office. Anyway, I think we've probably seen enough. No, don't come down, Mister, er, we'll show ourselves out.' And with that they were gone. In the depths of Hedley House, the grand-father clock chimed and the ancestors sagged wearily in their frames. It was a quarter to ten. Wearily, I slumped down onto the floor, watching the particles of displaced dust as they danced in the air around me. Ahead of me, the long passage-way of the north wing receded into the distance.

It was along this stretch of corridor, I suddenly remem-bered, that I had first unravelled the bulky roll of writings that formed the Great Book of Arboria.

On the day that my grandmother had given me the book, the air raid siren had sounded, so that I did not get the chance to examine her gift straightaway. Nor, for various reasons, did I get the chance to examine it for a couple of days after that. I kept it by me, though, I even kept it under my pillow while I slept. It excited me just to have the book in my possession, just to hold it, just to toy with the knotted ribbons, just to allow the rough texture of its outer surface to tickle my fingertips. Now and again, it seemed as though some kind of undefined energy were passing into me from that tightly rolled bundle. Something was seeping in through my fingers, something was flowing along my nerves and my arteries, something was coursing around my whole body, something that was capable of jolting me awake like a sudden charge of electricity.

All of this somehow made it easier for me to put the deaths of my parents to the back of my mind. For two days I hung in a state of frustrated anticipation but, on the third day, I found myself at last alone. I wondered what would be the best way to examine such a long roll of paper. The monks and the scholars of the middle ages must have had some kind of reading stand, I reasoned, something specially designed to support a half-unwound scroll. But Hedley House had nothing like this and, if ever there had been such a thing, it was now long gone. Eventually I decided that what I really needed to do was to unwind the scroll to its full length on a flat surface, so that I would be able to examine the whole of it at once. I considered venturing out into the open air and carrying out my task on the terrace, but I was reluctant to risk the hazards of wind and rain. Eventually, I hit upon the idea of using the long corridor. Even in those wartime days the north wing of the house was unoccupied, but it had not yet begun to deteriorate too badly, and my grandmother still managed to keep it fairly clean.

Checking that I was unobserved, I retrieved my precious burden from its hiding place in my bedroom, tucked it under my arm and ventured out onto the landing. As I rounded the corner, the perspective of the corridor stretched inscrutably ahead of me. The architect who had designed this part of the building, I remembered, had built the doors at the far end to a slightly smaller scale than the nearer ones, with the aim of giving an exaggerated impression of distance. But, optical illusion or no, I estimated that the corridor would be just long enough for the work that lay ahead of me.

As I knelt on the floor to unroll the yards of flaking parchment, I could sense the Great Book squirming restlessly in my grip, like a hibernating beast reluctant to be exposed to the daylight. The scroll was displaying an annoying inclination to roll itself back up so, to counteract this, I kicked off my shoes and placed them as paperweights at both ends. After a few moments it seemed to settle down. From the walls of the corridor, the portraits of my long dead ancestors, in their beards and their ruffs and their wimples, gazed down with impassive curiosity.

Rising to my feet, I started to make an examination of what lay before me. The Great Book of Arboria extended along some thirty feet of the corridor. I could see now that it consisted of around a dozen or twenty separate documents, all attached to one another in a long strip. The newer sections, the ones that were on the outside when the scroll was rolled up, were written on thick paper, and were fastened together with glue or sticky tape. But as I got closer to the centre of the roll, to what must have been the oldest part, paper gave way to thick, yellow parchment, and glue and tape gave way to crude, black stitching. Eventually, the parchment was superseded by an even thicker material, brownish and brittle and coarse, perhaps some kind of leather or hide.

Kneeling down again, I started to look more closely at the words on the scroll. I did not recognise the most recent handwriting but, in the section that came immediately before it, I was startled to recognise an unformed, juvenile version of my father's script. Before that, I discovered a passage inscribed in the crabbed, forward-slanting script of the Victorian age. Perhaps this was the work of my grandfather, I pondered – or my grandmother? It was, after all, my mother's family from whom Hedley House had acquired its name . . .

As I edged my way along on my hands and knees, it seemed that I was edging slowly backwards in time. At every stage, the handwriting became harder to decipher, each entry appearing more angular, more forbidding than the one before. Soon I was peering at an impenetrable tangle of gothic script. I could not make out any of the words now. I could barely even identify the letters. I began to wonder if this part had been written not in English, but in some other language, perhaps Latin. Eventually, burrowing my way to the heart of the scroll, to the part that was inscribed on hide, I found that I could not recognise even a single character. Thin, spiky forms appeared before my eyes, forms that looked more like stick men than letters. The writing swam before me, the stick men seeming to caper mockingly in their uneven rows. How old is this writing, I wondered. How old is Arboria?

'Aren't those runes?' I leapt to my feet, startled to hear Janny's voice. She had been standing just behind me, peering over my shoulder. 'Sorry,' she went on. 'I thought you'd heard me. It's runic script. They say it's one of the oldest forms of writing. Do you know how to read it?'

'No I don't.' I made a lame attempt to brush the dust from my bare knees. 'How could I? I haven't even heard of— What did you say? Runes? What do you know about them?'

'Oh, not much,' said Janny vaguely. 'You pick these things up, don't you?'

As summer gave way to autumn, and autumn to winter, Hitler's bombing raids on London continued with ferocious intensity. To me, though, the war might just as well have been happening in some other universe. My overriding preoccupation was with the Great Book of Arboria. Night after night, barricaded behind my bedroom door, I pored over the scroll, squinting in the candlelight at the disparately shaped characters, hoping against hope to extract some sense from them. Once or twice, Janny asked me how my work was progressing, but in truth I was reluctant to speak to her about it and, after a while, she stopped asking. From Robert too I kept my work a secret. This task, I sensed, was mine and mine alone.

But one morning, emerging red-eyed and haggard from my room, I bumped into my brother on the landing. 'Heavens, Ken,' he commented, 'you look a bit of a state. I hope you haven't been playing with yourself.'

'I don't know what you mean!' I replied, indignantly but not very truthfully.

My brother's attitude suddenly changed. 'I'm sorry,' he said. 'I suppose you must still be a bit upset about Mother and Father . . .'

'It's all right,' I replied abruptly. 'It's not that.' But, as I elbowed my way past him and into the bathroom, I could feel the tears pricking at the back of my eyes.

*

Bit by bit, the scroll started to yield up some of its secrets, the voices of the various contributors seeming to whisper to me from the depths of the past. The Victorian handwriting straightened up and opened out to me. Even the gothic script started to untangle itself and to hint at something of what it concealed. Only the runic characters remained stubbornly indecipherable.

Some of the writings dealt with the history of Hedley House. I discovered that the oldest part of the house, my grandmother's part, was at least four hundred years old. The house stood on the crest of a hill. The hill offered a stronghold that would have been easy to defend, so it came as no surprise to learn that there had been other settlements on the site before Hedley House. I remembered that, at the top of the hill where the ice house stood, there lay the remains of another building, a square plot of ground enclosed by the humped remnants of a mound and ditch. This had always been referred to in the family as 'the villa'. I had therefore always imagined that it had been a Roman building but, according to the long-dead writer, this structure was not Roman at all, but was in fact a hill-fort originating from the New Stone Age.

'*The Romans forbore to build at this place,*' my invisible friend whispered to me. '*There was some aspect about the place that struck fear into them. Even the Roman road turns aside from its path to shun this place.*' It was true. The Romans, I knew, were famous for building their roads dead straight, but here, at Hedley House, their engineers had made a surprising exception, with the result that the grounds of Hedley House were skirted on the west side by a long, curving bend in the road. What was it about the place, I wondered, what was it that the Romans had dreaded so much? They surely weren't bothered by a hillfort! There must have been something else here, some-thing that even their practically minded engineers had sensed, something that lurked beneath the ground, something that lin-gered in the caves beneath the earth. Something that was older than the Romans, something that was older even than the men of the Stone Age. Something that had lived here from the very beginnings of time itself. Something that perhaps still lived here today.

And then I remembered that night in the clearing, the night when the Good People had come out of the darkness and danced.

When it was not too cold, I made my way through the garden gate to take a walk in the Arborian forest, kicking through drifts of rustling leaves and snapping twigs. At the log store I would always steal a glance through the doorway, but Tommy Pelling, like many of the creatures in the forest, preferred to spend the colder months in hibernation. As I strode out along the track, I could feel the ground hard beneath my feet. Above my head, the trees were bare and soon, I knew, there would be ice on the lake. Nothing stirred in the forest except for the occa-sional squirrel or rabbit. It was as though the land itself were hibernating, as though it knew that nothing else was going to happen until the spring. On the far side of the water, I sup-posed, the Barbarians would be skulking in their mud huts. Sometimes I hid under one of the willow trees, my eyes raking the far shore of the lake, but not a trace of them could I find. Even Davy Hearn was nowhere to be seen. I suppose I could have crossed over the bridge to look for him but, remembering Robert's stern prohibition against crossing the water, I still chose not to do this.

Week followed week, and the bombing continued. When we heard the howl of the sirens, it was the signal for all of us to hurry down to the shelter. One November evening, I found myself unusually restless, and as I prowled to and fro, I noticed that I was not the only one in Hedley House who was afflicted in this way. Janny, usually steady handed, dropped and broke a couple of plates while drying up. My grandmother was filling her pipe about twice as often as usual. Only Robert, impassive, continued with his homework, unaffected by the nervous tension of those around him.

It was almost a relief when the sirens sounded. Robert put down his books and briskly donned his ARP helmet. My grandmother collected up her pipe and her matches, while Janny and I made a hasty tour of the house to check that all the blackout curtains were in place. By the time we had returned to the kitchen, Robert was standing out on the terrace fidgeting with his torch, impatient to lead the way down to the ice house.

'Hurry along, all of you,' he badgered us. 'Hitler's not going to sit around waiting for us to make ourselves comfortable.' He started to lead the way across the vegetable patch.

Preparing to follow him, I noticed at the last moment that my grandmother was still not ready. I turned back. She was standing by the kitchen door, just straightening up, and I realised that she had been putting something on the back doorstep. It was a saucer of milk. My grandmother was facing away from me, and she could not have known that I had seen her. Janny was standing close by, though, and I could tell that she had noticed.

'Come along, come along!' It was Robert's voice again. 'What's the point of having a shelter if we're going to hang around by the back door all night? Do you want us all to be killed? Is that it?' I could imagine my father using exactly the same words. With a rueful grin, I followed my brother down to the shelter. The matter of the milk would have to be dealt with at a later time.

Robert was the first to turn in that night. As soon as we were safely installed in the sitting area, he disappeared into the bunk room with a couple of candles and his homework books. Meanwhile, my grandmother had been lighting the oil stove. The three of us pulled up chairs and did our best to make ourselves comfortable. After a little while, the old lady's head dropped back and she began to snore.

Janny's curiosity soon got the better of her. 'You don't have a cat, do you?' she began. I shook my head. 'I think I've seen people putting milk out for the hedgehogs, though,' she continued.

'We don't get many hedgehogs round here,' I replied warily.

'So what is it?'

I wanted to say, 'I don't know.' I wanted to say, 'I can't tell you.' I wanted to say, 'It's nothing to do with you.' But somehow, I knew that I had to tell Janny the truth. 'It's something that we used to do when we were little,' I began reluctantly. 'Gran told me there was someone who looked after the house, someone who made sure that everyone in the house was safe.' Janny was eyeing me with a steady gaze, not attempting to hurry me, calm in the knowledge that the truth was about to emerge. 'He was a sort of guardian spirit,' I went on. 'Gran called him a hobgoblin. He had looked after the house ever since it was built.' I started to speak faster, relieved that I was at last able to unburden myself. 'He wasn't the same as us. We never saw him, well, hardly ever, but we had to make sure that he always had something to eat and drink. So we used to put out a saucer of milk at night, sometimes a biscuit or a crust of bread as well. We used to say that if we looked after him, he would look after us. I haven't thought about it for years. Gran used to say that he was one of the Good People.'

'And in the morning?' Janny's prompting was gentle but relentless.

'That's the funny thing. In the morning, the milk was always gone.'

'Perhaps the fairies drank it.' In the yellow flicker of the oil stove, I could not see whether Janny was smiling or not. She sounded perfectly serious, though.

'He was called Tommy,' I said finally. 'The milk was for Tommy Pelling.' There was a few moments' silence. To my surprise, I could feel the sting of tears behind my eyes. Then, very gently, I felt the touch of Janny's hand on my wrist.

'I do understand, Kenny,' she said quietly. 'Maybe more than you realise. I knew someone once . . .' For a long moment she was quiet, and I could find nothing to say either. 'And I'm like you in another way,' she went on at last. 'I don't have a mammy and a daddy either.'

But before Janny could say any more, my grandmother stirred uneasily in her sleep and, at the same moment, I became aware of a distant, low rumble. It began quietly, then it started to increase steadily in volume, growing into a deep-throated, threatening, booming roar. Soon, the sound seemed to be coming from every direction at once, from left and right, from behind and in front, from above and beneath. Janny withdrew her hand, my grandmother sat up and opened her eyes, and Robert emerged from the bunk room, once more strapping his tin hat onto his head. In the meantime, the noise continued steadily and inexorably. In the dim light, all four of us stared at one another.

'They're bombing somewhere,' said Robert finally. It was a statement of the obvious, but nobody said anything. 'I don't think it's all that close, but it sounds as if someone's getting hit pretty hard.' He stepped towards the iron doors. 'I'm going to take a look. Ken, come with me. The rest of you, you'd better wait here.'

'Is it safe?' said Janny.

'As I said, the bombing's not close,' Robert replied. 'We'll be all right for a couple of ticks. Come on, Ken, let's go and see.' He eased the doors open just enough for us to squeeze through, then pushed them shut behind us. We scrambled up the side of the hill to a place just above the doors. We didn't need the torch, because the sky to the west was glowing crimson and yellow. Above us, we could hear the sinister drone of enemy aircraft and, from somewhere to the north, there came the rattle of anti-aircraft fire. The rumble of the bombs sounded much louder out in the open, but I could tell that it was coming from a long distance away.

'Well, I don't envy the people over there,' said Robert finally. 'But it's not Tollcester, at any rate. It's in the wrong direction for that. I reckon it must be about twenty miles from here. Come on, let's get back inside. It's best not to worry the ladies.' Smiling inwardly at his pompous turn of phrase, I followed Robert back towards the shelter. Twenty minutes later, the noise continued unabated.

Listening to the wireless the next day, I discovered that the target of the bombing had been Coventry. Hundreds of people had died that night, and the city's beautiful cathedral lay in ruins. That winter, and the following spring, was dominated by the German bombings. Much of our time was spent either sitting around the kitchen table waiting for the sirens, or huddled in the air raid shelter waiting for the all-clear. From time to time I noticed my grandmother putting out saucers of milk, and after a while it dawned on me that, whenever she did this, it was a sign that a particularly destructive and violent raid was due to follow. For a time, Arboria was forgotten. It was not until one afternoon the following April that I ventured into the forest again.

It was a warm afternoon, and we had all, for different reasons, decided to spend it in the open air. My grandmother was in the kitchen garden, making a tentative assault with her hoe on the weeds that sprouted between the rows of carrots and turnips. She was becoming a little forgetful, I noticed, and occasionally paused in her tracks, as if uncertain what she was supposed to be doing. Partly because of this, I had offered to help her, and was following behind her with a basket, collecting up leaves and weeds for the compost heap. Whenever she looked the other way, though, I would take the opportunity to uproot a young carrot from the ground and to slip it into the side pocket of my shorts.

After a while, I became bored with this and wandered away to explore the patch of waste ground to the north side of the house. Here I discovered Robert, wearing his ARP helmet as usual, and Janny, who was pushing a small wheelbarrow. Robert was scavenging on the ground, collecting up anything that was made of metal: an old saucepan, a broken coal-shovel, a rusty bucket. 'It's for the Spitfire Fund,' he explained as I approached. 'It's salvage. We're supposed to collect up bits of scrap metal, and they get melted down and made into aeroplanes. Every little helps, you know.'

'Dad used to say they'd take down the railings,' I remembered. 'Do you think they ever will?'

'I expect so,' Robert mused. 'They've been talking about cutting them down in London. It was on the wireless. For the iron, I suppose.' He fingered the strap of his helmet. 'But it really depends how long the war goes on. Here, let's take a breather.' He tossed the dented lid of a kettle into the cart, and the three of us sat down together on the scrubby grass.

I produced the carrots. 'Here,' I said. 'I've got three. One each.' I handed my booty around and we sat munching contentedly. A watery sun had broken through, and the air around us smelled of fresh vegetation and the sweat of young bodies.

To a visitor who had not heard about the war, we would have presented a sorry sight. Our hair was unkempt, and our fingernails were filthy. Our clothes had started to become threadbare and, although none of us was getting fat on our sparse wartime diet, all three of us had grown over the past year. Janny's faded blouse was becoming immodestly tight across the bust, while Robert and I, both still in short trousers, were starting to display rather more thigh than was considered proper in those repressive days. Lately we had all had our feet measured and, while Janny and Robert had been allowed new shoes, I had just failed to qualify, and my scuffed old sandals had started to pinch my feet. Glancing at my brother's profile, I noticed that the outline of his features had begun to harden, to take on a more definite shape. In many ways, it occurred to me, Robert had started to act more like a man than a boy. Yet there were still days when he seemed ready to shrug off his responsibilities and return to the games of our childhood. Today, it turned out, was going to be one of those days.

'Fancy going to Arboria?' he suggested impulsively. All three of us sprang to our feet and started running pell-mell towards the vegetable patch and the garden gate. Robert, some distance in the lead, vaulted smoothly over the fence by the greenhouse, while Janny astonished me by turning three perfect cartwheels, her grey pleated skirt flapping gaily about her legs as she whirled upside down through the air. Then Robert heaved the gate open and we all elbowed our way through.

Inside his brick hut, Tommy Pelling was busy stacking logs. He looked up when he heard us coming. 'Beautiful day, Master Robert, Master Kenneth, Miss Janny. Lovely to see you all again. I think it's going to be a fine summer . . .'

His final words were lost as he turned back to his work, but we had better things to do that day than to discuss the weather with Tommy. Down the track to the lake we raced, hardly giving ourselves time to take in everything that had happened since our last visit. Here, a dead tree had fallen across our path, and a new way had to be found around it. There, a bank had collapsed after some heavy rain, and once again a detour had to be improvised. On every twig, the fresh leaves of springtime were sprouting while, from the undergrowth all around us, came the cheepings and squawkings of young birds and animals. But there was another noise too, a noise that was not so easy to identify. Beneath my feet, somewhere far beneath the earth, I could feel once more the slow, deep rhythmic pulsation with which I was starting to become familiar, that same deep rhythm that had propelled the dancers through the midnight revels in the forest. The pulse of the earth was beating again now, beating beneath our feet as we ran. It dawned on me that

I could recognise the presence of the Good People. Janny, I was sure, would have recognised it too. About Robert, I was not quite so certain.

Soon, the three of us were huddled together in our favourite hiding place, the cool, green cavern under the willow tree by the shore of the lake. Shading our eyes, we peered out across the water. Janny was the first to break the silence. 'I can see him,' she whispered. 'Davy Hearn. He's back in the forest. Just there.' She pointed a slim, white finger. Sure enough, there among the bushes on the far shore, I could make out Davy's crouching figure. Almost hidden in the undergrowth, he was making his way stealthily along the shoreline. Not a leaf rustled at his passing, so deftly did he thread his way through the forest. He arrived at a spot almost opposite our hiding place, glanced both ways and then stepped clear of the concealing thickets and stood before us on the shore. 'I think he's alone,' Robert said after a moment. 'No sign of the Barbarians. I wonder where they've gone?'

Now that Davy was standing upright, we could see that he too had been growing. He was wearing the same ragged old shirt, but now it had lost most of its buttons and was displaying a chest that looked harder and more muscular than it had done six months before. His torn corduroy breeches seemed to have grown shorter, now barely covering his sturdy knees. Hands in pockets, he took in the view in a leisurely fashion.

'Cheeky devil,' breathed Robert.

'Ssshhh!' Janny raised a finger to her lips. 'What's that?'

I strained my ears. This time, I heard it. I caught Robert's eye, and I knew that he had heard it too. From the far shore of the lake, muffled by the undergrowth, but still unmistakable, all three of us had heard the chink of metal. I shaded my eyes.

There, almost hidden by the bushes, were four or five Barbarian warriors, spears at the ready, their armour glinting in the dappled shade of the forest.

'Anyone would think they owned the place,' Robert continued after a moment, his hushed voice betraying an undertone of indignation. 'Arboria belongs to us, not to Davy and his Barbarians. It's time we taught young Hearn a lesson!'

'Why don't we start a campaign?' I broke in. 'Let's rally the Arborian army!'

Robert drew his lips tightly together for a moment. 'I'm not sure we really need to start a full-scale war,' he continued in a more measured tone. 'Arborians against Barbarians? No, not straight away. Let's find out a bit more about them first. Why don't we try and locate their camp, see how many of them there are, and what we're up against. Then perhaps we might call in the army.' He glanced at me, then at Janny. 'Let's make it a proper campaign. And, as High Lord, it will be my job to lead it.' In the silence that followed, Robert adjusted the strap of his helmet in what struck me as a rather conceited way. As he did this, Janny took a thoughtful look at him. Then she turned her head and took a thoughtful look at the boy who stood on the far side of the lake.

'Our very own campaign,' she said, half to herself. 'That sounds like fun. When do we start?'

Robert glanced at his wristwatch. 'Not today,' he said. My brother, as usual, was right. It was growing late, and supper time was approaching, so we agreed that the campaign against Davy Hearn and the Barbarians would have to be postponed until another time. Slowly, we gathered up our things and made our way back up the track to Hedley House. In the kitchen, though, a new surprise awaited us. Seated at the long table was a stolid-looking, dark-haired girl with an anxious expression on her face. The three of us halted in our tracks.

'There's a new little visitor come to stay,' my grandmother explained. 'She's an evacuee, Janny, like you. Her English isn't very good, so you'll have to be a bit patient with her.' She turned to the girl. 'Nadia, these boys are my grandsons Robert and Kenneth,' she indicated each of us in turn, 'and this is Janet Grogan. We call her Janny, so I expect you can too.' She turned back to us. 'She's called Nadia. Introduce yourself, Nadia.' The girl stood up, and I could see that, although probably about the same age as me, she was a good head shorter. She made a rather stiff curtsey.

'Good afternoon,' said the girl in heavily accented English. 'My name is Nadia Skolomowski and my mother and father are in internment camp.'

Getting to know Nadia was a slow, difficult business. She was a shy, awkward creature, and both Robert and I quickly became frustrated by her stilted manners and her halting English. Janny, more compassionate by nature, was prepared to make more of an effort, and as time went by, she began to learn something of Nadia's story.

'Her family escaped from Europe just before the war started,' Janny explained. 'They were afraid of what the Nazis might do to them, they'd heard all kinds of rumours I suppose, so they ran away to England. They travelled hundreds of miles in lorries and goods trains, and they ended up having to do the last bit across France on foot. They lost everything they owned apart from the bags they were carrying. And then the British government decided that they were Enemy Aliens and they got locked up anyway, and Nadia got sent to us. It doesn't seem fair, does it, after everything they've been through.' I had to agree with this although, I'm sorry to say, I still didn't find Nadia any easier to like. 'You should try and be nicer to her,' Janny rebuked me one day. 'She's had a terrible time and she's finding it really hard to trust anybody.'

A week had passed since we had seen Davy Hearn on the shore of the lake. Robert had been at school every day, while Janny and I had, as usual, spent as little time there as we could get away with. My grandmother was supposed to have written to the school about the arrangements for Nadia's education but, in her increasingly absent-minded state, she had so far neglected to do anything about it. But now it was Saturday again, and we were all ready to make a start on the campaign against Davy Hearn and the Barbarians. The four of us were sitting cross-legged on the roughly planed floorboards of the House in the Air, just finishing off the picnic that my grand-mother had prepared for us. Janny was in charge of the picnic basket. Robert's tin helmet lay on the floor beside him, while next to me lay the Great Book. Nadia, doubtless rather baffled by our curious world of Arborians and Barbarians, had never-theless tagged along with us, stumbling haltingly across the bumpy ground. She had not yet overcome her shyness, and seemed happiest when close to Janny. Tommy Pelling, sensing some unusual goings-on, had temporarily forsaken his log store and sat next to me on the floor. There was a gentle breeze, and the house was rocking to and fro on its creaking ropes.

'We need to gather intelligence,' said Robert importantly. 'Infiltrate the Barbarian camp. Find out what their plans are.'

'Why did nobody think of making sugar sandwiches before the War?' Janny pondered.

'I suppose sugar wasn't so hard to get in those days,' I said. 'Lucky for us that Mother had the idea of stockpiling it,'

Robert observed. There was a moment's uneasy silence before he continued. 'Now, about this campaign . . .'

'How are we going to find out where the Barbarians have made their camp?' I said. 'We don't really know anything about their part of the forest.'

Robert frowned in concentration. I noticed that, when he stopped frowning, a faint vertical line remained visible between his eyebrows. 'We could wait for Davy Hearn to appear at the lakeside,' he suggested. 'Then we could follow him and see where he goes.' He thought this over for a moment. 'No, that wouldn't work,' he went on. 'Davy can move about without making a sound, but one of us would make too much noise. He'd hear us straight away.'

There was a long silence while everyone tried to come up with another idea. Finally Tommy whispered to me. 'If I might make so bold, Master Kenneth, perhaps Master Robert might not have thought of spying on the enemy from above. From the top of a tree, perhaps.'

'Tommy's had an idea,' I broke in excitedly. 'We could watch Davy from up in the branches. He'd never think of looking for anyone up there.'

'I'm good at climbing trees,' Janny interposed.

Robert did not respond to this. 'Aerial surveillance might just work,' he mused. 'But how would we get across to the other side of the lake? We couldn't use the bridge. The boards are all loose, so that would make a lot of noise too.'

'What about the place where the lake gets narrow?' said Janny excitedly. 'You know, next to the waterfall. The branches of the trees there are all sort of tangled up with the branches of the ones on the other side. A good climber should be able to get across.' She licked a few grains of sugar from her lips.

'Perhaps we could swim,' Nadia suggested hesitantly.

For a moment, we all stared at her. Then, ignoring her suggestion, Robert continued. 'I wouldn't fancy climbing,' he said. 'And I don't reckon Ken would be much use either.' There was another silence. The two girls exchanged a glance, but neither of them said anything.

'Miss Janny is a more than capable climber,' observed Tommy.

'Yes, why don't you let me go?' Janny exclaimed. 'I am supposed to be the Chief Scout, after all. And you've seen how good I am at climbing trees.'

There was a brief silence, while Robert considered this. 'All right,' he said finally. 'If you really think you can do it. But wait a minute, how will you be able to hear what the Barbarians are saying? You'll be too high up to make any sense of it.'

Janny looked crestfallen. 'Oh,' she said. 'I never thought of that.'

'And as well as that, the Barbarians have got their own language,' I pointed out. 'I've read all about it in the Great Book.'

'What language do they speak?' Nadia enquired. Once again, everyone ignored her.

'I think I might be able to understand them,' I went on, ' and I don't suppose anybody else could. But I'm not sure I could get through to their camp without them hearing me.'

'Perhaps I should admit to some familiarity with the Barbarian tongue,' said Tommy quietly. There was another silence. Robert put his helmet back on his head and continued to frown. Janny stood up, crossed over to the window and leaned her folded arms on the sill close to where Tommy was sitting. After a moment, Nadia followed her. I noticed that she was frowning, and caught myself wondering whether she too could see Tommy. Then I started to unroll the Great Book, hoping against hope that I might find some inspiration there.

Eventually, a solution was found. Janny would observe Davy Hearn's movements from her tree-top vantage point but I would have to be the one who did the listening, relying on Tommy to interpret any difficult words or sentences. While Janny spied on Davy's movements from above, I would conceal myself near the bridge. As soon as Davy was out of earshot, Janny would signal that it was safe to follow him.

'How will you signal to each other?' Robert was saying.

'Maybe we could imitate bird calls?' I said.

'Don't be daft,' Robert broke in. 'That sort of thing only works in story books. You'll be keeping Janny in sight, won't you? All she'll have to do is point the way. But how will Tommy keep up with you?' I turned around to seek Tommy's advice but he was no longer there. During our discussion, I realised, he must have slipped quietly away. With an effort, I brought my mind back to the conversation.

'Shall we start this afternoon?' Janny was begging Robert.

Robert glanced at his wristwatch. 'Better not,' he concluded. 'Gran will be expecting us back for tea in three quarters of an hour. We could do it tomorrow morning, though. I'll skip church. I don't suppose anyone will notice.' His face took on a more serious expression. 'It'll be dangerous, though. Those Barbarians are desperate characters by all accounts. Neither of you must take any silly risks.'

A thought occurred to me. 'Where will you be, Rob, while all this is going on?'

'I shall be here, overseeing the operation from headquarters,' said my brother importantly. 'I'll probably need to have the Arborian bowmen standing by, just in case things get out of hand. You never know, the Barbarians might get wind of our plans and mount a counter-attack.' He glanced in Nadia's direction. Discouraged by her earlier rebuff, she had taken no further part in the discussion. 'You can stay here with me,' he offered ungraciously. 'Do you think you're up to looking after the refreshments?'

'Rob,' I ventured tentatively, 'can I use this?' While he was speaking, I had reached across to where he was sitting, taken hold of the helmet and tried it on for size. But, seeing me, Robert at once sprang forward to snatch it away. For a moment, we wrestled on the ground, but it wasn't much of a contest. Robert was bigger than me and older than me, and within seconds he had repossessed his property and returned to his place.

'You keep your hands off!' he snapped, his eyes blazing with anger. 'That was Dad's helmet! And now it's mine!' Startled by this passionate outburst, I could only mumble my apologies.

'Come on boys,' said Janny quietly. 'It's only an old tin hat.' United again by her apparent lack of understanding, we both glared at her.

As Janny had pointed out, the trees that grew the nearest to the waterfall had branches that overhung the stream, so that a skilled climber could easily cross to the far side without resorting to the bridge. Early on Sunday morning, therefore, we took up our positions. I crouched down behind the jagged rocks next to the falls, while Janny glanced about her looking for a suitable tree to climb. Robert remained at the House in the Air in the taciturn company of Nadia, ready to call up the Arborian army if its help were required.

'Where's Tommy?' Janny hissed anxiously.

'Don't worry,' I replied, probably sounding more confident than I felt. 'Tommy will be here when we need him.'

With a shrug, Janny continued to inspect her surroundings. 'This one will do pretty well,' she said at last. 'It's plenty tall enough, the trunk's good and knobby, and there are branches quite low down.' With brisk efficiency, she kicked off her socks and sandals. 'Good luck,' I whispered. Within seconds, she was halfway up the trunk, her white, bony legs working like pistons, her fingers seeking whatever purchase might offer itself, her pale red hair flapping like a flag behind her.

I watched Janny's progress. She soon found an overhanging branch that interlocked with the branches of several other trees. Silently she stole out along it, her bare feet seeking their grip with practised ease, her hands lightly tracing their way along a higher branch to secure whatever support she needed. Reaching a point where the branch began to dip, she lightly transferred her weight to the branch of a tree that grew on the far side of the stream. Quickly she stepped along to the stouter end, then negotiated her way around the trunk to a suitable vantage point. Then she dropped down neatly into a seated position, her back against the trunk, her knees drawn up under her chin. Without the least exertion, Janny had secured a lookout point high above the land of the Barbarians. She craned around to look at me. I waved up at her, and she waved back. I smiled at her lack of concern, then started to settle myself more comfortably into my own hiding place. There was nothing to do now but to wait for Davy Hearn to appear.

Down among the rocks I waited. Far up in the air Janny waited. Back at the House in the Air, Robert and Nadia waited. We did not have long to wait. Within a quarter of an hour, our adversary appeared at his usual place beside the water. Davy

Hearn was wearing the same torn shirt and the same shabby breeches in which we had seen him the previous day. His feet, as always, were bare and brown. This time, though, there was a sense of purpose to his visit. Swiftly and silently, he crouched at the lakeside, his dark, curly head was only inches from the surface of the water. For nearly a minute, he gazed into the murky depths, then, almost too swiftly for me to see, he shot his bare arm into the water and pulled out a fat, black, wriggling fish. Without a moment's hesitation, he dashed its head three times against a rock, weighed its limp form in his hands, then laid it beside him. Before long, there were nine fish laid in a neat row. The boy rose to his knees, drew a length of twine from his pocket, and neatly threaded the fish together. Then, carrying this odd bundle in one hand, he sprang to his feet, turned around, and vanished into the undergrowth.

I looked up. Janny, ever alert, was already standing upright. She looked down at me to check that I was ready, selected a branch that pointed in the right direction, and stepped lightly out along it. As she did this, I started to edge my way towards the bridge. I could not see Davy Hearn, but I could still see Janny. She was on the branch of another tree now, a slim branch that bowed slightly under her weight. She glanced back towards me, and gave me a swift thumbs-up sign. Cautiously, I stepped out onto the rickety decking. The boards creaked a little under my weight, but I felt confident that Davy would by now be out of earshot. Quickly, I ran across. For the first time in my life, I was in the land of the Barbarians. Across the water, Robert and Nadia waited patiently with the Arborian army. Over here, though, Janny and I were on our own.

At first, the forest felt little different from the forest of Arboria. High above me, I could follow the slight figure of

Janny as she made her way nimbly from branch to branch. Stealthily I moved along the track, keeping her in sight but remaining at a safe distance, so that Davy Hearn would not hear my footsteps. The girl seemed almost to be running on air now, her slender form weightless as it darted through the sky. And I was running too, racing along the track, careering around its twists and turns. Brambles snagged at my bare knees, and a vicious stitch snipped at my side. Faster and faster Janny soared, and faster and faster I ran, until it seemed that my legs could support me no longer, until it seemed that my lungs would burst, until it seemed that my heart would beat itself to a standstill. At last, Janny paused in her flight, signalled to me to stop, settled herself astride a branch.

My nostrils twitched. There was a smell of wood smoke. Realising that we must be very close indeed to the Barbarians' camp, I started to advance more cautiously. Ahead of me, the ground rose to a crest. I headed off to my right, following a narrow track that sliced its way through a patch of bracken. Nearing the top of the rise, I dropped to my hands and knees to peer over the ridge. There before me was a small, grassy clearing surrounded by tall trees. On the far side there stood a cluster of huts. These were of a domed shape, rather like igloos, but they were built from curved branches cunningly woven together, the gaps stuffed with handfuls of moss. This, I guessed, would provide a reasonably weatherproof shelter. Next to the huts, there stood a pile of roughly stacked logs and, close by, a huge mound of earth, from the top of which a thin column of smoke spiralled skywards. Closer to me, on a patch of bare ground, surrounded by a ring of big stones, a small wood fire was burning. Around the fire, a group of people were sitting in a circle.

They were ragged-looking people: men, women and children. Their skin was dark, their eyes were dark and their hair was dark. The grown-ups looked tired and dirty, but the children, although dirty too, looked more lively. Some of the grown-ups were smoking pipes. One of the women had a pair of thick knitting needles, and was engaged in making a dark, lumpy garment. I noticed that the men were not wearing their armour or carrying their spears. I wondered what had happened to their battle equipment. Perhaps it's stored in one of the huts, I said to myself. Yes, that must be it.

After a time, another person emerged from one of the huts. It was Davy Hearn, and he was carrying the fish that he had caught, now trimmed of their tails and speared along a sturdy wooden skewer that passed through their eye sockets. Davy stepped forward into the circle, approached the fire, and hung the fish up to bake. Like the others, he was ragged and dirty. He looked bigger and stronger than any of the other children, but he had not yet acquired the air of weariness and resignation that was apparent in the grown-ups. Compared with them, he glowed with energy, his strength still unwasted, his flame still unquenched. I watched him with renewed interest as he went about his work, then, remembering the real purpose of my presence, I tried to concentrate on what was being said. This could well be my one and only chance to learn the secret plans of the Barbarians.

'Master Kenneth?' With a start, I recognised Tommy Pelling's voice. I glanced to one side and discovered his wiry form crouched beside me on the bank. 'Look at the fish, Master Kenneth,' Tommy whispered to me. 'How many do you see?'

Straining my eyes, I started to count the fish that hung above the fire. 'One, two, three . . . I think I can see eight. Yes, that's it, eight.'

'And how many did you see the young gentleman catch?'

I thought for a moment. 'Nine. I'm sure it was nine. So what happened to the other one?'

With a gnarled finger, Tommy directed my gaze towards a small group of Barbarians who squatted just to the right of our hiding place. There were two old women, who could well have been sisters, and they were crouching over a low rock. For a moment I could not make out what they were doing. Then I realised. On top of the rock lay the last fish that Davy had caught. One of the women had slit open its stomach, while the other was carrying out a minute examination of its contents, laying out the entrails in an intricate pattern on the flat surface and muttering something in a voice that was too low for me to hear. As she did this, the other Barbarians began to rise to their feet and move towards the place where she was squatting. 'Tommy?' I whispered. But when I turned round to look for him, Tommy Pelling had vanished. For a few more moments, I remained in place, hoping to discover some more clues. Soon, though, I found that I could no longer ignore the delicious scent of the roasting fish. I tried once again to turn my mind to my task but, aware now of my hunger, I found that my concentration had deserted me. I looked above me to where Janny was perched. She offered me a tentative thumbs-up, to which I responded with a more definite version of the signal. Straight away she was on her feet, tiptoeing back along the branch. I eased myself back down the slope and, as soon as it felt safe to do so, rose to my feet and followed her back towards the bridge.

'So what did you hear?' Janny demanded. We had made our way back to the waterfall, Janny through the air and I along the ground, and now we were back on our own side, bathing our throbbing feet in the stream. Rinsing the mud from my legs, I noticed that the hairs on my shins had started to grow longer and darker.

'Are those nettle stings? Here, try this.' Janny handed me a dock leaf.

'Thanks.' I dabbed cautiously at the angry red bumps until the pain began to dull. 'It's the black fish,' I said finally. 'I don't reckon the Barbarians catch them just to eat. Those two old women, you must have seen them too, they were cutting up one of the fish and spreading out all its guts on a rock. And the others were watching them do it. It was as if they were looking for something in there, something that . . . I don't know . . .'

'Something more than just a cooked lunch,' Janny hazarded.

'I suppose so. Perhaps there's something about it in the Great Book. I'll have a look later.'

'Not a bad idea,' Janny replied. 'But I guess you're probably better with books than I am. Are you ready to get dressed again?' Painfully, I started to ease my swollen feet back into my shoes. After that, we walked slowly back up the slope towards the garden gate. Outside Tommy Pelling's hut, our ears briefly caught the sound of snoring. We passed through the gate and back into the vegetable garden. 'Ken?' said Janny suddenly. I turned to look at her. Her upturned face was white and anxious. 'Why have they cut the trees down?'

'They're charcoal burners,' I explained reluctantly 'That's what Davy's people are. They come every year. We let them cut a few logs and burn them for the charcoal. They don't really do any damage.'

\*

126

Three weeks went by before we were able to continue the campaign against the Barbarians. During the week, Robert was at school, and I was reluctant to do any more scouting without the reassurance of his presence. Sundays were out of the question for the time being, as Robert's recent absence from church had, after all, been noticed and reported on by the vicar. This left only Saturdays, but for the next couple of weekends even this was impossible. Other things had been planned for us; a village fête one week, a lunchtime visit to Uncle Magnus and Aunt Dottie the next. Finally, however, we were able to assemble once more at the House in the Air. Robert, as usual, was wearing the ARP helmet. Janny had managed to acquire an old pair of Robert's khaki shorts. These were slightly too large for her, so she was also sporting a green elastic belt with a snake clasp. Nadia, reluctantly tolerated by Robert and me, sat in sullen silence.

'I've had a good look through the Book,' I began. ' I've been trying to find out why the Barbarians are so interested in the lake.'

'And?' said Robert briskly.

'Well, I found this,' I offered. '"*In the depths of the lake, there lies buried a thing of great moment, a thing whose nature shall remain forever hidden from the eyes of men, a thing whose true nature is perhaps known only to the black fish that circle there. Many have tried in times past to learn the true nature of this thing, but none to this day has been rewarded for his pains.*"'
I could tell that Robert was interested now, and so was Janny. As I continued, their eyes were riveted on me. '"*It has long been told that the one who learns the nature of this thing will—*"'. Sorry, I can't read the next bit, it's on quite an old section of the scroll. It's gone all smudgy. Here, take a look.'

The four of us were on our hands and knees now, even Nadia was drawn into the mystery. Our heads almost touching, we peered at the jumble of letters in front of us. The day was warm, and I could not help noticing the mingled scent of our bodies.

'Sorry,' Robert declared finally. 'Can't make head nor tail of it. What about you, Jan?'

'Not a hope,' said Janny. 'The next bit looks like runic script, but I don't really know how to read it.' Robert turned his gaze towards me. I shook my head. Finally, he turned towards Nadia. 'Don't suppose you've any idea?' he said, making a grudging effort to include her. But she too shook her head. 'Oh well,' Robert went on. 'Let's look at what we do know. There's something buried in the lake, something that's important to everyone. And it seems that it's the black fish that hold the key to what it's all about. I suppose that's why you saw those two old women cutting that one up and looking inside it. But whether we can work it all out before the Barbarians do, well, that's another question. I certainly don't fancy diving into that water.'

'I can swim,' said Nadia timidly.

Robert ignored her. 'I suppose we could try cutting up one of the fish.'

'Ugh!' said Janny. There was another silence.

'We could declare war,' I suggested.

'Seems a bit drastic,' Robert mused. 'We don't want mass casualties.'

'Well, there is one other thing,' I said. 'Here. "*Duel of the Champions. For the resolution of disputes, each party shall appoint a fighting man, and the two champions shall do battle. Then, whosoever shall win the battle, shall be deemed also to have won the*

128

*dispute. Thus shall the shedding of the blood of the many be fore-
stalled . . ."'*

'Quiet!' Robert interrupted me. 'Did you hear something?'
For a moment, I could hear nothing but the creak of the ropes
that supported the House in the Air. With its usual gentle
rhythm, the house was swaying to and fro, to and fro . . . But
suddenly, I felt a shift in that rhythm, a very slight shift, but just
enough to tell me that something was wrong. I exchanged
glances with the others, and I knew that they had sensed something too. 'There's someone out there,' Robert hissed. 'It must
be a Barbarian spy.'

Our nerves tingling, we held ourselves utterly still. Sure
enough, my ears could now detect the faint hiss of breath. It
was coming from just outside the room.

'I am the smallest,' whispered Nadia unexpectedly. 'I shall go
to the window.' Before we could stop her, she had wriggled
around on the floor and crawled across to the sill. She raised her
head, then quickly ducked down again. The House lurched on
its ropes.

'Three of them,' breathed Nadia. 'But I think that perhaps
they saw me.'

'Stay there,' Robert replied. 'Jan, you look after her. Ken,
come with me.'

We two boys tiptoed across to the door, while the girls obediently hung back. But we were too late. By the time we were
outside, our fleet-footed visitors were halfway down the ladder.
I was just in time to catch a glimpse of a dark figure vanishing
among the branches below.

We turned round and collided with the girls, who had been
craning over our shoulders to see what was happening. 'How
much do you think they heard?' said Janny.

'We'd better be prepared for the worst,' said Robert. '"Duel of Champions" it has to be.' He paused, checking that he had our attention. 'So let's see if I've got this right, Ken. We send out our best man, and the Barbarians do the same. They fight each other and, whoever loses, their side has to do what the winner demands.' He glanced at me and I nodded. 'Well, I'm the High Lord,' he continued. 'I'll fight for the Arborians. I can't ask anyone else to do that. We just need a time and a place. I suggest twelve o'clock next Saturday. At the bridge. All agreed?'

'I'll write a notice and post it on the handrail,' I offered.

'Twelve o'clock,' said Nadia dreamily. 'Robert shall be our champion.'

The days of that week dragged by, but at last the appointed hour arrived. We Arborians assembled in disciplined formation at our end of the bridge. Robert stood at the head of the party, with Janny, Nadia, Tommy Pelling and myself lined up close behind him. On the far side of the bridge, I could make out the figure of Davy Hearn. Behind him stood a row of Barbarian warriors, silent and ready. I looked at Robert and he looked at me. 'Let's hope the Arborian army is standing by!' he said in a low voice. For a moment, it seemed that I could hear a rustle of breath, a tautening of bowstrings, among the trees behind me but, with an effort, I concentrated my attention on the scene ahead. As the long hand of Robert's wristwatch crawled towards the top of its dial, my brother stripped off his school pullover and handed it to Nadia. Then, without once looking behind him, he stepped forward. Janny and I patted him on the shoulders. 'Good luck,' we breathed in unison.

At the far end of the bridge, mirroring Robert's action,

Davy Hearn stepped forward from the ranks of his supporters, glancing briefly behind him as he came. Silently, the two boys moved into position at opposite ends of the bridge, Robert in his tin helmet, shorts, sandals and singlet, Davy in his tattered breeches, bare-chested and bare-headed. As the water gushed and foamed noisily over the lichen-covered rocks beneath them, the two combatants sized each other up. Their bodies seemed charged with nervous energy, and that energy communicated itself to the surrounding company. Behind each champion, his supporters waited, silent and tense.

Robert took a step forward. Davy Hearn did not move.

Robert took another step. Still Davy remained motionless.

'Why won't he come out onto the bridge?' I whispered to Janny. 'Is he afraid of Robert?'

'I think it's the running water that scares him,' Janny replied. 'Remember that old superstition?'

'It is the same in my country too,' Nadia said unexpectedly. 'They will not cross a moving stream.'

I didn't have time to ask who she meant by *they*, because, while we had been talking, Robert had slowly advanced the last few feet towards the unyielding Davy. Suddenly the two boys lunged towards one another, each gripping his opponent by the shoulders. A roar went up from the Barbarians, echoed by an answering roar from the Arborians in the forest behind me. The two champions locked together, and I could now see that, although Robert was the taller and longer-limbed, Davy had the advantage in breadth and in muscle. But, while Davy was halfway to being naked, Robert's head and feet at least were well-protected. The two were grappling with each other like wrestlers now, each trying to drag his opponent towards his own bank of the stream. Davy's body glistened with sweat, and Robert's singlet had damp patches under the arms. 'I don't trust Davy Hearn,' I whispered to Janny. 'I'm sure he'll have some dirty trick up his sleeve.'

'He has no sleeves,' observed Nadia, with a straight face.

Janny giggled. 'He looks all right without them , though!'

I glared at the pair of them. 'Robert's going to win,' I hissed furiously.

Sure enough, Robert had succeeded in dragging his enemy halfway across the bridge. As the pair of them struggled, the fragile structure began to tremble under their feet. Robert had gained the upper hand now, while Davy's strength was waning visibly. Even above the noise of the stream and the shouts of the supporters, I could hear the breath rasping in his throat.

'It's the running water,' breathed Janny. 'I told you. It's sapping his strength.'

Now Robert was forcing Davy down. The young Barbarian was hardly putting up a struggle, and his knees had started to sag. On the far bank, the Barbarian warriors tensed themselves, tightening their grip on their spears. Behind me, bowstrings were pulled back as the Arborians prepared to retaliate.

'Yield!' roared Robert. Davy shook his head. Robert forced him down another inch. Davy slackened his grip on the other boy's shoulders, clutched at the handrail for support. Under his feet, a rotting board cracked. 'Yield!' roared Robert again. Once more Davy shook his head. Suddenly, the boy's bare feet skidded on a patch of moss and he was down. Robert in his tin hat loomed over him. 'Yield!' Robert roared for a third time, but once more the response was a shake of the head. Now Robert lunged forwards and downwards and, as he did this, Davy twisted to one side. I could feel Janny's hand gripping my arm in alarm. Suddenly, Davy toppled over the edge of the bridge, and now he was hanging at full length above the raging water, his fingers clutching at the edge of the decking, his face as white as paper. Robert towered over him in triumph.

Suddenly frightened by the force of his anger, I could restrain myself no longer. 'That's enough, Rob,' I called. 'You don't want to kill him!'

Robert turned towards me. For a moment he said nothing, perhaps allowing himself one more moment to savour his victory. Then, with a shrug, he dropped to his knees and offered the other boy his hand. Davy clung on to this unexpected lifeline, his breath coming in ragged sobs. As he allowed my brother to haul him to safety, Davy seemed close to tears. Staggering unsteadily to his feet, he appeared to have shrunk several inches in stature. He was deflated, his youthful energy gone from him. Shrugging off Robert's arm, he lurched a pace backwards towards his own side of the stream. As he stepped off the far end of the bridge, his own people moved forwards towards him. Rough hands were laid on his sagging shoulders, and I could hear a dark murmur of voices.

'What are they doing?' said Nadia.

'Listen,' said Janny.

Those voices were almost below the threshold of my hearing, but they seemed to carry within them a power, a force, a black energy, that flowed through their hands into the young Barbarian's body. All at once, Davy was revitalised. His chest filled with life-giving breath, his shoulders broadened and drew back, and his spine straightened up until he seemed to have grown almost taller than before. The colour rushed back to his pale cheeks, his eyes narrowed, his lips tightened. Before Robert could grasp what was happening, Davy stormed forwards and dealt my brother a tremendous blow to the side of the neck.

Just then, from somewhere behind me, I heard a subdued word of command. Startled, I glanced over my shoulder and there, in full view at the edge of the forest, stood a row of Arborian foot soldiers. Their heads were bare, and their hair hung to their shoulders in long, pale locks. Each one wore a leather jerkin and breeches bound with gaiters, and each one carried a longbow and a quiver of arrows. Their sergeant caught my eye and nodded curtly. A flood of relief surged through me. I knew at once that my party was safe, that the Barbarians would never defeat us.

I turned around once more. To my horror, I could see that Robert had been caught off guard. Reeling under the impact of Davy's blow, he was lurching dangerously to one side. Suddenly, he lost his balance and, as he fell, the handrail of the bridge caught him low down on his hip. Like a gymnast in a slow-motion film, he somersaulted over the rail, spun through the air, and landed with a clumsy splash in the rapids below. Sick with fear, I heard the clang of his helmet as it dashed against a rock.

'Oh, Master Robert,' gasped Tommy Pelling.

For a moment, Davy Hearn remained where he was. Then, abruptly, he turned on his heel and strode off, back in the direction of the Barbarian horde. From the far side of the water, there arose a deafening roar of triumph and a savage clatter of spears as his people welcomed their champion back among them. On our own side, the Arborians stood grim and silent, awaiting their next order.

'We've got to get Robert out!' I cried. 'He must have fallen fifteen feet!' Down we scrambled over the rocks to where the High Lord lay. He was spread-eagled across the bed of the stream, his helmet skewed at an alarming angle, his clothes plastered to his motionless body by the raging water. As the stream gushed over him, it carried away with it vivid streaks of blood. For a moment I feared the worst. Then Robert lifted his head.

'Beastly trick,' he breathed. 'After I'd gone and rescued him, too. Worst thing, though – I think I've lost my wristwatch.'

Janny and Nadia looked at each other in relief. 'Come on,' I said, for once taking charge of the situation. 'Let's try and get him back to the house and assess the damage.' We manhandled him up the bank and on to the path. Davy Hearn, I noticed, had disappeared back into the forest with the Barbarian forces. And, on our own side of the water, the Arborians, too, had vanished without trace.

*Five*

## ACROSS THE BRIDGE

$\mathscr{I}$ was awoken this morning by the sound of violent hammering. Do you have nightmares, Jamie? I had been dreaming yet again about the fight on the bridge between my brother and Davy Hearn, and at first the noise wove itself into the fabric of my dream, blending in with the thumping of the Barbarians' spear shafts on the ground. It took me a few moments to collect my senses, to disentangle myself from the bedclothes, to locate my slippers, to remember who I was and where I was. While I was doing these things, the sound of the hammering continued, gradually increasing in intensity until the whole of Hedley House seemed to shake to its foundations. I realised at last that someone was banging at the kitchen door.

'All right, all right, I'm coming, no need to break it down,' I mumbled as I negotiated my way around the kitchen furniture and the umbrella stand. While I was doing this, the hammering ceased and I caught a brief glimpse of somebody's silhouette peering in at the side window of the porch. I wrestled with the rusty old bolts, wrenched the big iron key around in the lock and finally threw open the door. A thin, rather nervous-looking lad was standing there. To me, he appeared about fifteen years old. He was wearing a large, clumsy-looking pair of trainers, a baggy pair of shorts, a bright orange jacket and a baseball cap that bore some sort of ornate crest above its peak. Over his shoulder he carried a bulging sack, and in his right hand he held a white envelope. Finally shrugging off the last of my interrupted sleep, I realised that this was the uniform worn in the twenty-first century by employees of Royal Mail.

'Recorded Delivery for Mr Storey?' It sounded more like a question than a statement.

'That's me. Aren't you a bit young to be delivering letters?' The only response to this was a feeble grin. I signed a piece of paper, and the postman handed me the envelope together with half a dozen other pieces of correspondence. Then he turned on his heel and hastily made his way down the path.

Pulling the door shut behind me, I stumbled back into the kitchen, deposited the letters on the table and turned to the stove to boil the kettle. Having done this, I drew up a chair, pulled my nightshirt about my shoulders against the chill, took a long draught of tea, and then began to open the post.

For some reason, I kept the recorded delivery letter until last. But, while I examined and discarded the advertisements for credit cards and special offers and once-in-a-lifetime holidays, the slim, official-looking packet seemed to glower at me with a menacing eye. At last, having tossed the final circular through the open doors of the stove, I could ignore it no longer. I slit open the envelope and unfolded a single sheet of paper. My hands trembled as they held it.

The letter bore the crest of Tollcester District Council, but my eyes were reluctant to focus on the paper. Isolated phrases swam into view: '. . . following our recent inspection under the

1985 Housing Act . . .' That must refer to those two officious women who had come poking their noses in the other week. '. . . property declared unfit for human habitation . . .' Well, how dare they! I had seen the way they had wrinkled their noses at the damp patches on the plaster, the way they had shuddered when I showed them the downstairs lavatory. But what business was it of theirs? '. . . District Council now minded to take action . . .' Minded to take action? What on earth did that mean? Were they going to send somebody round to repair the plaster, to scour away the reassuring brown stains from the lavatory pan? I tried once more to extract some sense from the labyrinth of bureaucratic jargon, but whatever meaning it might have had eluded me. It made about as much sense as the runic script in the Great Book of Arboria. The signature at the bottom of the page was indecipherable. All I could glean from the letter was that somebody at the council did not approve of the state of Hedley House, and somebody wanted to do something about it.

Well, let them, I thought. We can soon see them off, Tommy Pelling and I. Oh yes, we can see them off all right. Like we saw off those reporters. Like we saw off those developers. Like we saw off Davy Hearn and the Barbarian horde.

But perhaps the letter frightened me more than I wanted to admit, or perhaps it was just because I had once again started thinking about Tommy Pelling and Davy Hearn and the Arborians and the Barbarians. Anyway, without really considering what I was doing or why, I found myself heading for the back door. In the porch, I abandoned my slippers in favour of a stout pair of Wellingtons, strapped the old ARP helmet onto my head and, with my nightshirt still flapping around me, made my way across the vegetable patch and through the garden gate.

Before long, I was standing at the side of the lake. The willows had grown much taller, of course, and their branches drooped lower over the water. Some of them had become intertwined with their neighbours, so that they looked more like a gigantic, unruly hedge than a row of trees, but I managed nevertheless to slip through a gap and down to the edge of the water. I found myself opposite the place where Davy Hearn used to come to catch fish.

The day on which Davy had pushed my brother Robert into the stream, I remembered, had been a Saturday, and Robert had been determined to return to school the following Monday. When Janny and Nadia and I rescued him from the stream he had been determinedly cheerful and, to our relief, he did not seem to have any difficulty standing up and walking. By the time we got him back to the house, though, he was forced to admit that he was actually in quite a lot of pain. Reluctantly, he agreed to be stripped of his soaking clothes and subjected to my grandmother's beady-eyed scrutiny.

'That's a nasty bruise on your neck,' muttered the old lady as she ran her gnarled fingers over Robert's injuries. 'A big one, but it'll soon heal. And these cuts, nothing that a bit of iodine and sticking plaster won't cure. But what's this?' As she ran her hands around his shoulders and upper chest, Robert suddenly winced with pain. 'Something's not right here,' the old lady concluded. 'Nadia, get the kettle on the stove. Janny, run and get the doctor. Oh no, Kenneth, you stay here. You and I need another talk.'

So Robert perched uncomfortably on one of the kitchen chairs, waiting for Nadia to make the tea and waiting for the doctor to arrive. My grandmother, in the meantime, led me into her parlour, closed the door and started to fill her pipe. Having completed this task to her satisfaction, she struck a match and inhaled deeply. After a long moment, she exhaled a plume of blue, aromatic smoke.

'Who did this to your brother?'

'We were just mucking about . . .'

'Don't lie to me, Kenneth,' the old lady interrupted sharply. 'I thought we knew each other better than that. He's been fighting, hasn't he? Who was it? Was it Davy Hearn?' I nodded silently. She continued to stare at me.

'They were on the bridge,' I said finally. 'Robert saved Davy from falling. And then Davy pushed Robert into the stream and ran away.'

'Still fighting for the bridge,' my grandmother mused, half to herself. 'After all these years. That Davy Hearn, he's always been a bad lot.' I considered this for a moment. It struck me that I really knew very little about my brother's adversary.

'What do you know about Davy?' I hazarded.

'Davy Hearn the gardener's boy,' my grandmother replied. 'That's what we always used to call him. Back before the war, he used to help old Ned Hearn. I don't know if he really was Ned's son, though. Some said he was, others said he wasn't. But when Ned died, Davy ran away. Went to live in the forest with the charcoal burners or some such people, that's what I heard anyway.'

'He's still there,' I replied. 'We saw the charcoal burners' camp, Janny and me. But we don't have a gardener any more, do we? Davy can't still be the gardener's boy.'

'There's always been a gardener's boy at Hedley House,' said my grandmother slowly, 'even when I was a little girl all those years ago. Come to think of it, he was called Davy Hearn too.'

140

'But Davy's just a boy like Robert and me,' I replied wildly. 'He can't be more than about fourteen, can he? He can't have been here all this time.'

My grandmother blew out another long stream of smoke. 'Can't he?' she said.

For a moment, I wondered whether Davy might have been one of the Good People. I was about to ask my grandmother about this when I was interrupted by the distant clatter of the doorbell. Doctor Solloway had arrived and my enquiries, for the moment, would have to be postponed.

It turned out that, when he fell, Robert had broken his collarbone. He was taken to the hospital in Tollcester, and eventually returned home the next day with his arm in a sling. Much to his annoyance, he had to miss the next week of school and, even when he was allowed to return, his arm remained bandaged for several weeks more. In the classroom, he struggled manfully to write with his left hand; in chemistry, he dropped test tubes and flasks; at sports, he sat on the sidelines, twitching with irritability. At home, he was surly with my grandmother and short-tempered with Janny and Nadia and me. I waited for a couple of weeks before raising the subject of Arboria.

'When are we going to carry on with the campaign?' I asked him finally.

'Oh, for heaven's sake, Ken . . .' he snapped. Then, hastily, he collected himself. 'I think we'd better leave it for a bit. It was Arboria that got me into this mess, wasn't it?' I turned to the girls for support, but Nadia looked the other way, and Janny pressed her lips together and shook her head. At any rate, we all knew better than to argue with my brother when he was in this kind of mood. Without his leadership, though, the campaign against the Barbarians would have to be postponed.

I waited until both Robert and Nadia had left the room. 'I don't think we could manage it without Robert,' I admitted to Janny when we were alone. 'Rob's always been in charge. No one else could be the High Lord. Especially since Father . . . you know. We'll just have to wait until he's better again.'

'I'm sure he'll come round,' said Janny, touching my wrist for an instant. 'But maybe we need to give him a little bit more time.'

In the event, it wasn't until the start of the Christmas holidays that the three of us managed to persuade Robert to come back with us into the forest. Over the course of the school term, he had gradually recovered from his injuries, and the doctor had agreed that he could go back to doing sports in the new year. His spirits, however, had been slower to mend than his body.

'Just for an hour,' Janny coaxed him. 'It might do you a bit of good.'

'It will not be the same if you are not there,' Nadia added.

'Very well then,' Robert conceded. He had started to sound slightly more cheerful. 'Arboria it is. I've probably been indoors for too long, anyway.' It was a crisp December morning, and there was something of a holiday atmosphere as the four of us set off across the vegetable patch and through the garden gate.

The frost on the forest floor was thick enough to reveal a single line of small footprints that led from the door of the log store and down the hill.

'What has Tommy been doing?' said Nadia.

Robert cast an expert eye over the tracks. 'Look at the depth of the heel marks. He's been running.'

142

'But where to?' I put in. Then another thought occurred to me. 'Or what from?'

'Come on,' Robert replied. 'Let's go and find out.'

As we strode down the forest track towards the lake, we could feel the crunch of the frost and the crack of the frozen puddles beneath our heavy shoes. All around us, the trees stood tall and stately, their trunks inclined this way and that, none completely vertical, none quite parallel with its neighbour. Above us, the bare branches formed an irregular lattice that cast alternating patches of light and shade across the ground. Soon, we rounded the bend and the lake came into view.

'It is beautiful,' breathed Nadia.

'It freezes in really cold weather and we get ice,' said Robert. We were strung out along the waterside path now, the bare heads of the willow trees nodding gently below us.

'Have you got a set of skates?' Janny called back to him.

'Maybe in one of the bedrooms in the old wing,' Robert replied. 'You know, in the corridor with all those old paintings. Hey, can you hear that?'

All three of us stopped in our tracks. Sure enough, from somewhere in the distance ahead of us, an unfamiliar sound echoed menacingly through the Arborian forest.

'It must be the Barbarians.' I frowned in bewilderment. 'What are they up to now?'

Robert raised a finger for silence. 'Sounds like hammering to me,' he said after a moment, 'hammering and sawing. What's going on? Is somebody building something?' He beckoned us forwards. 'Quietly now.' With a flood of relief, I knew that Robert was back in charge. My patience had been rewarded, and the High Lord had at last returned to his people.

In wary silence we continued along the track, passing the bridge and making our way along the right bank of the stream. As we drew closer, the sound became more distinct. It was coming from somewhere in front of us and to our right. Suddenly our ears were split by an agonising creaking noise, followed by a clatter of branches and an earth-shaking crash. Nadia covered her ears with her hands.

'It's not building work,' said Robert finally. 'Someone's felling trees!'

'Could it be the charcoal burners?' suggested Janny.

'They moved on months ago,' I replied.

'Come on,' Robert exclaimed, 'let's take a look!' Suddenly, the four of us broke into an urgent run. Finally recovering his energy, Robert took the lead, with Janny running a close second. I was trailing some way behind in third place, while Nadia brought up the rear. Moments later, though, we caught up with the others. Robert and Janny had pulled up short and were peering out from behind the trunk of a huge oak tree. Janny twisted around and put a cautionary finger to her lips. Checking our pace, Nadia and I crept up to join them, our lungs still burning from the chase. I could see now that we were at the edge of a clearing. But it was at a place where there had never been a clearing before.

With shocking brutality a great, raw wound had been slashed through the ancient woodland. A score of tall, ancient trees had been felled and, on the far side from the four of us, there stood a small cluster of khaki-coloured tents and a couple of powerful trucks. All around us, people were at work. Some were busily swinging axes, others were wielding long two-handed saws, others were stacking logs on the back of one of the trucks. There was even a mobile canteen with two big shiny tea urns. I glanced around the clearing. I could sense that others, too, had come to look. Quite close to where we were standing, I could make out the insubstantial figure of Tommy Pelling. Slightly further away, scattered here and there, among the surrounding trees, small groups of Arborians were peering incredulously out at the scene before us. In one place, I could even make out the coppery glint of Barbarian armour.

With an effort, I concentrated my attention once more on what was taking place in the clearing. Standing quite close to us were two people who seemed to be in charge of the operation. They were wearing baggy, coarse-textured breeches, thick plain shirts and heavy dark-blue jackets that came down to their hips. Around their heads were tied turbans made from gaily coloured strips of cloth, and these provided the only touch of colour in the scene. Even under their shapeless clothes, though, I could see that these lumberjacks were unusually broad in the hip, unusually full in the chest. I cast my eyes around the other members of their team. It dawned on me at last that all of the intruders in our forest were women.

'The Lumberjills,' whispered Robert. 'I've heard of them, but I've never seen them before. It's because of the war effort. While the men are away fighting, the government's getting the women to do the men's jobs. Didn't you see that newsreel where Princess Elizabeth was learning to drive a truck?'

'In my country it is the same,' Nadia remarked. 'The women and the girls work on the farms and drive the tractors.'

'I saw a woman driving a bus,' I remembered. 'When we went into Tollcester. And Frank Carberry has taken on a couple of women at the print works.' I could feel my voice rising in agitation. 'But what are they doing in Arboria? They aren't supposed to be here.'

145

Robert poked me, rather hard, in the arm. 'Ssshh,' he hissed. 'They'll hear you.' The silence that followed was interrupted by an unexpected sniff from Janny. The three of us turned to look at her.

'I don't know how they can do that,' she gasped, and I could see that there were tears in her eyes. 'Cutting down the trees. How could anyone do that? I could never be a Lumberjill.' I felt her hand clutching at my arm. 'I love the forest . . .'

'Who's that there?' The chief Lumberjill spoke with a thick Scottish accent. 'Come out where we can take a look at ye.' She and her lieutenant were walking towards us. Too confused even to run away, the four of us stepped out into view, Janny still sniffing back her sobs.

'Och, it's only two wee lads and two lassies,' said the lieutenant. 'Come to play in the woods, have ye?'

'It's nae safe for them here,' snapped her sterner colleague. 'We're felling trees. It's too dangerous. Get along with ye now, away to your mammies.' Her stern tone brooked no argument. Burning with humiliation, we slunk away into the forest, back along the path that led back to the garden gate and Hedley House. For a time, each of us was wrapped in solitary silence. Robert was the first to speak.

'Janny's right!' he erupted indignantly. 'They've no business chopping down the trees! They're our trees and our forest! What are those people doing here?'

'Actually, Rob . . .' I interrupted him cautiously. 'I'm not sure the forest *is* strictly ours. I saw it in the Great Book. Most of this land never actually belonged to Hedley House. I think it belongs to Helsing Fold Farm.'

'Why are you always so pedantic?' Robert snapped.

'Kenneth is only saying . . .' Nadia began.

'It doesn't matter who the forest belongs to,' Janny cried passionately. 'It was beautiful and now they've spoiled it.' Her freckled face was pale and her cheeks were streaked with tears and grime.

Christmas came and went in poverty-stricken wartime fashion. The weather that winter was severe, and it wasn't until the New Year that any of us managed to get out of doors again. Early in January we were finally sent outside to shovel snow from the paths. We were all wrapped up tightly in our threadbare overcoats and worn-out scarves but, even in gloves, our fingers were frozen. Robert, as always, wore his ARP helmet, while Janny and Nadia were sporting rakish-looking berets. I had a woollen hat, knitted by my grandmother, with a colourful pom-pom on the top. Our breath made white clouds in the air around us, our noses were shining, and Janny's eyes, as always, were red and sore. In the distance, the bare branches of the Great Tree, and the branches of all the other trees, were delicately outlined in white, sketching a fine lattice against the bleak winter sky. Robert and I equipped ourselves with two spades from the garden, while the girls were issued with a pair of coal shovels. 'Let's pile all the snow up over here, then we can build a snowman later,' Robert ordered us. 'We can use pebbles for his eyes, and give him one of Dad's old pipes to smoke.'

'He's got to have a hat,' Janny suggested. 'He could wear that old tin helmet of yours. No, only joking!' she added hastily as Robert bore down on her, grinning, with a large handful of loose snow. 'Not down my neck!' she laughed, twisting from side to side in his grip.

Dropping my spade, I too snatched up a large handful of

snow, pressed it into a hasty snowball, and lobbed it in the general direction of my brother. It missed him by a couple of feet and struck Nadia on the shoulder, disintegrating into white fragments on the dark fabric of her coat. For a moment she appeared dumbstruck then, warming to the idea, Nadia too stooped slowly down and collected a fistful of snow. A moment later, all four of us were pelting each other at random with more or less well-constructed snowballs, laughing and shouting and stumbling awkwardly about in the heavy drifts that surrounded Hedley House. Nadia had finally abandoned her reserve and, after that, I started to find it easier to enjoy her company.

A few days later, the temperature rose a couple of degrees and the snow began to melt. Robert and Janny caught the bus into Tollcester, Janny to run some errands for my grandmother, Robert to visit Uncle Magnus. Since my father's death, Magnus had been dividing his time between the two family businesses, and we had seen little of him at Hedley House.

'Nadia,' I suggested tentatively, 'would you like to visit Arboria?'

'Oh, yes please,' she replied eagerly. 'I like Arboria very much.'

And so we made our way in single file across the bare vegetable patch, through the garden gate, and down the track that led to the side of the lake.

At Tommy's hut, there were no footprints on the ground, and no signs of activity from within. Although little snow remained, the air still felt cold, so I set a brisk pace. Before long, though, I realised that Nadia had started to fall behind.

'Slowly, please,' she protested. 'I cannot walk too fast.'

Noticing her slow, halting steps, I waited for her to catch up. 'I am sorry,' she explained. 'My legs are not strong. When I was a little girl, I had bad sickness.' Embarrassed by my own lack of consideration, I slowed my pace, allowing Nadia to walk beside me and, as we walked, we started to talk. I noticed that her English had improved a great deal since her arrival. I started telling her the English names for all the trees, and I told her how the ice house had got its name, and I told her the story of how my grandfather had built the House in the Air, and I even told her about the other tree houses where the Arborians lived. In due course we arrived at the side of the lake, close by the waterfall and the rocks.

'I like your forest, Kenneth,' she said. 'It reminds me of the forests in my own country.'

'Did you live in the forest?'

'No, not in the forest, in the city. In an apartment in a big building. With my mother and my father and my sister Luda. Luda was training for the ballet. And now I have lost them all. Oh Kenneth, I miss them so much.'

'One day you'll see them again,' I encouraged her. 'But my parents have gone for ever. It's quite a while now. I still miss them.' It was the first time that I had actually said the words, perhaps even the first time that I had acknowledged the fact. Suddenly, I felt a sense of comradeship with this odd, awkward girl. 'What was it like,' I asked her, 'where you grew up?'

So Nadia told me about the city of her birth, and about the workshop where her father had run his furrier's business, and about the family's flight across Europe, and about the tiny room in London where they had lived until the day of that fateful knock on the door. And I told her about the Arborians and the Barbarians and the Good People, and I told her about the Great Book and about the wealth of legend and wisdom and history that lay buried within it.

'I like you, Kenneth.' Impulsively, she took hold of my arm. 'You are funny. Your stories, they make me laugh.'

'I like you too.' The words escaped my lips before I had time to consider what I was saying. Perhaps I was just being polite. At any rate, we walked on for a little way, still arm in arm, arriving a little later at the bridge. Pausing for a rest, we leaned side by side on the handrail, listening to the tumult of the wild waters as they danced and splashed beneath us. 'This is the best view of the lake,' I said after a time. 'This is our side, the Arborian side. The Barbarians live on the other side.'

'I like to swim. Can I swim in the lake?'

'Maybe later. I'll ask Robert. Perhaps when the weather's warmer.'

Still arm in arm, we rested for a little while longer. Then we turned around and started to make our way back to Hedley House. Soon, it would be teatime.

Over the weeks and the months that followed, I found myself spending quite a lot of my time in Nadia's company. Meanwhile, I couldn't help noticing, Robert was spending quite a lot of time with Janny. Sometimes, of course, Robert and I would still do things together, and sometimes the two girls would band together on some mysterious feminine business. And, now and then, one or other of us might decide to go and do something on their own, and then the others would have to amuse themselves as best they could. In my most private moments, though, I had to admit to myself that it was still really Janny that I wanted to be with. Robert, however, seemed to have the upper hand in that department, or at least he did for the time being.

On the subject of Nadia, my grandmother, unusually, had little to say. 'There's more going on in that little head than you might think,' she said to me once. On another, even more cryptic occasion, she said simply, 'She's a deep one, that girl. She has swum in mysterious waters.' It was to be a while, though, before I began to get an inkling of what it was that she meant.

When Nadia was not in my company, I noticed, she would often wander off alone into the forest, strolling amongst the trees and along the shore of the lake. I wondered idly what she did there. I knew, of course, that the forest reminded her of her native land. Perhaps she was homesick and that's where she felt most at peace. At any rate, on the day in early spring when Robert and Janny and I decided that it was once more time to visit the House in the Air, Nadia was nowhere to be seen.

It was our first visit to the House since the winter. I had unrolled a length of the Great Book across the floorboards, and was still trying to discover exactly what it might be that lay buried in the lake. Janny had borrowed a broom and was carrying out some rudimentary spring cleaning, her eyes streaming with irritation from the dust, while Tommy Pelling crouched in a corner holding the dustpan. Robert had brought my father's binoculars, and was scanning the horizon, trying to discover whether the Lumberjills were up to any more mischief.

'They're definitely back in the forest,' he said. ' I can hear them. I just can't see them. They must have moved somewhere else.'

'Ken, would you mind tidying that scroll away?' pleaded Janny. 'I'm trying to sweep up round here.'

'If it's not too much trouble, Master Kenneth,' Tommy added politely.

'All right, you win,' I conceded. 'I'll look at it later.' I started to roll up the yellowing length of parchment that I had been studying. 'Here, Rob, any chance of a look through those binoculars?'

'All right then. Just for a minute.' My brother reluctantly handed me the binoculars, and I stationed myself at a suitable vantage point by the window. At first, I could make no sense of the two blurred, intersecting circles that swam before my eyes. Then I became aware of the light touch of Robert's hand, guiding my fingers towards the knurled focus wheel. 'You always were a bit of a butterfingers with these,' he commented. 'Here, just turn this gently until it becomes sharp.' I did as I was told and, after a moment, the two circles suddenly coalesced and the silhouetted forms of some branches jolted into view. 'Is that OK?' Robert asked. 'Now try scanning it from side to side – no, not like that, you've got to do it gently.'

After a few false starts, I managed to acquire the knack of scanning along the horizon with the glasses. 'Can't see any Lumberjills over there,' I reported. 'I'll try nearer the lake. Whoops!' Janny had jogged my arm with the broom. 'I've lost it again. Oh yes, there we are. I can see the lake now, or just a bit of it between the trees. I think I can see somebody there. Rob! It's Nadia. And she's on the far side of the lake! She's on the Barbarian side! What on earth is she doing?'

On either side of me I could feel the bodies of my two companions pressing up, anxious to have their turn. Elbowing them away, I peered through the lenses in fascinated silence as Nadia scrambled clumsily down to the edge of the water, kicked off her shoes and socks, and then started to unbutton her cardigan. I could feel my heart thumping harder than usual as she stripped off her blouse and her skirt and finally shed even her shabby-looking underwear. I knew that I should not have been looking at her, but for some reason I found it impossible to avert my gaze. For a long moment, Nadia stood there naked, and then she took an unsteady step forward and, suddenly, plunged into the water.

The instant that she began to swim, Nadia became a different being altogether. On land she had moved with a painful, halting gait, but here she was in her element. Like a torpedo she shafted through the water, leaving hardly a ripple behind her. Effortlessly, she turned on to her back, on to her side, plunged below the surface only to emerge several yards away, breathing evenly, her composure miraculously intact. Around her, the black fish gathered in a circle, curious to inspect their new companion, anxious perhaps to pay their respects to one of their own kind.

'What's she doing?' demanded Robert. 'Let's have a look.'

'You've jogged me again,' I complained. 'I've lost her now.' I scanned to and fro along the lakeside, trying to re-locate the object of my scrutiny. 'Hello, there's somebody else there as well.'

So I was not the only one interested in Nadia's display. There, standing on top of a large boulder at the water's edge, was Davy Hearn, his body tense, his eyes seemingly riveted on something that lay outside the small circle of my field of view. But it was obvious to me what it was that was causing him such excitement. In the silence, I could almost feel the accelerated rhythm of his breathing. And then, as I watched, his hand began to steal down towards the front of his breeches.

At that moment, Robert snatched the binoculars away from me. He fidgeted around with them for a moment until he had located the object of my curiosity. 'Good Lord,' he exclaimed, 'she hasn't got a stitch on! I suppose she thinks nobody's watching.' I could see him scanning to and fro along the lakeside. Suddenly, with a sharp intake of breath, he froze. I realised that he must have spotted Davy. 'The horrible, filthy brute!' Robert blurted out. 'But he's on his own this time. I say we go and teach him a lesson!'

'What's he doing?' demanded Janny, struggling to get possession of the binoculars.

'Come on, Ken!' shouted Robert. 'Janny, you stay here!'

'But what . . .'

'Oh, Miss Janny,' said Tommy mournfully. 'Sometimes it's better not to look.'

Seconds later, Robert and I were at the bottom of the ladder, tearing along the track that led to the lakeside. By the time that we reached the water's edge, though, Nadia had finished her swim and had started to get dressed again. But just as she was fastening the buttons of her blouse, Davy Hearn emerged from the bushes behind her. Startled, the girl spun around to face him. With lightning speed, he seized her by her arms.

'Hey!' Robert yelled. 'Leave her alone!' Without thinking what we were doing, we ran across the bridge, scrambled up the rocks that flanked the waterfall and fought our way through the bushes that grew along the shoreline. Ahead of us, we could hear the sounds of a scuffle and raised voices. Moments later, the two of us burst out of the undergrowth. With a blood-curdling yell, Robert hurled himself down the slope towards the two struggling figures at the water's edge. Startled, Davy spun around to face him, but he could not hope to stand up to Robert's breakneck speed and furious rage. Within seconds, it was over. Robert had delivered two powerful blows, and Davy was on the ground, showing no inclination to get up.

'That'll teach you,' said Robert grimly. 'One-all, I think.'

I handed the tearful Nadia her cardigan. 'You finish getting dressed,' I suggested. 'And then we'll take you home.' On the bridge, we paused for a few minutes to collect our wits, the three of us leaning up against the handrail.

'Well, we've given young Hearn another scare,' mused Robert, 'but I daresay he'll be back again in his own time. And, Nadia, perhaps swimming in the lake isn't such a bright idea.'

'But I love to swim,' Nadia complained. 'If I cannot swim, I am nothing.'

'Nadia should be safe enough if she stays on our side of the water,' I suggested by way of compromise. 'We know that Davy doesn't like to cross the bridge.'

'Yes, that's fair enough, ' Robert agreed. 'But no more nakedness. Nadia, we'd best see if we can find you something to wear. Maybe there's an old bathing costume in Mother's dressing table.'

'Very well,' said Nadia stolidly. 'If that will make everyone happy.' We stopped on the bridge for a little longer, leaning up against the twisted old rail, staring at the white blur of the waterfall as it tumbled over the rocks below us, allowing its spray to cool our faces and arms.

Gazing at the descending column of water, I noticed that it was also moving, with a slow, pendulum-like regularity, from side to side, cascading first to the left, then edging its slow way across to the right, then working its way just as slowly back to the left. I found myself wondering on which side it had first started, and on which side it would finally finish. And then I found myself wondering on which side of the water Nadia really belonged.

'Time to go.' Robert's decisive voice broke in on my

thoughts. Easing himself upright, my brother turned back towards Hedley House. We all started walking, Robert taking the lead, Nadia and I some way behind. Nadia clung to my arm as she walked, the side of her face pressed hard against my sleeve. Perhaps I could have taken the opportunity to bring myself closer to her but I did nothing. In my innermost heart, I still couldn't stop wishing that the face against my shoulder had been Janny's.

It was a few weeks before I saw Davy Hearn again. One Saturday, Nadia and Janny, having unsuccessfully ransacked my mother's dressing table for a bathing costume, had taken the bus into Tollcester to see if they could find anything suitable in the shops. While they were away, Robert and I decided to make another attempt to locate the Lumberjills' camp.

We were trudging along the track that led us beyond the waterfall. It had been a wet spring, and our shoes were squelching in the mud, but the sun was shining and we had allowed our coats to flap open. I could hear distant footfalls in the undergrowth, and I knew that the Arborian bowmen were keeping pace with us, ready to step in at the first sign of trouble.

'I realise that this part of the forest doesn't really belong to us,' I was explaining to Robert. 'But the Lumberjills are committing an injury to the land of Arboria. And we're its guardians, even if we're not the owners. It's all in the Great Book, I can show you later on. "*Whoever shall cause hurt to the sacred land, or to the trees, or to the waters, or to the soil of that land, so shall he face the implacable wrath of the Good People. So shall he face the Hand of Fire.*" I wonder what the "Hand of Fire" is? Anyway, Rob, it's all there. So we really ought to see what we can do to stop them.'

'You and I need to have a talk about Arboria,' Robert interposed. 'There are things that we need to discuss, Ken, important things. But all right, let's see if we can find where they're camped.' For a moment, I wondered what it was that Robert wanted to discuss with me, but my attention was quickly diverted back to Arboria, because my ears had caught the sound of axes and saws. Robert had noticed them too. 'Come on,' he beckoned me. 'It's this way.' Leaving the track, we crept stealthily up a patch of rising ground and soon found ourselves, on our hands and knees, peering over the top of a bush into the Lumberjills' camp. Robert had finally been granted a pair of long trousers, but, even at the age of fourteen, I was still in shorts and long socks. At least it would be easier for me to get myself cleaned up afterwards, I caught myself thinking.

It was mid-morning by this time; the Lumberjills had stopped work and had formed into a line at their mobile canteen, where they were collecting cups of tea and slices of bread and margarine. Robert reached into his coat pocket and produced a rather soggy-looking packet of sandwiches. 'Here,' he offered. 'If they're having a break, we might as well have one too.' I unwrapped my share of the feast, took a tentative bite, and shuddered at the all too familiar taste of Spam and National Wheatmeal bread. Robert noticed my disgust and grinned. 'You'd better get used to it, Ken. I reckon we'll be eating it for quite a while yet. We'll probably end up eating horse meat before the war's over.'

For a brief time we chewed in silence. In the clearing, the Lumberjills had formed into small groups and were sitting on logs and trailers, eating and drinking, smoking cigarettes, and chattering noisily in their sharp Scottish accent. 'There's quite a lot of them,' I observed. 'There must be at least twenty, maybe twenty-five. And they all look quite strong. They'll put up quite a fight. We'll need to marshal the whole of the Arborian army. Do you think—'

'Listen, Ken,' my brother interrupted me. 'I've got to talk to you. I'm finishing school soon, and I'm going to go and work for Uncle Magnus.'

I stared at him in disbelief. 'But Rob, I thought you liked it at school.'

'I do – I did, but for heaven's sake, Ken, there's a war on and I really want to start doing my bit. I'll have finished my School Certificate soon, and I can't really see any point in hanging around for Highers. I can't join the army till I'm eighteen, but at least I can get a job and do something useful.'

'So you'll still catch the bus into Tollcester?'

'No, I won't be catching the bus. I'm going to go and stay with Magnus. It's better that way. He wants me to help out at the print works.' He paused, then added importantly, 'They've got a big order of propaganda leaflets. And they're going to be printing books, too. They have to do it on cheap paper, though. It's called the War Economy Standard.'

My heart was pounding in my throat. 'But what about Arboria?'

'Look, Ken,' said Robert gently, 'we're not kids any more. Arboria was all very well in its day, but really, don't you think it's time . . .'

There were tears in my eyes. 'Arboria's all around us,' I cried, my voice suddenly unsteady. 'It's always been here. I'll never leave Arboria, never. And I thought you were going to stay here too . . .'

'Oh, Ken,' Robert was struggling to keep the dismay out of his voice. 'I know Arboria always meant a lot to you. Maybe it meant more to you than it meant to me, but it was only a game, wasn't it? A kids' game? But we're not kids any more, are we? You're going to be the man of the house now, you're going to have to try and be more responsible, try to get your feet back on the ground. You can't go on living in a make-believe world for ever. Gran's not getting any younger, and someone will have to look after the girls . . .'

'I'm going for a walk,' I interrupted him. Suddenly I felt alone, abandoned, desolate. 'I'm going to see if I can find Tommy Pelling.' My head reeling, I rose abruptly to my feet and, half-running, half-staggering, made my way back towards the Great Tree. I needed to find a place where I could be myself again, a place where I could recover my composure, a place where I would be safe in the company of my small, insubstantial friend.

For the next few nights I slept fitfully, my thoughts in turmoil, my bedclothes a damp, tangled mess, my pyjamas twisted uncomfortably around my thighs and body. Disjointed scraps of dreamstuff jostled for position with shards of memory, until I no longer knew for certain what was real and what was imagined. Strangely, though, I dreamed not of my treacherous brother Robert, but of our old enemy Davy Hearn. Davy playing his pipes at the window of the garden room . . . Davy strutting bare-chested at the head of the bridge . . . Davy spying on the naked Nadia from the safety of the undergrowth . . .

Davy in the Lumberjills' camp.

An unsettling image started to form in my mind. For I could see Davy now, Davy sitting cockily astride a pile of roughly sawn logs, Davy surrounded by an admiring cluster of young women. One of them was ruffling his tangled hair, another was smoothing the legs of his breeches, another was slipping a cigarette between his full lips . . .

Had Davy really been there in the clearing, had he been there while Robert was giving me his terrible news, had he been there while I was choking on my Spam sandwich? Or had I spun the whole scene together in my dreams?

I awoke with a jolt. Perhaps, after all, I had only dreamed it. I reached under my pillow, felt for the reassuring bulk of the Great Book. It was still there. Relieved, I turned towards the window. Silhouetted against the moonlight, I could just detect the dim outline of the Great Tree and, beyond it, I could see the other tree houses too, the tree houses of the Arborians. In the background, I could hear the hum and the murmur of the wounded forest, the ripple of the black fish in the lake, the crackle of the fire in the Barbarian camp. But there was another sound too, a faint, muffled pulsation that came from far beneath the ground, from the depths of the caves at the heart of the earth. I had heard that sound before. I had heard it on the night of the dance. Now it told me that the Good People were starting to take notice of what was happening, that the Good People had begun to stir. Perhaps the Good People would come and rescue the forest, it occurred to me. Perhaps it was to the Good People that I must turn for help . . .

I awoke again at dawn, and I knew all at once what Davy Hearn had been doing in the Lumberjills' camp. Davy had been spying on the Lumberjills too! We Arborians may have had our differences with the Barbarians but, like us, Davy and his Barbarians were children of the forest, and they did not welcome intruders any more than we did. Perhaps the Arborians and the Barbarians could join their armies together . . . Perhaps their combined strength would be enough to drive the Lumberjills from our land. At any rate, I realised, it was Davy Hearn who held the key. It was Davy who could persuade the Barbarians to help us. But which one of us was to speak to Davy? Who was it who would act as the intermediary? I didn't think I would be brave enough to talk to him. Robert would be brave enough, of course, but, after everything that had happened between them, I didn't think that Davy would be prepared to listen to him. Then there were the girls, but we surely couldn't ask the girls to do it.

My thoughts had begun to chase each other around in circles when, all of a sudden, the spell was broken by a quiet, discreet cough. I opened my eyes. On the windowsill, softly outlined against the sunrise, perched the tenuous form of Tommy Pelling. 'Master Kenneth – if I might make so bold? Perhaps *I* could be of service to you . . .' After that, I fell asleep again.

The attack on the Lumberjills' camp required several weeks of careful planning and preparation. Robert showed no inclination to become involved in the project, so I concluded, reluctantly, that I was going to have to take charge of it. I set off alone to explore the forest tracks that encircled the clearing, and I managed to identify a number of trees that I reckoned would not be too hard to climb in the dark. Using my pocketknife, I carved signs on the bark, so that we would know the right ones when the time came.

As my plan started to fall into shape, I decided that it would be safe to confide in Janny, but Nadia still seemed a fragile and uncertain ally, so I deemed it wiser to leave her out of things for the time being. Then there was the question of Davy Hearn. There was still something about his presence that troubled me, so that I found myself reluctant to meet him face to face. In the end, I decided to accept Tommy Pelling's offer of help and, true to his promise, my small friend proved to be a resourceful messenger. In due course he brought back word that, on this occasion, Arborians and Barbarians would be fighting side by side.

Concerning my older brother, I found it harder to come to any decision. I knew that his presence would give me strength and confidence but, at the same time, I dreaded another of his bitter outbursts of sarcasm. As a result, I fought shy of speaking to him and decided to take a chance on engaging his enthusiasm at the last moment. In the end, my opportunity arrived with only a short time to spare. Nadia had slipped away after tea to visit my grandmother so, while Janny finished washing the dishes, I steeled myself to confront Robert across the kitchen table. My brother had just sat the last of his examinations, and was now getting ready to start his job at the print works. He had been preoccupied lately, but I knew that, after a meal, he was most likely to be in a good mood. I took a deep breath. I had worked out what I was going to say. 'Rob,' I started, 'we're attacking the Lumberjills' camp tonight at dusk. I wish you'd come. You're still the High Lord, after all.'

Robert sighed. 'All right then, Ken. I don't want to let you down. But I want this to be the last time. Do you understand?'

'All right,' I said. 'And thanks.'

Robert sighed. 'What's the plan?'

So this was to be my moment. I beckoned to Janny, waited impatiently while she finished her work and hung up the tea towel. Finally she joined us. I waited until I had everyone's attention. 'It'll be dark,' I began excitedly, 'so we'll need torches, of course. And we'll each have to carry a saucepan and a ladle. And bring a knapsack too, unless you think you can climb one-handed . . .'

'Slow down, Ken,' Robert broke in. 'First things first. What plan have you got in mind? You haven't explained. Are we going to scare them away with our cooking?' Until this moment, I had still been hoping that Robert would take control at the last moment, that the High Lord would once more be safely in charge. But I knew now that Robert was intent on taking a back seat, that he was determined from now on to leave Arborian matters to me. I stared at him, hoping against hope that he would relent at the final moment, that he would spare me the ordeal of being in control. But my brother's expression did not change.

'We assemble at the garden gate at nightfall,' I said finally. 'Don't be late.'

A couple of hours later, as the evening sun was beginning to cast its orange glow across the sky behind Hedley House, the three of us were in position and ready to make a start. For a moment I thought of Nadia, probably asleep in bed by now, unaware of anything that was taking place. I wondered, once again, whether I should have included her in my plans, but I still wasn't sure that I could trust her completely. In any case, it was too late now to change anything. 'Let's go,' I said, with more confidence than I felt. It was a solemn moment. I led the way past the log store, along the track, past the lake and the falls, and onwards towards the Lumberjills' camp. By the time we reached the spot where Robert and I had had our fateful talk, dusk was well advanced. From the clearing, we could see the glimmer of torches behind canvas, and we could catch the faint, drowsy murmur of Scottish voices as our invaders settled down for the night.

'We're each going to climb up into a tree,' I whispered. 'I'll take you round and show you which ones. Four trees, one at each corner of the clearing.'

'There are only three of us,' Robert objected.

'Davy's going to help us,' I revealed. 'Don't you think that's a good idea? For once, we both want the same thing. He'll be along in a minute.'

Despite himself, Robert seemed impressed by this. 'You have been doing your homework,' he admitted. 'I'll give you that. Let's just hope he turns up. But you still haven't told me what the pans and ladles are for.'

'My idea,' said Janny. 'Something we do where I come from. We're going to give them the Rough Music. And Kenny's hoping that some of his friends in the forest will be good enough to help.'

It was not too dark for me to notice the tightening of Robert's lips. 'The Arborian army is standing by,' I explained. 'And Davy's bringing the Barbarian warriors with him. They're waiting in the forest now, all around us. Listen. Can't you hear them?' In the silence that followed, I could sense the tension of bowstrings, the poised spear points, the faint release of breath from a hundred throats. Robert, though, appeared to hear nothing. But he had agreed to help me, so he held his tongue.

At that moment, there was a rustle in the undergrowth beside us and Davy Hearn emerged. He carried neither knapsack nor torch, but his old tin whistle was slung on a leather thong around his sturdy neck. Silently, he extended his hand towards me, and for a moment we touched palms. His hand felt harder and warmer than mine, and the palm was rough, like sandpaper. Davy nodded courteously to Janny, and exchanged wary glances with Robert.

'Follow me now,' I addressed the others. 'I'll take you to your places and, when I've done that, I'll get myself into position. And, remember, everyone keep quiet until you hear me begin.' Davy and Janny nodded grimly. I caught Robert's eye too, but could detect nothing more than reluctant compliance.

Twenty-five minutes later, I had settled myself into the crook of my chosen tree. Far beneath me, I could still make out the last of the lights in the Lumberjills' camp. In my mind, I estimated the positions of my companions. Janny would be away to my right, Robert off to my left. Behind us, in the forest, rank upon rank of Arborian bowmen would be standing, silent and ready. Directly opposite to where I was stationed, Davy Hearn would be waiting in his tree, with the Barbarian spear carriers stationed dark and grim behind him. Our four trees formed a broad square, encompassing the clearing with geometric perfection. I drew a long breath, allowing the surrounding silence to seep into me. Was it my imagination, I wondered, or could I also feel, far below us, the quiet, intangible presence of the Good People, the people of the caves and the depths, the people on whose presence the success of the Rough Music ultimately depended? For a moment, I allowed the silence to possess me. Then, grasping my pan and my ladle, I struck the first note.

From left and from right, there echoed the answering tones, the high-pitched tinkle of Janny's milk pan, the deeper clang of Robert's frying pan. Working together, we gradually established a rhythm, gently at first, then more firmly, until the metallic notes began to ricochet from one corner of the clearing to the next, their paths tracing out a network of fine lines, weaving a menacing web across the air that divided us.

Then, from the caves beneath the earth, a dark choir of voices began to hum. As the rattle of the pans grew louder and more insistent, so the drone of the voices became more menacing, their harmonies the harsh discords of doom, their pitch and their volume ebbing and flowing like the sluggish tides of a black, underground river.

In the clearing, the flap of a tent was thrown open, a lone voice cried out in alarm.

Then, as the dark flood of noise started to throb to its grim crescendo, I heard at last the sound of Davy's whistle. This time it was not the plaintive air that he had played to Janny while she sat at the piano. This time shrill notes twisted this way and that with a terrifying agility that could not be second-guessed, this time the notes of the pipe slashed their way through the surrounding maze of sounds with all of the murderous intent of barbed wire slashing through flesh. All at once, around the clearing, a howling wind arose, a whirling, anguished, tumultuous hurricane of noise that whipped its way in and out of the trees, loosening their very roots in the earth, shaking every truck and every tent in the clearing, loosening every tent peg, rattling every plate in the canteen.

Then, from the depths of the forest there sounded a harsh word of command. From the ranks of the Arborian army, a flight of arrows whistled between the trees. At the same moment, from the Barbarian side, a heavy rain of spears descended. Cries of alarm from inside the clearing told us that several of the missiles had met their targets. Below me, terrified women were emerging from tents only to find more arrows burying themselves in tree trunks, more spears thudding into the ground. The wind whipped at tent canvas and at ground-sheets, it scattered logs and branches to left and to right, it upended trucks and trailers as though they were toys.

At last, the music began to fade. The throbbing earth settled slowly to rest, the howling wind abated. All that remained was the thin, discordant melody of a tin whistle at the lips of a wild boy, and the thin rattle of two saucepans and a frying pan from my grandmother's kitchen. Then, finally, there was silence. The Arborians and the Barbarians melted away into the forest while, beneath the earth, the Good People retreated once again to their deepest, darkest caves. Davy Hearn scrambled down from his tree and slunk away to wherever it was that he slept, and Robert, Janny and I shouldered our knapsacks and made our torchlit way back to Hedley House and our three narrow little beds. In the clearing, the terrified Lumberjills were left to tend to their wounded and to salvage what they could from the wreckage of their camp.

Just as I was falling asleep, I heard a familiar whisper in my ear. 'Well done, Master Kenneth.' It was Tommy Pelling's husky voice, and he sounded almost as if he were smiling. 'Well done indeed. I think we could say that you have truly given them what for!'

'You're right, Tommy,' I whispered, 'We've done it. They'll never come back here now.' Moments later, I fell into a dreamless sleep, the first proper sleep that I had enjoyed in weeks.

Later that day, when Robert and I finally bumped into each other again, my brother made no reference to the extraordinary events of the previous night, and I found myself wondering, once more, whether everything had been nothing but a dream. A few days later, though, I received some gratifying news.

'The Lumberjills have left the forest,' said Janny. 'I've heard folk talking in the village. Apparently there were 'unexpected difficulties', and they've decided to go and cut down someone else's trees instead.' Sniffing back a noseful of liquid snot, she treated me to an urchin-like grin. 'Seems like the Rough Music did the trick. And your invisible friends, of course.' It was a dry day, and we were in the garden, scavenging on the rubbish tip for any remaining pieces of scrap metal.

'I've found a couple of nails,' I said, 'But I don't think there's much else left.'

'I reckon you're wasting your time there.' It was Robert's booming voice. I could see him in the distance, resting against his hoe on the vegetable patch while Nadia stumbled along with a basket, collecting up the thistles and dandelions. Since that last, hard winter, my grandmother seemed to have lost much of her old spirit, and she was disinclined to venture out of doors if she could avoid it. My brother, though, responsible as ever, was making good use of his last weekend at Hedley House by helping with whatever heavy work needed doing. He was right about the rubbish, of course. The tip had been raked over and sifted and excavated and dismantled and reconstructed so thoroughly that those two nails were very probably the last two pieces of metal there.

While all these events were taking place, of course, the war against Hitler continued. The German aircraft were still making regular bombing raids on England but, that summer, there had been a change in the pattern of the assaults. The enemy had decided to carry out a series of attacks on some of the country's most ancient cathedral cities, and these attacks had become known as the 'Baedeker raids'. This rather odd name apparently came from a series of German guidebooks in which the cities were mentioned.

The cathedral at Tollcester was not one of the more famous monuments in the land, and the town had never really been troubled by more than the occasional tourist party. However, during the wartime years, Tollcester certainly received its fair share of bombs. The medieval market place that huddled close by the city walls was destroyed, and the old riverside dockyard and some of the factories that surrounded it were badly damaged too. One bomb fell on the Storey print works, although, fortunately, nobody was there that night apart from old Horace the watchman, and Horace was lucky enough to escape with nothing worse than a gash on his hand from a piece of shrapnel.

But Uncle Magnus was not going to let the operation of the factory be disrupted by anything as trivial as a German bomb. Work had to continue because, as well as books, there were other important contracts to fulfil for the government. Posters and leaflets were waiting to be printed, so new premises had to be found as quickly as possible. Everyone was pressed into service to salvage whatever could be recovered from the wreckage, and this army of helpers of course included Robert. Soberly dressed, carrying a surprisingly small suitcase and looking intimidatingly grown-up, he moved out of Hedley House on the morning following the bombing. Whether I liked it or not, I was now the man of the house, just as Robert had predicted.

I didn't like it much, and I certainly didn't find it easy. Despite having successfully organised the attack on the Lumberjills, I had felt no inclination to repeat the experience of being in charge. I had always looked to my brother to make the decisions and to take the lead in everything we did and now, suddenly, I was expected to do everything myself. My grandmother continued to do what she could in the kitchen, as well as retaining the responsibility for the weekly grocery order, but I soon found that Nadia and Janny were looking to me to take charge of the practical side of running the household. Sometimes I would find myself lying awake at night, worrying about leaking window frames, or about blackout curtains, or about new underwear, but at other times I slept like a corpse and defied every effort to wake me. I found the responsibility exhausting, and I realised that I was missing my family more than ever. Often, when I walked into a room, I found myself expecting my mother and father and brother still to be there, talking or arguing or playing cat's cradle.

When I did sleep, though, I dreamed about Arboria. I dreamed about an Arboria that had lost its High Lord, an enfeebled Arboria that struggled to keep at bay the dark forces of the Barbarians, an impotent Arboria that struggled to resist the sinister, alluring life force of Davy Hearn. For, with the Lumberjills gone from the forest, Arborians and Barbarians no longer had common cause, and the old state of hostility had been resumed.

A couple of nights after the first bombing raid on Tollcester, the air raid sirens sounded once more. It was my job now to assemble the household and to lead the way down to the shelter. The sirens were late sounding that night, though. Even as we made our way towards the kitchen door, the skies were already heavy with the menacing drone of the enemy bombers. The German aircraft were cruising low over Upper Helsing, a geometric formation of threatening crosses silhouetted against the moonlit clouds. Away to the north, the sky was riven by brilliant orange flashes, followed a split second later by the deafening roar of explosions. I was the first to leave the house.

'Come along, Gran,' I bellowed through the door. 'If they get any nearer, they'll be in the kitchen. Jan, can you give Nadia a hand?' There was another explosion, this one even nearer. Then something whistled through the air past my left ear, and landed with a stifling thud in the rubbish heap. For a long moment, I held my breath, waiting with utter dread for the blaze of fire and the roar of noise that would mean the end of everything. But nothing came.

After a moment, I allowed myself to draw a cautious breath. Then there was another explosion, this time a little further away. 'Come on,' I said. 'Let's hurry up and get underground.' The bomb that had fallen in the garden might still go off at any moment. I turned and led the way down the path and through the garden gate, while Janny marshalled the others at the rear.

Fortunately, I had remembered to check the batteries in all the torches, and we arrived at the shelter without further mishap. The key to the padlock was hidden in its usual place, and the lock opened easily because Janny, whose job this was, had been taking good care to oil it regularly. I heaved open the iron doors, and the four of us piled into the shelter, pulled the doors shut behind us, and started to light the candles. From inside, we could still hear the muffled drone of aircraft engines, the dull roar of explosions and, a little later, the comforting rattle of anti-aircraft fire.

For some reason, I didn't mention the bomb that had fallen near the house. After a while, it occurred to me that the others, who had still been indoors, might not have heard it. I didn't want to frighten them, so I decided to say nothing. Nobody else had much to say either, and soon we were all asleep.

When I awoke, I found myself alone in the bunk room. The candles had burned down almost to their stubs, and I could see in their yellow, flickering light that the other beds were unoccupied. I searched around for the alarm clock, but realised after a moment that I had forgotten to bring it. Tossing aside my two rough blankets, I jerked myself upright, thrust my feet into my shoes, pulled the curtains aside and made my way into the sitting area..

'Hello?' I called into the gloom. 'Janny? Nadia? Gran, are you there?' But there was no reply. I supposed that the others must have heard the all-clear and made their way back to Hedley House. Probably they had failed to wake me, and had decided to let me sleep. I searched about for a torch, but could not find one. Had we brought all four torches across from the house, or had one of them been left behind in the confusion? I racked my brains but could not remember.

Suddenly, I felt a surge of panic. What would happen if the others had forgotten about me and fastened the padlock? What would happen if I had been locked in? The iron doors were far too strong for me to break down and, out here in the forest, no-one would hear my cries for help. I would remain here for days, choking on the stale air. There was no food, no water. Where would I go to empty the chamber pot? How long would it take for me to starve to death? My heart thumping, I stumbled across to the steps that led up to the big doors, collecting on the way a painful bang on the shin from the oil stove. To my relief though, the doors were unlocked and stood slightly ajar. I let out a long, shuddering breath. Despite my father's fear of tramps, I thought, perhaps it was after all a bad idea to keep the doors locked. I could not remember ever seeing a tramp in the forest anyway.

It occurred to me then that my parents had been dead for over two years. My father and my mother had left me, and now Robert had left me too. Apart from my grandmother and two flighty girls, I was all alone. What was I going to do? Hastily, I collected myself. Robert was not dead. Robert had only gone to Tollcester. Robert would still be there to help me if I needed him. I stepped outside the shelter and took a long breath of the cool night air. The padlock, still unfastened, hung placidly in its hasp on the left-hand door, the key resting quietly in the key-hole. After a moment's hesitation, I unhooked the padlock and key and slipped them into my pocket.

I wondered what time it was. Several hours must have passed because, around me, all was dark and all was silent. The bombers had departed, the sirens had ceased their wailing, even the anti-aircraft guns were quiet. I was eager to return to my bed, but reluctant to grope my way back to Hedley House in the dark. I waited another moment, then stepped back into the shelter, pulled the doors shut behind me, and made my way down the steps and through to the bunk room where the candle stubs were still burning.

I was fully awake now, and I knew that there would be no point in trying to go back to sleep. What was I going to do? I cast my eyes around the room and noticed, for the first time in ages, the low doorway that stood in the corner of the far wall, half-concealed by Janny's bunk. For a moment, its outline seemed to shimmer and melt, as if it were uncertain of the exact form that it wanted to take. Then it settled back in to a slightly twisted rectangle. That's funny, I thought. Surely that was the door that was bricked up when my father had the alterations done? Oh well, I must just have remembered it wrongly . . .

I picked up one of the candlesticks. If I wasn't going to sleep, I might as well try a bit of exploring. The outline of the doorway stood out clearly before me, its lop-sided form the only definite shape in the surrounding murk. Cautiously, I reached out towards it; hesitantly, I brushed its rough surface with a fingertip. I sensed a faint vibration, my skin tingled in response to it and, for a moment, my ears caught the strains of distant music. I shivered. I knew now that, on the other side of that door, something was waiting for me, something was down there, enticing me towards it. What kind of thing it was, I could not tell. Perhaps it was wonderful; perhaps it was dangerous. But, I realised, if I turned away now, the chance might never come to me again. For a long moment, I hesitated, luxuriating in a delicious feeling of uncertainty.

Then I pushed harder at the door and, with a reluctant creak, it began to yield.

## Six

## BENEATH THE EARTH

$\mathcal{B}$efore me, I could see nothing but blackness. Cautiously, I stepped through the doorway but, instead of solid ground, my foot encountered only empty air. Terrified of losing my balance, I made a clumsy grab at the rough wooden frame, and just managed to recover. I held out my candle at arm's length and peered into the gloom. I could see now that I was standing at the head of a flight of steps, worn-looking stone steps that stretched down ahead of me into the dark. From a long way away, I could hear what sounded like music, or at least the deep, dark rhythm of some music as yet unknown.

Steadying myself against the wall with my free hand, I began slowly to descend. The steps beneath my feet were uneven, and the roof above my head was low, as if the staircase had been built for a race of beings who were a good head shorter than the men and women of today. But the music drew me onward. Stooping awkwardly beneath the low roof, my feet fumbling for each step, I made my cautious way ahead, my right hand grasping the candlestick, my left hand seeking what purchase it could against the rough, slightly slimy wall. In the distance, the eerie sound continued to beckon me. Perhaps it is the music of the Good People, it occurred to me. Perhaps they are luring me down into their realm.

It was a long descent. After a time I paused, looking behind me to try and gauge how far I had come. Far above, I could just make out the tiny, dim shape of the doorway to the ice house, faintly outlined by the unsteady glow of the candle that still flickered in the bunk room. The line of the staircase must have been crooked, though, because the next time I stopped and turned around, I could no longer see the light.

Ahead of me, the ground began to level out. I had come to the bottom of the stairs, and I now found myself in a gently sloping corridor. The ceiling was higher than before, so that I was able to walk upright, and the ground beneath my feet seemed flat enough for me to step out with more confidence. Here and there, I noticed, the walls on either side bore cryptic symbols, convoluted shapes daubed in rough dark ochre. It occurred to me that they looked rather like the runic figures in the oldest part of the Great Book, and I wondered whether the ancient authors of the book might also have been the builders of this tunnel.

Abruptly, a gust of wind extinguished my candle flame. Startled, I allowed what remained of the candle to slip from my grasp. I heard a faint rattle as it rolled away across the floor. Frightened now and not knowing what to do, I stood marooned in the darkness, until, with infinite trepidation, I managed to gather the courage to move forwards once more. Now, as my feet carried me along, I started to become aware of a faint, dull glow ahead of me, a colourless glow that was slowly becoming more distinct the closer I drew. The music was growing clearer too. I could make out the sounds of chattering percussion weaving in and out of the rhythmic pulsation. But my ears could discern no melody, no harmony. What I was hearing, I began to realise, was more like the harsh rattle of machinery than the soft tones of music. As I drew closer to the light, the air around me was becoming warmer, but it was a dry, choking warmth, not at all pleasant. Involuntarily, my steps were beginning to quicken. Suddenly, I rounded a bend and came upon a sight that left me breathless.

I was standing at the edge of a vast, dust-choked cavern, a cavern dimly illuminated by the colourless, directionless glow that I had seen ahead of me in the corridor. On either side of me stood rows of heavy benches in long, parallel ranks that seemed to recede in the infinite distance to little more than pinpoints. Arranged at regular intervals along the surface of the benches were rows of machines. Each machine was bulky and square and metallic, each machine was identical to its neighbour and it was from these machines that the noise was coming. Above each bench and running along its length, there spun a long, cylindrical shaft, from which loosely flapping drive bands supplied the power. Alongside the shafts there hung dusty loops of electrical cable, thick humming pipes for water, thin rattling pipes for compressed air, and thin hissing pipes for gas. In places, the pipes were leaking and a nauseous mixture of compressed air, water and gas seeped out into the atmosphere. The noise and the smell and the heat and the steam and the relentless, humming vibration of the place struck me like a blow to the stomach.

Slowly, as my eyes started to grow accustomed to the dim light, I began to take in more details of the scene before me. With a shock, I realised that alongside the benches there stood rows of people, people who seemed little more than slaves to the machines, people who bore an unmistakable air of tiredness and defeat, people whose robotic movements seemed to be driven purely by the relentless rhythm of the factory. The sound that had drawn me here, I now realised, had not been music at all. It had been the roar and shudder of the machinery. I wondered who was in charge of this place, what was its purpose, who were the unhappy souls who laboured here. Surely, with all this misery around me, this could not be the realm of the Good People?

Still nobody had noticed me. I cast my gaze around, struggling to gain a better understanding of this terrifying underground world in which I had arrived. Some of the gangways between the benches, I could now see, were patrolled by groups of people who appeared to be in charge of the slaves. These people were dressed in crisp, black, sharply tailored uniforms, ornamented with braid and buttons and badges. On their heads they wore peaked caps, their eyes were shielded by black goggles, and in their hands they carried sleek, vicious-looking batons. They looked cruel and hard and merciless None of the slaves at the machines dared to pause in their work, none dared to speak to his fellows, none dared even to look to one side. The guards who patrolled the gangways clearly maintained a rule of iron. These guards, I knew at once, must not be allowed to see me.

Impelled by a heady mixture of fear and curiosity, I ducked my head and moved stealthily along the gangway between two rows of benches, until I could get a closer view of the slaves who worked at the machines. Each one stood wearily in his place, each one seemingly indifferent to the deafening noise and the unrelenting vibration and the choking, stinking fumes. Each one wore an identical grey outfit, a plain, rough suit of clothes that buttoned up to the neck, coats with no pockets and no collar and trousers with no turn-ups. The slaves seemed undernourished, their meagre frames hardly more than skeletons. I peered more closely at them. Their faces displayed the harsh lines of pain and anxiety, their skin bore the dull patina of despair. But, although each face was different, each face was in some way familiar to me. So where had I seen them before? Why did I know them? I racked my brains, but the answer eluded me.

But then I came upon a face that I recognised at once. A face with a distinctive, blunt nose, a distinctive long upper lip, a distinctive pair of resolute grey-green eyes. I knew that face. It had the same nose, the same lips, the same eyes that had stared at me across the kitchen table during a thousand family meals. It had the same nose, lips and eyes that had grinned at me from beneath the rim of a black tin helmet in the House in the Air.

'Robert?' I breathed. 'Robert?' But my brother did not respond. 'Why have they brought you here? What have they done to you?' A thick, bitter tide of despair was welling up inside me, a sour, inexorable flood of loss and longing that I was powerless to resist. 'What have they done to you?' I sobbed. 'What have they done to you?' But still my brother made no reply. He did not look at me. He did not indicate in any way that he had heard. Then, too late, I realised that although Robert had not heard me, there were others who had. The slaves at the nearby machines had stopped their work and were staring at me, row upon row of those strange yet half-familiar, stricken faces. Untended, the machines quickly started to run out of control, the driving belts flailing wildly from side to side, shards of material and fountains of liquid and hissing jets of steam shooting out uncontrolled. 'Robert,' I howled again, 'what have they done to you? What have they done to you?'

Now I realised that other people had seen me too. In the distance, several of the patrolling groups of guards had started to converge on my position. Red warning lights were flashing, the throaty roar of klaxons was adding its blood-chilling howl to the overwhelming din. The guards were coming rapidly closer, they were advancing purposefully towards me, their batons poised. 'Robert,' I moaned, 'what have they done to you?' But my strength was starting to fail now, my voice was starting to lose its power, my lungs were choking with the escaping gases. 'What have they done?' I groaned. Knowing now that there was no escape, I sank to my knees. Then the guards were upon me. Boots and batons thudded into my ribs, my shoulder blades, my kneecaps. I could feel the cracking of my bones, could sense the warmth and wetness of my seeping blood. I was on my back now, my arms raised to protect my face. Strong, rough hands grabbed my arms and legs, and I felt myself dragged along the floor, grit and rubbish snagging on my clothes, the din of the machinery and the wail of the klaxons reverberating through my shuddering frame.

Suddenly, high up in the rock wall in the distance, I caught a glimpse of two figures standing on a balcony, two figures outlined in a wavering bluish light, two figures who looked down upon the factory floor from a quiet place far above. Their forms seemed somehow familiar to me and, all at once, I recognised them; a tall, bearded man and a slim, graceful lady. 'Help me!' I begged them. 'Lord Owen! Lady Margaret! Help me!' For a moment they cast their gaze in my direction, but then I was dragged once more from their sight, dragged to the side of the room, dragged down staircases, dragged along corridors. At last, bruised and bleeding all over, I was thrown into a low, dank space. A heavy door slammed into a frame, a rusty key turned in a lock, and I was alone in darkness and silence.

And then, bit by bit, I began to understand what had happened to Robert. It was the Good People who had stolen my brother away from me. It was the Good People who had kidnapped him. It was the Good People who had set him to work in this terrible place. 'You haven't put him in a factory,' I moaned, as the light behind my eyes began to dim. 'You've dragged him down to Hell.'

After what seemed an endless, endless time, I opened my eyes and found that I could see once more although, at first, I could make no sense of the distorted perspectives that receded before me. Then, slowly, it dawned upon me that I was lying on my side on the rough concrete floor of the air raid shelter. In the foreground of my field of view there loomed the iron legs and the faded mattress of one of the bunk beds. In the distance I was able to identify the short flight of stone steps leading up to the pair of iron doors that opened into the forest. The doors were standing slightly ajar, and through the crack there shafted a narrow blade of daylight. It must be morning, I concluded. The others must have gone back to the house.

Cautiously, I eased myself into a sitting position, wincing in pain as I did so. The muscles of my legs were aching furiously, and I detected blood oozing from, among other places, my right shin and the left side of my skull. I reached out and fumbled about me on the floor. My questing hand encountered something cold and smooth and rounded, something with a canvas strap attached to it. It was my father's old ARP helmet.

I placed it clumsily on my head. Then I rose unsteadily to my feet and made my way through the double doors, wondering what awaited me in the world outside the shelter. I must have presented a ghastly sight. I was caked in mud and blood and dust, my clothes were torn, my eyes were wild, my hair was awry, and the helmet on my head listed at a crazy angle. Fortunately, though, there was nobody there to witness my disarray.

The sun was low on the horizon and I concluded from its position that the time was early morning. The forest lay still, in the air there was a faint hint of mist, and on the ground there lay a fine coating of dew. Each detail of my surroundings stood out with hallucinatory clarity. It was as if every object had been outlined with a fine, silver pencil; every leaf, every blade of grass, every thread of every cobweb. Above all of this filigree detail, there towered the gnarled, crooked forms of the ancient trees of Arboria. High in the branches of the trees, I could make out the irregular shapes of the tree houses. But there was no light showing behind the canvas. The Arborians were asleep.

For a moment, my sense of direction deserted me. I found myself turning this way and that, uncertain which route to take. Then, thankfully, some familiar landmark offered me an impromptu signpost, something in my mind seemed to snap into focus, and I set off in what I knew was the direction of home. As I made my way out of the forest, the mist began to clear, and I strode with renewed confidence back up the path that led to the garden gate and across the vegetable patch to the kitchen door of Hedley House. Then I remembered the bomb that had landed in the garden. Somewhere close to me it was still lying, still waiting to explode. Had it happened only the previous night? Baffled, I shook my head. I was starting to feel tired. Once again, I dismissed the bomb from my mind and continued on my way.

The door had not been bolted. In the silent kitchen, I splashed cold water on my face and hands and knees and then, without bothering to dry myself, I made my way upstairs to the landing. But when I reached the top of the stairs, instead of passing through the archway that led to my room in the old part of the house, I turned the opposite way, heading towards the rooms that fronted the building. Here, there was a place where I knew I would be safe. I threw open the door of my parents' bedroom and, without bothering to get undressed or even to remove my shoes, I flung myself face down on the bed and instantly fell headlong into a bottomless pit of sleep.

When at last I awoke, I found myself in some high, cold, remote place. Through the reverse end of a telescope, or some kind of distorting lens, I was looking down upon a room, a room that had pink wallpaper on its walls, a room that had in it a wardrobe, chest of drawers and a dressing table, a room that had at its centre a huge double bed with a pink satin coverlet. Across the coverlet, there sprawled the motionless body of a boy. His hair was uncombed, his clothes were bloodstained and filthy, and his shoes had left muddy streaks on the satin.

Then, in the corner of the room, a door opened softly, and two people entered the room. They were two girls, a dark girl and a pale girl, and they seemed to be interested in something that lay on the dressing table. After a moment, I recognised the object of their interest as a box of make-up. For a time, the make-up absorbed the girls' attention, so that they did not notice the boy until, finally, the pale girl happened to glance in the mirror. 'Oooohh!' she screamed. 'It's Kenny! My God, Nad, he really gave me a turn! What's he doing here?'

'I thought he had gone back into the forest,' replied her companion in halting English. 'But what has happened to him? Has he hurt himself?' The two of them turned around and stepped anxiously across to the bed.

'That's a bad cut,' said the pale girl, dabbing cautiously at the boy's shin with a grubby handkerchief. 'He'll need some ointment on that. And what's happened to his poor head? Nadia, you'd better run and fetch Mrs Hedley. Kenny? Kenny? Can't you wake up?'

Kenny? Nadia? Mrs Hedley? The names sounded familiar but, for the moment, I was unable to place them.

The boy on the bed stirred drowsily. 'I went down the steps,' he mumbled. 'I found Robert. The Good People have stolen him away. And then they saw me. And they came for me with their sticks. And they locked me in a cell.' He was speaking with a voice that I thought I recognised, but the sound carried a dull, distant, confusing echo. 'Am I still in the cell?' he mumbled. 'Am I still in the cell?'

'Just lie still,' ordered the pale girl. 'Your gran's coming. I expect she'll get the doctor.' With an oddly tender impulse, she leaned forward and smoothed the boy's hair away from his eyes. 'You are a silly boy, Kenny. But we'll look after you.' She dabbed at her nose with the same handkerchief, and I noticed that she had been crying.

A little while later, the other girl came back into the room with an old lady. A little while after that, a plump, bald-headed man arrived, carrying a black leather bag. I decided that he must be the doctor. He approached the bed and started to examine the boy.

After a time, the doctor left the room and, a little while after that, the old lady and the dark-haired girl left the room too. The other girl, the one who had been crying, stood for a while beside the bed, staring down at the boy. Then she crossed to the window and quietly drew the heavy blackout curtains across and, as she did that, the scene faded from view.

A rusty key grated in a lock. A door creaked open and, silhouetted against the dull light from outside, three tall figures in dark uniforms loomed above me. Alarmed, I glanced quickly around me. I was lying on my side on the hard stone floor of a small, windowless cell. One of my visitors stepped towards me, the tread of his heavy boots echoing blackly from wall to wall. Shivering, I rolled onto my back, half-rose, edged myself into the corner furthest from the door. The guard approached closer, crouched down, prodded me with his baton, while his two companions watched impassively from the doorway. 'What do you want?' I stammered.

Without speaking, the guard doffed his cap, pushed his goggles back onto the top of his head. Even in that dim light, I could now see that he was not much older than me. And surely I knew that dark skin, that tangled hair, those crooked teeth . . . The guard fixed me with an unblinking, slightly hooded stare. Behind him, I noticed, his two companions had also unmasked themselves. Waves of long hair cascaded from beneath their caps, and I just had time to recognise the fair-haired girl and the dark-haired girl that I had seen in the pink room earlier. Then the boy crouched down beside me, blocking them from my view. I could feel his hot breath scorching my face, his rank scent corroding my nostrils. He prodded me gently on the shoulder with his baton, then ran it down lightly over my ribcage, across my groin, along the inside of my thigh. Uncomfortably, I became aware of something stirring at the pit of my stomach and, even more uncomfortably, I could sense by a change in their breathing that the two girls were aware of it too. For an instant, I felt myself possessed by a vertiginous wave of fear. Then the guard withdrew the baton.

'Has the little boy lost his big brother?' he said at length. I realised that this was the first time I had heard his voice. His pointed tongue darted out and licked his full lips.

'He is alive, isn't he?' I whimpered. 'Robert is alive? Have the Good People stolen him away?' The boy did not reply, but continued to stare into my eyes. With his baton, he prodded me in the chest, harder this time. I felt a bone crack. 'I know you've got him,' I blundered on, tears in my eyes. 'Just tell me what I have to do to get him back. Just tell me!'

For a long moment he stared at me. 'We've got him sure enough,' he said finally. 'And you'll know in good time what it is that you have to do.' He narrowed his eyes a little further and smiled faintly. For a moment, the pressure on my chest continued to increase then, abruptly, he sprang to his feet and spun around. The two girls at the doorway drew aside to allow him to pass. Then they too turned away. With a metallic clang, the door banged shut, and I was alone once more.

The next time I opened my eyes, I was looking down on the pink room again. The old lady was just bringing in a visitor to see the boy in the bed. The visitor was a bulky, middle-aged man in a heavy tweed overcoat.

'Just for a minute, Magnus,' the old lady was saying. 'He's still very weak.'

The big man stepped forward uncertainly and looked down

on the boy's frail form. A little distance away, the old lady waited in silence. 'I don't see how he can stay here in the long term,' the man said finally, his meaty hands beating time as he spoke. 'We've got to listen to what Doctor Solloway says, haven't we? What was the expression he used? "Nervous exhaustion", that was it. "Nervous exhaustion brought about by delayed shock." Doubtless because of what happened to poor old Toni and Hugh. Not to mention the strain of managing the household on his own. Kenneth was never a strong one, was he? Never quite the man his brother was. I don't suppose he could cope with it all.' There was a long silence. 'And what about those ridiculous games in the woods?' the man continued finally. The pitch of his voice was rising now in anger. 'Heaven knows what nonsense he's been getting up to! Unhealthy, that's what I call it. It can't be good for a growing boy. Can't you see it's all been too much for him, Mrs H? The doctor says he's had a complete mental breakdown. It could take him months to recover. His mind might even be permanently damaged.' The man looked down at the boy in silence for a few moments, then turned away from the bed to face the old lady once more. 'He'll probably never be able to manage on his own,' he continued finally. His voice was calmer now, his hands steadier. 'Why won't you let him come and stay with Dottie and me? And his brother will be there too. Maybe the three of us can knock some sense into him.'

'I know you mean it for the best, Magnus,' the old lady replied, but in her voice I could detect a thin core of steel. 'But this is still Kenneth's home. All the familiar things are here around him. The house, the garden, the forest . . .' She paused for a moment before continuing. 'It won't do him any good to be uprooted, not at the moment, anyway. Not with the state his nerves are in. Remember that the doctor said rest and quiet, too.'

I wondered for a moment about the boy's brother. Why had his brother never been to see him? I wondered whether the big man was telling the truth. Perhaps the brother had gone away for good. Perhaps the Good People were holding him captive. Perhaps he had died and was never coming back. I watched for a while as the old lady and the man continued to argue, but I could no longer hear their words. Presently, the two of them left the room, and the boy was alone again. Later, the pale girl came and drew the curtains once more. Before she too left the room, she bent down briefly to kiss the boy. I could see that she had been crying again.

I found myself back in my underground cell, but this time, rather than being in darkness, the little room was dimly illuminated by a dull glow. For a time I lay there, allowing my eyes to take in the surroundings, the rough stone walls and floor, the heavy iron door. Then, cautiously, I started to straighten myself up, rubbed my aching limbs to restore my circulation and rose to my feet. Making a cautious inspection, I discovered, to my surprise, that the door of the cell was standing slightly ajar. I peered through the crack. There was nobody in sight.

Heart in mouth, I pulled the door towards me and slipped through the gap, only to find myself in a long, dank corridor with rows of identical iron doors lining the walls on either side. It was like a bizarre, distorted version of the long corridor at Hedley House. I looked both ways, then chose a direction at random and started to walk. Rather than walking down the centre of the corridor, though, I found myself instinctively hugging the left-hand wall. Soon, I came to a place where my corridor met another. It didn't seem to matter which way I went, so once again I picked a direction and continued.

At the next corner, I came in sight of a distant group of guards marching towards me. Panic-stricken, I cast about for an alcove in which to hide myself but, finding nothing, I squeezed myself tightly up against the wall, hoping that this would somehow make me less conspicuous. To my astonishment, the guards walked straight past me, as if they had seen nothing. Emboldened by this, I walked on, making my way along more corridors, across hallways, up and down staircases. From time to time I encountered other groups of people, but none of them paid me any attention.

Eventually, I came upon a row of doors that seemed somehow more interesting than the others. I was not sure what I was looking for, but I knew in some way that, behind one of these doors, I would find whatever it was that I needed. But how was I to know which door to open? Uncertainly, I tried one. The handle turned in my grip, but the door would not shift. I tried again, then abandoned my attempt and continued on my way.

The next door I tried was not locked. I pushed at it gently. It opened a crack, but then it seemed to encounter some obstacle and, try as I might, I could push it no further. So I pulled it shut again and carried on.

Then I saw it. From beneath the next door, there glowed a thin line of wavering blue light. At once, I knew that it was the same blue light that I had glimpsed behind the distant figures of the Lord and Lady on my very first day in this place. Perhaps the Lord and Lady were behind this door. Perhaps they would be able to help me. Summoning up all my courage, I tapped twice at the door. There was no answer, so I tapped again, louder this time. Still I heard nothing. My heart thumping, I turned the handle and pushed. As the door opened, the unearthly blue light flooded out and, momentarily dazzled, I shielded my eyes. 'Hello?' I called. 'Can anybody help me?' But still there was no reply. Squinting between my fingers, I stepped into the room, slowly lowering my hands as my eyes adjusted to the glare. I looked around me. There was nobody there.

For no particular reason, I had expected to find myself in another rough, windowless cell like my own, but this room was quite different. The floor was covered with a richly patterned carpet, and the walls were smoothly plastered but, above me, the ceiling receded away into darkness. In this mysterious void, there drifted several dozen pale globes, seemingly suspended freely in space, and it was from these globes that the eerily shifting blue light was coming. For a time, I stared up at them, before reluctantly casting my gaze downwards. Opposite me, I could now see, there stood a row of carved upright chairs. It struck me that there was something odd about the chairs, but it took me a moment to grasp that they had been arranged with their backs towards the door. This, I now saw, was because, on the wall in front of them, there was a long, curving glass window. The room, I realised, was some kind of observation gallery. I stepped forward, my tread muffled by the carpet. Pushing one of the chairs aside, I leaned on the sill and peered through the glass.

Below me, bathed in the familiar glow, I could see the whole of the factory floor. There were the long lines of benches, there were the rotating shafts that drove the machines, there were the pipes that carried the water, the air and the gas, and there were the grey-clad slaves, each standing impassively in his or her place, each repeating the same endless sequence of movements. But, although I could see everything that was taking place below me, the thick glass had the effect of insulating all my other senses. I could not feel the heat, I could not hear the noise, I could not smell the overpowering stench of oil and sweat and blood. I felt myself relaxing slightly. Somehow, protected as I now was against the worst aspects of that factory, the room below me had begun to feel less threatening, more acceptable. Even the patrolling groups of guards seemed somehow more reassuring.

Fascinated now, despite myself, I continued to stare down and, as I stared, I started to notice a number of details that had not struck me before. In the distance, away to my left, there stood a row of enormous hoppers, like huge funnels, one at the end of each bench. Into these, I assumed, must go whatever raw material was needed to fuel the machines. At one of the hoppers, a party of guards were standing on stepladders. They seemed to be filling the hopper with something but, at this distance, I could not make out what it was that was being tossed into the opening. Then I looked in the other direction, and I could see that, at the far right-hand end of the benches, there stood a row of wooden crates into which moving belts were depositing whatever was the final product of the factory. I could make out pile upon pile of small identical objects but, once again, I was unable to identify them. Desperate to satisfy my curiosity, I decided to make my way down to the factory floor and take a closer look. Quickly I glanced around me. There, in one corner of the room, was a small doorway that I had not noticed before. Ducking quickly through the opening, I found myself at the top of a long flight of iron steps. I took a deep breath and began my descent.

As I went down the staircase, the noise and the heat and the stench of the factory struck me once more with the force of a battering ram. Drawn forward by the hypnotic rhythm of the machines, I quickened my pace, taking the steps two at a time, until I was once again on the factory floor. I wanted to find Robert, and I wanted to know what was going into those hoppers and what was coming out at the other end. I threaded my way between the rows of benches, zigzagging in the direction of the hoppers, making impromptu detours to avoid the patrolling guards. Then, all at once, I caught a glimpse of something that brought me up short. One of the machines stood silent. Nobody was tending it. Somebody's place was unoccupied.

Puzzled, I stepped towards the abandoned bench, raised my hand to feel the surface of the machine. It was cold. Trembling now, I ran my palms over the rough wooden surface of the bench, fumbling among the dust and swarf and fluff, searching for anything that might give me a clue. Then, at last, my questing fingers encountered something small and cool and flat, something that had a soft, flexible leather strap attached to it. With a pang of horror, I recognised Robert's wristwatch, the same wristwatch that he had lost on the day when he had fought with Davy Hearn on the wooden bridge. Hastily, I shoved the watch into my pocket.

Turning away from the bench, I could see that, in the distance, a couple of guards were dragging something large and heavy in the direction of the hoppers. Reckless now, dizzy with shock at my discovery, reeling under the impact of the noise and the dust, I hurried along between the benches, shoving people aside, overturning anything that obstructed my path. Now I was breaking into a sweat as I ran, twisting an ankle as

I skidded on a patch of oil, striking my hip a numbing blow as I collided with the corner of a bench. I started to become aware of a choking, putrid smell.

Suddenly, I reached the end of the gangway and, from here, I could finally see what was happening. Into the hoppers were going the decaying remains of every type of living being. I could see jagged strips of skin and hide; I could see the stinking, half-dismembered skeletons of the black fish from the lake; I could see the broken bodies of dogs and cats. And then I saw a long, shining bone, a bone that still bore reeking chunks of bloody flesh, a bone that still bore torn scraps of grey cloth. Stunned, I drew back, swallowing hard to choke back a sudden, bitter-tasting flux of vomit.

The guards had seen me now, but I no longer cared. I offered no resistance as they dragged me back to my cell. Exhausted, filthy and beaten as I was, it suddenly seemed the safest place to be. The grating of the key in the lock brought me nothing but relief.

The boy in the bed stirred, turned over, settled once more into uneasy sleep. Something in the room was different, though. Something was there that hadn't been there before. For a moment, I was unable to identify it. Then I saw. On the bedside table beside the boy, there lay a wristwatch, surely the same wristwatch that had been lost in the river, the same wristwatch that I had found on the abandoned workbench in the factory. The watch was still ticking. How strange, I thought to myself. How strange. How did it get there?

The weeks passed, and the fields outside the boy's bedroom window turned slowly from fresh summer green to rich autumn gold, and from rich autumn gold to deep winter brown.

Gradually, the injuries to his body healed but, for some reason, he still showed no inclination to get out of bed, and people continued to come into the room to look after him. I watched the two girls bringing him bowls of soup and doses of medicine, and I watched them carrying away his chamber pots and his soiled pyjamas. Once, when they thought he was asleep, I saw them experimenting again with the perfume and lipstick on the dressing table, the dark girl with fumbling fingers, the pale girl with a quicker, surer touch. On another occasion, I heard them bickering over which of them should give the boy his medicine.

Now and then, the old lady would put in an appearance too, and I watched her as she sat in the corner chair, reading or sipping a cup of green tea. Sometimes, when the boy was awake, she told him stories, stories about the Good People who lived deep under the earth beneath Hedley House, stories about the Good People who would sometimes steal away a child from our world to their own. At first, I was afraid that these stories might unsettle the boy, but they seemed to have the opposite effect. After listening to the old lady's stories, the boy always slept soundly.

On one occasion, I saw the old lady sewing. She was stitching something together from oddly sized scraps of bright, flower-patterned material. In the subdued light of her surroundings, her work shone out in a blaze of greens and blues and reds. The pattern of the fabric looked oddly familiar to me but, try as I might, I could not identify it. At length, the old lady reached the end of the seam that she was sewing, nipped off the end of the cotton, folded her work away. Then she crossed to the window. This time, though, she did not draw the curtains. This time, she left them open so that the boy could look out at the countryside that stretched away into the blue distance.

'Master Kenneth? Master Kenneth?' It was Tommy's voice once again and I knew by the sound of its echo that Tommy was sitting beside me in my little stone cell.

'Tommy?' I replied, and I noticed that my own voice carried an echo too. 'That boy? The boy in the bed? He's me, isn't he? So am I here, or am I in bed? What is this place, Tommy?'

'You and I are in the realm of the Good People, Master Kenneth,' Tommy reminded me gently. 'I am here because I belong here, but you are here because you have come to seek your brother. Everyone will come to this place in time, of course, but perhaps it is still too early for you. Perhaps your time is yet to come. Perhaps you would prefer to go home.'

'Oh Tommy, I do want to go home,' I begged. 'Can you show me the way?'

'If you've made your choice, Master Kenneth. If you're truly certain.' I heard the patter of footsteps, the creak of a key in a lock and, a moment later, the door opened and I could see Tommy's slight form silhouetted against the light. I rose to my feet and stepped towards the doorway and out into the corridor. Tommy was hopping impatiently from foot to foot but, as soon as he saw me, he started off briskly in the same direction that I had taken all that time ago. Together now, we followed the same corridors, we took the same turnings, we climbed the same staircases, we traversed the same hallways. I knew now that my days in this place were nearing their end, and I stepped forward with confidence. No longer afraid of the guards and their batons, I spurned the safety of the walls and strode boldly along the centre of the corridor, so that Tommy found himself struggling to keep pace with me. At last, we arrived at the door that led to the room of the blue lights. Tommy paused, his small hand resting lightly on the handle, until he had recovered his breath.

'Are you ready, Master Kenneth?' he said at last.

'Yes, Tommy, I'm ready,' I replied.

My small friend tapped twice at the door, then, without waiting for an invitation, he stepped softly inside. 'My Lord,' he announced. 'My Lady. May I present Master Kenneth Storey, from Hedley House?'

I entered the room. There was the same blue light cast by the drifting globes, the same smoothly plastered walls and ceiling, the same beautifully patterned carpet, the same row of upright chairs and the same long, curving window. This time, though, the room was not empty, because two people were standing within. They were facing away from me, looking out of the window, their hands resting on the backs of the chairs. My heart pounding, I stepped forward and, as I did so, they turned to face me, their heavy robes billowing gently about them. Before me stood a tall, bearded man and a slim, graceful lady. But, although they faced me, my eyes seemed unable to focus on their features.

'Lord Owen,' said Tommy quietly, 'and Lady Margaret. The Lord and Lady of the Good People.'

'Kenneth Storey,' said the tall man, and his voice was quiet, but rich and resonant. 'What is it that you seek here?'

'If you please, sir,' I stammered, 'I am looking for my brother Robert.'

'Robert Storey was here,' said the Lady, and her voice was cool and sweet and mellow. 'But he is here no longer. You have searched here long enough, Kenneth.'

'Where must I look, then?' I said. I tried once more to look at their faces, but still I found that, each time I tried, my gaze was somehow deflected to the side.

'You must look for him in your world,' said the Lord, 'not in ours. In your own world, you will find everything that you need in order to do what you have to do.' For a moment, I found myself thinking about the Great Book of Arboria. But then I realised that the Lady had started to speak.

'You shall come to our world soon enough,' she was saying. 'All shall come in time to the realm of the Good People.'

'Very well,' I said. 'May I go now?'

'You may go,' said the Lord and Lady together, and it was as though a weight had fallen from my shoulders. 'Farewell, Kenneth,' they said. 'Farewell for now.' Their voices fitted side by side into each other, like two pieces of a jigsaw puzzle, and then, at last, I could see their faces. There before me were the features of my mother and father, looking just as they had looked the last time I had seen them. Suddenly, tears filled my eyes and, for a long moment, I was too overcome to move, too overcome even to speak.

At last, I felt a gentle tug at my sleeve.

'Come, Master Kenneth,' said Tommy softly. 'Best not outstay our time.' I nodded dumbly, wiped my eyes and my nose. The two tall figures of the Lord and Lady remained in the room, but now their faces were once more lost to my view.

Tommy drew me towards the small door that led to the iron staircase. Down we ran, down once more from the cool air of the gallery into the choking smoke and heat of the factory, down among the rows of benches, down among the patrols of guards, down among the sinister hoppers and the robot-like

197

slaves. This time, though, as we passed along the gangways, the slaves turned around from their work; they turned around to face us and to cheer us on our way. And, this time, I understood at last who it was that toiled here, because the faces of the slaves were the same faces that I had seen in Hedley House every day of my life. They were the faces that looked out at me from the crumbling gilt frames of the family portraits, the faces that lined the hallway and the staircase and the long corridor, they were the faces of the people who had lived at Hedley House for as long as anyone could remember, the faces of my ancestors: the Hedleys and the Storeys.

Finally, we reached the line of big wooden crates into which the moving belts were ceaselessly tipping their load. Here, then, I would find the answer to my final question. Nervously, I approached one of the crates, nervously I peered on tiptoe over its edge. The small objects that filled it, I could now see, were about the size of my palm, round and flat and smooth and black. I reached into the crate, picked out one of the objects, examined it in my hand. It was some kind of container, I realised, a flat casket with a tightly fitting lid attached to it by a miniature hinge. I eased my thumbnail into the crack between casket and lid, and the lid popped open.

The casket was filled with some kind of ointment, a thick ointment with a smooth, glossy surface. But beneath that surface, I could now see, something was stirring. Shielding my eyes against the dim glow of the factory, I peered harder. Before me, in the depths of the casket, there danced countless tiny pinpoints of blue light, pinpoints that circled endlessly around each other like a thousand dancers following some unfathomable choreography. For a long time I stared. Perhaps, it occurred to me, these lights are not pinpoints after all.

Perhaps they are really planets or stars, celestial bodies performing their neverending dance across the distant, empty reaches of outer space, too far away for me ever to reach. All at once, I felt myself drawn in among them, drawn into their strange, abstract world. Easily, too easily, I gave myself up to its alluring, unearthly geometry, gladly abandoning all notions of time and space.

They were pulling me towards them now, taking me with them wherever they chose to go, downwards, they were drawing me downwards, down among the black fish in the dark depths of the lake, down into the deep realm beneath the earth, into the realm where the ghosts of my ancestors toil for ever at their machines, down into the realm where Lord Owen and Lady Margaret look on for ever with silent neutrality.

Perhaps, after all, this was the place where I belonged. A place where there was no difference between past and future, no difference between inward and outward, no difference between good and bad, no difference even between life and death, just drifting, endlessly drifting . . . were we planets, I wondered, or were we atoms? And, after all, what did it matter? For time unknown I drifted with them, no longer certain of the difference between left and right, between forward and backward, between up and down, just drifting, endlessly drifting . . .

I awoke with a jolt. I was sitting bolt upright in bed and, from outside the window, I could hear a strange noise. It must have been the noise that had woken me. It sounded like someone repeatedly striking a metal object with a heavy hammer.

For the first time in months, my curiosity got the better of me. Summoning the whole of my depleted strength, I levered myself up into a sitting position, edged my reluctant body over to the side of the bed, and carefully lowered my feet to the floor. Inch by inch, I forced myself upright, my flaccid limbs groaning in protest. As I made my way across the room, my nostrils pricked up at a sharp, pungent smell that was wafting in from the garden. Slowly, painfully, I staggered across to the window, leaning heavily on the various pieces of furniture as I went. I peered through. Now, at last, I could see what it was that was causing the noise.

Standing in a loose group around the front gates of Hedley House were half-a-dozen men, among whom I recognised my Uncle Magnus, dapper as ever in his tweeds. The other men were all wearing shabby overalls, and I guessed that they must have been the labourers from one of our factories. The men in overalls were all wielding large saws or hammers. One man seemed to be responsible for the smell that I had noticed, because he was operating what I recognised as an oxyacetylene cutter which was producing a dazzling flame. In a welter of banging and hacking and sparks and smoke, the small working party was busily engaged in cutting down the tall iron railings that fronted the house.

Reeling in shock, I clutched at the window frame for support. Magnus must be made to stop what he was doing, I told myself, but I knew that, in my enfeebled state, I had no means of forcing him to do so.

'Uncle Magnus!' I called. There was no response. My voice was simply not strong enough to attract the men's attention. I tried again, this time summoning up my entire reserve of strength. 'Uncle Magnus!' I bawled. 'What are you doing?' This time, the men paused in their work, the noise stopped, and a couple of heads turned in the direction of my window. The effort of raising my voice had been too much for me, though. As my uncle started to walk towards the house, I could feel my legs giving way beneath me. I clutched at the curtains, but my arms were too weak to support me. Entangled in yards of dusty black serge, I collapsed to the floor.

When I came to my senses, I was in bed again. Uncle Magnus was standing just inside the doorway, shuffling his feet uneasily. 'Hello, Ken,' he ventured, sounding surprisingly timid for such a large man. 'Your gran tells me you're starting to feel a bit stronger.'

'Am I? I suppose I must be,' I conceded, struggling to prop myself up on my pillows. 'Why are you taking the railings down?' I realised that my heart was racing and my throat was dry.

'The government wants to commandeer them for salvage,' my uncle explained unhappily. 'All the railings from people's houses. Going to melt them down to make aeroplanes and bombs and so on. All very well for the ordinary folk, I suppose, but I know your mother would never have wanted it. She was very proud of those railings, you know. Because of the Hedley crest on them.' I stared at him blankly. 'She would never have wanted them cut down. And of course she was doing her bit in other ways. Such as taking in those evacuees. And Operation Dynamo.' For a moment, a wistful look came into my uncle's eye. Then he rallied himself briskly. 'So I thought we'd better act quickly. Cut down the railings and get them out of harm's way. For the duration, as it were.'

Magnus's bizarre logic was beyond me. 'What are you going to do with them?' I said faintly.

'Oh, I think we can manage to tuck them away somewhere safe,' he responded airily. 'But mum's the word, eh? Careless talk costs lives, don't you know?' He winked at me and tapped the side of his nose with a fat finger.

Partially reassured, but too bewildered to frame a rational response, I sank back down onto my pillows. When I opened my eyes a little while later, the noise had stopped and the smell had gone. My uncle was nowhere to be seen, and the railings were nowhere to be seen either. The two stone gateposts at the front of Hedley House stood tall and naked and lonely.

Just before teatime, Janny and Nadia arrived in my room to give me my medicine, and I was astonished to see that they were wearing, not their usual drab skirts and cardigans, but a matching pair of brilliantly vivid summer dresses in multi-coloured floral designs.

'Do you like them?' said Janny. 'We've been helping your gran to make them up over the winter. We thought it would be a nice surprise for you.' The two girls performed an improvised pirouette to display their new outfits to the best advantage. The skirts swirled around them, offering a tantalising glimpse of calves and knees. 'We have grown too tall for the old out-fits,' Nadia explained. 'They are all too tight, too short. So we have made new ones. It is better?'

'Yes,' I replied lamely. 'It is better.'

The transformation was indeed startling. Instead of the two shabby-looking schoolgirls of the previous autumn, I was now confronted by a pair of gorgeously attired young ladies whom I could scarcely recognise as my old playmates. Their dresses, I could now see, were constructed from a patchwork of violently conflicting flower patterns. There were large yellow roses on a dark green background, there were tiny blue daisies on a white background, and there was a latticework of red tulips and pink magnolias on a carpet of leaves. In defiance of the austere wartime fashion, the dresses were cut full in the skirt, and the bodices were designed to display the girls' busts in a manner that verged on the immodest. On their feet, Nadia and Janny were no longer wearing the clumsy, tight-fitting lace-up shoes that I remembered from before my illness. They both had sandals but these sandals, I realised, were not the sort of sandals that could have been bought in any of the shoe shops in Tollcester. They had been cobbled together from randomly sized scraps of leather and suede, all in different colours and textures. Their toes were sharply pointed, and the fastenings consisted of a haphazard collection of laces, buckles and old watch straps. They had obviously been made by hand, and I found myself wondering who had done the work. I remembered then the piece of needlework on which my grandmother had been working that day when I had seen her sitting in the corner chair. The old lady must have been busy with her work for most of the winter. But where had I seen that fabric before? I racked my brains but could not remember. Finally, Janny took pity on me.

'It's the old curtains,' she laughed. 'From before the blackout.'

'We found them in a chest,' added Nadia. 'In one of the old bedrooms. And Silvano made the shoes.'

I didn't ask just then who Silvano was, because I had started to think about that day at the very beginning of the war, the day when I had helped my grandmother to take down the old curtains and put up the dark, heavy drapes for the air raids. 'We'll put them away for the duration,' the old lady had said, as we packed the loosely folded armfuls of fabric into the huge old oak chest. But now it seemed that Hedley House had grown tired of waiting. Hedley House had decided that it was time to put the curtains to a new use.

From that day onwards, I began, gradually but noticeably, to recover my strength. I learned from my grandmother that I had had some kind of mental breakdown, that I had remained in my parents' bed all the way through the autumn and winter, and that, at one stage, my family had almost given me up for dead. I suppose that, if all this had happened in today's world, I would have been offered counselling or psychotherapy or hypnosis, and there would have been any number of highly qualified people doing their best to help me with my recovery. But I did not have any of these things. All I had was a few months of rest, and the only person who was there to help me was Tommy Pelling. So, with Tommy's help, I had done the best that I could and I suppose that, in my own fashion, I did eventually manage to come to terms with everyday life once more.

Sitting up on my pillows, enjoying the view through the window, I could see that the new spring was already well advanced. My parents' bedroom had not been touched since the night of my mother and father's fatal accident and, inside the room, everything remained exactly as it had been left, as if at any moment the two of them might step back through the door and once more take up their places in my life. My father's suits and my mother's dresses hung silently in their places in the tall, camphor-scented wardrobe; the scent bottles and the hair brushes remained in their usual precise positions on the dressing table; the pairs of shoes, purposeful, heavy lace-ups and dainty, frivolous high heels, stood patiently in line. At the window, the blackout curtains hung with portentous solemnity. My own occupation of the room had made little impression. Apart from my pyjamas and dressing gown, my clothes had remained in my own bedroom. The Great Book of Arboria had been brought in to the room for me, but I had been too depleted in strength even to look at that, so I had tucked it away out of sight behind my pillows.

One aspect of my illness, however, remained a mystery to everyone around me. Time after time, when I awoke, my feet were found to be scratched and scarred and caked in dust and mud.

'Do you think he's been sleepwalking?' I heard Janny say.

'I do not think so,' Nadia replied thoughtfully. 'Often I wake in the night. And I never hear him.' I glanced once again at my brother's wristwatch. That watch had been lost in the stream. So how, I wondered, had it found its way onto my bedside table?

Soon, I started to join the others for meals, and I started once again to do my share of the household chores. I decided to move out of my parents' room and back into my own quarters. From the back part of the house, I would be able to see the Great Tree and, with the Great Tree once more in my line of sight, I would be able to turn my attention back to the important business of Arboria. I knew now that, in the Great Book, I would discover everything that I needed to know in order to bring back my missing brother, just as Lord Owen had hinted. I realised that I had neglected my study for too long. I needed to be free now, free to concentrate on the one thing that really mattered. I needed to be free to concentrate on the vital task of restoring my beloved High Lord to his rightful place at the head of the Arborian people.

During the months that I had spent in bed, I discovered, life at Hedley House had not been standing still. Janny and Nadia had managed to get part time jobs helping Mr Lazenby with the potato planting at Helsing Fold Farm. They had made some new friends there too, and had taken to spending quite a lot of their free time with them, whether there was work to be done or not. 'You might like it at the farm,' Janny suggested. 'There's a whole gang of us that help out there.'

'Girls from the Land Army,' Nadia added.

'They come from all over,' said Janny. 'Cornwall, Wales. All sorts of places. Everybody's got different ways of talking.' We were in the kitchen, preparing a pile of carrots for our lunch. Janny was at the sink washing them clean of soil. Nadia and I were sitting at the table; I was chopping off the feathery leaves with the big vegetable knife while Nadia, with unexpected dexterity, was wielding the peeler. Periodically, one or other of us would sweep the leaves and peelings into the pig bin.

'And the Italians, too,' said Nadia. 'I like the Italians best.'

'Italians?' I said after a time. 'What Italians? Hey, Jan, hasn't anybody sharpened this knife since last year? Have you seen the oilstone?'

'I think it's in the drawer, just next to you,' Janny replied without turning her head. 'Oh yes, there's a Prisoner of War camp at Helsing Fold. They came and put the huts up over the winter. Really quick, they were. Some of the prisoners help on the farm. They're really nice. There's Silvano, he's the one that makes the shoes, then there's Gabrieli . . .'

'Gabrieli with his accordion.' Nadia picked up the thread of the narrative. 'Such funny little tunes he knows.' The two girls giggled.

'Doesn't it bother your eyes, Jan, working on the farm?' I broke in irritably. 'All the dust and so on?'

'Oh, I've got some new ointment,' said Janny. 'Your grandmother gave it to me.'

'Here,' said Nadia. I looked down.

She was pushing something towards me, across the pitted surface of the kitchen table. It was a smooth, flat, black casket with a tightly fitting lid secured by a miniature hinge. For a moment, I could not believe what I saw. The casket in Nadia's hand was exactly the same as the caskets that I had found in the realm of the Good People. I stared at it incredulously.

'Did Gran get that in Tollcester?' I said finally. I wondered what kind of shop might be selling such a thing.

'No, she doesn't go to Tollcester,' Janny explained from her place at the sink. 'I don't think she gets it from the chemist. But it's really good for my eyes.'

'I put it on my legs, too,' Nadia chipped in. 'I think it helps me to walk better.'

'It's got all kinds of magical properties,' Janny giggled. Nadia withdrew the casket and, with a rather secretive air, slipped it back into the pocket of her dress.

'Would it help us to find Robert?' I said suddenly.

Janny and Nadia exchanged puzzled glances. 'Robert's in Tollcester,' said Janny. 'At the print works. Don't you remember?'

'No.' I shook my head vehemently. 'He's in the realm of the Good People. Under the ground. Or at least he was. The Good People were looking after him. But he's gone from there now. So we've got to go and find him.'

The girls looked at each other again, alarmed now. 'Ken,' Janny began slowly. 'Don't you think . . .'

But at that moment, the door to my grandmother's parlour creaked open and her wrinkled old face emerged through the crack. 'Carrots again?' she complained. 'I'm getting a bit sick of carrots. Still, I suppose they'll be good for Janny's eyes.' So the conversation turned to other things, and then it was time for lunch, and after that, there was the washing up, so the discussion about Robert was not continued. After the girls' unsettling response, I didn't feel brave enough to raise the subject again.

'What are we going to do with you, Ken?' Janny said to me one afternoon. 'You surely can't go on wearing those old things for ever.' The two girls and I were sitting at the kitchen table. In the absence of any obvious alternative, I was still wearing the threadbare shorts and grey pullover that I had had since I was about twelve.

'It's all right for you,' I grumbled, 'with your new dresses. I don't suppose anybody's bothered to make any clothes for me.'

The grandfather clock in the hallway was just striking four o'clock. Janny filled the kettle and put it on the hob, while Nadia assembled four cups and four saucers and arranged them on the tea tray. Still rather disorientated, I slumped at the table and watched distractedly as the girls went about their work. When the tea things were all in place, Nadia tapped at the door of my grandmother's parlour.

'Mrs Hedley?' she called. 'Is everything now ready? We have brought Kenneth to see you.'

'Come in, all of you,' came the muffled reply. 'I won't get up for a minute.'

In single file, we made our way through the door. Janny placed the tray on the small table next to the fireplace. From her fireside chair, my grandmother peered up at me through her usual haze of pipe smoke. 'In the top drawer,' she said finally. Nadia made her way over to the tall chest, pulled open a drawer and brought out a bundle wrapped in crumpled white tissue paper.

'We have made new clothes for you too, Kenneth,' she explained.

'We were going to wait for your birthday,' added Janny. 'But then we thought that you might want them straightaway.'

In a daze, I unwrapped the layers of tissue and carefully unfolded the garments that lay within. Here was a pair of long trousers, trousers that had neither pockets nor turn-ups, narrow trousers whose waist fastened, not with buttons but like pyjamas, with a cotton drawstring. Here was a tunic, pocketless again and collarless, a tunic that buttoned right up to the neck with four large round buttons. With a start, I realised that the outfit was identical in design to the grey overalls that the slaves had been wearing in the realm of the Good People. But, even in the dim light of my grandmother's parlour, I could see that the tunic and trousers that I held in my hands were not grey. Like the girls' new dresses, my clothes had been cut and stitched from the remains of the old curtains of Hedley House. My new outfit was ablaze with flowers of every hue, flowers large and flowers small, flowers that glowed red and orange, flowers that blazed purple and blue and gold. As I held it, my hands were shaking, and all the colours in the petals seemed to merge together through a veil of mist.

'It's beautiful,' I stuttered, 'but when am I going to wear it?'

'You'll wear it soon enough,' my grandmother replied. 'You mark my words.'

But I could hardly make out what she was saying. It seemed as though she were speaking to me from some other place, some place an immense distance away. My hearing was fading, my vision was blurring, and my legs seemed no longer capable of bearing my weight. My knees started to buckle under me, my new clothes slipped from my grasp, and now I was feeling giddy . . .

'Try and catch him, Nad!' It was Janny's voice, but even her sharp vowels could barely cut through the dark mist that had risen up to encircle me. 'I think he's going again.'

Once again, the blackness rose up. But in those last moments, as I slipped away from the solid world of Hedley House, I had finally begun to grasp what I must do to bring my High Lord Robert back to the land of Arboria.

## Seven

# LORDS OF MISRULE

*O*nce again I'm sitting in the café at the bus station, once again I'm staring at the froth on the surface of the lukewarm coffee in the chipped mug in front of me. The café has been quieter and emptier than usual these last few mornings, and that's because the group of schoolchildren has not been in here lately. There's nothing here to remind me of them except for the scribblings of graffiti on the doors of the left luggage lockers. The children aren't here, of course, because the school holidays have begun.

You know how it feels on the first morning of the school holidays, Jamie? You wake up an hour later than usual, you yawn and you stretch yourself. The sun is shining through the gap in the curtains, but you know that can just lie there. You don't have to rush downstairs for breakfast, you don't have to snatch up your school bag and race down the road for the bus. The whole day stretches ahead of you, and you can do exactly as you please for every hour of that day, and the next day too, and the next, and the next. For the whole summer, you can climb trees in the forest, you can catch fish in the stream, you can take the bus into town or you can ride your bike up the

211

lane, you can kick a ball against the wall or you can stop in bed until dinner time. It feels as though the holiday will last for ever.

But then one day you discover that there's only a week left before you have to go back to school, and then there's only half a week, and then at last there's only one single day. At the start of that terrible day, you lie in bed staring out of the window as usual, and then you start to remember all of the things that you meant to do but never got around to doing. Because now you have run out of time, and tomorrow you will have to go back to school. You start to remember about the homework that you haven't done, about the sports kit that never got washed, about the bus and the dinner money. Suddenly, even though the sun is still shining, you don't feel like doing anything any more.

Well, that's the way that I have felt for as many years as I can remember. There have been so many things in my life that I have never got around to doing, and now I know that I've no time left to do any of them. Of course, it's partly because I'm nearly eighty now and I probably haven't got much longer anyway. But, more than that, it's because, before long, I'm going to have to leave Hedley House. And when I leave Hedley House, the house is going to be demolished by the property developers, and the trees in the forest are going to be felled, and the roots of the trees are going to be wrenched from the ground, and the lake is going to be drained, and that will be the end of Arboria. Of course, I don't know exactly when it's going to happen but, as I wake each morning, I know with greater and greater certainty that the end is approaching. The developers want me to go, the council want me to go, even my own family want me to go. What can one frail old man do against them all? As far as the law is concerned, the forest doesn't belong to me, the garden doesn't belong to me, even Hedley House itself doesn't belong to me, although I've lived in that house all my life. All I really have is my scroll of ancient scribblings and my little company of ghosts.

I wonder what my grandmother and my mother and my father would have thought. I wonder what all my ghosts will think when the bulldozers finally move in, when the walls of the house buckle inwards and the roof collapses, when the lake is drained of its water, when the very roots of the trees are torn screaming from the earth? Even after all these years, my ghosts have continued to haunt the house and the forest and the lake, the mournful sound of their voices echoing from the caverns, rippling across the waters, murmuring amongst the trees. I can still hear Janny Grogan's tears, I can still hear Davy Hearn's lilting music. I can still see Nadia Skolomowski in her bathing suit, swimming to and fro across the lake, to and fro, to and fro . . .

I wonder about Tommy Pelling too. I wonder about Tommy even more than I wonder about the others, because Tommy has been here longer than any of us, Tommy has been here since the very, very beginning. Tommy was here before the Arborians, and he was before the Barbarians. Sometimes, I even wonder whether Tommy was here before the Good People arrived.

I wonder what Tommy will do?

On that day when my grandmother showed me my new outfit, my strength seemed once again to desert me. Doctor Solloway would probably have said that I had suffered a relapse. At any rate, although I didn't actually go back to bed, for the next couple of weeks I couldn't summon the energy to go out of doors. I remained within the walls of Hedley House, wandering in my pyjamas from room to room, picking up ornaments or staring at pictures.

I took a particular interest in my parents' bedroom because, from its window, I could see across to Helsing Fold Farm. Here, at least, there were signs of new life. In the fields, people were picking the new crop of potatoes and, through my father's binoculars, I could make out the distant figures of Janny and Nadia helping with the work. I watched them sitting by the hedgerow, and I watched them swigging in turn from a bottle of lemonade.

One day I watched them exchanging banter with a dark-haired young man. I peered more closely at the man, assuming at first that he must have been one of the Italian prisoners of war. When he turned towards me, though, I was startled to recognise the features of Davy Hearn. Davy was grinning, sharing a joke with the girls, touching them lightly on the shoulder as they laughed together. Everyone is out in the fields except me, I thought glumly. Even Davy Hearn is out there doing his bit. Alone in the house, I was starting to feel neglected and abandoned, but somehow I still could not bring myself to venture outside again.

But I could at least make the effort to read. Lounging half-dressed on a sofa or across a bed, I returned once more to my study of the Great Book of Arboria. Along the dusty corridor of the disused wing, I unravelled yard after yard of its crumbling parchment, still puzzling over its arcane phraseology, endlessly sifting through its paragraphs for any further clues I could find about what I must do to bring my brother back to the forest. I was beginning to get a fleeting sense of what was needed, and I felt convinced that, somewhere within the tangle of writings, the answer would lie concealed. But, as I pored over the ancient script, I was reminded yet again of how helpless I was without the others. I thought then of Nadia and of Janny, the two girls out in the fields, happily absorbed into their own world of potatoes and Italians and Davy Hearn, and I began to understand that it was not just my family that I had lost. Remembering the night on which we had frightened the Lumberjills away from the forest, I was reminded of the combined power that my companions and I had once been able to wield. Now, though, I could sense that the two girls were drifting away from me, starting to discover a world of their own, starting to live in a world that was perhaps more grown-up than the world that I lived in. Whatever it was that had to be done, I realised, it was going to have to be done soon. For Arboria and for me and for Robert, time was beginning to run out. If I delayed things for much longer, I would lose my chance for ever.

It was my grandmother who finally stirred me into action.

It was a bright spring day, although the air inside Hedley House still felt chilly and slightly damp. Around lunchtime, I wandered downstairs to see if there was any food to be had. The tiles in the hallway felt clammy against the soles of my feet. I could hear no voices from the kitchen, no music from the garden room, I could hear nothing but the dull tick of the clock. The girls, I guessed, must still be out in the fields with their new friends. I made my way into the kitchen and laid a cautious hand on top of the black iron stove. It was barely warm, and the fire inside it had burned down to little more than a layer of ash. I tossed a couple of logs into the firebox, then turned around to look for the kettle. As I did this, I was surprised to see the old lady standing in the open doorway of her parlour.

'Will you sit down and have a cup of tea with me, Kenny?' she said. I followed her into the room. Soon, we were seated on either side of the fireplace, sipping her aromatic green tea. Although the ordinary sort of tea had been rationed since the start of the war, my grandmother had somehow managed to maintain a supply of her own peculiar leaves.

Rather than engaging me in conversation, though, the old lady returned to the task in which she had obviously been engaged before my arrival. Putting aside her cup and saucer, she reached down beside her chair and pulled out a tangled mass of ribbons from her work basket. She spread them out on her lap and began slowly to unravel them, her gnarled fingers teasing away at the knots and twists, separating red from blue and yellow from green. I watched her for a time, absorbed like her in the disentangling of one coloured strand from another. 'Here,' I said eventually, 'let me help.' Leaning towards her, I took hold of a trailing end of green ribbon, allowing her to untwist the other colours from around it.

'Do you remember the ribbons, Kenny?' she said after a while. 'We always used to get them out at this time.'

For a moment, my mind seemed a blank. Then it came back to me. 'The Maypole Dance,' I said slowly. 'For the Spring Festival. On the village green. I'd completely forgotten.'

'We used to do it every year,' my grandmother continued. I noticed that her voice had taken on a sing-song tone, as if reciting a bedtime fairy story to a small child. 'Right from when I was a little girl. And my grandmother remembers it too, from when she was a little girl. And her grandmother before her, I daresay. The Maypole Dance and the Saint George Play.'

'Back before the war,' I added.

'Yes, back before the war,' she echoed me. 'That's right. People stopped bothering with it when the war began. I suppose it didn't seem important any more.' For a while we were both silent, engrossed once more in disentangling the ribbons, laying out the separate strands as we unravelled them from the central puzzle of knots. I found myself wondering whether the war that she referred to was the same war that was going on now. Or was she thinking of the First World War? Or the Boer War? Or the Crimean War?

'First there would be the play,' the old lady continued after a while, 'and after that there would be the dance. St George was in the play, of course, and there was the Dragon too, and then there was the Maiden, and there was the Doctor. Once upon a time there used to be the Devil as well, but that was long ago, long before my time.'

'Were you ever in the play?' I asked.

'Once or twice,' my grandmother reminisced. 'I remember being the Maiden. I had a long white robe and long, flowing golden locks. But then another year I was just one of the People. We all used to dress ourselves up and paint our faces and put bows in our hair, all the children in the village. And then we used to act out the story. It was always the same, every year. It began with the Dragon striking terror into the hearts of the People. And the People were sore afraid! And then the Dragon captured the Maiden, and Saint George had to fight him to get her back. And after a long, long battle, the Dragon was slain and the Maiden was saved.'

'. . . but her honour was no longer intact,' I added.

'No longer intact,' the old lady agreed. 'Of course, I didn't know what that bit meant at the time. But I expect you're old enough to understand now.' Momentarily embarrassed, I blushed. 'Yes, I can see that you do,' she continued. Now, where was I?'

'The Maiden was saved,' I prompted her, 'but Saint George—'

'But Saint George suffered a mortal wound,' my grand-mother continued, 'and it seemed that all was lost. But then the People called for the Doctor . . .'

'I was the Doctor one year,' I said suddenly. 'Robert was St George and I was the Doctor.'

'Yes, you were. Robert was ten and you were eight. Your mother was so proud of you both.' The tail of the red ribbon suddenly came free. My grandmother rolled it up and laid it on the arm of her chair. 'The people called for the Doctor,' she continued, 'and then the Doctor made his examination, and he declared that Saint George wasn't dead after all, but he had been spirited away to the Other World, where the Good People were taking care of him.' The yellow ribbon was free now, and my grandmother rolled that one up as well.

'And the only way the people of the village could get him back,' I broke in, 'was to dance the Maypole Dance all day and all night . . .'

'. . . in the way it had always been danced.' The two of us recited the final few words together, my grandmother's cracked old contralto blending with my recently broken tenor in brief, spontaneous harmony. Just as this happened, the last ends of ribbon fell apart from one another, and there was another silence while the two of us rolled them up and arranged all the rolls in a line.

'At the end of the dance,' my grandmother said at length, 'the spirit of Saint George would return from the Other World, and then the Saint would come back to life and marry the Maiden, and the People would give three cheers. And then there would be feasting and drinking. There used to be a special punch that the grown-ups drank. St George's Brew, it was called. There used to be a copy of the recipe in the kitchen, but I don't know what happened to it. It's a long time since I last saw it.' For a few moments, her eyes seemed focused on something far beyond the walls of Hedley House. Then, with a shiver, she collected herself. 'I don't suppose there's much chance of feasting these days,' she concluded wryly, 'what with the rationing and all the shortages.' We both picked up our cups and took thoughtful draughts of lukewarm tea.

'I think I might have seen the recipe for the brew in the Great Book,' I said after a time. 'And there was something about the play as well. Its true meaning wasn't really about Saint George, was it? It was a kind of – what do you call it? – metaphor, that's it. What it was really supposed to be about was making the crops grow again after the winter. "*By breathing life once again into the chosen one, so life shall come once more to the soil of the land.*" Something like that, anyway. Saint George dying and then being brought back to life. The same as Jesus at Easter, I suppose. Dying on the cross and then coming alive again. Easter's in the spring, isn't it?'

'And that's when the crops grow again,' my grandmother broke in. 'They die in the winter and they grow again in the spring. The farmers used to say that the dance brought them fertile soil and sweet rain and good luck.' There was another silence while we both considered the implications of this.

'Or like Robert,' I said suddenly. 'I saw him. I know I did. The doctor tried to tell me it was a dream, but I know it was real. I went down the steps from the ice house, into the caves, and I saw him working in some kind of factory. And I know I was there, because I saw the dirt on my feet afterwards. I thought they'd taken him down to hell. And then, when I went again, he'd disappeared. There was no-one in his place. And then they told me I'd have to look in my own world. Not in theirs.'

'Stolen away by the Good People,' said my grandmother unexpectedly. 'Stolen away to be their slave. To toil in their workshops. People used to say that that's what they did to people who offended them. And then you had to pay them a forfeit to get someone back again.' She fell silent for a moment. 'You still miss Robert, don't you?' she said finally.

Tight-lipped, I could only nod my head. I didn't trust myself to speak, because my eyes had started to fill with tears. After a little while, in a very small voice, I said: 'Do you think, if Janny and Nadia and I did the Maypole Dance again, Robert might come back to us?'

My grandmother looked at me. It was a strange look, shrewd and compassionate and bleak, all at the same time. 'I suppose he might,' she said eventually. 'If you feel that's what you need to do, then perhaps you should do it. Folk always used to say that the Maypole Dance would call up the magic of the Good People from deep under the ground. Just a story, I suppose, but some of the old folk used to set a lot of store by it. Anyway,' she concluded briskly, 'It's about time you got yourself out of doors again.'

Over the next few days, I immersed myself once more in the bulky scroll of writings that made up the Great Book of Arboria. I had no trouble finding the recipe for the Saint George's Brew and, with my grandmother's help, I succeeded in identifying nearly all of the ingredients. Most of them came from plants that could be found in the woods and fields around the village, one or two of them lurked in the musky depths of the kitchen store cupboard, and there was one particular aromatic essence that would require a trip to the chemist's shop in Tollcester. I discovered that I was becoming quite excited at the prospect of another trip on the bus.

The story of the Saint George play turned out to be in the Great Book too, although I could find no trace of the role that the Devil supposedly once took in it. I wondered briefly whether the Dragon fathered a child when he deprived the Maiden of her honour, but could find no answer to this either. I wondered briefly what sort of child the two of them might have produced.

In another section of the scroll, one of the gothic-lettered parts, I found a series of diagrams that apparently constituted the instructions for the Maypole Dance. These looked rather like the curves and triangles and parallelograms that I had once been made to draw in the geometry class at school, although they were far more complicated. All the figures seemed to interlock with each other like the pieces of a puzzle, and at each apex I could see strange symbols that I thought might possibly have been Greek. Robert would have been able to understand all this, I told myself glumly. For a moment, I wondered once again where Robert was and what he was doing, but then I dismissed the thought and returned to my study of the charts. Eventually, though, I was forced to admit defeat. The symbols meant nothing to me. What was I going to do? Perhaps my grandmother might remember the steps of the dance. Old Ned Hearn might once have remembered too, but of course it was too late now to ask him. Perhaps Davy might know something about it. I wondered how best to approach him.

After a time, I found that the letters on the scroll were beginning to swim to and fro before my eyes. My head was pounding, and I took this as a sign that I had spent long enough indoors. I decided, for the first time in months, to pay a visit to Arboria. As usual, there was no sign of either of the girls in the house, but I suspected that on this occasion, even if I had bumped into Janny or Nadia, I would probably not have invited them to join me. For some reason, this was an excursion that I needed to make on my own. I shouldered my knapsack, slipped quietly out of the back door, crossed over the vegetable patch and unlatched the garden gate.

It was another bright day, but there had been some heavy rain over the past couple of weeks, and the ground was quite wet underfoot. Over the past few months, I discovered, my feet had been growing rather faster than the rest of my body, and my ageing sandals had finally started to split, so that my socks were soon uncomfortably wet. I peered in through the doorway of Tommy Pelling's little brick hut but, inside, it was dark and silent. I wondered where Tommy had gone.

As I squelched my way along, I stared down at the plants and wild flowers that grew on either side of the track, looking out for the various leaves and petals and berries that I would need to make the Saint George's Brew. I quickly detected the pungent scent of wild garlic, and dandelion leaves were also easy to find. I stumbled upon a mountain ash tree and tried to peel off a strip of its bark, but soon decided that I would need to come back another day with my penknife.

Arriving at the double doors of the ice house, I paused for a moment and reached into my side pocket. The padlock was still there, and so was the key. Suddenly, I remembered the small, oddly shaped doorway that had led me from the bunk room, down the staircase to the realm of the Good People. I wondered if the door would still be there the next time I ventured inside. I shivered, remembering my strange experiences at the bottom of that staircase. I didn't want to think about that door any more. I slipped the padlock back into its hasp and turned the key.

After that, I continued downhill towards the shore of the lake, my sandals squishing soggily as I went. It was a still day, and the surface of the water was dotted with broken reeds, leaves and other small pieces of debris. As I made my way along the line of willow trees, I peered across at the far bank, wondering if I might catch a glimpse of Davy Hearn or any of his Barbarian companions, but all was quiet. Eventually I reached the foot of the lake but, rather than clamber down the rocks towards the bridge, I decided to make my way back up the track that led to the Great Tree. On my way, I managed to identify a useful collection of wild mushrooms, and these I slipped into my knapsack along with my other booty.

Soon, the Great Tree towered before me. I had not set out with the idea of climbing it, but now it occurred to me that this was exactly what I needed to do. I could see that the rope ladder was still in place, although someone had tucked it away behind a branch. It took a moment to free it and to satisfy myself that it was secure. I kicked off my wet sandals and socks, thinking briefly of Janny as I did so. An instant later, I was in the air.

As the forest floor fell away beneath me, so too did all the misery and boredom and loneliness and frustration of the last months. Higher and higher I climbed up that wildly swaying ladder and, as I did so, the strength seemed to flow back into my limbs, and the courage seemed to flow back into my heart. Below me, dimly at first but then more clearly, I could feel that deep pulsation that told me that the Good People were still busy in their caves. Moments later, I was inside the House in the Air.

'Good afternoon, Master Kenneth,' a familiar voice greeted me. 'I see you've been collecting herbs. Would you perhaps be thinking about the May Day festivities?'

It turned out that Tommy and I were the first visitors of the year. The floor of the house was once again choked with the leaves of the previous autumn, but the dustpan and broom still stood in the corner. We cleared a working space in the middle of the floor and stood together in the doorway, watching the dead leaves as they fluttered and crackled down to earth. After this, I fished in my knapsack for the binoculars and perched myself next to Tommy on the sill, our feet dangling down outside.

I focused the binoculars and scanned to and fro across the forest. Far away, I could see the line of mountains, a dim purple silhouette that looked like nothing more than a strip of cardboard cut with scissors into an irregular zigzag. I wondered for a moment if I'd ever get to the mountains. Then I refocused the binoculars and looked closer to home. In the middle distance, spiralling up into the sky from somewhere on the far side of the lake, there rose a thin, grey column of wood smoke. I could tell from his excited fidgeting that Tommy had seen it too.

'I do believe that the charcoal burners are here again, Master Kenneth. Back in the forest once more.' At that moment, it struck me that the Maypole Dance should take place, not on the village green as it once used to do but, instead, in a clearing somewhere here in the forest. The more I thought about this idea, the more I liked it. And it needn't be just me and Janny and Nadia. Perhaps the Arborians would join in the dance as well. Perhaps even the Barbarians would join in, as they had when we chased the Lumberjills from their camp. Surely the combined magic of all of us would force Robert to come home again? Perhaps the charcoal burners would let us use one of their clearings. Perhaps they would even help us to build a maypole. But then it occurred to me that, in order to enlist the charcoal burners, I would first have to approach Davy Hearn. I was still a bit frightened of Davy, I admitted to myself. I didn't really feel up to tackling him. I found myself chewing a fingernail in perplexity.

'Pardon me, Master Kenneth,' said Tommy quietly. 'Miss Janny and Miss Nadia appear to be on cordial terms with Master Davy. Perhaps one of the young ladies might care to have a word with him?'

A few days after this, I was lying on my bed studying the Great Book, when slowly, at the fringe of my consciousness, I started to become aware of faint strains of music drifting up from somewhere in the house. Recognising the dissonant timbre of the grand piano in the garden room, I realised that Janny must be at home. This was a chance too good to miss. I hastily rolled up the scroll, tucked it under my arm, and scrambled down the stairs two at a time.

As I drew nearer to the source of the sound, I recognised the music as a piano sonata by Beethoven. It was a piece that my mother sometimes used to play, and for one precious, terrifying moment, it seemed to me that I might open the doors of the room and find her seated once more at the keyboard, while my father lounged in his armchair, smoking his pipe, and Robert sat at the table dealing out a game of patience. My heart pounding, I ran the last few steps and pushed open the door.

Of course, my family weren't there. In the garden room I found Janny sitting at the piano, frowning in concentration at my mother's thick, yellowing volume of Beethoven. Nadia sat close beside her, preparing to turn a page of the music. In the sidelong light from the French windows, countless motes of dust hung suspended, softening the detail of the scene and, for a long moment, I stood there unobserved. Then Janny caught sight of me, and abruptly ceased her performance. Nadia too looked up in alarm. I noticed that Janny's eyes and nose appeared even redder than usual. As the two girls stared at me, I realised that I had not worked out what it was that I was going to say.

'Come and have a look at this,' I hazarded. Aware of their startled gaze, I dropped to my knees and started to unroll a length of the Great Book along the dusty carpet, searching for the section with the strange diagrams. The two girls got up slowly from the keyboard and approached me warily. Nadia dropped down clumsily to kneel beside me, but Janny remained standing. I pointed to the maze of lines, curves and symbols on the scroll. Nadia peered at it for a moment, shoving her dark hair out of the way of her eyes.

'But these are – what do you call them – choreographer's charts,' she said. 'Long ago I have seen something like this. My sister Luda, when she was in the ballet. Before they . . .'

'Can you read it?' I interrupted, amazed at my good luck.

'Perhaps,' Nadia replied. 'It is not quite the same. But I think I can try.'

'Is this for that maypole thing?' Janny, intrigued now despite herself, joined us on her knees. 'Mrs Hedley was talking about it.'

'The Maypole Dance,' I corrected her. 'That's right. It's an ancient tradition. We should try to keep it going.' The two of them looked at me sceptically. 'It's supposed to make the crops grow again in the spring. There's a recipe for a special drink as well,' I continued, my enthusiasm taking over. 'Saint George's Brew, it's called. The children aren't supposed to have any. But we're not really children any more, are we? And besides, there's no-one to stop us now.' A warning voice somewhere at the edge of my mind told me not to mention Robert. Quickly I unrolled another section of the scroll, nearly overturning a standard lamp in my haste. Janny scrutinised the list of ingredients, coughing once or twice at the dust that we were stirring up.

'It sounds like powerful stuff,' she observed finally. 'Especially those mushrooms. Lethal, they are! Folk say that those things can make you see snakes and all sorts. You can't blame them for believing in magic if they drank a concoction like that. Still, at least none of the ingredients are on the ration.'

'I've found most of the things in the forest,' I said, running a finger down the list. 'Except that one. That will have to come from the chemist in Tollcester. I think it's a yellow powder; Robert mentioned it once when he was doing his chemistry homework. But that last thing, I'm not sure what that is at all.' The three of us peered at the list in perplexity.

'I know,' said Nadia finally. 'That is its name in Latin. It is some kind of pond weed, it grows in the lake, but only in the middle. I can swim out and get some.'

'And then we'll have all the ingredients,' said Janny, her earlier reserve now completely abandoned. 'We could make it

227

in that big iron pot in the kitchen. Your grandmother could help us, Kenny. And then we could all have a turn at stirring it.'

'So can you show me what to do in the dance?' I hazarded. 'If you want to come, that is.'

'I will come,' Nadia replied. 'But maybe I just sit and watch.'

'I'll come too,' said Janny eagerly. She turned to the other girl. 'We could ask some other people too,' she suggested. 'Have a good drink of that – what's it called – Saint George's Brew. Maybe make some sandwiches. Dance round the maypole. Come on, Nad, it'll be good fun. We can all dress up, do our hair . . .' As the two of them continued to chatter excitedly, I slowly rolled up the scroll and took my leave. I don't think they saw me go. It seemed that, even without my help, the arrangements for the Maypole Dance were falling into place.

Over the next few days, the three of us started to collect together all the necessary ingredients for the brew. In the woods we gathered the bark and the petals and the roots and the mushrooms and the berries. Under Janny's watchful eye, Nadia swam out to the middle of the lake to collect a few fronds of the elusive pond weed and, when this task had been successfully accomplished, we set out to find a place at the edge of the stream from which we could collect a basinful of cold, clear water.

'I know it doesn't actually say so in the recipe,' Janny pointed out, 'but somehow I've got a feeling that running water would be the best thing to use.'

'I'm sure it says it somewhere else in the book,' I mused.

'Maybe it will keep away the evil spirits,' giggled Nadia. 'In my country, the old people say so.'

'There's one plant that only grows on the other side of the stream,' I remembered. 'What are we going to do about that?'

'Perhaps Davy can help us,' Nadia suggested. 'Tomorrow I shall ask him.'

'We'll see him at the farm,' said Janny thoughtfully.

A couple of days after that, we caught the bus into Tollcester. The girls wanted to buy ribbons for their hair, but they had trouble finding the right colours. This meant that it was some way into the afternoon before we even started to look for a chemist's shop. Our usual man, though, was unwilling to let us have any of the mysterious yellow powder. 'You're too young to sign the poison book,' he said grimly. 'Now be off with you.' And so we were forced to trail round several more places before we finally found a chemist, in a shabby street of run-down shops, who lacked the scruples of the others.

'Don't take it all at once,' was his only comment as he pocketed most of our spare change. Nothing was said about signing a book. We made our way back towards the Broadgate in high spirits, dodging to and fro between the long lines of people queuing up outside the butchers' and grocers' shops. In the end, though, hot and footsore, we were only just in time for the last bus back to Lower Helsing, and we were so short of money that I had to pretend to be thirteen, so that I could pay half-fare. By the time we arrived back at Hedley House, we were all feeling tired and bad-tempered.

'Have you talked to Davy Hearn yet,' I reminded Janny, 'about finding a clearing in the forest, and getting a maypole from the charcoal burners?'

'Can't you stop going on about it?' Janny snapped. 'We've spent all day getting your stupid powder. We ended up having to run practically the whole length of the Broadgate to catch that bus. Look, I've said I'll talk to Davy, and I'm going to. I expect he'll be at the farm again tomorrow.'

229

'Janny does not mean to speak sharply,' Nadia explained later. 'Truly she is excited. But sometimes she becomes a little . . . on edge.' She paused, then added meaningfully, 'It happens to us girls. At certain times.' I gave what I hoped was a wise nod, but I don't think I really understood what she meant.

Soon it was Saturday, and Saturday was to be the day of the Maypole Dance. After breakfast, the three of us gathered around the long kitchen table and carefully spread out the ingredients for the brew. Nadia poured the water from the stream into the big iron pot and started warming it on top of the stove. 'It has a handle on each side,' she observed. 'So that we can carry it more easily to the place of the dance.'

While Nadia watched the pot, Janny and I sat at the table. Using the best kitchen knife, and working on the reverse side of the bread board, I began to slice up the pale mushrooms and the red and purple berries and the wilting green leaves. As I did this, Janny passed the ingredients across to me one by one. Once or twice during the task, our fingers brushed together, but neither of us looked up at the other.

The yellow powder had to be dissolved in a glass of milk, while the various tangled roots and curling slivers of bark needed to be shredded with the cheese grater, which resulted in a certain amount of damage to the grater. It also succeeded in giving me a cut finger, as I tried to force the last stubborn piece of bark through the mesh.

'There's going to be a bit of my blood in the brew now,' I pointed out. 'Do you think it will make any difference?'

'Shouldn't think so,' said Janny absently. She had taken the grater away from me and was trying to rescue the last scraps of material from the back of it. She looked up. 'Actually, it's given me an idea.' I tried to get her to tell me what she had in mind but she averted her eyes again and refused to say any more.

'The water has started to boil,' said Nadia anxiously. 'Are you ready?'

I tipped the small glass of milky mixture into the pan, while Janny carefully scraped in the soggy, multicoloured mess from the bread board, leaving behind a livid, raw-looking stain that no amount of scrubbing would ever subsequently succeed in removing. With a big wooden ladle, Nadia started to stir the bubbling liquid, until the contents of the pan had begun to mingle together into something that looked rather like vegetable soup. After a while, Nadia passed the ladle to Janny, stepping back from her place at the stove to give the other girl her turn.

Janny wrinkled up her long nose. 'It's gruesome,' she complained. 'How long do we need to stir it for?' I noticed that her eyes were red and streaming.

'Here,' I offered. 'Let me have a go.' The brew was thick and clingy, dragging against the bowl of the ladle. An acrid, bluish vapour rose from the bubbling surface of the liquid, giving me a tingling sensation at the back of my eyes and nose. I touched the underside of my nose to stop myself from sneezing. It was an actor's trick that my mother had taught me.

'You've all taken a turn with the spoon. That's good.' It was my grandmother's voice. Absorbed as we had become in our task, none of us had noticed the creak of her parlour door, none of us had heard her soft, slippered footfall on the tiled floor. 'When you have stirred the pot for a little longer, you must each have a taste of the mixture. Then you must each add something of your own.'

Her cracked old voice seemed to carry a note of authority.

Janny opened the cutlery drawer in the kitchen table and handed each of us a large tablespoon. Each stepped up in turn to sample the brew.

'Ugh!' shuddered Nadia.

'Never!' exclaimed Janny.

'Can we put some sugar in it?' I suggested.

After that, following my grandmother's suggestion, Nadia contributed a smear of the mysterious ointment from the little casket that my grandmother had given to the girls. I detached a fragment from a disintegrating corner of the Great Book, and crumbled the flaking parchment into the pot. About her contribution, though, Janny remained tight-lipped.

'It's a secret,' she said. 'I'll put it in later. And you're not to watch. Come on, Nad, time to get ready.'

'Will you come to the dance, Mrs Hedley?' suggested Nadia.

My grandmother smiled faintly. 'Don't be such a silly girl. I suppose it's kind of you to ask, but no, you're not going to see me dancing again. And you youngsters wouldn't want an old woman like me coming along with you. I'd only stop you enjoying yourselves.'

While this exchange was going on, I moved the pot to the coolest part of the stove, settled the heavy lid tightly on top of it, and left the brew to infuse in its own time. My grandmother agreed to keep an eye on it, while I too made my way upstairs to get dressed. As the old lady turned away from me, I noticed that she was smiling again. This time, though, it was a more private kind of smile. As I made my way out into the hall I could hear her, humming faintly to herself.

Entering my bedroom, I discovered, laid out neatly on the bed, the flower-patterned suit that my grandmother and the girls had made for me from the old curtain material. Janny and

Nadia, it would seem, had decided that this was to be my costume for the Maypole Dance.

Scarcely knowing what I was doing, I stepped out of my shoes and, undoing my buttons, allowed all of my outer clothing to drop to the floor. Then, catching sight of my threadbare socks and frayed underwear, I discarded these too and stood naked for a moment in front of the mirror. It seemed for a moment as if I were looking at myself through the eyes of a stranger, as if the body in the mirror no longer belonged to me. Then, wincing at the sight of my bony frame with its protruding hip bones and sprouting tufts of hair, I turned hastily towards my bed and stepped quickly into my new trousers and tunic. I looked in the mirror again. The trousers were rather loose around my hips but fitted more snugly lower down. The legs, slightly too long, fell in concertina-like folds around my ankles. The tunic, tight in the waist but looser around the chest, concealed the narrowness of my shoulders. I raised my eyebrows. On the whole, I was pleased with what I saw. Then, picking up a comb from the dressing table, I started to experiment with my hair, parting it first on the left, then on the right. My long fringe fell across one eye. I brushed it roughly aside with my fingers.

'Ooh Kenny, you look good enough to eat!' It was Janny's voice. I realised with a start that she and Nadia had been watching me from the doorway.

'You startled me! How long have you been there?'

'Long enough, I think!' said Nadia. They both giggled.

'No, really,' Janny continued. 'You look much better in long trousers. You might even turn out quite presentable one day.' I could feel myself blushing. 'Come on,' she said. 'Finishing touches.' They turned around and started to walk across the landing.

I noticed that both girls were wearing their flower-patterned dresses. The bodices fastened at the back, and Janny's top few buttons were still undone, presumably because the cack-handed Nadia had been unable to fasten them for her. Not thinking, I followed them.

Suddenly we were in my parents' bedroom. Nadia sat down on the stool in front of the dressing table. She opened my grandmother's casket and began to spread the ointment on her legs. Janny and I lounged on the bed watching her. It was like watching a scene in a film. Suddenly, I found myself feeling rather light-headed, and it struck me that my spoonful of the magic brew had started to take effect. Then Nadia's voice broke in on my thoughts.

'I will dance better now!' she exclaimed, rubbing the last of the ointment onto her knees. She then handed the ointment to Janny, still sprawling languidly beside me on the bed, who proceeded to anoint her eyes. Then, rummaging in the drawers of the dressing table, Nadia drew out my mother's make-up box, and upended it on the satin bedcover. From inside it there cascaded a jumble of variously coloured sticks of greasepaint, thick ones and thin ones, that my mother had used in her days as an actress. A musty, powdery, faintly oily smell tickled my nostrils.

'Do you think she would mind?' said Nadia.

For a moment I was nonplussed. 'I don't suppose so,' I replied after a moment. 'She used to let me play with it. She made me up to look like an old man once. Lots of lines and wrinkles.'

'Come on then, Nad,' said Janny, seating herself on the dressing table stool. 'We'll do each other first. Then we'll see what we can do for our gorgeous Kenny.' She picked a couple of sticks of greasepaint from the muddle that lay before us.

'What do you think? Number Five or Number Nine?' With unpractised hands, Nadia started to apply a foundation layer to Janny's narrow face. 'Rouge on the cheeks,' demanded Janny. 'Gosh, you can't see my freckles now. And how about some of that blue one on my eyelids? I'll look like a film star!' Nadia fumbled around under Janny's direction until both girls were happy with the effect. 'Your turn now, Nad. Why don't we give you some freckles, since I've lost mine?' I watched while the two of them transformed their young faces into doll-like masks with delicately arched eyebrows and bright red cheeks and lips.

'Kenneth's turn now,' said Nadia. 'Sit down.'

'Let's turn him around the other way,' suggested Janny. 'Away from the mirror. We'll give him a surprise.' So I stared out of the window at the distant fields while the light fingers of the two girls applied greasepaint and powder and rouge to my cheeks. As I sat there, placidly allowing them to carry out their work on me, I started to relax, once again feeling the tingling, soporific warmth of the magic brew. It's beginning, I mused, it's beginning. The magic that will bring Robert back. Soon my High Lord will be with me in Arboria again. I refocused my eyes on the horizon, enjoying the gentle tickling sensation of paint being applied to my face.

'Now you can turn around,' said Nadia at last.

I turned. The face that stared out at me from the mirror was the crudely painted face of a clown, a dead white face with a huge red grinning mouth, panda eyes, broad raised eyebrows and a bright red nose. For a second, I stared at myself. Then I burst into laughter.

'Come on,' said Janny, 'let's do his hair.' She began experimentally gathering my hair into tufts.

'I'll get the ribbons,' said Nadia. She dashed out of the room, returning seconds later with a handful of hair ribbons and a pair of nail scissors.

'Cut the ribbon up,' commanded Janny. 'Cut it into pieces about six inches long. Then you hold his hair, and I'll tie it.' I watched in fascination as Nadia gathered my fringe together in handfuls and Janny secured it with green and yellow ribbons. 'It's a bit long on this side,' Janny observed. 'Give us the scissors, I'll even it up a bit. There, that's better.' A handful of my hair fell to the floor. For some reason I found this very funny and started to laugh again. It's working, I thought, the magic brew is definitely working.

'It looks very good,' said Nadia, when the job was completed to everyone's satisfaction. 'I think I want my hair the same, like Kenneth's. It has grown too long. Many women have short haircuts now. It is more – practical.' Nadia giggled unexpectedly and, still giggling, took my place on the stool. I cut the lengths of ribbon while, once again, Janny gathered the hair into bunches, tied it and trimmed it. By now, all three of us were shaking with fits of laughter.

'Now me,' begged Janny. 'I want to be the same as you. I don't want to be different. I want to be practical too.' This time, Nadia cut the ribbons while I, marginally less ham-fisted, tied the bows and snipped away at Janny's hair. Soon, the bedroom floor was littered with discarded locks, dark brown from Nadia's head, light brown from mine and sandy from Janny's.

'Will you do my buttons, Ken?' said Janny. I leaned down to do as she asked, noticing how thin her neck looked now that it was fully exposed. Between the two unfastened sides of her dress, the vertebrae stuck out sharply beneath her pale, freckled skin. Slowly, I did up the three buttons, allowing myself to inhale as I did so the mingled scents of the greasepaint, her hair and her body. And then at last we were ready, two dancing dolls and a gangling clown, in our flowered costumes, painted faces, beribboned hair and pale, naked feet. We made our way downstairs to the kitchen, where the air was now heavy with the vapour of the bubbling brew. As we passed across the hallway, my ancestors seemed to smile down at us from their frames, while the grandfather clock ticked on impassively.

'It's going to be quite heavy to carry,' Janny observed. She was standing in front of the stove, testing the weight of the pan. 'Maybe it will be easier if we drink a bit more before we go.'

'We should perhaps use gold or silver goblets,' suggested Nadia. She was sitting opposite me at the kitchen table, and the two of us were sorting through the rolls of ribbon that my grandmother had found in her work basket. I was not sure whether she was joking or not.

'I think all the good silver got sold before the war,' I said. 'Mother said that the family was running a bit short of money. But there are probably some ordinary glasses in the cocktail cabinet. You know, that big sideboard thing in the garden room.'

'Let's just make do with these,' said Janny decisively. She had collected three rather ordinary china mugs from the draining board and was scooping generous measures of the brew into each of them. She transferred the drinks to the table and, sitting down with Nadia and me, raised her mug in rather a formal way.

'Here's to a short life and a merry one,' she said, and took a long draught.

'Where did you hear that?' I asked, slightly alarmed. 'It sounds a bit morbid, doesn't it?'

'I'm not sure,' Janny giggled. 'It's just something we used to say.'

I was about to ask her who 'we' were when Nadia broke in. 'Oh, Kenneth, don't be such a wet squib,' she rebuked me. 'A short life and a merry one.' She took a draught of the brew.

'All right. A short life and a merry one,' I said reluctantly. Then I too raised my mug to my lips and drank.

It was as though the world had stopped for a moment on its axis and then started again in a slightly different gear. The brew felt hot on my tongue and cold in my throat. It made my eyes water and my nose tingle. My head felt like feathers, and my feet felt like lead. I looked at the others, and I could see that they too were struggling to assimilate a barrage of conflicting sensations.

After a little while, Nadia lifted her mug again, this time rather unsteadily. 'A night of gods and monsters,' she proposed.

'Gods and monsters,' Janny repeated promptly.

'Gods and monsters,' I said, swallowing with a bit more enthusiasm this time. I could feel the unsettling glow of the liquid seeping through my body, coursing along every nerve, along every artery. My fingers were stroking the edge of the table, and I could feel every twist, every ripple of the grain in the wood. I stared at the table top. Its outline seemed to be shifting, a foreshortened rectangle that was gradually melting into a parallelogram, into a rhombus . . .

'Hadn't we better start making the sandwiches?' I heard myself saying.

'Oh, bother the sandwiches. You can't really be hungry, can you?' I recognised Janny's voice, echoing towards me down a

238

long, swirling tunnel of sound. 'Have you got all those ribbons sorted out for the maypole?'

'Everything is ready.' This time Nadia was speaking. Her accent suddenly sounded stronger than usual. I found myself wondering, for a moment, which country she actually came from. She had never told me.

'Put the ribbons in your pocket, Kenneth.' Rising slowly to my feet, I did as she asked, counting out the rolls of ribbon as I did so. When I got to eight, I began to become confused, and had to put everything back on the table and start again. The girls started to laugh again.

'What's the matter?' I demanded, affronted. 'What have I done now?'

'Nothing, Kenneth,' Janny giggled. 'I think you're doing really well. Come on, drink up. No, let's leave the mugs here. I've put the ladle in the pan.' All three of us drained our mugs and started making our way towards the back door. Janny and I, both around the same height, each took a handle of the big pan, which now felt somewhat lighter than before. We headed out across the vegetable patch with Nadia bringing up the rear.

The garden gate was hanging open when we reached it, and I was startled to see my grandmother standing beside it smoking her pipe. Glancing down at the ground, I noticed that her feet were bare. 'Enjoy yourselves,' she smiled. 'Remember the steps of the dance and you can't go wrong.'

'But I never learned the steps,' I blurted out in a panic.

'Then let the others lead you, Kenny,' she replied. We had passed through the gate now, and her voice was coming from behind us, slowly receding into the distance. 'Let the others lead you, Kenny. Let the others lead you . . .' With the pan and ladle clanking and slopping between us, we stumbled down the path that drew us into the heart of the Arborian forest.

'Slow down!' pleaded Nadia. 'I can't keep up with you!' I realised that Janny and I had accelerated almost to a run. We checked our pace, allowing Nadia to catch up with us.

'Nadia's right,' said Janny. 'There's plenty of time. We've got all night if we need it.' I made another conscious effort to slacken my pace, and so did Janny. We continued at a leisurely stroll and, as we did so, I noticed for the first time that the forest was starting to come alive around us. By now, we had drawn level with the steep path that led up to the ice house, and I could hear that from around us and ahead of us, a growing murmur of voices had begun to arise. In the distance, I could detect the faint, ethereal strains of music and, from beneath my feet, the earth itself had begun once more its slow, deep, rhythmic pounding. I felt my heart quicken as it occurred to me that the Good People had begun to take an interest in our Maypole Dance.

We made our stately way along the shore of the lake, arriving in due course at the waterfall. Here, before I could grasp what was happening, I felt myself drawn towards the threshold of the bridge. 'Where are we going?' I cried out in alarm. 'Where's the maypole? Why are we crossing over?'

'It's all right,' Janny reassured me. 'We've arranged it all with Davy.'

'Davy Hearn, he has matters in hand,' echoed Nadia. 'Davy, he can fix everything.' No longer in control of my legs and feet, I felt myself being borne inexorably across to the far shore of the lake, the forbidden shore where lurked the Barbarian horde. We continued now along unknown pathways. Still uneasy, I was nevertheless borne along by the excitement of the others. The track twisted this way and that, drawing us deep into the heart of the Barbarian land. Everything began to feel different. The trees on either side of us were leaning crazily to one side and the other, and suddenly I could hear more voices in the distance, but this time different voices. These voices were not the familiar voices of our Arborian friends. These were the harsh, mocking tones of the Barbarians, and the Barbarian voices were growing more distinct every moment. The forest rang now with shouts and cries, with threats and with curses. My feelings were in turmoil, panic and laughter struggling with each other like two wrestlers, each one grappling to gain the upper hand.

'Listen to the music!' cried Janny suddenly. I listened. Along with the voices, the music had been growing louder by the second, and now I could hear the tense, bouncing rhythm of an accordion, interwoven with the lithe, sinuous melody of Davy Hearn's tin whistle. Suddenly, the forest fell away to either side of us and we were in a clearing. Encircling us were the wild, distorted forms of the trees, their twisted branches groping menacingly into the turbulent sky. But beneath our feet there stretched a wide, smooth circle of lush turf and, in the centre of that circle, stood the maypole.

It was a long, straight, slender column that must once have been the trunk of a tree, perhaps a tall mountain ash. Its stem was adorned with intricate symbols and, as I drew closer to it, I could see that these were the same runic symbols that I had found in the oldest parts of the Great Book and on the walls of the underground tunnel. This time, though, the angular, writhing forms of the runes appeared, not in flat black and white, but carved in deep relief and richly decorated with every colour in the paint box. Tentatively approaching it, I skimmed its surface with my hands, allowing the crisp peaks and deep troughs of the carvings to caress my palms and fingers. As its magic seeped into me through my fingertips, I found myself hugging the pole more tightly. Looking up, I could see that its summit was ringed about with a circle of large, intricately worked brass hooks. I became aware of the chanting voices around me. 'The ribbons,' they seemed to be saying. 'Where are the ribbons?' Suddenly, startlingly, I felt a hand thrusting itself into my trouser pocket. Involuntarily, I pulled away.

'It's only me,' said Janny. 'What ever did you think? We need the ribbons now.' I allowed her to feel around for them in the depths of my pocket but, as she did so, I could also feel myself beginning to react to her touch in a way that embarrassed me. She seemed to be spending longer than necessary on her task. 'I think that's the lot,' she said finally, with a grin. Then, turning away from me, she seized the maypole with both hands, and suddenly hoisted herself up. Moments later, she was far above my head, her pale hands and feet gripping the sides of the pole as she climbed, her long, lean arms and legs carrying her upwards with swift, unconscious co-ordination. I watched in bewilderment as she settled herself at the top and, leaning forwards at an alarming angle, began to fasten the ends of the ribbons to the brass hooks. While she continued with this task, I wandered away and took stock of my surroundings.

Towards the far side of the clearing, a small log fire was burning, and on top of this stood the iron pot that contained the Saint George's Brew. It was hot now, and a dense vapour was rising from its surface. Around this fire, people had started to cluster. I recognised the tall, fair figures of the Arborians and, mingling among them, the darker, stockier forms of the Barbarians. Hostilities seemed, for the moment, to have been suspended. There must have been plenty of brew in the pot, because cups were being passed around and everybody seemed to be having their share. A little way away, an olive-skinned man with a thick moustache was sitting on the stump of a tree with a small accordion across his knees, squeezing out a rollicking jig. This, I realised, must be the Italian prisoner, Gabrieli. Beside Gabrieli stood Davy Hearn, accompanying him on his pipes. Davy was naked to the waist, wearing nothing but a dark pair of knee breeches that clung tightly to his flanks and thighs. Around his head, twisting in and out of his dark, curly hair, he wore a garland of wild flowers. When he saw me, he narrowed his eyes menacingly, then dropped me a wink. Confused, I turned away, only to find myself face to face with Janny, now safely back on solid ground.

'Time for the dance,' she smiled. 'Here's your ribbon, Kenny.' She passed me the end of a red ribbon which, I could see, was dangling down from one of the hooks at the top of the maypole. Clutching it as I had been told, I took a few steps backwards, only to find myself standing in a broad ring of people. Each of us was holding on to one end of a ribbon, and the other ends of the ribbons were attached to the top of the pole. It was rather like the framework of an enormous tent, although there seemed to be far more ribbons than I could remember seeing on my grandmother's kitchen table.

For a moment, there was silence. Then Gabrieli played a brief salute on his accordion and the Maypole Dance began.

As the dancers around me poised themselves for their first steps, I found myself rooted to the spot, my mind a blank, my feet paralysed. Then a voice behind me whispered, 'Turn to your right,' so I turned to my right, only to be faced by someone hurtling towards me holding a green ribbon. Quickly,

I ducked down under the ribbon and, as I straightened up again, someone else appeared, this time clutching a blue ribbon. I raised my ribbon, and the other dancer ducked down beneath it.

At last, I understood what was required of me. For a brief, vertiginous moment, it seemed as though I were perched on top of the maypole and could see the whole intricate inter-weaving of the dancers and the ribbons taking place far below. All at once, my own fragile strand in the pattern became clear. Suddenly, my feet were carrying me forward of their own accord, twisting and ducking among the other dancers, plung-ing like the black fish in the lake, my ribbon plaiting and unplaiting with countless others. As the music grew louder and louder, and our steps grew faster and faster, our bodies were brushing closer and closer together with each other. Janny's narrow figure came flying past me, her mouth open wide in a yell of delight. Now I caught a glimpse of Nadia's broader form as she threaded her unsteady way in and out among Arborians and Barbarians, her eyes shining with excite-ment. Now I could see Davy Hearn, his pipes abandoned, his garland of flowers streaming out wildly behind him, his bare torso glistening with sweat. I could see Tommy Pelling too, faithful Tommy, threading his solitary path amongst the dancers, his narrow silver ribbon weaving its way into the multicoloured canopy that was beginning to take shape above our heads.

Suddenly, the end of my ribbon flew out of my hands, and I realised that the pattern was complete. The interlacing colours had wrapped the stem of the maypole in a motley garment that bore the trace of every dancer's steps, that bore the record of every skip and every hop, every dive and every twist. From all around the clearing, there erupted a wild outburst of clapping and cheering. There were other people out there, I realised, other people who had come to watch the dance. I stole a glance in the direction of the onlookers. It was dusk now, but I could still make out the dim forms among the trees, because each one of them, man, woman and child, bore with them a pale blue, luminous globe and the globes, between them, cast a spectral, shifting blue light around the fringes of the clearing.

I stared at them, entranced. After a time, I noticed that two of the figures among the watchers stood straighter and more dignified than the rest. There was a tall, bearded man, and a slim, graceful lady. On this night of nights, Lord Owen and Lady Margaret had come with the Good People from the caverns beneath the earth to look on at the Maypole Dance.

The music had stopped a few moments earlier, but now it suddenly started again, louder and faster even than before. I had time for just one more glimpse of the Lord and Lady before I found myself whisked back into the dance, unfettered by the interlocking grid-work of the ribbons, free now to go wherever and however I pleased. The next time that I had a chance to look, my two stately guests were no longer there.

By this time, night had begun to advance, but the circle of little lamps around the edge of the clearing was now lighting the way more brightly, both for the dancers and for the watchers. My belly fired by the Saint George's Brew, I flung myself wildly into the throng, the swirling tide of the dance bearing me around and around, now this way, now that, I was no longer conscious of who I was or why I was there. Catching glimpses of the faces of my companions, I found myself growing uneasy. During the Maypole Dance, the other dancers had been ablaze with joy, but now all at once they seemed threatening, their features distorted by cruelty and derision. One twisted face after another swam into view, leering crazily at me before lurching on its way. 'Kenneth thinks he can dance,' they seemed to be taunting me. 'Kenneth thinks he can dance.'

The ground began to sway under my feet, and the surrounding trees tilted dangerously under the darkening sky. Tripping over recumbent bodies, I stumbled on, narrowly missing the embers of the log fire. I saw Davy Hearn staggering towards me, his dark face twisted into a leer. Suddenly he threw his body forwards, kicked his legs into the air and, upside down now, danced a few swaggering steps on his hands. With a sickening lurch of horror, I realised that his lower half was clad, not in worn black breeches, but in long, shaggy fur. Suddenly, before my eyes, he spread his legs wide apart, treating me to a startling, grisly view of his private parts. No sooner had I seen this than Davy somersaulted over to land on his feet in front of me. His garland had slipped away from his head now, and I could see that from his forehead, there sprouted two small horns. I turned and fled, shrieking, into the forest.

The derisive laughter of Davy and the others rang behind me as I ran wildly in whatever direction my legs would lead me. Branches reached out to claw at my clothing, writhing tangles of roots clutched at my ankles. Unearthly shrieks and howls assailed my ears from every direction. Suddenly I found myself stumbling across the rocks that overlooked the lake. I pulled myself up short, just in time to avoid a ducking, and paused to collect my wits. My heart was pounding like a pneumatic drill but, as I gazed out across the waters, my composure gradually began to return. In the far distance, I could still hear the music of Gabrieli's's accordion. In the half-light, the water shimmered with a dim, phosphorescent glow. Beneath its surface, I could make out the shadowy forms of the black fish, circling and dipping in their own mysterious dance. For a moment, I found myself alone in an oasis of calm.

One fish was swimming towards me now, a fish that seemed suddenly much larger than the others. I watched it as it approached. Then I realised that it wasn't a fish. It was a woman, a naked woman. Or, at least, it was a woman from the waist up. Because instead of legs, she had fins and scales and a tail. Suddenly, the creature turned over onto its back. With a start, I recognised the inverted features of Nadia. 'Come in the water, Kenneth,' she crooned at me, 'come in the water.' For a moment, her face seemed suspended in space. Then, with a rippling laugh, she plunged back into the depths, her arms windmilling above her head, the scales glistening on her breasts and hips.

Panic-stricken, I turned around and started to run again, heading back this time towards the clearing where the dance was taking place. At the meeting of two paths I hesitated, feeling torn now, unable to decide between the terrors of the clearing or the horrors of the lake. All at once, a figure dropped lightly down from a tree, barring my way. It was a girl, a girl of about my own height, a girl wearing a flower-patterned dress, with crudely applied makeup on her face and coloured ribbons in her jagged cropped hair.

'Hello, Ken,' said Janny. 'Why are you in such a hurry?'

My body glowed with a massive surge of relief. 'Thank goodness it's you,' I mumbled. 'I saw – at least I thought I saw . . .' My legs started to give way beneath me. Janny took my arm and guided me towards a small, dim glade, where I was able to rest against the solid trunk of an oak tree.

'Poor Kenny,' Janny murmured. 'What a night you've had. But you're safe now.' It dawned on me that her face was very close to mine, much closer than I might have expected in the course of any normal conversation. I could see the lights and patterns of the dance reflected in her eyes, their red rims forming miniature frames around the tiny, swirling images. For a moment, it seemed that I was once again watching the black fish as they circled in the lake. Then I realised that Janny was still talking. 'Yes, you're safe now,' she was repeating in a whisper, 'Kenny and Janny are safe now.' She brought her face closer still, until I could feel her lips inquisitively brushing mine. I could smell the greasepaint that she wore and, intermingled with it, another, riper, sharper smell. I found that I was quite enjoying the mixture of sensations.

'There,' said Janny. 'That's better, isn't it?' With the tip of her tongue, she started to trace a row of little circles among the hairs on my top lip. I had to admit it, it did feel better. Now her tongue was starting to follow the outlines of my mouth in further, intricate detail. Gently at first, then with increasing potency, the tiny, moist, flickering exploration was unleashing charges of electricity in me, lightning bolts that were suddenly scorching through my flesh like fire through a timber-framed building. I could feel her hands now, working their way down my sides, starting to investigate the front of my trousers. My head was spinning and, lower down, my body had started to respond in a manner that was impossible to disguise. Moaning softly, I allowed her to continue.

Suddenly, I felt a heavy hand on my shoulder, felt someone dragging Janny away from me. By this time, though, her touch had set me on a course from which there was no turning back. Quite unequal to taking in this new intrusion, I sank to my knees until, a long moment later, I came, with a shudder, to my senses. Then, horribly embarrassed, I looked up. Standing in front of me, soberly dressed in a plain grey suit, was my brother Robert.

'Oh, for God's sake, Ken,' he barked impatiently. I noticed his eyes straying downwards. 'You are such a disgusting little brute. What the hell do you think you're playing at?'

'It's the Maypole Dance,' I managed to stutter. 'Didn't you come through the clearing? Didn't you see all the people dancing?'

'I don't know about that,' snapped Robert. 'All I saw was a pack of silly kids larking around like idiots. Christ, Ken, I do worry about you sometimes. Now come on, let's go back indoors and get you cleaned up.' He seized me by the elbow and marched me back towards the bridge.

And that was the end of the Maypole Dance. On the way back to Hedley House, though, it struck me that perhaps, in an unexpected way, the dance had managed after all to work some of its magic. I may have been intoxicated, I may have been terrified, I may have been humiliated but, despite all this, my dearest wish had been fulfilled. My brother Robert, the High Lord of Arboria, had returned once more to his people.

## Eight

# THE CRAGS AND THE POOL

*I* must seem pretty ridiculous to you, Jamie. A crazy old man with a long beard, a tin helmet and the faded remains of a pair of flower-patterned pyjamas. A crazy old man screaming abuse from the top of a tree. You'll probably think I'm even more ridiculous when I tell you that I'm now actually living in the tree. It's the only safe place left, so I have moved into the House in the Air, and I have taken Tommy Pelling with me, and the Great Tree is our home now. You can't see Tommy, I'm the only one who can see him and, even to me, there's hardly more than a faint outline visible.

After those two officious council women had been to inspect Hedley House, I started to get quite a lot of letters from Tollcester District Council. I threw them all away, of course, and I didn't read them. This was probably a mistake, because later on something called a Deferred Action Notice arrived. I didn't understand that either, so I threw it away too. After that, I had a couple of letters from Robert. I didn't open them – I stopped opening his letters years ago – but I could see that it was his handwriting on the envelopes.

Well, today I made my patrol of Arboria as I always do, and

everything seemed normal. I could hear Janny weeping in her usual place, and I could hear Nadia splashing about in the lake, and I could even hear the sound of Davy Hearn's old tin whistle drifting along on the breeze. On my way back from the bridge, I could see that the tree-felling was still going on on the patch of land between the Great Tree and the Tollcester Road, so I avoided going that way. I took the short route and made my way back past the ice house to the garden gate. I had my usual struggle getting across the vegetable patch – I don't know why I still call it that, it's been completely overgrown for the best part of fifty years. Then, when I arrived at the back door of the house, I discovered that, while I was taking my walk, someone had been there. And I couldn't get into the house, because someone had nailed a couple of thick wooden planks across the door.

When I saw those planks, I felt a horrible surge of panic well up inside me. I ran round to the kitchen window and I couldn't get in that way either, because someone had nailed a big sheet of board over it. Then I ran on to the next window and, sure enough, that one had been boarded up too. I made my way right around the house, and every window and door was boarded up, even the windows on the top floor, even the windows in the disused wing where nobody had been for years and years. My heart was pounding furiously. When I got to the front door, I found a notice nailed there saying that the property had been condemned and that nobody was to go inside it.

Of course, I had known for quite some time that people wanted me to leave Hedley House. The council wanted me to leave, the property developers wanted me to leave, even my own family wanted me to leave. Robert has let me stay here since the end of the war but, for the last fifty years, I have lived here alone. I suppose I have always known in my heart that, one day, the family would be forced to sell Hedley House. Well, they might want to get me out, I told myself, they might want to get me out, but they'll have to wait till I'm dead before they do. It's my home, it's the only home I've ever known, and I'm not going to give it up without a fight.

So here I am living in a tree in the forest. It's not so bad up here. The years have been quite kind to the House in the Air. There's still enough of a roof to keep me dry, and there's still enough of a floor for me to get a fair night's sleep. There's a windowsill where Tommy can perch, and I've still got my old binoculars, so I can keep an eye on everything that's happening.

If I chose to look towards the Tollcester Road, I would be able to watch the men cutting the trees down. I prefer to look the other way, though, so that I can ignore what they are doing. When I look the other way, I can see right across to the lake, and beyond the lake I can see the Barbarian land, and beyond the Barbarian land I can see all the way to the purple mountains in the far distance. Through the gaps in the trees I can see what's left of the bridge. I can see the rock where Davy Hearn used to sit and catch the black fish, and I can even see the place where Nadia used to dive into the water. And, when I think about Nadia diving into the water, I start to remember what happened on the day after the Maypole Dance.

By the time I awoke that day, the morning was well advanced. My flowered tunic was twisted uncomfortably around my shoulders, its buttons unfastened. On the floor, my trousers lay in a crumpled heap and my helmet had been abandoned upside down. Cautiously I sat up in bed. I didn't seem to have a headache or any other sort of pain but, as I cast my gaze about the room, I noticed that the colours of the wallpaper and the eiderdown seemed somehow paler and more washed-out than usual. Surprised at this, I looked again at my discarded trousers and I could see now that the pattern on them, too, had become more subdued, less vivid than it had been the previous night. Even the uncompromising black of the curtains seemed more like a medium grey.

Puzzling over this, I first sat up on the edge of the bed and then eased myself to my feet. This operation did not present me with any difficulties but, as I walked the few steps necessary to retrieve my clothing, I had the feeling that my feet were not connecting very firmly with the floor. Having made myself as respectable as I could manage, I stepped out on to the landing and made my way down to the kitchen. It felt as if I were floating down the staircase, drifting through the air in an unsettling new world of muted colours, of muffled sounds, of weightless movement through space.

When I arrived in the kitchen, I found Robert and Janny sitting at the big table with a pot of tea and a round of toast. Robert was wearing his grey suit and tie, while Janny was still in her nightclothes. Of my grandmother, there was no sign. Robert gestured at me to join them. 'Help yourself,' said Janny. Her words seemed to echo distantly towards me as if from some faraway place. After the events of the previous night, I had been hoping that she would show a bit more interest in me.

So I sat and I drank and I ate. The tea was almost flavourless and, as I chewed on a mouthful of toast, it seemed to dissolve into nothing in my mouth. Unable to meet Janny's eye, I stared out of the window. The sky and the bushes and the trees looked like a watercolour painting that had been allowed to fade in the sun. The whole world had become insubstantial, a shimmering veil that now barely concealed whatever grim reality lay beneath.

'What's happened?' I blurted out. 'Where's everything gone?'

'You need to get yourself in hand, Ken.' Robert was speaking to me. 'Are you really sure you wouldn't be better off staying with me at Magnus and Dottie's place? You're really becoming quite . . .'

'I'm happy here,' I blurted out. 'I'm happy in Arboria. It's just my eyes. Everything seems a bit . . . pale.'

'Try some of this,' suggested Janny. Her tone was brusque. There was no acknowledgement of what had passed between us. With an effort, I looked over to see what she was showing me. Across the pale, scrubbed surface of the table, her white hand was sliding the small casket that contained her special ointment. Suddenly, my eyes were riveted on that casket. Alone among all the objects in the room, it had retained its colour. In the misty wash that bathed my surroundings, it had become a hard, bright, sharp focal point. Cautiously I stretched out my hand, allowed my fingers to connect with its gunmetal surface. It felt solid, smooth, still slightly warm from Janny's touch. With a fingernail I prised open the lid. Beneath the slick, glossy surface of the ointment, I could make out a multitude of tiny lights, pale blue pinpoints that seemed to dance around each other in endless warp and weft. Their dance reminded me of the lights that I had seen reflected in Janny's eyes, of the black fish that swam in the lake . . . Fascinated, I stared into the casket, drawn into its depths as if by some irresistible magnetic force.

After a time, I realised that Janny was talking to me. '. . . on your eyelids,' her voice was saying. 'Not too much. And then a bit on the tips of your ears . . .' I did as she bade me. For a moment, the ointment stung my eyes and ears painfully. Then, slowly, the colour and the sharpness began to return to my vision. '. . . and rub what's left into your hands . . .' she was saying. I could hear her much more clearly now and I couldn't help noticing that her tone carried more indifference than compassion. But, as the ointment started to seep into my skin, I found myself becoming aware once more of the cold tiles beneath my feet, of the hard kitchen chair pressing into my thighs. I noticed that my two companions were staring at me.

'That's better,' I said finally.

'Thank heaven for that,' said Robert. 'Lord knows what was in that muck you were drinking last night.' At that moment, the clock in the hallway began to chime. 'Anyway, Magnus said he'd pick me up at eleven. We're going to be busy. We've got all sorts of things to do. Keep in touch, Ken. And Janny – try to keep him out of mischief.' He glanced at her anxiously, then rose abruptly to his feet and left the room. Alone again with Janny, I felt suddenly uncertain.

'Janny, about yesterday,' I began hesitantly.

'It doesn't matter,' she interrupted me. 'It was nothing. It was a stupid mistake. Forget about it. I have.' And with that she too rose to her feet and left the room.

I thought briefly of going after her but decided, on second thoughts, to give her a little time to herself. I finished my breakfast and dumped the dishes in the sink. My grandmother would attend to them later. Then I went back to my room and lay for a while on my bed, staring at the impenetrable calligraphy in the Great Book. After a while I realised that I wasn't taking in any of what I was reading, so I shoved the scroll aside and went back down to the kitchen. Nobody was about. For a moment I hesitated. Janny's casket of ointment, I noticed, was still on the table. Without quite knowing why I did it, I picked it up and slipped it into my pocket. Then I opened the back door and headed out across the vegetable patch and through the garden gate.

Arboria felt rather subdued that afternoon. Tommy was still fast asleep in the log store, his snores echoing faintly from its murky depths. The Arborians, I guessed, would still be asleep in their tree houses, recovering from the exertions of the previous night. The air was calm, the branches were unmoving, even the animals and birds seemed quieter than usual.

As I walked, I started to sift through the previous day's events in my mind. Had all those things really happened, I wondered, or had it all been a result of too much strong brew on an empty stomach? Had I really seen Nadia swimming like a mermaid in the lake? Had I really witnessed Davy Hearn's shocking display of acrobatics? And, if I could find my way back to that clearing, would I still find the maypole standing erect at its crux, would I still find the coloured ribbons woven tightly around it? Had I really danced with the Arborians and the Barbarians? Had the Good People really been there looking on? Had I really seen Lord Owen and Lady Margaret? Or had Robert been right in his accusation? Had we just been a bunch of silly kids larking about?

Unable to answer any of these questions, I started instead to relive my encounter with Janny. I could still taste her tongue on my lips, I could still feel the touch of her hands at my sides, and I was still reeling from that other sensation, that overwhelming tide of warmth and confusion and shame that I had not wanted to come. But still it was me that she chose, I told myself. I'm still the one that she wants. I'm still the one that she was waiting for. The two of us are soul mates. We were made for each other. Given a little more time, she's bound to understand that.

As I pondered on this, my thoughts were suddenly interrupted by the sound of splashing and shouting. There was someone else about after all. I realised that my feet had carried me down to the side of the lake, and that someone was swimming in the water. I scrambled down the bank, threaded my way between the willow trees and seated myself on a dry stretch of bank, where I could get a clear view of what was happening.

The swimmer, I could now see, was Nadia. She was no longer wearing fins and a tail, but was clad today in a more conventional black bathing costume. I watched her as she swam up and down the length of the lake. Her streamlined form was slicing cleanly through the water, leaving scarcely a ripple behind her. The shadows of the overhanging trees formed a shifting pattern across her shoulders. From time to time she turned over in the water, swimming now on her front, now on her back, now on her front again. The wet costume clung to her body, displaying a figure that, I couldn't help noticing, seemed rather more mature than when I had first glimpsed it. So, at least that part of last night's events had been real. I realised that Nadia had not noticed me so, abandoning for the time being my thoughts of Janny, I sat back and allowed myself to enjoy the spectacle.

But the entertainment was destined to be short-lived. A moment later, I was annoyed to discover that I was not the only person watching from the banks of the lake. On the far shore, Davy Hearn was sitting in his usual place. In his hands he held his whistle and, although the mouthpiece was some way away from his lips, I could see that his fingertips were bobbing restlessly over the holes in the stem as if they were making some secret, silent music for his ears alone. Davy too was watching Nadia as she swam up and down, his face turning slowly to the left, and then slowly back to the right. For a moment, our eyes met. He gave me a very slight nod of acknowledgement, smiled a small, mysterious smile, then turned his attention once more to the girl in the water.

Uneasy now, I rose to my feet, with the aim of moving to a more secluded spot but, as I turned around to walk along the shoreline, I caught sight of Janny. She too was sitting on the bank, a little way away from me. She sat in a hunched position, her pale knees drawn up against her chest, her thin arms hugging her shins. Unlike Davy, though, she was not turning her head from side to side. Her eyes were not following the girl in the water, but instead were riveted upon the boy on the far bank. I made my way along the water's edge and sat down next to her. Perhaps this was my chance to put matters right.

'Hello,' I said. 'I was just taking a walk.'

Startled, she twisted around to look at me. Her expression was somewhere between alarm and disgust. Her eyes were looking very red and I could see that she had been crying again. 'Kenneth,' she said. 'Please leave me alone.' With a loud, liquid sniff, she stood up and moved away from me, settling herself a little further along the shoreline. Once again, I decided not to follow her. Give her time, I thought, give her time.

So there we all stayed. Nadia swam up and down, up and down. Janny hugged her knees. Davy fingered his tin whistle. And as I shifted my gaze from one of my companions to another, I began slowly to understand what was really happening to the four of us.

After a while, I noticed something else that I had not seen straight away: a small but significant detail. On the far bank, on the flat rock next to where Davy was sitting, lay a small, colourful, neatly folded bundle. At first, I could not identify it but, after a time, it dawned on me that it was Nadia's flower-patterned summer dress.

Nadia, I realised, had undressed for her swim on the Barbarian side of the lake.

The weeks and the months that followed these discoveries were a lonely time for me. I badly wanted to talk to Janny about what had happened on the night of the Maypole Dance, but she continued to avoid me. When she did speak, her utterances were monosyllabic. She stopped coming to Arboria and, before long, she didn't even seem prepared to stay in the same room as me. She didn't ask for her ointment back, and I didn't feel inclined to offer it to her. I reasoned that, when she needed it, she would have to talk to me once more. But, for some reason, she never mentioned it again. I realised that she was spending a lot more time out of the house. I had no idea where she was going and what she was doing, but I was pretty sure that she wasn't going to school. After a while, I managed to persuade myself that I no longer cared.

With Nadia, on the other hand, I remained on speaking terms, and Nadia remained a regular visitor to the forest. I soon noticed, though, that her purpose in going there was no longer the same as mine. She had never been particularly happy running or climbing or sitting in the tree house so, once we had passed through the garden gate, we tended to go our separate ways, Nadia taking one path and I taking another. As often as not, I noticed that Nadia would make her halting way down the track that led to the lake. She told me that she spent her days diving and swimming in the water. I didn't doubt this for a moment, but I couldn't help suspecting that she had also started to take more than a passing interest in Davy Hearn.

Tormented by these suspicions, I started to avoid the lake altogether, and instead took to spending most of my time at the House in the Air. Light-headed from my scanty diet of jam sandwiches and raw carrots, I spent hour after hour puzzling over the Great Book, searching obsessively for the answers to the questions that continued to gnaw away at me. Who were the Good People? What were they doing down there in those caves? What did they want from me? Arboria and the Great Book were like an addictive drug, so that the more time I gave to them, the more time I wanted to give. On some days, I became so engrossed in my mystical world that I was scarcely able to find my way back to Hedley House. On such days, the garden gate would loom threateningly at the top of the track, a grim harbinger of the dreary world that must one day take the place of my magical kingdom. From time to time I noticed Tommy Pelling watching me from his place on the sill, but it seemed that Tommy had nothing more to say. He just stared at me with his big, sad eyes. One day, even Tommy stayed away, and I found myself utterly alone. I was feeling wretched that day, wretched and abandoned. Weary of wrestling with the mysteries of the Great Book, I put it aside, sat back against the hard wooden wall, made myself as comfortable as I could, and allowed my eyes to close.

It was just then, just on the cusp between waking and sleeping, that I heard the music. It was a different music, but I didn't realise that straight away. It started, as it so often did, with the slow, deep, pulsating rhythm that echoed from the caves beneath the earth. Slowly at first, then with greater urgency, the rhythm established itself, a rhythm that grew in intensity, a rhythmic call that demanded a response. I found myself waiting for an answering phrase from the trees or from the water but, when the answer came, it was not at all what I had expected. It was more like a challenge than an answer. It was a jagged, contrary statement that cut brutally across the deeper rhythm, a statement that asserted a logic and a metre of its own. More voices joined in then, contrary voices, each voice fighting its own corner, and I found my attention being tugged now this way, now that, unable to apprehend a nodal point, unable to cling on to anything that would bring the jarring sounds into focus. The music swelled quickly into a hideous cacophony that had no harmony, no sense of purpose. It's like an argument, I thought. No, it's worse than that. It's like a war. It's as if the Good People were fighting among themselves.

Involuntarily, I rose to my feet. I was shaking all over. My breath was coming in quick gasps and the skin felt clammy. I clapped my hands over my ears, but I could still hear the noise, I could even feel it through the floorboards under my feet. 'Stop it!' I cried. 'Stop it! It's horrible! You're tearing Arboria apart!' I dashed to the doorway, swung myself hand over hand down the ladder, raced for the garden gate. I stumbled as I ran, my feet unsure of their ground, my hands clamped over my ears to defend me from the terrifying din. I tugged the gate open, blundered through it, kicked it shut behind me.

The music stopped instantly, and I collapsed to the ground. I felt weak, exhausted, confused. Every limb was aching and there were tears in my eyes. Once again, the colours around me seemed pale, the sounds muted. Gasping for breath, I reached into the side pocket of my trousers. My fingers closed around the casket that contained Janny's ointment.

'Janny hates me,' I moaned to myself. 'Janny hates me.'

All that winter, I saw nothing of Robert. It seemed that the print works and the knicker factory were occupying all of his time. What little news I had of him was brought, on his fleeting visits, by Uncle Magnus. The print works, finally established in its new premises, was continuing to produce propaganda leaflets in regular, bulky consignments. The knicker factory, meanwhile, was being fitted with new machines for stitching parachutes, and it was this operation that had been keeping my uncle and my brother busy for so long. As it turned out, there were still a number of technical hitches, and it wasn't until the following spring that the parachutes were finally in production.

It was shortly after that Uncle Magnus arrived at Hedley House with his mysterious parcel. 'Hello, Kenny-boy,' he boomed. 'Got a little something here. Is your gran at home?' Curious despite myself, I showed him into the kitchen. I tapped at the door of my grandmother's parlour and, rather to my surprise, she emerged to join us.

'Hello, Mrs H.,' said Magnus. 'Nice to see you. How are you keeping?'

'I don't get out so much these days,' the old lady complained. 'We're none of us getting any younger. And it's so hard to keep warm, what with all these shortages.' Magnus nodded in agreement as he eased his tweed-clad bulk into one of the rickety kitchen chairs.

'Just as well we cut down those railings when we did,

though,' he remarked. 'No, no, don't bother with the kettle, Mrs H., I shan't be here for long. I just wanted to drop this off.' He indicated the parcel, which now rested at the far end of the long table. 'You've probably heard on the wireless, it seems that Mr Churchill's government has finally decided to requisition all the ornamental ironwork. They've got men going up and down all the streets cutting down people's railings and taking them away. They're going to melt them all down to make guns or bombs or whatever. Toni would have turned in her grave if we'd let them take those gates. She had a bit of a soft spot for the gates, you know, and for the railings. Because of the old Hedley crest, I suppose.' For a moment he stared out of the window, seemingly lost in thought. Just then, though, my grandmother deposited the heavy tea tray on the table.

'Won't you stay and drink a cup now that you're here?'

'Oh, Mrs H., you shouldn't have,' said Magnus. 'Still, now that you've made it . . .'

'Where did you hide them?' I broke in. Magnus looked bewildered. 'The railings,' I persisted. 'Where did you hide them when the men cut them down?'

'Never you mind, young Kenneth,' he replied with a wink. 'Careless talk costs lives, don't you know? Anyway, I daresay you'll find out in good time. Can't see this war lasting much longer now that the Yanks are on side.'

'Got any gum, chum?' Nadia had arrived at the back door, her hair still dripping from her daily swim. The American forces had been setting up an air base just the other side of Tollcester, and their servicemen had arrived in England with generous supplies of chewing gum, Lucky Strike cigarettes, nylon stockings and catchphrases. The catchphrases, at least, had penetrated as far as Upper Helsing.

'You want to be careful, young lady,' said Magnus sternly. 'A nice-looking girl like you can't afford to go about asking for trouble.' He eyed her up and down for a moment in what seemed a rather wistful way, then, realising that everyone was looking at him, he took a hasty gulp of tea. 'I'd better give you what I've come to give you,' he spluttered, 'and then I'll be on my way.'

'What is in it?' Nadia had joined us at the table and was inspecting the parcel, running a speculative finger along the knotted white string that secured it.

'Why don't you open it and see?' Magnus suggested. 'Don't cut the string, though. I'll need to take that away with me. Make do and mend, that's what they're saying nowadays.'

Nadia's fingers had already started to worry away at the knots in the string, struggling to tease them apart with her closely chewed nails. My grandmother and I looked on.

Finally I could wait no longer. 'Go back under again, then try pulling the end,' I blurted out.

'It is coming,' Nadia replied distractedly. 'Be patient, Kenneth.' An instant later, the final knot came apart, the string slipped to the floor, and the brown paper parted with a crackle to reveal what lay within.

It was a stack of folded cloth, pale and slightly shiny in appearance. Freed from the restraining influence of its wrappings, the pile started gently to collapse, layer slithering over layer as gravity asserted itself. Nadia reached out quickly to rescue the escaping pieces. Gently, she touched one to her cheek. 'It feels lovely,' she breathed. 'So smooth. Is it silk?'

'Parachute silk,' Magnus agreed. 'Well, it's the off-cuts, actually. They're too small for us to use, so we're giving them away. Thought they might come in handy for your needlework or whatever. Some of our ladies use it for making, er, well, you know . . .' He broke off in embarrassment.

'Petticoats,' my grandmother said. 'Such lovely silk petticoats we used to wear before the war.' Once more, I caught myself wondering which war she meant. She had unfolded one of the pieces of silk and was running it through her hands. It was of a generous size, but its shape was irregular and awkward. 'Such beautiful stuff. I could make you a petticoat, Nadia. Or how about a nightgown? Do you have anything nice to wear in bed? I don't suppose you've had a new nightgown since before the war began.'

'A new nightgown,' Nadia echoed wistfully. 'My nightgown has worn out entirely. For such a long time there have been no new ones.'

I was just wondering whether I would be allowed to have a new pair of silk pyjamas when Janny appeared at the door. Her hands were thrust deep into the pockets of her green raincoat and her jaw was champing rhythmically and rather noisily at something in her mouth. I realised after a moment that she had managed to get hold of some chewing gum. I wondered if it had come from one of the Americans at the Tollcester air base.

As usual, I half-hoped that she would meet my gaze but, as usual, she avoided me. 'Hello, all,' she said. 'Hi, Magnus. What's that you've brought? Parachute silk?'

'Will you have a cup of tea, Janny?' suggested my grandmother.

'No thanks, Mrs Hedley, I'm just going to put some stockings on, then I'm going straight out again.' She reached across the table and stroked the silk with her fingertips. 'Are we all getting new knickers? We'll have to be careful they don't fall down.

Slippery stuff, that parachute silk!' She disappeared in the direction of her bedroom.

Nadia hastily covered her mouth, trying, unsuccessfully, to suppress a fit of giggles.


I was slowly becoming resigned to my solitary life in Arboria, without the High Lord or my other companions, when Robert finally made a visit to Hedley House. He was wearing, as he always did now, his office suit and tie. At the back door he hesitated, and I realised that he was waiting to be invited in.

'Would you like a cup of tea?' I offered reflexively.

'Don't let's bother about tea,' he replied. 'Look, Ken, there are things we need to talk about. It's a fine day. Let's go for a stroll.' I followed him back into the garden, and we began to walk slowly along the flagged terrace in the direction of the French windows. I noticed that there were quite a lot of weeds sprouting between the flagstones. Robert noticed as well. 'That gardener's boy is hardly pulling his weight,' my brother observed. 'What's his name, Danny? Denny? This place is starting to go downhill.'

'Davy,' I prompted. 'Davy Hearn. He doesn't do so much in the garden these days. I suppose I could ask—'

'Look, Ken, I didn't come here to talk about the garden,' Robert interrupted me. 'Well, no, in a way I suppose I did. But it's not just the garden. It's Hedley House too, it's Gran, it's everything. I just don't see how you're going to cope with it all, just the two of you.'

'We've got Nadia here to help us, and Janny as well.' Robert seemed to have forgotten about our two house guests. 'Although Gran's not very quick on her feet any more . . .'

'Ken, those girls are just evacuees. They'll be going home

any day now. They can't stop here, not once the war's over, and that's not going to be very long. Can't you see that the place is starting to get run down? Maybe you don't realise it, but Magnus and Dottie have been paying out of their own money to keep Hedley House going; they've been paying all the bills. And they've still got to run the factories, plus shelling out for their own house. You can't expect them to keep doing it for ever.'

'Magnus doesn't seem bothered.' I was trying to resist what I knew was coming. 'He was here only the other day. He never said anything.'

'Magnus still thinks you're coping. He doesn't really notice things. And he doesn't know you like I know you.'

We had by now arrived at the front wall that adjoined the Tollcester Road. From the brickwork of the wall, the stumps of the railings protruded, their sawn-off ends now dull with rust. We stood side by side between the two stone columns in the space where the tall iron gates had once hung, at the very spot from which we had waved goodbye to our parents those few short years ago. The sign board that I had painted on the day of their funeral was hanging askew now, dangling crookedly by one nail. For a moment I stared at a spider spinning her web across the corner of it. Then, looking back at the house, I noticed that the paint on the front door had started to peel, and that several of the window panes were cracked.

'I'm nearly eighteen now, Ken,' said Robert. 'I'll be getting my call-up papers any day. I'll have to go off and fight. It could be anywhere in the world. I might not even come back. You're only fifteen. You're still a boy. I know you've got Gran, and I know that she's your legal guardian and all that, but she's getting frail, and she's getting forgetful, and she's not going to live for ever. I just want to make sure that you're going to be OK.'

'I'll be OK,' I replied, trying to show more confidence than I felt. 'We all will.' The two of us started walking again, heading in the direction of the disused wing. How strange, I thought. Robert's my brother, isn't he? But now he's behaving more as if he were my father. He's even talking like an older person. He's been spending too much time with Magnus. I kicked out at a clump of tall nettles that were growing across our path.

We walked on in silence, and I noticed that, although Robert must by now have reached his adult height, I was an inch or two taller. My face was starting to display the first unruly sproutings of a moustache and beard, but my brother's face, I observed, was sternly clean-shaven. I shrugged self-consciously, suddenly aware of the tightness of my old v-neck pullover around my shoulders, of the pinch of my disintegrating sandals. As we approached the rubbish heap, I steered Robert carefully away from the place where I knew the German bomb still lay waiting to explode.

'Ken, I've got to ask you this,' my brother began. 'Although I know what you're probably going to say. But I'm going to ask you anyway. I want you and Gran to come and live with Magnus and Dottie. While I'm away, at least. Please say you'll think about it.' We had stopped walking once more. Robert turned to face me. I could feel tears in my eyes.

'I can't, Rob. It's all this . . .' I gestured in the direction of the forest. From where we were standing, we could see the mass of trees that grew behind the garden wall. We walked on around the next corner, until the vegetable patch and the branches of the Great Tree came into view.

'Arboria?' Robert said quietly.

'Yes. Arboria,' I replied. 'I belong here, Rob. Don't you see that? I belong to Arboria, and Arboria belongs to me. You and I, we both used to be a part of it once. And I can never leave it, never, even if you think *you* can.' Before I knew what I was doing, I realised that I had been leading him across the vegetable patch and up to the garden gate. I stood with my hand on the latch, while Robert held back a couple of steps.

'Don't you remember?' I pleaded. 'Tommy Pelling? The Arborians? The Barbarians? I'm still the Keeper of the Great Book, you know. I still study it every day. And, Rob, you're still the High Lord. We want you to come back. We're your people. All of us.'

'Oh, Ken, what's going to happen to you?' My brother sounded close to despair. 'Don't you understand? All that stuff was a game, a kids' game. It was just make-believe. But I've grown up now, and so have you. You can't go on believing it for ever. People will think you're mad. The girls probably think you're mad already. Haven't you seen the way they look at you? You're going to destroy yourself. If you don't leave here soon, you'll end up being carted away in a brown van.' I did not reply to this, but I could not meet his eye. I was staring at the latch on the gate, my vision misted now with tears.

'Very well,' said Robert finally. 'I've said my piece.' He paused for a moment. 'Look, Ken, I may not be able to come again for a while. There's so much work to be done at the factory before I get my call-up. But if you change your mind, or if there's anything you need, anything at all, you're to get in touch with Magnus or Dottie or me. Will you promise me you'll do that?'

'All right,' I said. I hesitated before continuing, then took a deep breath and plunged on. 'Rob, there is one thing. And I promise I'll never ask you again. But please come to Arboria with me, Rob. Come now. Just this one last time.'

I still couldn't look at him, but I could hear him giving a long sigh.

'Oh, Ken, Ken, Ken,' he said finally. 'You know I'll come. But this time really has got to be the last time. Do you promise?'

'I promise.' I turned and started to run back towards the house.

'Where are you going now?' Robert called after me.

'To get the binoculars,' I shouted. 'And we'll need the bows and arrows too. I think the Barbarians are preparing for a big attack.' I returned a few moments later to find Robert still in his place. It was a warm day, and he had taken off his jacket and tie and was waiting for me in his shirt sleeves and braces. I handed him his bow and a quiver full of arrows. Then I opened the gate and beckoned him through.

As we passed by the log store, I could see Tommy Pelling staring out at us. After a long, inquisitive look, though, he withdrew once more into the gloom. For one reason or another, he did not want to join our expedition. Very well, I thought. It looks as if I'll be taking charge again. Sure enough, as we strode off down the track, I found that I was setting the pace, while Robert hung back a couple of steps behind.

'Come on,' I encouraged him. 'The Barbarians won't wait for us, you know.' From the direction of the lake, I could already hear the tramp of their feet, the clatter of their spears. 'They're going to attack the tree houses,' I called to Robert, who was now several paces to my rear. 'We'll have to get to the Great Tree and muster the army.'

'Oh yes,' I heard Robert reply. 'The Arborian bowmen. Do you still see them? And what about Tommy Pelling? Do you still see him too?'

'Of course I still see them. And didn't you see Tommy just now? I don't think he's very well, though, he didn't want to come out today. But I expect the bowmen will be along in a minute.' I could hear the clatter of the Barbarians' feet in the distance now as they marched over the bridge. They were marching into Arborian territory! Nearer at hand, though, I could hear the rustle of undergrowth, the zing of bowstrings, the rustle of flights as the Arborian bowmen assembled among the trees, readying themselves for the attack. And, far below us, down the steps at the back of the ice house, down in the deep caves at the heart of the earth itself, I could sense the murmur of the Good People, as they too readied themselves for what was to come.

'We're nearly there now,' I called back over my shoulder. 'We've got to defend the Great Tree at all costs. Look, the rope ladder's ready. Do you want to go up first?' Cautiously, Robert placed a foot on the bottom rung of the ladder, testing its strength before he started to climb. In the forest, the Barbarians were drawing nearer. 'Quickly, quickly, they're nearly here!' I was dancing from foot to foot in exasperation, anxiously watching Robert as he ascended the ladder. He seemed unfamiliar with the task, his movements awkward and painfully slow. I waited until he had reached the first platform, then I too started to climb. Of the two of us, Robert had always been the natural athlete, but I realised with a shock that I had now overtaken him, not only in height, but in strength and agility too.

As I climbed, I heard something hiss through the air and

thud into the trunk of the tree. Beside me, a spear had buried itself in the living wood, its shaft quivering angrily. The Barbarians must be even nearer than I had imagined! Why weren't the Arborians shooting back? I hastened to reach the safety of the branches.

We tumbled through the doorway of the House in the Air, feeling it sway giddily on its ropes. I waited until it had steadied itself, then I seized the binoculars, crossed over to the window, crouched down and looked out. The bushes on the ground were shifting and rustling as rank upon rank of Barbarian warriors strode through the undergrowth, the points of their spears rearing fiercely up above their helmeted heads. Wildly I looked this way and that. In every direction, ranks of warriors were converging on the House in the Air! Where was the Arborian army? Alarmed, I turned towards Robert. He was standing in the far corner of the room, stooped forward and breathing hard. 'Quite a climb,' he panted. 'I must be out of condition.'

'Robert,' I wailed, 'what's happened? The Barbarians are here! Where are the Arborians? There must have been an ambush! There's just the two of us against the whole Barbarian army!'

'Just you and me against the world?' my brother replied. 'So this is it? What do you want me to do, then?' I stared at him in disbelief. The very roots of the Great Tree were vibrating now with the tramp of the enemy's feet, but the valiant troops of the Arborian army were nowhere to be seen. Perhaps they were lying dead somewhere, with spears buried in their backs. We were in the most desperate of situations, and the High Lord was asking *me* what to do!

'Shoot!' I screamed, panic-stricken. 'Shoot them, Robert,

before they kill us! Shoot! Shoot! Shoot! What are you waiting for?'

'Right-ho,' he replied. 'I think I'm OK again now.' Seemingly unconcerned about the fate of Arboria, my brother nevertheless crossed over to one of the windows and loosed an arrow randomly into the air. Meanwhile, I was firing shaft after shaft, and each shaft flew straight and true into the heart of a Barbarian warrior. One after another, the enemy fell. Still they kept coming but, as they came, I was ready for them; and now, as Barbarian after Barbarian screamed and died, the Good People began to sing to me, and their song, stern and dark, was dense with bitter satisfaction at each death. As the song swelled in volume and in power, so too did my arrows fly faster and straighter, each one unerringly striking its mark, until the blood of the enemy formed a huge red pool on the forest floor below. Robert fired another lackadaisical shot. 'I think I got one that time,' he remarked, although his tone lacked conviction. He frowned. 'I say, what's all that noise?'

'It's the Good People!' I replied. 'Don't you know them? They're singing their hymn of victory!' I continued my barrage of fire, my quiver bottomless, my bowstring vibrating joyously as each shaft sliced through the air into its target. 'We're going to win, Rob, we're going to win!' But, as yet another volley of arrows soared, as the sombre music of the Good People grew ever louder and ever deeper, my brother no longer looked as if he was in any state to win anything. Glancing towards him in alarm, I was just in time to see him drop his bow. He staggered back from the window, sinking to his knees, his hands pressed tightly over his ears. For a moment, I feared that he had been hit but, a moment later, I realised that it was not a Barbarian spear that had felled him.

'What's going on?' he gasped. 'What's that horrible noise? Is it those kids with their pots and pans again? Can't you get them to stop?' His face had gone a deathly white, his mouth was hanging open and his eyes were bulging. Anxiously I shouldered my bow and knelt at his side. 'What's happening?' he panted again. 'What are we doing here?'

I grasped his shoulders. He felt suddenly small and frail, and he was trembling violently. 'Oh God,' he continued. 'Can't you get that racket to stop? What's happening to my eyes? I can't see! What have you done to me?'

I reached into my side pocket for Janny's ointment. Thankfully, it was still there. 'Here,' I said to him, 'try this.' I dipped a finger into the casket and applied the salve to his eyelids. At once, his face tightened, and his breathing seemed to quicken. Then he gave a sudden roar of pain.

'What is that stuff?' he howled. 'It's burning . . . it's like . . . I can't . . .' Panic-stricken now, I stared at him helplessly as he clutched at his eyes. 'You've got to get me out of here, Ken,' he moaned. 'Get me home. Get some cold water in my eyes.' I stood back in horror as he groped his way to the door, fumbled at the top rungs of the ladder, began his clumsy unseeing descent into the hurricane of Barbarian spears. How could I defend him against the onslaught of this unruly mob? There was only one thing for it. Seized by a sudden inspiration, I drew a grubby handkerchief from my pocket and waved it frantically at the horde below.

'Man injured,' I cried. 'Ambulance party! Make way!' The fusillade of spears abated, and the song of the Good People ceased abruptly. As we began to descend, the whole forest held its breath. I followed Robert down the steps until we reached the final length of rope ladder. Heart in mouth, I waited on the

274

platform with my flag, watching him swaying helplessly to and fro until, at last, he loosed his grip and landed with an undignified bump on the forest floor. Respectful of the white flag that I bore, the Barbarians hung back, I swung myself down and hastened to my brother's side.

'Try some more ointment,' I suggested, reaching in my pocket for the casket.

'No Ken, I've had enough,' he groaned. 'Can't we go now?'

So, watched by rank upon rank of silent Barbarian warriors, I helped my poor sightless brother to his feet, I offered him my arm to support him, and I guided him gently back along the track that led to the garden gate. As we limped the last few yards, though, a great savage cry suddenly broke out from the Barbarian ranks, and a volley of spears came whistling past us. One of them glanced off my right shoulder but, thankfully, my High Lord was spared further hurt.

By the time we reached the kitchen door of Hedley House, Robert's sight had begun to return to him. Irritably shrugging away my arm, he blundered through the jumble of coats and sticks that littered the porch and staggered across to the sink. Slumped against the cracked glaze of its side, he ran the tap and clumsily splashed cold water into his eyes, overturning the piled-up dishes in the process. A stack of enamel saucepans toppled from their place and landed with a crash on the kitchen floor. Disturbed by the commotion, my grandmother emerged from her parlour and hobbled towards us.

'What have you done to yourself, Robbie?' the old lady fussed. 'Come along. Sit down.' Stooping over him, my grandmother made a careful inspection of his injuries, prising his eyelids apart with her tobacco-stained fingers and dabbing at the corners with the hem of her handkerchief. Finally satisfied, she straightened up. 'You really must be more careful what you put in your eyes,' she said, fixing the two of us with a piercing glare. 'And you, Kenny, you must be careful what you give to people. Some medicines are much stronger than others.'

She extended a hand towards me. For a moment, I didn't understand what she meant. Then her meaning dawned on me, and, reluctantly, I reached into my pocket for the casket of ointment. She glanced at it with a sniff, then tucked it away somewhere beneath the folds of her apron. Then, without another word, she turned away from us and started to make her halting way back towards her parlour door. Robert waited until the latch had clicked back into place.

'My God, Ken,' he burst out finally. 'I'm not even going to ask what that stuff was. And I don't want you to try and explain all those noises in the woods either. Or any of the other weird things that you've been getting up to. I've got just one thing to say to you, and it's this: I'm not having anything more to do with Arborians or Barbarians or poisonous brews or invisible arrows or maypole dancing or bloody fairies either! I keep telling myself that I'm too old to believe in it any more, but sometimes it all begins to seem just too real again. I never thought I'd hear myself saying this, but it really scares me now, the whole lot of it scares me rigid. What would happen if we all let ourselves keep believing it? It just frightens me to think that you're getting yourself mixed up in something so crazy, so dangerous. So if you want to keep playing at it, then fine, that's up to you, but from now on I wash my hands of the whole shooting match. From now on, Ken, you're on your own.' He paused to catch his breath after this tirade. 'And, for Pete's sake, get that shoulder bandaged up. You're dripping blood everywhere.'

I glanced down at my shoulder. Sure enough, it was oozing blood from where the Barbarian spear had slashed it. But, before I had even had time to reply, Robert rose abruptly to his feet and strode from the room. A moment later, I heard the rapid tread of his feet on the stairs, followed by the banging of his bedroom door. I looked again at my bleeding shoulder. Robert was right, I thought. I'd better get this bandaged.

Slowly, I forgot the wounding force of Robert's words. One morning a couple of weeks later, I was lolling on my bed studying a passage in the Great Book. I was clad in my favourite costume for this pursuit, namely my flower-patterned trousers and tunic and Robert's ARP helmet. I had located a passage in the scroll that explained the uses of the special ointment, and I was starting to feel that I finally had the subject within my grasp. *'The Eyes of a Mortal Man or Woman'*, I read, *'will become Tender and will start to Weep when they look upon Things that they are not Permitted to See. The Ointment that is kept in the Black Casket . . .'*
At that moment though, my line of thought was interrupted by a loud knock at the front door of the house. Swearing under my breath, I tried to ignore it, assuming that someone else would eventually answer the call. I tried to shut my ears to the noise and concentrate on my study. *'The Eyes of a Man or Woman of the Good People, on the other Hand . . .'* I realised that the knocking was getting louder. I could no longer disregard it. Janny and Nadia had both gone out, it occurred to me, and, from behind her parlour door, my grandmother probably hadn't heard the noise at all. Abandoning the scroll, I hastily belted on my dressing gown and padded downstairs to investigate. I threw open the front door. Standing on the step was a soldier in khaki battledress and beret.

'Can I help you . . .' I began.

'Ken,' said the soldier. Belatedly, I recognised my visitor as Robert. Behind him, framed by the two lonely gateposts of Hedley House, a car stood waiting, the idling note of its engine drifting towards me in the early summer haze.

'I've only got a minute,' Robert went on awkwardly. 'I thought I'd better let you know. My papers have come, sooner than I expected, actually. The car's waiting for me now. I just wanted to say—'

'You can't go!' I interrupted him. 'When will you come back? What are we going to do?' To my surprise, a hollow sensation of panic was starting to spiral up from the depths of my belly.

'I don't know, Ken,' said Robert. 'You and Gran are going to have to look after things now.' His outline appeared blurred, and his voice boomed distantly across the gulf that separated us. 'Look, Ken, I want you to remember all those things I said when we took our walk the other week. I'm not going to be around for a while, but Magnus and Dottie are still here. Just remember that you can call them if you need to. Or if things get too much for Gran.'

'Magnus and Dottie,' I repeated faintly. In my rising consternation, I could think of no suitable reply. Suddenly I became aware of the awkward weight of my headgear. I loosened the strap, removed the helmet and held it out towards my brother.

'Do you need this?' I said haltingly.

'Oh Ken, it's only a stupid helmet,' he snapped. 'Of course I don't need it.'

I stared down at it. 'It was Dad's,' I said slowly. 'Then it was yours. And now it's mine. Are you sure?'

'I expect they'll give me a new one,' Robert replied. Slowly, I replaced the helmet on my head. For a moment, time hung suspended, each second seeming like an hour. Then the car that was waiting in the lane pipped its horn. 'Look, I've got to go,' said Robert suddenly. 'Duty calls and all that.' He extended his right arm towards me and, rather awkwardly, we shook hands. 'Say goodbye to Gran,' he added. 'And Ken . . .' For a moment, I thought I could detect a crack in his firm voice. '. . . for Pete's sake, don't do anything daft.'

We stared at each other. Then he turned sharply on his heel and marched briskly down the drive towards the waiting car. I waited until the car had driven away, then I closed the front door of Hedley House and made my way slowly down the corridor towards my grandmother's parlour. As I approached the doorway that led to the kitchen, time seemed to stretch ahead of me in an infinite, empty expanse. The perspective of the corridor twisted and curved before my eyes, the cold soundless tiles absorbed the tread of my bare feet like cotton wool, and the portraits of my ancestors stared inscrutably down at me. From within each cracked frame, a pair of eyes followed my progress. Entering the kitchen, I nearly lost my balance, and had to cling to the edge of the long table for support. Clumsily, I fumbled my way around it. My grandmother's door, I noticed, was open, her wrinkled face peering anxiously out.

'Who was that?' she asked me. 'It sounded like Robert.'

'Robert's gone,' I said. 'Robert's a soldier now.'

'Kenny . . .' she began, but I didn't want to stop and talk to her. My feet were drawing me, pace by unsteady pace, in the direction of the kitchen door. Frantically I stripped off my dressing gown, tossed it among the coats and jackets that hung in the porch. Then, tightening the chinstrap on my helmet, I stumbled out of the door and across the vegetable patch, clawing like a drowning man for the latch that secured the garden gate. Arboria was calling me as it had never called me before. Nothing could be allowed to stand in my way.

Tearing open the gate with trembling hands, I set off at an unsteady jog past Tommy's hut and down the track. Downhill I raced, my bare feet picking their way among the roots and brambles, my equilibrium miraculously reasserting itself after every stumble. The trees and rocks and flowers around me formed a jouncing, jarring, swirling background to my headlong dash. As I ran, I wondered whether any Barbarian warriors might be lying in ambush. I could only trust to luck. On and on I ran, past the ice house, past the Great Tree, down now to the bank that fringed the western shore of the lake. Because somewhere I could hear music, somewhere I could hear a faint, thin, trickle of music, and the music was drawing me inexorably onwards.

I skidded muddily down the slope and lurched to an ungainly halt between two of the willow trees that fringed the water. A moment later, the jarring colours and blurred shapes of the forest juddered to a halt too, the lakeside view jolting into crisp focus and vivid colour as I paused to recover my breath. I gazed at the scene before me, allowing myself to take in what was happening.

On the far bank, directly opposite to my position, sat Davy Hearn. The music that had drawn me, I now realised, was coming from his tin whistle. It was a strange, angular, unearthly melody, a melody that seemed all twists and corners. Davy's gaze, I noticed, was directed not at me, but towards a spot further along his own bank.

Following the direction of his eyes, I realised that Davy was watching Nadia. Unable to avert my eyes, I looked at Nadia too.

She was standing on top of a high rock, facing out across the water. She was clad in her black bathing costume, and I could not help noticing the contrast between her slender legs and her powerful torso. As I watched, she took a deep breath, swung her arms back behind her, then seemed to topple forward into space. Suddenly, in mid air, her body straightened up into a sleek, streamlined form that hung suspended for a moment, then plunged in a straight, clean dive into the water. A moment later, her dripping head broke the surface and she struck out once more for the shore. As she scrambled back up the rocks, Davy continued to play on his whistle, the weird angles of his melody forming an unsettling counterpoint to the girl's breath-taking athletic display.

This time, Nadia climbed higher, her strong arms doing most of the work as her frail legs scrambled for purchase. I watched in silence as she positioned herself once again, finding her way to a higher rock that overhung a deeper stretch of water. Again, she stood in silence for a moment, her wet body gleaming. Then once more she plunged forwards, once more she hung suspended in space, once more she entered the water with hardly a ripple. And once more she swam the few strokes back to the shore.

And now Nadia was climbing up to the highest rock of all, up to the tall rock that overlooked the deepest part of the lake, the tall rock that overlooked the place where the black fish went to sleep at night. Mesmerised, I gaped at the stir of muscles beneath the glistening sheen of her costume; entranced, I shielded my eyes as she stood, at last, silhouetted against the morning sun. I could make out her shape, the curves of her hips and her waist, the jagged outline of her untidy hair. I could not see the expression on her face but I knew, somehow, that she was aware of the two pairs of eyes that looked on admiringly, longingly, hungrily. Suddenly I became aware of my own excitement, shafting up from the depths of my being like a deadly blade.

Once more, Nadia dived. She could only have been in the air for a second, but it seemed like an eternity, an eternity during which the whole universe was focused upon this sleek, beautiful, plunging girl, an eternity frozen in time while two earthbound boys looked on enthralled. Davy's music ceased mid-note, as his lips parted in wonder.

I had expected the girl once more to enter the water like an arrow piercing a target, but this time it was different. This time, Nadia's body seemed to collide violently with the surface of the lake, as if her flight had been broken by a solid stone floor. There was a thud and a splash and a sudden disjointing, followed by a scream, followed by another scream, this one prolonged and piteous. My jaw dropped in horror and incomprehension as Nadia's limbs thrashed frantically, as her body writhed in distress, as her mouth gaped open in sudden pain and fright. Wildly, I turned and raced along the shore. Surely Davy will help her, I told myself as I clattered over the wooden bridge. Surely Davy will know what to do. But when I arrived panting at the place where he had been sitting, Davy Hearn was nowhere to be seen. Nadia was still in the lake, though, her struggles feebler now, her cries weaker. The water that surrounded her was turning an ominous red.

I plunged into the lake and, half-wading, half-swimming, struck out towards the stricken girl. Seconds later, I was at her side. 'Try and keep still!' I shouted. 'Try and keep still!' But Nadia took no notice. Her arms clutched spasmodically at my neck; thick blood bubbled from her nose and mouth. I grasped her shoulders, tried to pull her free from whatever was holding her, but, try as I might, she seemed to be stuck fast. So, treading water, I felt my way along her shuddering body, trying to discover what it was that had trapped her. And then I found it. Something was protruding from the small of her back, something long and hard and sharp. Panic-stricken, I continued my frantic search, supporting myself all the while by treading water. Here was a second spike, and a third. More blood was coming from these wounds. I could see it seeping into the water in slow, regular spurts. Nadia's movements had all but ceased now, her screams little more than a thin, hopeless wail. I ran my hands around the girl's waist, trying to identify what it was that had pierced her. Then, suddenly, I knew. Between two rocks, wedged upright beneath the waters of the lake, was a length of sturdy, spiked iron railing.

Hopelessly I looked on as Nadia's struggles dwindled to nothing, helplessly I was forced to listen as her cries faded at last to silence, as the last bubble of blood burst with a splash on her lips. Finally, she was still. Nadia Skolomowski had died in my arms, impaled on the sawn-off railings that my Uncle Magnus had thrown into the lake.

Slowly, the full horror of my situation dawned on me. I was up to my armpits in mud and blood and water with a dead girl who was stuck fast and who couldn't be moved. A jumble of confused thoughts came chasing suddenly into my head. I don't know what to do, I thought. I'll have to tell someone. But, if I tell someone, I'm going to get blamed. They'll think I killed Nadia. They'll think that nobody's looking after me properly.

I won't be allowed to stay here, I'll be put in an institution, I'll be taken away from Arboria.

All at once, I knew what I had to do. Taking a deep breath, I ducked down under the water, feeling this time for the base of the railings, trying to discover how they had become wedged in position. One end, I could now tell, was stuck fast in a cleft in the rocks, entangled in pond weed, half-buried in mud.

My lungs bursting, I abandoned my task and broke surface, gasping for air. Nadia's form lay limp now, her head face-down in the water, her limbs splayed out starfish-like. I took another breath and plunged down again, this time making for the other end of the railing.

This end didn't seem to be wedged. It was resting up against something that felt like the rotting branch of a tree. I let my hands explore it. It didn't seem to be stuck too tightly. Now, if I could just get my hands underneath . . .

Suddenly the branch shifted and the railings started to topple towards me, then settled again, this time at an angle in the water. I made for the surface once more, coming briefly face to face with Nadia's staring, lifeless features as I did so. I could see now that the railings had shifted a bit, but not enough. They had become wedged again. Now, though, only Nadia's lower half was visible above the surface, her two white legs thrust into the air like the legs of some macabre acrobat.

I dived once more, this time hoping to free the other end of the railing from the cleft in which it was wedged. I braced my back against the rock, pushing with my legs. The railings shifted by a fraction of an inch. Another gasp of air, another breath, another push. Again the railings shifted a tiny amount. One more try. They shifted again but this time it was more than just a fraction. The railings toppled into the grim depths of the lake, carrying the girl's lifeless form with them. I just had time to scramble out of the way. As the waters closed over Nadia for the last time, one by one the black fish appeared, and began to circle inquisitively around the red stain in the water.

Hurriedly, I scrabbled up onto the bank. My clothes were filthy with mud and blood, my helmet was dented, and I was shaking all over. The High Lord was gone from Arboria, and now the Good People had exacted their retribution. But Nadia was safely hidden, and nobody need know what had happened to her. Davy Hearn would know, of course, but Davy, I sensed, had reasons of his own for remaining silent. So at least I was safe now. All I needed to do was to work out what I was going to tell my grandmother.

As I made my lonely way back to Hedley House, I could hear, in the distance, the sound of weeping. As I approached closer, the weeping grew louder, echoing around and around and around. The weeping, I suddenly realised, was going to be with me for the rest of my life. The weeping was never going to end.

*Nine*

# THE IRON DOORS

*N*ever before had I felt so reluctant to return to Hedley House. My feet dragged like boulders on the ground, every second that passed felt like an hour, every step that I took felt like a hundred miles. I could barely muster the strength to heave open the garden gate and, when I reached the vegetable patch, its overgrown tendrils and shoots clung to my wet clothes, dragging me down, holding me back from the task that I had to face. Eventually, though, heart in mouth, I arrived at the kitchen door. My dressing gown still lay where I had abandoned it in the porch, and I pulled it on over my filthy clothes, trying as best I could to conceal my dishevelled state from whoever might be about.

As it turned out, though, I was not faced with any immediate confrontations. The kitchen was quiet and, apart from the unbroken background tick of the grandfather clock, there was no noise from the rest of the house either. Noticing that the door to my grandmother's parlour stood ajar, I peered cautiously through the gap and caught a glimpse of the old lady dozing in her chair. Relieved, I quietly withdrew and tiptoed my way across the hall and up the stairs. On the landing, an inspection of the bedrooms revealed that Janny was not at home. I supposed that she must have been making one of her increasingly frequent visits to Tollcester. Well, I thought, at least I have a little time to clean myself up and to work out what to say to everyone.

I stepped across the landing and into the bathroom, shoved the plug into the plughole of the stained enamel bath and turned on both taps. The Ascot heater shuddered into life with a disgruntled roar, and a thick stream of yellowish water gushed into the bath. Shedding my dressing gown, I stepped into the tub, still wearing my trousers and tunic. Soon, I was immersed up to the neck. I watched the steam rising from the surface of the water, condensing on the windows and on the mirror. It was a long time since I had filled the bathtub up to the brim. Since the beginning of the war, even King George had permitted himself only five inches of water. I watched with mild curiosity as the mud and the blood seeped from my clothes, and the water slowly turned to a murky reddish-brown colour. A frond of pond weed detached itself from my ankle. I plucked it from the water and tossed it into the lavatory bowl.

A little later, having towelled myself down and put my dressing gown back on, I made my way to the disused wing of the house and hung my dripping outfit on a clothes horse in one of the abandoned rooms. Here, I guessed, it would be likely to remain undiscovered for the foreseeable future. Then, returning to the main part of the house, I went into Nadia's bedroom and shut the door. I was not sure what I was going to do, but I knew that nobody must discover that I had been there.

At the bottom of the rickety wardrobe I discovered the small, battered suitcase that Nadia had been carrying on the day she arrived at Hedley House. It contained only a bundle of fading letters in a language that I could not read. I pulled open the drawers of the small chest and threw their contents into the case, together with a skirt and a cardigan that had been hanging up. Between the grubby sheets of the narrow bed, I discovered a threadbare nightdress. This too I deposited in the case. Its luxurious silken replacement, it occurred to me, had failed to materialise. There was nothing else in the room. No toys, no books, no photographs. I felt a sudden pang of regret. Nadia had arrived at Hedley House, she had danced in the clearing, she had swum in the lake, and now she was gone. Soon her few pathetic belongings would be gone too. A few childish clothes, a brush and a comb, a bundle of letters in an unknown language. In the chaos of war, the girl's family had vanished and, for nearly three years, not one person had tried to get in touch with her. I closed the lid of the suitcase and headed for the stairs. Every trace of Nadia's presence was going to be eradicated from Hedley House, I decided. I was not going to shoulder the blame for her disappearance.

Janny, it seemed, had still not returned from her outing. In the kitchen, I peered once more around the door of my grandmother's room, hoping to find her asleep. But, at the sound of my tread on the threshold, she stirred in her chair and opened her eyes.

'Kenny,' she mumbled, 'is that you? Is that your dressing gown you're wearing?'

For a moment, I felt as though my heart had stopped beating. 'I was just having a bath, Gran,' I improvised frantically. 'I thought I heard you calling. Is there anything you want?'

'Could you put the kettle on the stove?' she said. 'I might make a cup of tea in a little while. But I'll shut my eyes again first, for a few minutes. I've got a headache just now, Kenny.

Perhaps we can have a little talk later on.' She closed her eyes and, a moment later, she was asleep again. I let out a long, relieved breath. Thank goodness she hadn't noticed the suitcase, I said to myself. Thank goodness I didn't have to come up with a story about that. I filled the kettle, carried it over to the stove, and placed it on the hotplate. Then, clutching the case, I set out once more towards the garden gate.

Luckily for me, my return journey to the lake was unobserved. I would certainly have struggled to explain why I was taking a walk in the forest in my bare feet and my dressing gown, carrying a small, cheap suitcase.

The forest was silent. Not a bird or an animal stirred, not a leaf or a twig rustled on a branch. There was no trace of the Arborians, no trace of the Barbarians, no trace even of the Good People. It was as if the whole of Arboria was in mourning for Nadia. Just once, I caught the briefest of glimpses of Tommy Pelling, perched above me on the branch of a tall ash tree but, when I looked again, he was gone. At any rate, I knew that, even if he had seen me, even if he had seen Davy, even if he had seen Nadia's final, fatal plunge into the lake, faithful Tommy would never have given me away.

When I crossed the bridge to the far side of the stream, there was still no sign of the Barbarians, and no sign of Davy Hearn either. I scrambled up to the place on the rocks from which Nadia had been diving. Her brown sandals still lay there side by side, her summer dress still lay there neatly folded. I opened the case and thrust the clothes inside. Then, scouting quickly around, I picked up seven or eight large stones and laid them on top of the other things. Then I closed the lid of the case, crammed it shut and jiggled the two catches into place. Then I clambered up to the high place on the rocks from which Nadia had made her last dive, and I hurled the suitcase into the empty space that yawned before me. For a moment, it spiralled through the air. Then, with hardly a splash, it struck the water and sank instantly. A few bubbles broke the surface, and then all was still. For a moment, I half-wondered whether the black fish might put in an appearance but, as it turned out, there was no sign of them.

I turned around and started to make my way back towards the bridge. Now that I had taken care of Nadia's things, I told myself, I would be able to explain her sudden disappearance. It was simple, really. Once she was here. But now she is gone. As I made my way homewards, it started to rain.

Emerging from the vegetable patch, I was alarmed to see dark wisps of smoke curling up from under the kitchen door. Putting aside all thoughts of the dead girl and her suitcase, I raced inside to find the air dense with stinking black smoke. The kettle that I had left on the hob had boiled dry! Instinctively, I snatched at its handle then, in sudden pain, hastily withdrew my hand. I glanced frantically around, sucking at my scorched fingers, searching for something that I could use. On the rail by the stove hung a couple of tea towels. I grabbed them, wrapped them around the handle of the kettle and tossed it out of the back door. It landed with a very final sounding hiss in the damp vegetation of the vegetable patch.

I looked in on my grandmother and found her still sleeping. There was no sign of Janny. Uncertain what to do, I paced to and fro, ate a piece of dry bread, stared out of the window at the rain, rummaged in cupboards looking for another kettle. But all the kettles, it seemed, had been melted down to make

Spitfires for the Battle of Britain. From now on, I realised, Hedley House would be boiling its water in a saucepan.

Eventually it started to grow dark and I went up to my room. I sat up in bed for a while, scrolling through the Great Book in search of some words of comfort and guidance, while the rain drummed at the windows and Nadia's pale ghost splashed to and fro in the murky waters of the lake. When I awoke late the next day, I found myself still entangled in twisted yards of flaking parchment.

Rain was still falling, and I guessed from the state of the garden that it had been raining all night. For a while I continued my hopeless search through the Great Book until, finally drawn by hunger and thirst, I made my disorientated way downstairs.

As my feet padded down the threadbare stair carpet, my ears caught the sound of the piano echoing up faintly from below, and I realised that Janny must have returned home from Tollcester, although I could not be certain whether she had arrived that morning or late the previous night. Crossing over to the other side of the hallway, I pushed open the double doors and stepped through.

The dusty air in the garden room was ringing with a jarring sequence of unrelated notes. Janny was seated at the piano striking the bass keys in a seemingly random fashion. Their muddy, out-of-tune resonance set up an unsettling vibration deep in the pit of my stomach. For a moment, I stood at the threshold, uncertain what to do. Then, slowly, I approached the piano. Janny looked up at me for a moment, then stared down again at the keyboard. I could see now that she had been crying. Her hair was uncombed and her clothes were dishevelled. Cautiously, I seated myself next to her at the piano bench. To my surprise, she did not move away from me.

'Jan?' I said. She withdrew her hands from the keys, allowed the last note to die away, then turned her face towards me. Her eyes and nose were red, and the grimy traces of tears streaked her pale cheeks.

'Kenny?' she stuttered. 'What's happened to Nadia? All her things have gone.' I took a deep breath. I had a story prepared now. Here was my first chance to test it.

'She had to leave,' I said. 'Her parents came for her. It was yesterday, while you were out. One of the billeting officers was with them.'

'Weren't her parents interned? Shut away in a camp somewhere? A camp for enemy aliens?'

'Yes, that's right,' I conceded. 'They were. But now they've been released. The war's nearly over, I suppose. People are being set free. Nadia packed her things, and she went with them.' For a moment, Janny said nothing. My heart pounding in my throat, I too said nothing. Would she challenge my explanation?

'Poor Nadia,' she said finally. 'I'll miss her so much. We were like sisters, almost. We had so much in common. Didn't she leave a note or anything?'

'They were in a hurry,' I improvised. 'The car couldn't wait. She said she'd miss you too. She said she'd write.'

'I wonder if I'll ever see her again?' Janny mused unhappily. There was another long, intense silence. Then she seemed to rally. 'So I suppose it's just you and me now,' she said finally. 'And your gran, of course. Did she have to sign any papers or anything?'

'Gran was asleep,' I said truthfully. ' I didn't want to wake her. So I signed the papers. And the billeting officer witnessed it, because of me not being twenty-one. It all happened so quickly.'

The girl stood up, crossed slowly to the French windows and stared out across the terrace to where the Great Tree of Arboria towered over the garden wall. Raindrops ran like tears down the window panes. I noticed a wide, ugly ladder in one of Janny's stockings.

'Ken,' she said after a while, 'I'm getting worried about your gran. She always seems to be asleep these days. And when she's awake she's usually got a headache. Do you think anything's wrong?'

'I don't know,' I replied. 'Perhaps we should see if we can get Doctor Solloway to come and talk to her.' I stepped across to stand beside the wraithlike girl at the window. On a sudden impulse, I placed my hand on her shoulder. Irritably, she shrugged it off. For a moment, I expected her to flounce out of the room, but she merely edged a couple of inches away from me, continuing to stare out of the window, her sharply drawn profile outlined against the rain-streaked glass.

'It's best if you don't,' she said. 'Oh, Kenny, I know you mean well, but—'

'It's all right,' I broke in. 'It doesn't matter. What are you going to do today? Are you going in to Tollcester again?'

She shook her head violently, pressed her narrow lips together. I realised that she had begun to cry once more. 'I'm fed up with Tollcester,' she snapped with unexpected vehemence. 'I'm not going there again. I'm fed up with Tollcester and fed up with the Americans. And Kenny, I'm fed up with this war too.' There was a silence before she continued. 'I might go for a walk in the forest. Maybe down to the lake. If the rain ever clears up.'

And so we stood there at the window, together but separated, side by side but not face to face, talking at last but never touching. After a long time, Janny turned back to the piano, sat down on the bench, took up once more her monotonous refrain. Hopelessly, I turned away from her, heading back again towards the other part of the house. We can't call the doctor, I was thinking. If we do, Gran will have to go to hospital. And then we won't be allowed to stop here. If Gran goes into hospital, I'll have to leave Hedley House. And then I'll never see Arboria again. And I'll never see Janny again, either.

The rain continued for several days, and Hedley House remained our prison. Janny, indifferent now to the glittering allure of Tollcester, mooched aimlessly around the house, slouching along the corridors from room to room, staring out of the windows at the rain, sitting at the piano in the garden room hitting random sequences of unrelated notes. While she was doing these things, I could be found slouching along other corridors or staring out of other windows. Sometimes I lounged in my room, continuing my increasingly fruitless scrutiny of the Great Book, and sometimes I called in on my grandmother to make her cups of tea or to complain about the weather. Once, I found myself sitting cross-legged on Nadia's empty, cold little bed. Fearing that Janny might discover me and start to guess at my guilty secret, I hastily withdrew from the room and closed the door. From time to time, I worried that someone might come looking for Nadia, but nobody ever did and, after a while, I found that I was no longer thinking about her so often.

The only place at which my wanderings and Janny's seemed to coincide was the kitchen. We had long ago abandoned the pretence of formal meals at the table, and were by now subsisting on unscheduled snacks of dry bread, or raw vegetables, or jam spooned straight from jar to mouth. From time to time,

Magnus would appear at the door with boxes of groceries and news of Robert.

'Got a letter this week,' my uncle informed us distractedly one day. He was sitting opposite me in the kitchen, his overcoat unbuttoned, his chubby fingers drumming restlessly on the grimy table top. Janny hovered in the background, leaning up against the stove, her arms folded resentfully across her chest. 'He's a tight-lipped bugger, though,' Magnus went on. 'Never says much. Seems that he's in some sort of holding camp, waiting for orders. He's probably heading for Germany, that seems to be where everything's happening nowadays. People are saying that the war hasn't got much longer to run.' He frowned, apparently considering the implications of this, then abruptly changed the subject. 'How's your gran, by the way? Having another one of her little naps?'

'It's probably best not to disturb her,' I began. 'But I'm sure there's nothing—'

'I think she might be quite ill,' Janny interrupted me. 'She never gets out of her chair. And her breathing's getting very noisy. And when she does try to get up, she gets giddy, and she has to sit down again. Do you think we ought to call the doctor?'

But Magnus had already risen, tight-lipped, from the table. He walked quickly across to my grandmother's door, tapped once, and went in without waiting for an answer. After a few moments, the door opened again and my uncle re-emerged. He looked pale and unhappy, and he seemed to have shrunk several inches in height. 'She's not right,' he said at once. 'You should have told me straight away, Ken. We'd better get old Solloway along as quick as we can.' His expression brooked no argument. I glanced across to where Janny stood, but I could see at once that she and my uncle were of one mind. I decided to remain silent. There was nothing for it but to go along with their plans.

Waiting for the doctor to arrive, I paced from room to room more restlessly than ever. What would happen if I was made to leave Hedley House? Would I be adopted? Would I be put in an orphanage? How would I get to Arboria then? Janny noticed my agitation and tried for once to be kind. 'You mustn't worry about your gran, Kenny,' she reassured me. 'I'm sure the doctor will do everything he can.' I nodded mutely. Janny had entirely misinterpreted my mood, but I deemed it wisest not to correct her.

When the doctor arrived, though, the news was better than I had expected; or, at any rate, it was better for me than I had expected. 'I think you're both old enough to understand this,' Doctor Solloway said to us. Janny and I stood side by side in the hallway, meekly awaiting his verdict. The doctor was at the front door, presumably anxious to hurry off to his next appointment. While his right hand gripped his battered leather bag, his left hand was unconsciously fingering the brass door knob. 'Yes, I think you're getting to be quite grown-up now, Kenneth and er, Janet. Mrs Hedley, you see, well, she's getting to be an old lady now and, to be frank, I think she's probably getting close to the end of her time. The best thing we can do for her, I suppose, is to keep her comfortable, yes, keep her comfortable and try not to move her. And I think it would be a good idea if she could stay here, stay at home where things are familiar. Perhaps someone could arrange for the nurse to call, yes, the nurse . . .'

Still muttering about the necessary arrangements, the doctor sidled out of the front door. A few moments later, we heard the dull roar of his car as he drove away. Janny and I looked at each other in silence. 'We can look after her, can't we?' said Janny finally. 'Us and the nurse? And your uncle and auntie, of course.' Secretly elated, I nodded. I was to be allowed to stay at Hedley House. I was to be allowed to stay at Hedley House with Janny. And one day, before very long, Hedley House would become mine. I could stay in Hedley House, and I could stay with Janny, and I could stay in Arboria for ever and ever and ever.

So Janny and I stayed at Hedley House, and we looked after my grandmother. We took it in turns to check that she was comfortable, we took it in turns to change her bedclothes, and we took it in turns to tidy her thin grey hair and to moisten her cracked old lips. She ate little, although she continued to demand cups of her special tea and, from time to time, her pipe. This I would fill, with fumbling hands, from the few sweet-smelling strands of tobacco that still clung to the sides of the old stone jar.

Occasionally, when circumstances forced Janny and me to carry out some small task together, our fingertips might touch briefly. However, if I was expecting the shared burden of caring for my grandmother to draw Janny closer to me, then I was destined for disappointment. Apart from sleeping under the same roof, apart from eating and drinking in the same kitchen, apart from looking after the same old lady, our lives no longer seemed to share any points of contact.

The rain continued for several days then, at last, I woke up one day to find a shaft of sunlight slanting obliquely into my bedroom. As I pulled open the dusty blackout curtains and clambered into my rancid-smelling clothes, I noticed the familiar sound of the piano reverberating distantly through the house. But as I stepped out onto the landing and started to make my way down the stairs, I realised that I was listening, not to the incoherent strumming of recent days, but to a proper piece of music, a piece of music that had both rhythm and melody.

For a moment, I wondered whether it was indeed Janny that I was hearing, but then I recognised the tune. My spirits lifted briefly. It was *Over the Hills and Far Away*, the first tune that I had ever heard Janny play, the tune that I had heard her play on the day when she had refused to go with the family to church, the tune that I had heard her play on the day when Davy Hearn had stepped boldly onto the terrace with his whistle and had joined in with the melody. Now the simple, plaintive song beckoned to me once again, drawing me, step by reluctant step, along the hallway and towards the double doors. Just as I turned the handle, though, the music stopped.

I opened the doors and stepped into the room. The last, haunting note still hung in the air, but the piano bench was unoccupied. I ran my fingertips across the shallow indentation in the worn, padded leather. It was warm. 'Janny?' I called. 'Are you hiding from me?' There was no reply. 'Janny? Jan?' I repeated. 'Was that you that I heard?' Still nothing. I walked slowly away from the piano and, as I did so, I felt a waft of fresh air in my face. At the French windows, the curtains were billowing gently in the light summer breeze. The final strains of the song still hung in the air. And the windows, I now noticed, were standing open. I stepped out onto the terrace, looked to the right, then looked to the left. From the shrubbery, there came a faint rustle of movement. Cautiously, I moved in the direction of the vegetable garden.

As I rounded the corner of the garden room, there came

once more a rustle from ahead of me. All my senses on the alert, I continued in the same direction, tiptoeing past the old part of Hedley House, past the kitchen and my grandmother's little parlour. Then I spotted the movement again, coming this time from the direction of the garden gate. Ears and eyes wide open, I began gently to push my way between the overgrown stems of cabbages and Brussels sprouts, drawn inexorably in the direction of Arboria. Moments later, when I reached my goal, I found the gate hanging open. As silently as I could, I stepped through.

'Master Kenneth?' Tommy began, but I had no time even for Tommy. As I made my way along the track, I could feel the forest stirring all around me, welcoming me back into its heart, welcoming me home. The undergrowth was alive with movement, the air crackled with the whisper of voices, the very ground vibrated beneath my feet. Following now a footprint, now a scent, now the twitch of a branch, I started to walk faster, hurrying along the track, rushing past the narrow path that led up to the doors of the ice house, breaking into a run as I rounded the bend above the waterfall and finally came in full view of the lake. Borne along now on tumbling rapids of dread, I raced down the path that skirted the lakeside, careering helter-skelter towards what I knew awaited me at the bridge. My gaze was riveted on the ground ahead of me, absorbing every clue, negotiating every obstacle. Each breath seared through my lungs like red hot wire; the shaggy tops of the willow trees flew past beneath me. At the spot that overlooked the bridge, I juddered to a halt, hands on knees, gulping for breath, eyes still fixed on the ground, not daring to look up because, in some curtained recess of my mind, I already knew what I was going to see. At last, I forced myself to raise my head. Yes, sure enough, there were two people standing on the bridge, and those two people were Janny Grogan and Davy Hearn.

I knew at once that they had not seen me. They were standing face to face, less than a footstep apart, and Janny's two slim freckled hands were clasped in Davy's larger, brown ones. Janny, shorter by half a head, was looking up into Davy's face, while Davy looked down at Janny. The roar of the water obliterated whatever words they were saying, but I did not need to hear any words to tell me what was happening. As I watched, the two distant figures drew closer together. Davy's arms reached out to encircle Janny's slender body and, at the same moment, Janny dropped her head and buried her face in Davy's shoulder.

'He's giving her a hug to comfort her,' I told myself. 'Janny's still sad about Nadia, and Davy is giving her a hug. There's nothing wrong with that.' But, unable to avert my gaze, I found myself biting my lip in apprehension. Then, as I looked helplessly on, Janny slowly lifted her face towards Davy, and Davy slowly tilted his head down towards Janny, and suddenly their lips were touching and their arms were clutching at each other's bodies, and then even I could see that what Davy and Janny were drawing from each other was something more than mere comfort.

With a groan, I spun around and started to run back in the direction from which I had come, longing desperately to take myself away from the thing that I had seen, longing desperately to take myself to some place where it had never happened, to some place where it had never been. I staggered as I ran, my knees scarcely able to bear my weight. My blood thumped like a cannon, deadening my hearing, and tears flooded my eyes, blurring my vision. As I ran, tidal waves of rage and hatred and envy surged through my heart, sharp mocking voices echoed around my head, the very ground seemed to throb in fury beneath my feet. Unbidden by my conscious self, my legs carried me back up the slope, back around the bend in the track, back past the doors of the ice house, back through the garden gate, back into the house and back up the stairs to my room. I slammed the door and threw myself on the bed. But the spiteful voices continued to reverberate around me and, far beneath Hedley House, the earth continued to pound. The Good People are angry, I said to myself. The Good People are angry and they're going to have their revenge. They're going to have their revenge, they're going to have their revenge, they're going to have their revenge . . .

After a time, I started to feel calmer. I sat up shakily at the edge of my bed; I reached down to straighten my socks; I felt for a handkerchief to clean up my face; I fumbled under my pillow for the reassuring bulk of the Great Book. But still the image of Janny and Davy's kiss lingered before my eyes. I could see once more the moment at which that first, tentative contact had started to turn into something fiercer, something more purposeful. I saw it again, and again, and again, like a neverending loop of film. My ears were numb with the roar of the waters, and with the vicious chatter of the voices, and with that vengeful, relentless pounding from the deep caves at the heart of the earth.

As that moment continued endlessly to repeat itself in my mind's eye, the truth dawned slowly upon me. I had known it all along, I realised; I had surely known it since that moment, all those years ago, when the narrow thread of Davy's melody had started to insinuate itself so gently into the warp and weft of Janny's harmony. Now, at last, I understood that the two of them, Janny Grogan and Davy Hearn, shared something between them, something that was special to the two of them, something that I could never have in common with them. Because Janny and Davy, I now knew, were both children of the forest, Janny the spirit of the air, and Davy the spirit of the woods. Both of them would find their true home here in Arboria, while I, no matter how hard I tried, could only ever truly belong in the grim corridors of Hedley House.

Just as these thoughts were taking shape in my mind, I became aware of another presence in the room. Sure enough, looking up, I caught a glimpse of the tenuous form of Tommy Pelling, perched at the corner of the sill, staring at me with his huge, sad eyes. But Tommy hovered at the very edge of my field of vision, just as the Good People had once done. When I tried to look directly at him, he was no longer there.

A couple of weeks later, the wireless brought the news that the Germans were deploying a new weapon against the towns and villages of England. At first it seemed strange and frightening but, as with everything else in the war, people soon got used to the idea. Its proper name was the V1 rocket, but everybody was calling it the Doodlebug. It looked like a small jet aeroplane, with a fuselage, an engine, wings and a tail, but it didn't have a pilot or anyone else on board. Instead, the space inside its body was packed with explosives. The Doodlebugs were launched from somewhere in the north of Germany. From there they travelled across the North Sea and, once they arrived over England, they somehow found their way to their target and came crashing down to earth. Then, of course, there would be a huge explosion, and all the nearby buildings would be destroyed, and all the people would be killed. They used to fly over our towns and villages making a sort of buzzing noise, and when the buzzing stopped, it meant that the Doodlebug's engines had cut out and that it was about to come down. It was only when the buzzing stopped that people really started to feel afraid.

The day that I heard on the wireless about the Doodlebugs, it was my turn to make my grandmother's tea. I was just taking the kettle from the stove when Janny passed through the kitchen on her way towards the back door. 'Are you doing Mrs Hedley?' she called over her shoulder. 'I'm just going for a walk. See you later.'

'See you later,' I repeated absently. Since the episode at the bridge, Janny had been taking quite a lot of walks: always, I noticed, in the direction of the forest. I was pretty certain that she was going to see Davy Hearn, but I didn't ask her, because I didn't want to hear about it, I didn't want to know about it, I didn't even want to think about it. I wanted to ignore what was happening. I suppose I still believed that if nothing was said then, somehow, it still wouldn't be real. And then Janny would still be on her own, she would still be lonely, there would still be a chance for me.

I arranged the teapot and my grandmother's cup and saucer on the tray, crossed over to the parlour door and, balancing the tray on my knee, unlatched the door and stepped inside. The room was dimly lit and the air was heavy, as always, with the mingled scents of wood smoke, tobacco smoke, rosemary and lavender and my grandmother's tired, sick old body. 'Gran,' I said, 'I've brought your tea.' She was sitting propped up in bed on a stack of pillows, her small wrinkled hands folded in front of her on the patchwork counterpane. As I spoke, she turned her head to look at me.

'Hugh?' she said slowly. 'No, it's Robbie, isn't it?'

'It's Kenneth,' I corrected her gently. 'Robbie's gone away. He's in the army now.'

'Robbie's gone away to war,' the old lady mused. Her voice had acquired a rather abstract, sing-song quality that struck some distant chord in my memory. 'Robbie's gone away to war, and Kenny's bringing me my tea.' I placed the tea tray on the bedside table, poured half a cup, and lifted it towards her. 'In a minute,' she said. 'It'll be too hot just now. I'll have it in a minute.' I returned the cup and saucer to the tray. She closed her eyes and, for a moment, it seemed that she was about to fall asleep. Then, abruptly, she looked at me again.

'What are you going to do today, Kenny?'

'I'm going to check the air raid shelter,' I began. Somehow, I needed to explain to her about the V1 weapon. 'Herr Hitler's got a new kind of bomb. It flies without a pilot, then its engine stops, then it crashes down somewhere and it explodes. The Germans have got a whole fleet of them.'

My grandmother turned away from me to look out of the window. Perhaps she was scanning the skies for the approaching armada of Doodlebugs. 'A whole fleet of flying bombs,' she mused. 'The power to destroy half the world. The Hand of Fire.' There was a long silence, during which she seemed to ponder the significance of this phrase. The words struck a chord in my mind, but where had I heard them before? Where had I heard them? Where . . . ? In the Great Book, perhaps . . .

I realised that my grandmother was staring intently at me. Her expression was harder now, more sharply focused. 'The retribution is coming, Kenny. A wrong has been done, a great wrong against the Good People. I can't see just what it is . . . But those who have transgressed against the Good People are due their just deserts. And they who wield the Hand of Fire have the power to destroy half the world.'

'I think the Doodlebugs come from Herr Hitler, Gran,' I said carefully. Had she somehow found out about Nadia? 'Not from the Good People. Anyway, I've been thinking. I reckon we might have to start going in the shelter again. So I've decided that I ought to go and check it.' Suddenly I remembered the bomb that had never gone off, the bomb that still lay somewhere in the waste ground at the side of the house. Was it safe now, or would it one day explode?

'We all used to go in the shelter,' the old lady reminisced. 'You and me, Kenny, and Robbie too, and then there were those two young girls, what were their names?'

'Janny Grogan,' I reminded her with an effort, 'and Nadia Skolomowski. Nadia's gone home, Gran, do you remember? Gone back to her own people? So now there's just Janny.'

'Now there's just Janny,' came the echo. 'Nadia's gone and now there's just Janny. Oh, Kenneth, I had such hopes of Janny at one time. I knew that she was special. I really felt that she might have been one of us. But now everything's changed, everything's different. Why do they always have to grow up?' She fell silent then, and for several long, uneasy moments neither of us said anything. When my grandmother eventually spoke again, it was in a different tone, brisker, more decisive. 'I don't think I can go down to the shelter again, Kenny,' she said to me. 'I can't seem to get about on my feet any more.'

'Perhaps we could carry you down,' I suggested, although I didn't feel much confidence in this idea. 'Or we could get you a bath chair. I expect Uncle Magnus would know where to find one.'

'You don't want to bother about a silly old woman like me,'

came the retort. 'I'll be gone from you soon enough. You young ones are the future. You must try to look after yourselves.' I could not think of anything to say to this, so once again I remained uneasily silent. 'How about fetching me my tea?' my grandmother suggested suddenly. 'It must be cool enough by now.'

It was only when I was on my way down towards the shelter that the old lady's words came back to me. '*The Hand of Fire . . . the power to destroy half the world.*' The phrase continued to strike a dim chord in my memory. I must have picked out something similar from among the tangle of writings in the Great Book. On the other hand, though, my grandmother no longer seemed to have all her wits about her, and for much of the time her words were no more than a jumble of nonsense. At any rate, I dismissed the thought from my mind for the time being, and made my way up the steep, narrow path that led to the ice house.

As I strolled along the path, I felt in the pocket of my trousers for the key that would unfasten the padlock, but the key was not there. Puzzled, I felt again in my two side pockets, in the left, then again in the right, but still there was nothing. I felt in my hip pocket too, I even felt in the breast pocket of my shirt, although I was certain that the key would not be there.

As I approached the two iron doors, though, the explanation became clear. The doors were standing slightly apart, and the padlock was dangling unfastened from its hasp with the key still in it. Someone had borrowed the key from my pocket, I realised. Someone had borrowed the key, and someone had let themselves into the shelter. I remembered my father's warnings about tramps. More cautiously now, I continued my approach.

As I drew closer to the doors, my ears pricked up at an unfamiliar sound. This sound, I was certain, was not one of the usual, friendly sounds of the forest, it was not a sound made by any of the ordinary woodland animals or birds. I listened harder. The sound continued. It was a faint, scratchy, repeating sound. It was a bit like the sound of chalk on a blackboard, a bit like the sound of a fingernail scratching along the side of a matchbox.

It was a bit like the sound of a set of iron bunks scraping against a hard concrete floor.

Heart in mouth, I slithered through the gap between the doors and fumbled my way down the steps. Then, for a moment, I waited in the gloom until my eyes started to adjust. The sitting area of the shelter, I could now see, was deserted. From the archway that led to the bunk room, though, there came a faint glimmer of candle light, and it was from the bunk room too that the sound was coming. I tiptoed across the room, groping my way between the randomly placed pieces of furniture. In the half-light, I collided with the oil stove, almost overturning it, and had to bite my lip to suppress an oath. Fortunately, the stove was cold. I wiped my paraffin-soaked hand on the rear of my trousers. Then I completed my crossing and, very gently, I inserted a hand between the flower-patterned curtains that screened off the doorway to the bunk room and put my ear to the opening. Now, with the curtains parted, I could hear more sounds, and the new sounds that I could hear were unmistakably human sounds. In precise unison with the scraping noise, I now registered a sharp, repeated intake of breath, somewhere between a cry and a moan. The voice that was making this sound was a girl's voice.

Fearful now of what awaited me, I edged forward through

the gap in the curtains. I could make out still more sounds now, the creak of bedsprings, the rustle of a straw mattress, the deeper grunting of a second voice. After a moment, I heard something else too, a faint, slippery hissing sound that might, perhaps, have been made by cool parachute silk sliding across warm skin.

Slowly, my eyes adjusted to the flickering light of the candle. I could now see that there were two people in the bunk room, and both of them were in the same bunk, the lower bunk in fact, the bunk that had once been occupied by my brother Robert. The two people in the bunk were Davy Hearn and my poor Janny. Neither of them had noticed me, presumably because their attention was entirely taken up with one another.

Innocent I may have been but, even to my naïve eyes, there was no doubting what Janny and Davy were doing and, from the practiced ease of their movements, it was apparent that this was not the first time they had done it. For a moment, transfixed by their utter absorption in the act, I continued to stare. Then, tears pricking at my eyes, I withdrew from the room, gently pulling the curtains back together, wearily slumping back against the wall that separated the two rooms of the shelter from one another. But still I could hear the sounds from next door. The rhythm was growing quicker now, the cries rising in pitch, the incidental scrapes and squeaks growing cruder and harsher. For a few moments I lingered there. Then, half-reluctantly, I turned away.

Slowly, I threaded my way back among the furniture of the outer room. My attention was focused now on the narrow slit of light that marked the position of the two iron doors, the iron doors that separated the two dark rooms of the ice house from the bright world that lay outside. As I mounted the short flight of steps, I could hear the sounds from the bunk room growing ever louder and quicker, approaching their final resolution, rolling helter-skelter now towards the culmination that I knew was inescapable. Turning my shoulder to the opening, I wormed my way between the doors and stood outside, blinking in the summer light.

The cacophony of sounds still rang out from the inner chamber, furious now in its intensity, mocking me with everything that I knew I would never have. I could not bear to listen to it any longer. Janny was never going to be mine, I suddenly realised. Very well, then. Davy Hearn could have her. He could have her for ever and ever.

I wiped away a tear. Then, gently, very gently, I pulled the two iron doors together. Softly, so softly, I clicked the padlock shut in its hasp. Quietly, more quietly than you could ever imagine, I turned the key in the lock.

Then I turned around, and I strode away down the track that led to the lake, and I walked along the edge of the water, and I walked out to the middle of the wooden bridge that connected the two banks of the stream, and I threw the key far away from me, and I watched it drop with a tiny splash into the foaming, swirling rapids.

I don't know how long I stood there, staring into the water as it cascaded down from the foot of the lake into the stream and over the rocks. Perhaps I had a moment of regret for what I had done, but the key to the padlock, I knew, was now gone for ever. It could never be recovered from the bed of the stream and, so far as I was aware, there wasn't a spare key anywhere in Hedley House. What would my two lovebirds do now, I wondered, what would they do when they discovered that the doors were padlocked and that they could no longer leave their nest? They would hammer at the doors, I supposed, they would pound at the cold metal with their fists, but the lock would not yield, the hinges would hold firm, the iron doors would not shift. The two of them would shout for help, of course, hoping against all hope that someone would hear them and come to their aid, but I knew that nobody would hear them, because nobody except me ever came into the forest. So nobody would pass by the entrance to the cave, nobody would pay any attention to them, nobody would come to help them until it was too late.

And then what? How long could two healthy young people survive with no food, with no water, with nothing but stale air to breathe? Once the candle had burned down to its stub, there would be no light, and once the stove had consumed its last drop of paraffin, there would be no heat. How long would they survive? A week? A month? I had no idea. At last, I tore my gaze away from the water, I forced myself to turn around and to face up to what I had done. Step by reluctant step I dragged my weary feet back along the track, dragged myself back along the side of the lake, dragged myself back at last to the steep, narrow path that led up to the doors of the cave.

Fearfully, I stood before those two tall, iron doors, staring at the rivets that secured their stout panels, staring at the thin lines of rust that streaked their surface, staring at the flat, heavy, implacable padlock that bound them together. I tried listening then, I pressed my ear up against the crack, but there was no sound from within. They must have fallen asleep, I decided. Janny and Davy had done what they came to do, and they had fallen asleep, their exhausted bodies wrapped around each other on the bed, their contented breath sweet in each other's ears. For the moment, they were happy. Perhaps they should be allowed to enjoy their last moments of happiness.

Perhaps they should be left alone now, left to the mercy of the Good People.

Nearby, among the trees, I noticed a fallen branch. Scarcely knowing what I was doing, I dragged the branch from where it lay and arranged it across the base of the doors. Then I went to look for another branch, and I laid it on top of the first. The twigs of the two branches seemed to reach out for each other, to twine together into a dense, perverse tangle. Two branches, I realised, would be much harder to shift than one. Then I fetched another branch and added that to the growing pile. After that I added another, until at last I had built a wall of branches that was as high as the doors themselves.

Still no sound came from within.

I stood back to inspect my handiwork. The doors were hardly visible now, but a sharp-eyed person might still, perhaps, make out the dull glint of iron here and there between the branches. I would need to fill in all the gaps, I would need to stuff every crack with whatever came to hand. In a frenzy now, I turned back towards the undergrowth, seized handfuls of leaves, handfuls of moss, uprooted wild plants, tore straggling lengths of ivy from the trunks of trees, and began to cram everything that I could find into the chinks in my wall of branches, until at last I was satisfied that not one glimpse of the iron doors remained. At last, my task was done. The wall that I had built completely covered the doors from top to bottom and, on either side of the opening, it blended invisibly into the side of the hill. In time, the grass and the bushes and the wild-flowers would grow across it, binding it for ever into the rich soil of Arboria. The iron doors had vanished for ever.

Weary and filthy, I made my way back towards Hedley House and, as I walked, I became aware of an eerie silence in the forest around me. But this silence, I knew at once, was not the silence of a deserted place. This silence was the silence of those who chose to remain silent. Because, in the gaps between the roots of every tree, the Good People were watching. In the bottomless depths of the lake, they were waiting. In the deepest caves at the heart of the earth, they were biding their time. Now, beneath my feet, I could feel once more that familiar, slow pounding, that deep, throbbing rhythm that told me that the Good People were once more awake. But the Good People are not angry with me, I told myself. They do not seek to reproach me or to punish me. They understand that I have merely done what had to be done. What I have done, I have done for them. I am not the one who is going to be punished.

Satisfied that all was well, I squared my shoulders, quickened my pace, and strode firmly ahead along the track that led back to the garden gate and Hedley House. The silence held until the very last moment, until the final instant when I placed my hand on the latch of the gate. And just then, in the distance, far, far away, I heard the faint sound of a muffled cry. For a moment, I listened, waiting for the other cries that I knew would follow. Perhaps, I thought, it is not too late to do something after all. Then, with a shrug, I passed through the gate, and I pulled the gate closed, and I clicked the latch down behind me. The cave was on the other side of the garden wall now. I could not hear the sound any more.

But although I could no longer hear the sound, I could find no way of protecting myself from the knowledge of what I had done. Night after night I lay awake, my imagination on fire. Night after night it seemed that I too was buried in that cave. Night after night my ears burned with the screams and the cries, the tearful recriminations, the futile pounding of fists against unyielding iron. Night after night, I too could feel the biting ache of chilled bones, the searing pain of hands bruised and fingernails bloody from clawing at hard concrete. Night after night, my throat throbbed with dehydration and my head reeled with delirium. Night after night, I choked on the mingled stink of damp earth and stale air and sweating bodies and human filth.

Then, after more nights than I wanted to count, the cries grew feebler, the ache grew duller, the fists could no longer pound, the nails could no longer tear, and at last there was nothing but a bed of rough concrete, and the sickly-sweet scent of damp earth, and the long stone staircase that led down, down, down to the twilit realm of the Good People.

And then Janny and Davy slept. And outside the cave, the cowslips and the dandelions started to grow, and the bindweed began to twist its way in among the branches that hid the iron doors, and the birds built their nests from the twigs and the leaves that filled the cracks. And then, one day, the baby birds hatched from their eggs, and in time they grew wings, and they took to the air, and they flew away to build nests of their own.

During the day, of course, normal life had to continue. With all the others gone, I had now acquired the sole responsibility for looking after my grandmother and, although she no longer seemed in complete command of her wits, it didn't take her long to notice Janny's absence.

'Where is she, that young girl?' the old lady demanded one day. 'The one that can climb trees. The one that started wearing stockings. She thought I didn't know, but I did. Why doesn't she come to see me any more? I used to like it when she came to see me.'

'Janny had to go home,' I replied. I had decided to use the same story that I had successfully concocted to explain Nadia's disappearance. 'Her family sent for her. They decided it was safe for her to live with them again.' What I knew of course, but what my grandmother did not know, was that Janny had not had a single letter from her family in all the time she had been staying at Hedley House and, so far as I was aware, she had not written a single letter to them either. I could not even remember hearing her mention her mother or father. To begin with, this had struck me as odd but, distracted by all the other odd events of the last few years, I had long since ceased to puzzle over it.

'She never said goodbye,' my grandmother persisted. 'Why didn't she come and see me before she went?'

'You were asleep, Gran.' I calmly repeated my earlier lie. 'We came in to see you, but we didn't want to wake you up.' The old lady nodded grudgingly. 'She said she'll write,' I continued wildly. 'When she gets home. I don't know whether she will or not.' For a long moment, my grandmother stared at me or, at least, one of her eyes stared at me. The other eye, I noticed, had lost its sense of direction, and was gazing distractedly into empty space, but the eye that stared at me had retained its full, penetrating force. That eye seemed to stare right through my lies and my pretences. That eye seemed to stare right through my wall of branches. It seemed to bore through the iron doors, it seemed to thrust its way right through to whatever vile scene had enacted itself in those final hours on the concrete floor of the ice house. Although she could not possibly have known what I had been forced to do, I found myself avoiding my grandmother's gaze.

'What's happened, Kenny?' the old lady said suddenly.

'Something isn't right. You can't hide yourself away from them, you know. You can't hide from the Good People. They're always watching. They watch and they wait. And, one day, they will remember. The Hand of Fire, Kenny, the Hand of Fire . . .'

But at that moment, her ramblings were interrupted by the distant growling of a Doodlebug. I pricked up my ears, but could hear nothing else. 'It sounds like an air raid, Gran,' I broke in. 'I'd better go and get ready, in case the sirens go. Shall I make you a cup of tea? I'll find a pan and boil some water . . .' I hurried from the room, fearing to look back, terrified lest that one all-seeing eye should penetrate the last remnants of my defences. Of course, I had no intention of going anywhere near the air raid shelter. If there was a raid, I'd have to hide under the kitchen table.

But of course there were to be no more raids, not on Tollcester, anyway. By this time, the Allied armies had entered Germany, and the war in Europe was heading for its final phase.

It was several weeks before I could bring myself to visit Arboria again. This delay, I persuaded myself, would allow enough time for me to be quite certain that there would no longer be any unwelcome noises coming from the ice house. By the time that I finally steeled myself to pass once more through the garden gate, autumn was well advanced. Thick drifts of brown leaves had blown into Tommy Pelling's doorway, had formed a carpet on the forest floor, had obscured the courses of all the paths.

Taking my first hesitant steps among those leaves, I found myself unable to discern the contours of the ground. As I stumbled uncertainly along, hidden roots clutched at my ankles, concealed stones deflected my feet. Several times I was forced to snatch at the branches of the trees or at the stems of the undergrowth for support but, as often as not, they proved treacherous allies. Once, I sank up to my knees in an unseen patch of deep mud and had to fight my way back to safety. At last, though, I found my way up the narrow track that led to the ice house.

Once more I stood before my wall of twigs and branches. All was silent. No voices cried for help, no fists beat at the unyielding iron. For a long, long time I stood there, just to be certain, just to be sure, but I heard nothing. At last, slowly, I turned around and started to head back down the slope, once more feeling my way cautiously through the drifts of leaves, wary now of the snares and ambushes that might lie beneath my feet. A few minutes later, I found myself back again on the main track. For a moment I paused, undecided, then I turned to my left and headed on downhill towards the shores of the lake. Apart from the rustle of leaves and the crackle of branches, there was nothing to be heard. For a long moment I waited. Then, sure enough, far beneath my feet, I felt once more that faint, distant pulsation that told me that the Good People were listening.

'What is it?' I heard myself saying. 'What do you want?'

For a long, long time, there was no reply. Then, somewhere in the far distance, I heard music. It was faint and it was far away. It was scarcely more than the song of a skylark borne on a distant breeze. I recognised it at once, though. It was the sound of Davy Hearn's tin whistle. I knew the tune, too. It was *Over the Hills and Far Away.*

At the sound of that tune, I turned and fled, careering down the track like a madman. At every step, I stumbled. Brambles tore at my clothes, nettles lashed at my skin, branches stabbed at my eyes. Half-lame, half-blind, I blundered on towards who knew where and, all the while, that accursed tune was threading its way among the trees, it was winding in and out of the copses and clearings, it was enmeshing me in a tangled web of broken melody. The faster I ran, the louder the music seemed to play, until I feared that my eardrums would burst with the force of it. Gasping for breath, my ribs aching, my face streaked with dirt and tears, I stumbled on, stumbled down the slope until at last the surface of the lake came into view. Then, at last, I could run no more. On a flat rock that overlooked the waters, I threw myself face down, my head cradled in my arms, weeping and choking and sobbing with exhaustion.

At last, the sound began to fade. At last, nothing remained but the passing echo of that departing song, borne softly away on the wind. Slowly, as the last strains of the melody died away, I sat up and tried once more to regain control. Pulling a grubby handkerchief from my pocket, I dabbed at my eyes and my nose and my cheeks, wiping away the grime and the snot and the blood and the tears that had intermingled there. Cautiously I inspected my body, checking myself for cuts and sprains and bruises. Slowly I stretched my tired limbs, gradually I allowed the throbbing in my skull to abate.

As the sky grew dark, I remained there by the lake, sitting up on that flat rock, hugging my knees, staring out across the water. Now all was once more silent, except for the faint rippling of the water as the black fish swam to and fro beneath the surface. Now all was silent, except for the faint susurration of my breath. Now all was silent.

But then I heard another sound. This time, it was the distant wail of a young girl weeping. I sank my head in my hands, knowing all too well what was to come.

Of course, Arboria wasn't the only thing that I had to worry about. Although my grandmother's condition didn't actually seem to be getting any worse, it didn't seem to be getting any better, either. It wasn't long before Uncle Magnus decided that something would have to be done. 'I don't see how anyone can expect you to look after her on your own, Ken,' he fretted. I was standing by the front door, willing him to leave, while he continued to pace up and down the hallway, his hands fidgeting restlessly in his trouser pockets, his unbuttoned overcoat flapping around his bulky frame.

'It's all right, Uncle,' I countered. 'She's really no bother at all.'

'It's not all right,' he continued, ignoring my interruption. 'A young lad like you. You should be out of doors, enjoying yourself. Fishing. Climbing trees. That sort of thing. You don't want to be shut up in a stuffy room with a sick old woman. Now listen to me Ken, I know we've been through this before, but—'

I knew what was coming. 'We're stopping here,' I broke in stubbornly. 'Gran and I. It's what Gran wants, and it's what I want. We're not leaving Hedley House.' I could feel myself shaking, and my voice was starting to crack. My uncle must have noticed it too, because he decided to draw back from a direct confrontation.

'Well, to be honest, the factory's keeping me pretty busy at the moment.' I could not help noticing a trace of relief in his voice. 'And Dottie's run off her feet, trying to keep our house going. Tell you what I'll do, though. I'll speak to old Solloway at the surgery. Try and remind him about getting the nurse to call in on the old girl now and again. At least save you from doing the dirty work. And I'll keep that grocery order going. Should be plenty for the pair of you, now that those two girls have gone home.'

I started to open the front door, and Magnus at last took the hint and began to walk down the drive towards his car. Magnanimous in victory, I strolled beside him and held open the door while he eased himself laboriously into the driver's seat of the old Humber. A comfortable smell of leather and tobacco and polished wood wafted up from the car's interior. 'Thanks for everything, Uncle,' I said. 'I do appreciate it. It will make life much easier for both of us.'

'Don't give it another thought, my boy.' He pressed the igni-tion switch, and the engine coughed noisily into life. 'Had a letter from young Robert the other day, by the way. They've sent him to Berlin. Seems that the final push is under way.'

Not responding to this, I closed the car door and stood at the roadside waving as the Humber roared away down the lane. As I made my way back indoors, I reflected on my uncle's offer. At least it had gained me a little more time. Of course, sooner or later, perhaps when the war was finally over, he would doubtless try once again to evict me from Hedley House. For the time being, though, I was safe.

Although my uncle continued to worry about my grand-mother's condition, he had shown little interest in the disappearance of Janny and Nadia. The story that I had pre-pared for my grandmother had proved sufficiently convincing for him too and, doubtless preoccupied with the day-to-day difficulties of running the print works and the knicker factory, he had not considered it necessary to check up on any of the details. I continued to worry, though, that someone would at some stage come looking for my missing companions.

By the winter of that year, the government had decided that there was no longer any risk from the Doodlebugs, and that the evacuees, who were still scattered all over the country, were to be sent home to the cities where their families awaited them. This started me worrying all over again. Daily, I expected the billeting officers or some other officials to come knocking on the door, demanding to collect Grogan, J. and Skolomowski, N. But, although every other evacuee in the neighbourhood was collected and dispatched, the billeting officers did not come to Hedley House. Nobody asked about Janny, and nobody asked about Nadia. Come to that, nobody asked about Davy Hearn either.

For some time, I fretted over this. Of course, I told myself, people are bound to go missing during a war. It must happen all the time. Documents get lost, lists get mistyped, mistakes are always happening. And perhaps Janny *was* an orphan. Perhaps Nadia's parents *did* die in the internment camp. And perhaps Davy Hearn had lost his family too. Davy had always lived a wild life, hadn't he, camping in the woods, sleeping under the stars. Perhaps there *was* nobody to ask about him. Briefly, I wondered about Davy's friends, the charcoal burners, who appeared in the woods every spring. But then I remembered that Davy seemed to be in the forest right through the year, whether the charcoal burners were camped there or not. But perhaps, after all, it was not so much of a coincidence that three lonely, ordinary children who had lost their families should all arrive at Hedley House at the same time. Perhaps it was not so much of a coincidence that three children should all go missing during the same summer. And perhaps it was not so much of a coincidence that, when all three of them disappeared, nobody in the world would notice.

But perhaps, I told myself, perhaps they were not such ordinary children after all. Perhaps none of them had ever had families. Perhaps each one of them belonged, not to a mother or to a father, not to a house or to a town, but perhaps each of them belonged instead to another world altogether, to a world where there are no mothers or fathers or teachers or soldiers, to a world where everyone can do exactly as they please from morning till night, to a world of woods and fields and trees and rivers and hills and valleys and wide blue sky and distant purple mountains.

Perhaps Nadia had belonged to the lake and to the stream and to the waterfall.

Perhaps Davy had belonged to the forest and to the clearing and to the riverbank.

And perhaps Janny, my precious Janny, had belonged to the tops of the trees, to the very tops, to the place where the branches reach right up to touch the sky.

Perhaps these three lost children had belonged, not to the world of women and men, but to the world of the Arborians, to the world of the Barbarians, to the world of the Great Book, to the world of the House in the Air. Perhaps, after all, they belonged to the world that lay beyond the garden gate.

Perhaps these three lost children belonged to the Good People.

And perhaps, one day, it would be the Good People who would come in anger to claim them back.

*Ten*

# THE HAND OF FIRE

*M*y story is nearly done now, Jamie. Soon you will understand.

My grandmother lived for another year, just long enough to witness the end of the war. Germany surrendered in the spring, and victory parades were held in every town and city in the land. Robert was still abroad with the army, of course, but my uncle Magnus organised a family outing to watch the parade in Tollcester. Actually, it was really more a works outing than a family outing. My uncle laid on a coach for all the people from the print works and the knicker factory, and there were a couple of spare seats for Aunt Dottie and me. We even managed to get my grandmother along, together with the nurse that Magnus had hired to come in each day and look after her. Gran couldn't walk any more, but Magnus got hold of a bath chair from somewhere and, between us all, we managed to help her in and out of the coach.

Everybody on the streets of Tollcester that day was in a good mood. The shopkeepers were handing out food and drink, there were rows of flags hanging up everywhere, and it all looked very festive after the drab years of the war. The parade was due to start at the top of Coventry Road, and from there it would travel up the Broadgate and through the old City Gateway for a service of thanksgiving at the cathedral. There were big crowds lining the streets to watch the fun, and we took our place among the people in the Broadgate, not that there was much left of the Broadgate after the bombings. Most of the medieval shops and houses had been destroyed, but the council had put up some temporary hoardings to hide the worst of the damage. The hoardings had been decorated with flags and victory banners, so it all looked quite cheerful in the end.

When people saw that Gran was in a bath chair, they were very kind to us and let us come to the front so that she could get a good view. I don't know whether she really understood what was happening, though. She could hardly speak any more, just the odd word now and again, but she could still just about manage a cup of tea or a puff at her pipe. Everyone was given little Union Jack flags to wave, and Gran managed to hold a flag, her knobbly old hand clenched around its splintery stick.

After what seemed like a very long time, we finally heard the band starting up in the distance, and after that it took an even longer time for the parade to come by the spot where we were standing. Apart from the band, there were people in all kinds of uniforms: the Army and the Air Force of course, the Air Raid Wardens, the Home Guard, the Police and even the Land Girls. The Boy Scouts and the Girl Guides were there too, and soon everyone was hoarse with cheering. Uncle Magnus cheered long and loud and, I thought, rather smugly. Aunt Dottie clapped her hands briskly and dutifully but didn't seem to have much to say to anybody. My grandmother didn't have the strength to cheer, but she managed to wave her flag feebly to and fro, although from time to time she seemed to forget what she was doing, and several times I had to bend down and pick up her flag from the pavement. The nurse, who usually seemed rather prim, was cheering more loudly and more wildly than anybody. I noticed after a time that she had tears running down her face. My own cheering, I suppose, was rather half-hearted, but I think I managed to convince everybody that I was enjoying myself.

At one point, my ears caught a small, hoarse, cheering voice that seemed to come from somewhere about the height of my waist. Looking down, I was surprised to catch a glimpse of Tommy Pelling, jumping up and down and clapping his small hands together. It was the only time I had ever seen him away from Hedley House.

After the parade, everybody crowded up to the cathedral for the service, but of course there wasn't room for everyone inside. Naturally the Mayor had a place, and all the important people from the council, but most of us had to pack into the cathedral close and listen to the service through big loud-speakers. The service seemed to go on longer than everything else that day, but in the end it was over, and then there was a lot of eating and drinking, during which Uncle Magnus got very merry, and even Aunt Dottie seemed to relax a bit. My grand-mother seemed very tired and bewildered, and in the end I could tell that she needed to go home.

Eventually we all clambered back onto the coach, and then there was a very long ride, because my uncle had decided that he wanted to drop all his workers off at their homes, so we spent several hours touring around all the back streets and villages where they lived. Gran and I were about the last to be

324

dropped, but eventually we were back inside Hedley House and it was just the two of us again.

Of course, that wasn't quite the end of the war. In the Far East, the war between America and Japan continued for another few months until the Americans dropped their atomic bombs on Hiroshima and Nagasaki. The two cities were completely destroyed, and hundreds of thousands of people were killed in an instant. After that, Japan surrendered too, and the war really was over.

On the night of the second bombing of Japan, I sat up with my grandmother listening to the news on the wireless. She was propped up in her bed with a cup of tea, looking like a tiny wrinkled doll on the great mound of white pillows that the nurse had arranged for her. I was sitting in one of the Windsor chairs next to the stove. As usual, I wasn't sure how much she had been understanding but, when I switched off the wireless and went over to her bed to make her comfortable for the night, she suddenly reached out with one of her thin arms and took hold of my wrist.

'*The Hand of Fire* . . .' she gasped hoarsely. '*The great conflagration from the skies* . . . See what men can do to one another, Kenny. See what they can do . . . *The Hand of Fire* . . . *The power to destroy half the world* . . .'

'It's all right, Gran.' Somewhat taken aback, I tried my best to reassure her. 'The war's over now. There won't be any more bombs.'

'Not the bombs . . .' She was starting to become agitated. She clutched at my wrist with surprising strength, her one good eye boring into mine with furious intensity. 'The Good People, Kenny . . . The Good People. One day, they will have their revenge . . . A great wrong has been done. *The Hand of*

*Fire . . . The power to destroy half the world . . .*' She released her hold on me then, slumped back against her pillows, closed her eyes.

'Good night, Gran.' Brushing my hair away from my face, I noticed that my forehead was sweating. 'There won't be any more bombs now.' I collected up her cup and saucer and emptied the ashes from her pipe into the stove. Then I waited until she was asleep. At last, I switched off the light and softly closed the door. I slept soundly that night but, threading its tortured path through my dreams, I could faintly discern the ragged noise of Janny's weeping.

The following morning, when I came downstairs, I was greeted by an eerie silence. After a moment, I realised that the tall clock in the hallway had stopped ticking. I could not remember this ever happening before. Panic-stricken, I ran straight to my grandmother's parlour, although, deep inside me, I already knew what had happened. Sure enough, during the night, the old lady had died in her sleep.

I don't remember too much about my grandmother's funeral. Her death affected me more than I had expected and, in the end, I was too upset to do much more than sit in my place and to stand up when the vicar told me to stand up. Uncle Magnus and Aunt Dottie made all the arrangements, but Robert appeared at the last minute, on compassionate leave from Germany, to take the role of chief mourner. He was still in his uniform and he seemed very grown-up and distant, but at least he did the job of shaking hands with everyone and saying the right things at the right times.

Afterwards, Magnus and Robert tried once again to persuade me to leave Hedley House, but once again I refused to consider it. I think I became rather hysterical, actually, and in the end the two of them once again gave in to me. Magnus muttered something about discussing it 'when things have calmed down a bit'. Over the next few months, my uncle tried several more times to persuade me to move in with him, but each time I became so upset that I think I rather frightened him, and in the end he left me alone.

Then, the year after the end of the war, my call-up papers arrived. The government wanted me to join the army, and I suspect that Magnus was hoping to take advantage of my absence and sell Hedley House while I was away. Robert had been discharged from the service by this time, and was living with Magnus and Dottie and working at the knicker factory again. It was Robert who went with me to the recruitment board, and it was Robert who accompanied me to the medical examination. After the doctor had listened to my chest and looked at my eyes and ears and feet, he asked me if I had any particular medical problems that I wanted to mention to him.

'Not really,' I said. 'As long as Tommy Pelling can come with me.'

'Tommy Pelling?' said the doctor. 'Who's he?'

'Oh, for God's sake, Ken . . .' I heard Robert muttering.

'Tommy's my special friend,' I said. 'I want Tommy to come with me.'

The doctor raised an eyebrow. 'Is he here now?'

'I expect so,' I said. 'Of course, you can't see him. Neither can I, most of the time. But he's here, all right.'

'Ken . . .' said Robert. The doctor and I both ignored him.

'What would happen if you had to leave Tommy Pelling behind?' asked the doctor cautiously. 'If you were posted over-seas, for example?'

'The Good People would be angry,' I replied. 'They would punish me.'

'The Good People?' The doctor had by now raised his second eyebrow.

'The Good People. They live on the other side of the garden gate. They've been there longer than anyone, in the caves under the earth. They're very vengeful. And they have the power to destroy half the world.'

The doctor asked me a few more questions, but by now he seemed to have made up his mind. Letters were written, papers were signed, and I was sent to see another doctor, this time a psychiatrist. In the end I was granted exemption from military service on the grounds of feeblemindedness. I was rather offended at being called feebleminded. I suppose I could have argued with them, but in the end I decided not to. I didn't want to see any more doctors because I knew that, if I did, I would probably have ended up being put in an institution, and I didn't want that. I wanted to go home to Hedley House.

So at Hedley House I stayed. After a while, Magnus and Robert gave up trying to move me and decided that it would be best for everyone if they just left me alone. The weekly boxes of groceries continued to arrive, and I suppose that Magnus must have carried on paying all the bills for the house, because nobody ever came to demand money for anything.

From time to time, Magnus or Robert would come to visit me. At least, they said they were coming to visit me, but I think they were mainly concerned about the state of the property. While I made tea for Magnus in the kitchen, Robert would go off and have a good look around, and then, a week or so later, a builder or a plumber would arrive to do some repairs. As the years went by, though, the gaps between the visits started to grow longer, and the repairs started to become more makeshift. But, at any rate, Hedley House didn't actually fall down, and I continued to live there pretty well undisturbed. After a while, I found myself slipping into a comfortable daily routine.

The morning was the time when I continued with my work on the Great Book. Although this proved to be an endlessly frustrating task, I never gave up hoping that one day the scroll would finally abandon its resistance and yield up its secrets, that one day I would achieve my longed-for breakthrough, that one day I would at last solve the riddle of Hedley House. But after many long years of fruitless effort, I can only resign myself to failure. Whatever secrets remain to be learned, it is too late for me to learn them now. I am determined, though, that the Great Book will not die with me, and that there will one day be someone else who will take up my task. Perhaps, Jamie, you are beginning to understand who I mean.

As well as reading the book, I have been writing in it too, adding my own contribution to those of my predecessors; not on parchment, of course, but on ordinary cheap typing paper. So my own story, my account of those long-ago wartime years, has now itself become a chapter in the Great Book of Arboria, a small part of a much greater story. One day, perhaps, my words will weave a spell for some other reader, just as the words that I have read there have woven a spell for me.

At times, though, the ghosts of Hedley House have proved too much of a distraction so, in the end, I decided that it would be easier if I carried out my task a safe distance away from Lower Helsing. That was when I discovered the café at the bus station. The staff here have raised no objection to my presence and, for the price of an occasional cup of their bitterly astringent coffee, I have been granted warmth and shelter and a Formica-topped table large enough to accommodate my increasingly bulky workload. Even the group of teenagers in the far corner seem to gain some amusement from my activities.

So much for my mornings. Afternoons have been my time for visiting Arboria. Each day, without fail, I hack my way across the vegetable patch and through the garden gate. Each day, wet or dry, I pause for a moment at the foot of the narrow path that leads up the hill to the ice house and the caves under the earth. Each day, warm or cool, I stride along the path that leads down the slope to the shores of the lake. Each day, bright or dim, I amble along the lakeside beneath the willow trees. And each day, calm or storm, I stand on the rickety wooden bridge, staring into the white torrent of water as it cascades over the rocks, wondering whether the key to the iron doors of the ice house still lies rusting somewhere in the depths.

Most days, though, there is nothing for me to see except for the trees and the branches, the lake and the waterfall, the roots and the boulders. Most days, there is nothing for me to hear except for the rush of the water and the other ordinary sounds of the forest; the rustle of the leaves, the song of the birds, the patter of the feet of small animals. But, once in a while, my ears catch other sounds too. Perhaps the joyful splash of a swimmer in the lake, perhaps the aching wail of a young girl's sobs, or perhaps the distant lilt of an old tin whistle, a tin whistle playing a half-forgotten song.

Once in a while, as I pause at the tumbledown hut where the logs used to be stored, I might even catch a sidelong glimpse of a slight, insubstantial figure that peers out at me with melancholy eyes, and then I know that Tommy Pelling is still here with me, still standing guard over the forests of Arboria. Tommy and I are the ones who must keep watch now. Tommy and I are the ones who must keep the sacred memory of Arboria alive.

Perhaps if I had had more strength of character, perhaps if I had not been feebleminded, I might have managed to tear myself away from Hedley House and Arboria and the Good People while I was still young. But it is too late now. I am old, I have stayed here for too long, and I am haunted by too many ghosts. I will never escape now from the things that have happened to me in this forest. The moment when I watched Nadia's suitcase spiralling through the air and vanishing into the black depths of the lake. The moment when I turned the key in the padlock, the moment when I secured the iron doors of the ice house against the two babes who slept within. The moment when I lay on the rock at the side of the lake and the air around me reverberated to the sound of Davy's melody. The moment when I clapped my hands to my ears, for fear that my ears might burst with the overpowering force of that sound. And the moment when I knew that, for as long as I lived, Janny's weeping would never leave me.

But I must not let myself forget that, as well as the sadness, Arboria also brought me much joy. There was the day when Janny shinned up the trunk of the Great Tree all the way to the House in the Air. There was the day when Nadia stripped off her clothes and plunged into the depths of the lake and swam. There was the day when Robert bounded down from the rocks and flung Davy Hearn into the water. There was the day when the four of us chased the Lumberjills from their camp with the Rough Music.

And then there was the night of the Maypole Dance.

That was the night when we all danced together in the clearing in the forest, Nadia and Davy and Tommy and Janny and me. That was the night when the Good People looked on as we danced round the maypole with the Arborians and the Barbarians. That was the night when Lord Owen and Lady Margaret stood at the edge of the clearing, watching with veiled eyes as we danced. Perhaps, in truth, that was the one and only time in my life at which I have known a pure moment of happiness. Perhaps I should be thankful, then, that the memory of that day, too, will stay with me for ever.

Each May Day, I make my way back to that clearing and try, as I have tried so many times, to remember the steps of the Maypole Dance. But the steps continue to elude me, and year after year I curse my rheumatic body and my fumbling feet, I curse my wayward steps and my failing memory. But at least, I tell myself, at least on that one great day in my life, I did dance here.

Perhaps, Jamie, perhaps you would say that I have not had much of a life. A mad old man in a tumbledown house with an overgrown garden and an overgrown wood and a stagnant pond. A mad old man with nothing more to show for his life than a crumbling scroll of indecipherable writings and a few scraps of memory.

To me, though, that is not the way it seems.

Once, you see, just once in my life, I danced by the light of the moon in that clearing in the woods. Just once in my life, I danced the Maypole Dance while the Good People looked on. Just once in my life, I drank Saint George's Brew, and I saw

Nadia's tail and I saw Davy's horns. Just once in my life, Janny Grogan came to me in the night, and I kissed Janny, and Janny kissed me. Perhaps to you it does not sound like much, but to me, in all my long life, it is the one truly great and wonderful thing that I have done.

I have lived at Hedley House for nearly eighty years now, but the house has never truly belonged to me. When my mother and father died, the house passed to my grandmother and, when my grandmother died, the house passed to my brother Robert. Robert never wanted to live here, though. Uncle Magnus and Aunt Dottie didn't have any children and I suppose that, in many ways, Robert was the nearest they had to a son. At any rate, he continued to live with them and, when Magnus eventually died, Robert inherited their house, as well as the print works and the knicker factory. This worried me at first but, as it turned out, it needn't have done. Despite all the harsh words that had passed between us, my brother understood more about me than anyone else ever has.

For many years, Robert left me alone and, for the rest of his life, I saw little of him. I did realise, though, that both Magnus and Robert had come to regard me as something of an embarrassment. I must have grown to look rather odd, with my ragged clothes and my long, white beard and my big, crumbling scroll of writings. My presence at family gatherings was not encouraged. I was not invited to Dottie's funeral, nor was I invited to Magnus's funeral, nor was I invited to Robert's wedding, which took place in the same year. And when Robert's son Nicholas was born the year after that, I was not invited to the christening. Of course, Jamie, you will recognise the names of Nicholas Storey and Robert Storey, because my brother Robert was your grandfather, and my nephew Nicholas, of course, is your father.

As Nicholas grew into a man, it became clear that he was destined one day to take control of the family businesses. But as the years rolled by, the businesses ceased to prosper. The knicker factory was the first to fail, priced out of the market by cheaply made underwear from the Far East. The print works suffered too, from competitors with more modern machinery, computers and other such things, I suppose. Over the years, though, your grandfather had become quite a stubborn old man, and he managed to keep the print works going, although he had to make many sacrifices in order to do so. But even in spite of all this, he never tried to dispose of Hedley House, although I am sure that the money would have been useful to him. He must have felt that he owed me some loyalty because, despite all his financial difficulties, he continued to leave me in peace.

But, as you know, Jamie, your grandfather eventually died earlier this year. Once again, I was excluded from the funeral but, soon afterwards, Nicholas came to see me. I had not met him for many years and, at first, I did not recognise my visitor.

'Uncle Kenneth?' The man who stood at the front door was in his early forties, and was wearing a well-cut, narrow-lapelled dark grey suit with a rather vividly patterned tie and extremely shiny black shoes. For a moment I stared stupidly at him. Then recognition dawned.

'You must be Nicholas,' I ventured. 'It's years since I last saw you. You used to have purple hair, it was in, what did you call it, a Mohican style. Do you still sniff glue?'

'That was all a long time ago.' Your father did not smile.

'Come into the kitchen,' I suggested. 'Would you like a cup

334

of tea?' He followed me along the hallway and down the step. I gestured to him to sit, but he remained standing in the doorway. Uneasy now, I crossed to the sink and started to fill a pan. I had never got around to replacing the kettle that I had burned on the day Nadia died.

'No tea, thank you,' he said rather stiffly. 'I shan't take up much of your time, Uncle Kenneth. Because I'm afraid that what I have to say is not going to be very pleasant.' I froze, with the pan still halfway to the tap. 'As you know, when my father died, I became the owner of Hedley House,' he continued. His words had the air of a carefully prepared speech. 'My father was content for you to stay here during his lifetime. In fact, he made great sacrifices in order that you could remain. I suppose you found him a soft touch. I warn you, Uncle Kenneth, you will not find me a soft touch.' Horrified, I could think of nothing to say. 'I can no longer afford to maintain Hedley House,' said Nicholas. 'I shall be putting it on the market. And I would prefer it if you could make alternative arrangements for yourself. As quickly as possible. Do you understand me?' I nodded, tongue-tied. 'I'll show myself out,' said Nicholas. 'And I'll be in touch again shortly.'

Your father returned a few days later. This time he was accompanied by another, younger, man, also in a business suit, and by a little boy, perhaps seven or eight years old, with straight, fair hair. The second man was an estate agent who had come to value the house. The little boy, of course, was you, Jamie.

'Don't bother about any tea,' said your father at once. 'This is Tony Gowers from Gowers and Harriman. I'll show him around the house, if you wouldn't mind keeping Jamie amused. I'm afraid Jamie's mother is a bit busy today. Jamie, this is your great-uncle Kenneth. Try to keep him out of mischief.'

I wasn't sure whether his last remark was directed at me or at you. At any rate, the two men strode off in the direction of the disused wing, and I was left wondering how a tired old man was supposed to entertain a lively young boy. You were staring up at me with your big grey eyes. I looked down at you awkwardly.

'Why are your clothes all ragged and torn?' you demanded.

'They're comfortable,' I replied. 'I like them like this. And, anyway, I don't have much money for new clothes. Would you like to come for a walk in the forest?'

So we made our way into the kitchen and through the back porch. You were fascinated by the jumble of ancient outdoor equipment that mouldered there.

'That's a funny hat,' you observed. 'What's it made of? What do the letters mean?'

'That's my tin hat,' I replied, unhooking it from where it hung. 'It's my special hat for going into the forest. Would you like to try it on?'

So you put on the tin hat, and then we made our way across the vegetable patch and through the garden gate.

'That's Tommy Pelling's little hut,' I said, as we stepped through the gate.

'Who's Tommy Pelling?' you asked.

'Tommy's my special friend,' I explained. 'Tommy looks after the house and the forest.'

'Where is he?' you demanded. 'Can I see Tommy Pelling?'

'Tommy's very shy,' I explained. 'But one day, perhaps.' We walked along the forest track as far as the Great Tree. 'Can you climb a tree?' I said. 'This one's easy. It's got its own rope ladder. Why don't I have a turn at wearing the hat?'

You proved to be an agile and fearless climber, and soon we were sitting side by side in the House in the Air. I showed you how to focus my binoculars, and you peered through them in the direction of the lake and the faraway purple mountains.

'Does anyone live there?' you said.

'That's the land of the Barbarians,' I explained. 'It's best not to go there. But the Great Tree, where we're sitting, that's in the Land of Arboria. You and I can be Arborians, if you like.' But just then I heard Nicholas calling to us from the house, so I knew that it was time for you to go.

'Thank you for looking after him,' said Nicholas curtly. 'I think we're done for now. I'll be in touch again soon. Don't forget, though, you should be making plans to find somewhere else to live.'

'Jamie was no trouble,' I replied, ignoring his last remark.

'Can I come again?' you said. 'I like you, Great Uncle Kenneth. Are you really eighty? You don't really seem like an old man at all.'

'We'll see,' said Nicholas. 'Perhaps your mother will have you.'

As it turned out, though, your mother was busy for quite a lot of the time, and you ended up accompanying your father on all his subsequent visits. Other estate agents needed to see the house, of course, and then there was a surveyor, and then there was someone from Rockingham Developments.

On each visit, you put on my tin hat, and I led you through the garden gate. I showed you the stream, and I showed you the lake, and I showed you the waterfall, and I showed you the bridge and, of course, I showed you Tommy Pelling's hut.

'When can I see Tommy Pelling?' you said.

'One day,' I said. 'Soon, perhaps.' Then I showed you how

to scramble along a branch, and how to shoot with a bow and arrow, and how to catch the black fish in your two hands. I told you stories, too, stories of the Arborians and the Barbarians and the Good People. I even let you have a look at the Great Book, but you were probably too young to understand anything in it. The only thing that I didn't show you was the ice house with its two iron doors, because I knew that you were too young to understand about that either. And then, one day, your father decided that he had brought all the people that he needed to bring, and you stopped coming to Hedley House.

After that, there were the people from the council, and then there were the letters, and then there were the boards across the windows and doors. By the time that the boards went up, everyone must have assumed that I had gone, but of course there was nowhere for me to go, nowhere except the House in the Air. So the House in the Air was where I went, and the House in the Air is where I have stayed ever since. And then the men with their chainsaws and their tractors moved into the forest and started cutting down the trees, and then there were the demonstrators and the reporters and the cameramen and now, at last, there are the excavators and the bulldozers, advancing upon Hedley House inch by inch.

I don't have any money to leave you, Jamie. I don't really have anything to leave behind me, except for my tin helmet, my binoculars and a scroll of ancient scribblings. I want you to have the scroll, though, but not yet, not until you are a little older. One day, you see, you are to be the Keeper of the Great Book of Arboria. For now, though, the Great Book has been left in a safe place. I wrapped it up yesterday morning, I wrapped the Great Book in a parcel with brown paper and string and sealing wax, and then I rode on the bus into Tollcester, and I placed my parcel in one of the left luggage lockers opposite the cafe at the bus station. I reckoned that it would be safe enough there. As I slipped the key into my pocket, I noticed a group of teenagers lounging in the café, the same teenagers that I had often seen there. The boy who was younger than the others, the one who usually sat on his own, was flicking through the pages of a science fiction magazine. He looked up, gave a slight nod in my direction, and then he returned to his reading.

Next I went to see a solicitor, at the firm in Tollcester who have always looked after the affairs of Hedley House. I handed the key to the left luggage locker to the solicitor, and the solicitor put the key in an envelope, and promised to keep it in a safe place until the day before your twelfth birthday. Then, on your birthday, the envelope will arrive through your letterbox, and you will become the Keeper of the Great Book. I think, by the time you are twelve, Jamie, you will be old enough to begin to understand what is in the Book. The chronicles of Arboria, and the history of the wars with the Barbarians, and the secret lore of the Good People, all of these will be yours. Perhaps one day you will unravel all of their secrets. I hope you will use them more wisely than I have done.

And now, as I sit here in the House in the Air, I am beginning once more to hear strange noises. There is the noise of the bulldozers, of course, there is the growl of the chainsaws and the excavators and all the other machinery. But now there are other noises too. From the far side of the water, from deep inside the land of the Barbarians, there drifts the melancholy lilt of a wild boy's tin whistle. From the surface of the water there sound the ripple and the splash of a girl who swims in the lake. And, from the dark caves beneath the earth, there echoes the doleful voice of another girl, a young girl with freckled skin and light red hair and light grey eyes with pale eyebrows, a young girl who weeps at every death, a young girl who weeps for the loss of the forest, a young girl who weeps for what might have been, but now can never be.

'Master Kenneth?' I recognise the voice of Tommy Pelling straight away, although it is many years since I have heard him speak. 'I'm so sorry, Master Kenneth. I tried to get it to stop. I spoke to the Good People. I even spoke to Lord Owen and Lady Margaret. But they are still angry, Master Kenneth, the Lord and Lady are still angry with you, and I couldn't persuade them. But I did try, Master Kenneth, I did try.'

I understand at once what he means because, in the dark caves far below the forest of Arboria, the Good People are beginning once more to stir. I can feel the anger of the Good People now. They are angry at the fall of the trees, they are angry at the destruction of the wild wood, they are angry at what we humans have done to the sacred land of Arboria. And, I realise at last, the Good People are angry with me.

Suddenly, my grandmother's words come back to me. In among the growling and the murmuring and the piping and the splashing and the weeping, I hear her dying words once again, her dying words spoken in her cracked old voice.

'*The Hand of Fire . . . The power to destroy half the world.*'

Yes. The Hand of Fire.

And now all the noises rise up and merge together into an unholy cacophony, and it is like one single, mighty, furious voice that roars with the force of an army, a voice that roars with the power to uproot trees, a voice that roars with the power to demolish houses, a voice that roars with the power to empty a lake, a voice that roars with the power to blow apart the two iron doors that for half a lifetime have kept guard over the blackest secrets of the darkest cave that lies there deep beneath the earth.

Only three souls can ever know those secrets. I know, of course, although for me there is but little time remaining. Tommy Pelling knows, but I can trust Tommy, I know that Tommy will never betray me.

And one day, Jamie, one day you will know my secrets too.

**SOUTH MIDLANDS TODAY**

**Camera Script Monday 6th December**

**Reporter JOAN HILDEGAARD**


**JOAN**

Well, hello again from Upper Helsing, and there's
been a dramatic and shocking development in the saga
of Hedley House, where yesterday demolition work was
halted by an explosion and an outbreak of fire. Fire
Officers were quickly called to the scene, and the
blaze was soon brought under control. But the
investigators have now told me that the fire may
have been caused by an incendiary bomb which fell
close to the house during the Second World War but
failed to explode at the time.

Following reports from Fire Officers, however,
local police were called in to examine the woodland
and outbuildings adjoining the property. It was
later reported that human remains had been
discovered in a cellar and in a pond. The latest
word from the forensic team is that there were three
bodies, all of them apparently belonging to young
people between thirteen and seventeen years of age.
The remains appear to have lain undiscovered on the
site for at least fifty years. An elderly man was
taken into custody earlier today, and I understand
that he has been detained pending psychiatric
reports.

Police are still looking for another man who was
observed by witnesses at the scene of the explosion.
He is described as being short and slight in build,

with prominent ears and thinning hair. When last
seen, he was dressed in old, ragged clothes. He is
not believed to be dangerous.

Well, that's all I can tell you just at the
moment, but I promise that, as soon as there are any
further developments in this horrifying story, you
will be the first to know.

This is Joan Hildegaard for *South Midlands Today*,
here at Upper Helsing.